A Parliament of Monsters

Gail Caress

Beachhead Books

Cover Art and Design by Gail Caress
Copyright 2011 by Gail Caress
Boston
All rights reserved.
ISBN: 0615517935
ISBN-13:9780615517933

*For my mother Ruth,
my daughter Jordan,
and my sons Adam,
Josh, and Alex*

Acknowledgments

With indescribable thanks to my hot-shot editor, cheerleader, best friend and husband Jay Caress, who has encouraged and challenged me to get this story to readers; to our dear friend Eric Tanquist, who has believed, edited, formatted, printed, acted as an agent, and not let the hope of publishing die and who has also spent countless hours on the process (thank you, Janet, too!); to the late and dearly missed Ralph McInerny, my mentor and friend, who made possible my position as a Visiting Scholar and Research Fellow at the University of Notre Dame, opening the vast resources of the Hesburgh Libraries to me; to the 5th and 6th grade classes at Trinity School who wanted to read this when it was published (you're out of college now but here it is!); to Mark Slouka, whose writing - especially *War of the Worlds* - has had a great impact on my thinking; to Sven Birkerts for his amazing insights in *The Gutenberg Elegies* (which I'm reading for the third time); and to all the fathers and mothers who quietly pray for their children.

Forward

Those of us whose lives have been changed by reading such novelists as C.S. Lewis, J.R.R. Tolkien, Michael O'Brien and Madeleine L'Engle always hope against hope that there will be new writers to carry on the great tradition. I believe that *A Parliament of Monsters* is a fulfillment of that hope. The novel combines a spell-binding plot with characters that pierce the reader's heart with their combination of human weakness and nobility.

Beautiful descriptions of love avoid all sentimentality because of the depth of the characterizations and the graphic use of sensory detail to highlight emotion.

Of special interest to contemporary readers is the use in the novel of computer lore into which is woven the history of Western mathematical knowledge. A masterful use of quotes from the poetic geniuses of the centuries provides a backdrop of cosmic beauty.

There will be joy for many readers in seeing the way the truths of faith permeate the novel in an organic way that is apologetic yet redolent of mercy.

Ronda Chervin

Chapter 1

February, 1999

Absence is the highest form of presence.
James Joyce

Existence is not a mystery unless you think it has a meaning.
Mason Cooley

Death was with her everywhere. The knowledge of it sat like a tentacled growth, centered in some vague but unassailable place in her mind or body. It was coldly indifferent when it squeezed her stomach as the airplane prepared to make its descent.

Patrick slept, his warm head on her arm, a matchbox car still clasped in his small hand, Legos scattered aimlessly around his feet. The bending of his tiny torso formed a perfect triangle with her arm. Her arm was alive in that golden proportion that connected her to him.

The plane lurched again. *"Hail Mary, full of grace ..."* The childhood habit erupted uncalled for in her mind, rote and meaningless. She almost hated herself for it. Maybe hate would have been better than nothing.

The cold liquid blue of the sky that had seemed unending was quickly replaced with dull white swirls of clouds. She felt no panic or loss of control as the plane sped through the atmospheric wilderness; she would have before. Now she had no illusion of control and instead, with a blink of her eyes she acknowledged the gray confusion as an extension of herself or maybe an annihilation. Even that became an alarmingly comforting possibility and she descended in a spiral of her own non-existence.

"Mommy, look! There it is!"

Patrick had awakened with a yelp as the landscape displayed itself from below. The foolishness of her inner indulgence left her breathless as she looked at Patrick's face. Sweaty ringlets of burnt copper stuck to his forehead — sleepy eyes, twinkling over a smile that broke her heart.

"There's the ocean, Mommy. It looks like the lake!"

His argument was succinct and well-delivered. Existential despair once again bit the dust as the plane hit the ground and shuddered to a stop. She held Patrick's hand as he pulled her down the aisle.

"Can we go swimming right away? Please?"

"Mommy wants to rest for a little while and then we'll see."

"*We'll see* usually means *No*," he said with no malice. He smiled up at her and she smiled back. He led her into the airport and she had no choice but to face the world.

Claire found to her relief upon checking in that the resort offered swimming classes for children in the smaller pool. When they got to their room she searched through the suitcase and found Patrick's faded blue trunks from last summer. She hadn't taken time to shop and she hoped they still fit.

He came out of the bathroom ready to go. He looked down at his rather snug blue trunks and then looked up. His eyes met hers. For a moment he seemed ageless and solemn, shifting shapes with his four-year-old self.

Then he was back. "Remember when Daddy swam with me on his back and was a big fish? That was fun. Do you think there will be lots of kids there? I want to practice my underwater tricks. Do you think they'll let me?"

How does he do it? She thought. *How do children handle death?* The day Michael died she thought Patrick would never stop crying. Great sobs shook his little body with such force that it was hard to hold him. The next morning he came into her room where she had not slept at all. He had his brown floppy stuffed dog under his arm and asked, "What's for breakfast?" as if nothing had happened. Were children's survival mechanisms so complex that they could compartmentalize things more easily? Or was it some sort of unhealthy denial that he would have to deal with someday? All she knew was that she had held on to his watertight compartments many times since just to stay afloat.

She reached across the lonely sea of her own pain and entered his room marked 'Daddy'.

"Yes, I remember you and Daddy in the pool. I don't think Mrs.

McNally liked it when he spouted water on her hair." They laughed together and she tickled him. "And I'm sure there will be some other kids … and we'll talk to the teacher about underwater tricks."

The lifeguard was a young woman who seemed to like the children. She said that Patrick would be fine for a couple of hours. Claire filled out all the forms and went back to their room and slept for a short time, then awakened abruptly and lay there for a few minutes in the darkened room. She longed for the gray mist again. She did not want to think.

She looked at her watch. Michael had given it to her. For some reason he had always insisted that she have a nice watch even though he was less concerned with time than almost anyone she knew. It was a bracelet, the band made of three strands of pale green glass beads bound together at intervals with delicate gold filigree. The case setting was gold, as were the hands. On the watch face was painted the figure of a beautiful woman with long streaming red hair, dressed in flowing robes who seemed suspended in mid-air. She was circled by a ring of stars, each star representing a number on the dial. Except for *6* which was the moon and *12* which was the sun. Michael had had it made especially for her but would not tell her anything else about it. He had given it to her on the day of Patrick's birth. It was to replace one with Celtic silver work that he had brought back from Ireland and given to her on their wedding day. Claire had lost that on the beach one summer and had anguished over it for months.

When he presented her with the new watch, she had asked him who the female figure was supposed to be … the Virgin Mary? No. An angel? No. He had said that he would answer her questions one day. She had never pressed him. God knows, he had given her time and space in so many things. It was only fair that she waited. It had been over four years and now she would never know. Time had run out. And yet the gold hands still moved lightly across the woman's arms, her face, her hair, her breasts, her feet … slowly and imperceptibly, still reaching and pointing to the heavens. Claire knew it was not for her that they now moved and reached and pointed, but for Patrick.

Her eyes focused on the time here and now: ten past two. She turned the watch ahead an hour to accommodate the time change.

She still had nearly an hour until Patrick was done. She put on a cooler dress. South Carolina was warmer than Chicago this time of year. Her feet looked bare and unnatural in her sandals. She walked over to the mirror to brush her reddish hair, which hung limply to her shoulders. She had no response to the image before her except to notice how the freckles stood out on her pale skin. Claire thought anxiously that she had forgotten to put sun block on Patrick. Well, it was late in the day.

She decided to walk around a bit. The resort grounds were enormous but she decided against a map from the lobby. There seemed to be miles of beach and that was the best landmark. The trails were marked well. The sun was low in the sky and the breeze was exactly the right temperature. The smell of blossoms and pine permeated the air. Claire, however, felt nothing but a neutral recognition of senses with no emotional connection.

Her mother had urged her to take this trip. Michael's family had agreed. *You need to get away from the house, from all the memories for awhile … get a fresh look on life,* her mother had said. She had even offered to keep Patrick, to let her spend some time alone.

But the thought of leaving her son was unthinkable. The child-like certainty of his existence had saved her again and again.

Her mother didn't understand that she could not get away from her memories or from the fact of Michael's death or from the knowledge of her own secret that splashed in and out of this tragedy like a slow poison. Her life was a mess no matter where she was. It was just a warmer and more fragrant mess here than it had been in Chicago.

She had ambled quite awhile when she found herself coming through a hedge of rhododendrons and the salt-tinged air signaled to her that this hill path led to the beach. Scattered at the feet of the larger bushes were small white blooms of evening primrose and pale violet flowers of what looked like peppermint. She didn't stoop to find out.

What no one else knew was that her thirty-two year old body, her still youthful shape, her quick and curious mind belied the fact of her true condition. A little over a year ago, after some months of experiencing occasional dizziness and some numbness in her hands, she had ended up in a chair in front of Doctor Quinlan's desk.

"Claire, the tests have confirmed my suspicions …"

He had looked at her with sincere fatherly concern. "Are you sure you don't want Michael here with you? Or your mother?"

George Quinlan had known her family for years. She wished then she had gone to a stranger. Why, after she had rethought and rejected so much of her childhood world, did she still live and move smack dab in the middle of it? She could have blamed it all on Michael, for even in the old days he was one of those people (one of those people? Was there anyone else like this?) for whom paradoxes and even contradictions seemed nothing more than long-lost eccentric relatives. But she had come to Doctor Quinlan all on her own and now he wanted to bring her mother into it. That's all she needed — her mother's stifling attention that always made her feel worse than better in almost every instance she could think of.

"Tell me the news and I'll pass it on. It's no big deal."

Of course it was no big deal and this was why, it finally had struck her, she had gone to Doctor Quinlan. This kind man, in her mind, was connected with minor childhood diseases: bronchitis, strep throat, and then there was that one food poisoning incident from Aunt Kathleen's potato salad and mono during sophomore year ….

She could tell from his face, however, that today it *was* a big deal and she held the arms of the chair tightly. She looked over his shoulder at the horribly tasteless Autumn Scene painting which had always hung right there on his wall; she clung to its familiarity and hoped desperately for anemia.

"You have a disease called Multiple Sclerosis …"

He continued giving her a rundown of the disease and what to expect in the days and months to come, but Claire had entered into a horrified daze. All she could think of was her mother's friend Peg who had M.S. and had died in a public nursing home, her body a shriveled tangle of twitching limbs. She had never seen her in that stage, but her mother's descriptions after her visits were sure to include morbid minute physical details.

"… no predicting at what speed it will progress. It may be years before …" Doctor Quinlan's voice drifted in and out.

Claire had always been repulsed, no, more *embarrassed* by any physical deformity or disability. She came to understand her reaction as a sense of shame; it did not preclude sympathy for the victim … but shame even so to be part of a race or a world that could produce or allow these tragedies to exist. Claire's world had always been one of precision. *Hell is inaccurate*, she had heard someone say. These mistakes of nature, these random miscalculations and deficient combinations of genes to her were desperate failures in her plan for the world. As a child she would turn away from people with Downs, or from wheelchairs or other handicapped paraphernalia. She had to leave the table when Grandpa's shaking hand would begin the laborious task of getting his after-dinner coffee to his mouth. She had recognized her own compulsive, phobic aspects especially when she became pregnant with Patrick. She had undergone weekly anxiety attacks for fear that her child might be handicapped in some way.

One day in the Jewel supermarket she had passed a woman pushing a child in a special wheelchair. It had a padded headrest and the child seemed semi-conscious as his head rolled roughly from side to side. She had no idea of his age, maybe six or seven. There was an unrelenting low growl coming out of his mouth except when replaced by a frequent shrieking wail that pierced the air of the entire store. Claire looked at the mother as she passed her in the aisle. She looked like an ordinary woman buying macaroni and cheese, coffee … ordinary things. The shrieks from the child did not seem to faze her. Claire had to forsake her shopping trip because there was nowhere in the store where she could not hear the child. She ran out of the door. She could not fathom the prospect of coping with such an unbearable situation.

"… an understandable and normal fear of not only being a burden on others but also the loss of independence and control …"

She had been to see Doctor Quinlan several times since. He made it clear that he was very much against keeping the news from Michael and her family. Claire kept saying that she just needed time. Michael never did find out and she was glad of that.

As she walked down the hill toward the beach, she seemed to be going against the flow. People were coming back from a day at the ocean. She found a wooden bench and sat down. She could make out several people still enjoying the day at some distance down the beach. Claire looked at her watch again. She was surprised to see almost an hour had passed. The sky behind her was making plans, no doubt, for a spectacular sunset, but the days were still short here and darkness would come soon, even in paradise. She had wandered farther than she thought. Patrick would be done any minute and she had to find her way back to the pool area. She stood up quickly and headed back up the hill. As she made the crest of the small dune, it happened again. She felt a weakness in her legs and began to lose her balance. Looking for something to hold on to, she reached for a tree to her right and grabbed it with both arms. She pushed her head against the rough bark, trying to center herself at that one point so the scattering of her consciousness would not be caught in the fragmented world that spun around her. She began to be alarmed about Patrick — how she would make it back.

Hearty laughter from someone coming over the hill made her open her eyes. She turned her head, still clinging to the tree. There was a group of three: a young man and woman and an older but very fit-looking blonde man. The younger woman was holding on to the blonde man's arm, looking admiringly up at him. They all noticed Claire at once, and the young woman came toward her quickly.

"Are you all right?" she asked sympathetically. Her voice had a pleasant melodic tone, with a slight accent Claire did not recognize. Her olive skin, her sleek dark hair and fine features combined to make an exquisite beauty. She looked deeply into Claire's eyes as she spoke, putting an arm around her shoulders.

Instead of gratitude, Claire felt embarrassment. The aura of the three radiated a perfect jet-set combination of wealth, beauty, health and ease of being that the Irish rarely develop no matter how much money they have (The Kennedys and Michael being the exceptions, of course). And here she was, dependent on these perfect strangers, an object of their pity; she hated this. She would never get used to it.

The blonde man moved over authoritatively and asked, "Are you staying here … at The Breakers?" His voice also had an accent. *German*, she thought.

"Yes," she answered. "I'm afraid I've wandered off and now I'm not feeling well."

The blonde man told the other two to head back and that he would meet them later.

"May I help you back to your quarters?"

Claire was tempted to decline, to say she'd be fine in a minute, but she wasn't sure she would be … and Patrick, poor Patrick.

"Oh, I'll probably be fine shortly, but I would be grateful for your help." She didn't feel so self-conscious with just him alone.

He put one arm around her waist firmly, the other supporting her elbow. He began to lead her back down toward the beach. "It's actually a shorter distance to walk back along the water this way. The trails meander somewhat."

He was amazingly strong. There was nothing forward in his touching her; Claire could sense that. He propelled her effortlessly down the dune. Her legs still felt strange. He didn't speak. She glanced at him out of the corner of her eye. He was not at all handsome although he had struck her so at first. His features, though tanned, were large and bumpy and seemed incongruous with the elite society where she had placed him. His manner was definitely one of self-confidence. He turned and caught her looking at him. She turned away. She could tell he sensed her embarrassment as she flushed. Still he didn't speak.

"My son will be waiting for me. He's having swimming lessons. I feel so foolish imposing on you like this."

His deep German voice was suddenly bright. "I hope you will not diminish the pleasure I have in assisting you by making me worry about your embarrassment. We all need help sometimes." He smiled at her. She could not imagine him needing help with anything.

"What do you and your son do when you are not vacationing in South Carolina?"

"We just lead ordinary lives somewhere else …" Claire wasn't sure if the caution she felt was because of him or herself.

She glanced up quickly again and this time she found him already looking at her. She tried to look away but his gaze did not allow it.

"We all think we're leading ordinary lives, but there are times when something breaks through to show us that we're not," he said and looked ahead again.

As they walked her strength seemed to return, somehow entering her body from his. Before she could react to the ridiculousness of *that* idea he was speaking again and gesturing.

"This is where we'll cut up and catch the trail to the pool area. Are you feeling any better?"

"Yes," she confessed and almost went on to say, felt she should say, *thanks very much, I'll be fine now* but she did not. She had the irrational desire to stay with this man as long as possible. There was something about him that exuded protective love … She caught herself up short. *What was she doing? Losing her mind as well as her body? Michael was dead so now she picks up a man on the beach?*

He released her waist and held her gently under one elbow. She looked at her watch again, turning it to find the face. He noticed its uniqueness and stared at the figure floating on the dial. He asked her about it. Claire explained that it was a gift. She didn't say "from my husband." She didn't want to let this man know everything about her. She noted the time and began to worry about Patrick again. She was almost twenty minutes late.

"I've got to hurry. My son will be frantic." She knew that Patrick wouldn't really be frantic, but he probably was a little concerned and she was feeling guilty at having enjoyed her rescue quite as much as she did.

"If we go between these two buildings we'll get to the pool sooner."

"I hope Patrick's all right!"

"Your son's name is Patrick? That's a fine name."

"His father insisted on it."

He smiled as he guided her quickly onward. He asked no more questions. He was not intrusive, just overwhelmingly present.

The open areas between the buildings were beautifully landscaped. Native shrubbery was intermingled with lovely flowers and plants. It was good to see things growing again; everything in Chicago was still dead. Every bloom here was perfect and every plant pruned meticulously.

"They must need an army of gardeners to keep these grounds so beautifully immaculate."

Claire said this knowing the hard work that she and Michael had put into their own gardens. She had not yet thought of the gardens without Michael. The seed catalogs that they had always looked through together on freezing winter nights must be sitting somewhere in a pile with other things that were lost in the fog of her grief.

As she spoke, Claire saw what she took to be one of the gardeners. Kneeling near a rose bush was a large ugly uniformed man. No, it was a woman with her hair pulled severely back. The contrast between this woman and the beauty and delicacy of the flowers caught Claire's attention. The woman's eyes seemed to fix on Claire, who was startled at the coldness they contained. The tall blonde stranger stopped and tightened his grip on Claire's arm slightly. She looked up at him. Something flickered across his face that frightened her. But she was not at all prepared for what happened as she turned back toward the gardener.

The woman was standing with an object in her hand. A gardening tool? All outward circumstances seemed very normal: people walking, gardener gardening, but now in a matter of seconds, things began happening in a supercharged dreamlike sequence. Claire realized with horror that the woman was reaching back to hurl the object at *her*.

She found herself being thrown to the ground, the blonde man next to her. The weapon shot past with a deadly *whishhh* and crashed into the building behind them. Claire caught a glimpse of it lying on the walkway. It was definitely not a gardening tool, but an unusual spear-like pole. But she had no time to dwell on it.

"Are you alright?" the blonde man asked. His German accent was very pronounced. She nodded.

"Hurry and go up to room two ninety-six in this building. You'll be safe there!" he said urgently as he helped her to her feet and pointed to the French doors.

"*Safe?* What's happening?" she blurted. But he was running off around the building toward where the woman had disappeared. Claire did as he said and hurried into the doorway. She looked wildly both ways for an elevator but there wasn't one in sight. She saw a stairway and moved toward it. Her mind was racing. "What in heaven's name is going on?" she muttered to no one. Was she dreaming? Had someone really tried to kill her? She scrambled up the stairs.

He had said *296*, hadn't he? She went out into the hallway. It looked like her own building but with a different color scheme. The elegant appointments seemed to mock her terrifying situation. *Widowed Invalid Murdered at Posh Resort*. Her legs were shaking again. She forced herself to move through the hall. She looked at a numbered door — *282*. She struggled further, eventually holding the wall as she pushed herself ahead. She looked at the room numbers again: *274*. She'd gone the wrong way as she had emerged from the stairway! She'd have to retrace her steps.

Her body refused to respond. What was happening downstairs? Outside? *Patrick! My God, what about Patrick!*

Confusion seeped into her brain again like a Morphean scent. Gray foam broke over her; two mighty waves from either side. Panic surfaced for one last gasp before the blackness.

Chapter 2

*There is a mystery that floats
between the tourist and the town.
Imagination estranges it from her.
She need not suffer or die here.
It is none of her affair.*
         Adrienne Rich

"Mommy! Mommy! Wake up! Please wake up!"

As Claire slowly opened her eyes she saw Patrick's stricken face above her own. Had he been already trying to fit the loss of his mother into the inscrutable puzzle of his young life?

He was still in his faded blue trunks. His red hair had dried sticking out in every direction at once.

"Mommy!" he exclaimed with joy as her eyes opened. "I *knew* you would wake up," he said confidently as he hugged her.

Claire looked around. Where was she? She saw her tan suitcase on the luggage holder. It was their own room. She looked past Patrick to see two unfamiliar faces. She pulled Patrick close again.

"Who are you and what's going on?" she asked with some anxiety in her voice.

"I'm Doctor Simmons, the hotel physician," the man answered with a Patrician southern drawl, "and this is Ms. More, the resort manager." Simmons had white hair and a white suit and made her think of fried chicken. Ms. More wore a conservative navy blazer and was gently wringing her manicured hands with a Please Don't Sue Us look on her anxious face. He went on: "Consuela here found you in the hallway of the Ocean View building." A Hispanic woman in a maid's uniform peeked timidly from the outskirts of Claire's vision. "She called Ms. More all in a flutter. I was summoned right away. Your vital signs seemed just fine. With the young gentleman's help we were able to get things properly sorted out and you back to your room."

The *young* gentleman … she certainly wouldn't have called him young, but then again this Doctor Simmons was speaking from a different perspective. She imagined the blonde stranger returning and helping them to find Patrick and their room. He probably even carried her here. Claire still felt shaky and her shoulder was sore, maybe she had hit it when she fell in the hallway, or when she was thrown to the ground outside.

"I think you may have had a reaction to the sun … with that fair skin of yours, and you just had a little fainting spell. We'll make arrangements for you to be taken to the hospital, if you …"

"No, I'll be alright, I think. What did the man say who helped you?" She wondered if the police had been called in. "Did you get his name?"

"Excuse me, ma'am. What man do you mean?" the doctor drawled in a kindly tone.

"You know, the 'young gentleman' who helped you find my son and our room and everything …"

The old man smiled and looked at Patrick. "The young gentleman I was referring to *was* your son. His swimming teacher brought him to the front desk and he helped us settle everything."

Patrick beamed.

"But what about the tall blonde man, the one with the German accent? Didn't he ask about me?" She looked at Consuela. "You must have seen this man, I'm sure he would have come back to check on me."

"No, *Señora*. I saw no one."

"Are you sure you wouldn't like to go the hospital, Mrs. O'Connell?" The old gentleman doctor asked once more. "Maybe it would be wise to get you checked out thoroughly."

She wondered now if her insistence on the phantom blonde man's existence made him think she'd incurred some kind of head injury or that perhaps she needed psychiatric care. She looked around the room. None of them knew what to think. How would they react if she told them the *whole* story?

"I'll be fine." Claire said. "*We'll* be fine," she said looking at Patrick.

Something kept her from mentioning the incident with the gardener. Was she protecting Patrick? Was she afraid to trust her own memory? Was she just typically embarrassed by the whole event? How could you be *embarrassed* about attempted murder?

Consuela and the two officials began to leave. She thanked them and Patrick closed the door.

"Was there really a man?' Patrick asked as he walked over to the bed where Claire was still lying.

"Yes, there was a man."

"Was he a good man or a bad man?" he asked before he climbed up on the bed with her.

"He was a good man."

As she said it she realized she knew absolutely nothing about this man, not even his name. But Patrick was satisfied and jumped up on the bed gingerly.

"You should have seen my underwater tricks!" he exclaimed proudly. He was doing it again. Scary and painful events were mere blips on his otherwise joyful and expectant childhood screen.

Claire felt weak and postponed any further investigation of her experience until the morning. They ordered room service and watched an old movie on cable. It was funny that at his young age, Patrick enjoyed old movies. He was fascinated with black and white film. Sometimes she felt that the bombardment of modernity was overwhelming to him. Unlike his friends and cousins, he sought refuge from fast-paced video games in boxes of Michael's old Tinker Toys and Lincoln Logs. He rarely touched her computer. Or he would draw. He especially loved to draw maps. He had always asked Michael and her, from the time he could talk, "Where does this road go? Where does it end? Can we drive to where it ends?"

She was not quite as indulgent as Michael, who would drive blocks and sometimes miles out of the way to satisfy Patrick's curiosity. Maybe it was his as well. One Sunday they had gone out for donuts and Michael had called over an hour later from some little town near the Iowa border. He put Patrick on the phone. *"We found the big river, Mommy!"*

When they'd arrive home, Patrick would draw a map, amazingly accurate but with wonderful embellishments of his own. Michael had put together a whole 'atlas' of Patrick's maps.

The movie was one her favorites and it helped to hold off the inevitable rush of reality with its decisions and unpleasantness. She was getting frighteningly good at not facing things. The door was locked and bolted and she had hung the Do Not Disturb sign on their doorknob, wishing the whole world would heed it.

Patrick fell asleep snuggled against her in his soft yellow pajamas. She reached for the remote and switched off the flickering black and whiteness as Lionel Barrymore was saying *"At our house a person can do what they like best"* while Spring Byington happily typed her novel in the living room and Ann Miller pirouetted across the floor.

As she lay there in the darkness Claire realized her utter exhaustion. She couldn't believe that they had only left Chicago early that morning. She wished that she had tried to ring Room *296* earlier in the evening, now it was too late. Besides, what would she have said? "Hello, is a tall blonde man there?" Amazingly she fell asleep without any more thoughts.

Upon awaking after an uneventful night's sleep, Claire decided against ringing Room *296*, believing it would be less awkward to go there in person. She would take Patrick to the morning swim and do some investigating on her own.

After breakfast she slathered Patrick with sun block and took him to the pool. He waved 'hi' to some of his new friends.

"Good bye, little boy," she said. "Have lots of fun and be careful. I'll be back before it's over to watch your tricks." A quick look of uncertainty passed his face.

"And," she said kneeling down by the edge of the pool where he was sitting, "Patrick, don't worry. I feel fine. I was just overtired yesterday. I'll even swim with you later."

At that he jumped into the pool and came up feet first. She clapped her hands when he surfaced. She checked him in with the lifeguard, a different one, thankfully; no explanations were necessary.

It was a beautiful morning. This time she got a map of the grounds from the concierge and walked toward the *Oceanview* building where the incident had happened. Everything was so normal again, people walking by in tennis or beach clothes; it didn't seem possible that anything unusual had ever taken place. As she neared the doorway, a sudden sharp pain shot through her shoulder when she looked at the place where the weapon had landed. She sucked in a breath of air and then let out a slight moan as she grabbed her shoulder. It was funny, she thought, that she hadn't noticed her soreness since she woke up, until now. Of course there was nothing on the ground. Someone would have removed it by this time. The blonde man, the woman who threw it, the police …

She hoped that *296* was the blonde man's suite; she had a lot of questions to ask him.

She located the clearly marked elevator that she had missed in her panic yesterday and rode it up to the second floor. It was *296* she was looking for, right? Her certainty foundered as she stood in front of the door. The details were all so hazy. What if she had remembered it wrong? But then what if she was right and the blonde man answered the door? Why should she bother him again? He had been nice enough to help her in the first place and had gotten involved in some sort of *Twilight Zone* attempt on her life. But if he had wanted to have any more contact with her he surely could have sought her out … checked on her safety. If she tracked him down, it might be awkward for both of them.

Still her curiosity won out. She didn't know how long she had been standing there, hand poised to knock, but now she let it strike the door, setting off a chain reaction as self-consciousness shoved her heart roughly and loudly against her chest. Did she want to see him again? Should she just have left it all alone and gone back to Patrick and tried to forget the whole thing? No, she had to report this to someone but she had to talk to him first. She knocked again. No one answered. No sound from within.

Claire walked back to the main lobby and talked to one of the clerks at the desk.

"Could you please tell me who is staying in room *296*?"

The young clerk had a smug look about him, and as he answered she realized that southern smugness was the worst because it was so polite. "It is against our policy, ma'am, as it is at any *reputable* hotel (was he sizing her up as a Motel-6er or what?), to ever give out the names of our guests." His nostrils flared in an annoying way.

"But a gentleman from that room — or I think he was from that room — helped me greatly yesterday and I was not able to thank him properly. I'm not going to harass him or anything …" She offered a half smile, hoping to warm him up a little.

"I'm sorry, but we cannot make *any* exceptions." He seemed so pleased to be enforcing this policy. She had never understood the type of person who got off on making sure lists of minor rules were followed. She looked at him. It was no use pleading with him; desperation only pleased this sort even more. She tried to look angry instead. That pushed some sort of small button.

"I could ring the room if you like," he said begrudgingly.

"No, thank you, I was just there and no one answered my knock. What about a message, could I leave one in the box for *296*?"

He looked a bit disappointed that she may have hit on a solution to her problem.

"Yes, I could do that for you." He handed her a piece of paper and a pen and cradled his condescending boyish face with the backs of his interlocked hands and waited.

Claire scribbled a rather ambiguous message, signed it 'Claire' and her room number. As she was folding it, he began to look at and click on the computer screen that held all of his *top-secret* information. Then he looked up at her with poorly disguised self-satisfaction.

"Oh, I'm afraid the message won't do you any good. The party in that room checked out several hours ago."

"Thank you," she said coolly as she crumpled the note and walked away. She had more to think about than this young man's lower-middle-management will to power. *What was she going to do now?* The only person who could verify her story was gone — if that even was his room. If not, she had no idea where he was anyway. Could she call the police and say "Someone tried to kill me yesterday but I decided not to report it until today?" She had no corroboration except for fainting in the hallway. The whole thing seemed more unbelievable as time went by. She went back to her room, slipped on her swimsuit and joined Patrick at the pool.

After lunch at the snack bar, they went down to the beach and she rented a cabana to stay out of the afternoon sun. When they ventured down to the water's edge to build sand castles she put on more sun block. As the sun beat down on their fair skin, she thought of Ireland, and the trick she'd played on those of her children who left her shores. Almost anywhere else they would go, they would always have to worry about the sun. Irish skin was meant to live in

Ireland, not South Carolina, she thought as she noticed the pinkness on the back of Patrick's neck and her own arms, in spite of the layers of sun block.

"Well, little boy, we've had enough sunshine for today." They rinsed the pails and shovels and headed back to their room.

As they passed a long hedge, a uniformed gardener stood up from his work. Claire jumped and held Patrick close.

"Sorry, Ma'am, Didn't mean to frighten you," the man said sheepishly.

"That's alright," Claire said, her heart still racing, "I guess I'm just a little nervous today.'

She kept hold of Patrick's hand and began walking again. Then she turned back to the gardener. "Do you by any chance know the names of the women who work on the grounds here with you? Actually, one in particular — she's quite tall, and wears her hair pulled straight back?"

"No, ma'am, there ain't no women that work with us. These are big grounds, but there are only six of us and ain't none of us women!" He laughed provincially at the thought.

"Oh, thank you then," Claire said, and they headed back toward the hotel.

Patrick took a nap in the cool of the air conditioned room. She tried to read a novel that she'd picked up at the airport. She'd hadn't brought any *good* books, she hadn't read much at all since Michael's death. She hadn't been able to concentrate; she still couldn't.

Claire slid open the balcony door stepped out and closed it softly behind her. She sat in the shaded chair hugging her legs, her chin resting on her knees. The ocean was beautiful, the surf rolling powerfully up on the sand. She wanted so much to enjoy it but instead, the beauty made her feel hollow and empty. She felt as if the sea of life had tricked her. Within her there were great chambers that had been carved out, expanded, and then filled by the beauty, the joy, the love, she had known with Michael. And now those chambers were still there, but they were empty. And this emptiness was not just the lack of something; it was a thing in itself: a demanding sucking void that collapsed upon itself again and again, pulling at her from within.

Of course there was Patrick. He still had his own place in her heart where they could laugh and sing and play; and she kept him there. But he was too much of a little boy to be let into the vast darkness of those cold chambers. Or maybe the place they lived was in him too. She couldn't sort it all out, not now. While he slept, she held her knees tightly to her chest, listened to the moaning wails of gulls piercing the air and cried for a long time, gently rocking herself in the azure blue of the sea and sky, and still she found no comfort.

The next morning Claire was awakened by a tapping at the door. It was too dark to see her watch. The bedside clock said five forty. Certainly housekeeping wouldn't be here that early. She heard the tapping again, this time more distinctly.

"Just a moment," she called as she searched for her robe. She went to the door and looked through the peephole. She couldn't see anyone. She left the safety latch on the door and opened it slightly and looked again. Nothing.

She decided it was time for them to go home. She couldn't fathom why she had stayed this long after the incident. She had not only herself to worry about; she might be putting Patrick in danger as well, with some deranged stalker lurking about. The tap on the door could have been a mistake, but for God's sake, somebody, some *Amazon woman* had thrown a *spear* at her and tried to kill her. It wasn't a vacation any more. When had it been? Maybe Patrick would be disappointed, but they had to leave.

But when she told Patrick they were leaving and began packing up their things, he said "That's okay. I miss Sean and Molly and Grandma and everybody." He was very close to his cousins and both sides of the family. He seemed glad to go home.

He climbed up on the bed where she was sitting and filling her carry-on bag with last minute things. He put his arms around her neck and whispered in her ear, "*And* I miss Daddy." It was as if he thought it would hurt less if he whispered it.

"I do, too, Patrick. I do, too."

Chapter 3

*The generous fort of generous kings
That had no fear of plundering,
Afterwards is pitied like a ghost,
And without him there, it's just an empty place.*
Medieval Irish Manuscript
(attributed to a widowed queen)

I call Christianity the one great curse, the enormous and innermost perversion, the one great instinct of revenge, for which no means are too venomous, too underhanded, too underground, or too petty — I call it the immortal blemish of mankind.
Friedrich Nietzsche

The airport limo dropped them at their door. Claire had called her mother once when they first arrived in South Carolina to let them know they'd arrived safely (per her mother's usual request). But she had not called anyone in her family to pick them up at the airport. She would call them in the morning after she figured out what to tell them. She was compiling quite a file of classified information. Doctor Quinlan had been her only accomplice in secrecy. Now she was connected in some bizarre symbiosis of knowledge with a strange blonde man with a German accent.

The driver helped them with the bags. As she walked up the sidewalk, she noticed that the only light on was the front porch one which had its own timer. She must have forgotten to check the other two timed lights before she left. Or maybe her mother had come over and cleaned the house and done things while she was gone. She was prone to do that more often recently. The late winter wind blew cold and hard. There were flurries of snow in the air. Patrick walked ahead of her, his stuffed floppy dog peering out from the top of his backpack. He always carried him that way so he could "see." He'd tried to help by carrying his own suitcase, but he was dragging — she'd had to wake him up when they'd arrived home in the big car.

She unlocked the front door and gave the driver a tip, then flipped on the switch in the hallway and closed the door behind them. Patrick's excitement at being home gave him a burst of new energy. He ran around turning on lamps saying, "There's our sofa, and our table and our good old chair." You would have thought they'd been gone for three months rather than three days.

Claire's chest tightened as she looked around the house. South Carolina might have been dangerous, but it *was* a diversion from these always-present physical reminders of Michael and their life together. She hated to admit that her mother might have been right about that. Still *wherever* she went, Michael's absence was supremely present.

She followed Patrick up the stairs, carrying his suitcase and her overnight case. He was in bed and asleep in no time, his second wind expiring with a contented sigh after he counted all of his stuffed animals surrounding his pillow to make sure they were still there.

Claire lay in the bed she had shared with Michael. In the glow of the bedside lamp, she was especially aware tonight of the religious icons, mostly old and ancient ones from Ireland — some real artifacts, some sentimental junk — that Michael had placed around their room. He had been very cautious in approaching her about it. Did she mind at all? If she did he could put them in his office. It had all happened gradually, piece by piece.

She had tried to be gracious about it, merely taking the enlightened view that they were objects of history and art. It had never really worked because of her own religious baggage, but it had been tolerable. But now they all seemed to be staring at her at once. There were pictures of saints and carvings of martyrs and statues of virgins. They had been Michael's dead friends, but now with him gone they seemed malevolent and barely tolerant of *her*. She would have to do something with them eventually.

She and Michael had ended up choosing such different paths when it came to religion. She never dreamed it would have turned out that way.

Claire and Michael had known each other since the second grade when her family had moved into St. Rita's Parish from Boston. Her father had come to Chicago to work with Uncle Joe in his dry cleaning business. They had worked hard and built it up together from a small operation to a chain of stores all over the city.

Claire was a good student, especially in math. She could be a bit cheeky, coming from a large and lively family of five children (of which she was number four) where she was always scrapping for her place in the lineup. She was obedient, though, and tried to follow the rules. She had been comfortable with the structure of the Church. Claire was painfully aware that she always fell short, but holiness had been at least a possibility that fit into her quest for accuracy. The Blessed Mother had been perfect and human. Her childhood imagination had captured Mary as an untouched virgin silence, coolly beautiful with porcelain skin, like the statue on the tiny altar she built herself in the corner of the bedroom she shared with Franny, her younger sister.

Michael was always crazy and unpredictable. By the fourth grade they were good friends, even though his wildness was always colliding with her sporadic but earnest attempts to be holy. In the fifth grade she decided she would be a nun. Michael would ridicule her continually after she made the mistake of telling him one day, and she would ask Our Lady to pray for him because she knew he wasn't *really* bad — just confused.

In the sixth grade, Brian McCarthy asked her to dance at the 'Spring Fling'. She enjoyed this so much that she gave up the idea of being a nun, seeing as nuns did not dance.

She and Michael continued to be best friends, and nothing ever came of Brian McCarthy. Michael said he was a creep, which she told him was not kind, but she never talked to Brian McCarthy much again.

One day when they were thirteen, they held hands on the way home from school. They never *talked* about the change in their relationship until much later. But from then on, they were in love. When she looked up at him, she saw not only his irresistible boyish good looks, but somehow she saw the man he was becoming.

He claimed later that he'd known since the first day she walked into St Rita's School that she was the only one for him. He had been, he said, just waiting to grow into it. His timing was perfect. He had reached for her hand and had held it ever since … until six weeks ago.

Michael was still wild in high school but not really crazy

anymore. He was quite serious about being wild. He developed a taste for poetry and literature and wine. He drank quite a bit, too much sometimes, but not usually with her. He and some of his buddies would get really drunk and do stupid things and get in trouble for awhile. He was very vocal about his growing disdain for the Catholic Church, its accepted rules of religion and the social conventions that they supported. He was unimpressed by Vatican II, as were the old nuns at St. Rita's, but in different ways, of course. He was usually championing one subversive cause or another, ranging from school policies to heretical cosmic theories. Even though subversion was not really 'in' anymore in the 80's, what with disco and Reaganomics and Young Upwardly Mobile buses loading daily for the future, nobody minded Michael.

While Claire pursued her study of mathematics, he would check in with excerpts from J.D. Salinger, Jack Kerouac, William Wordsworth, W.B. Yeats, and James Joyce.

He introduced her to a world of good people, intelligent and sophisticated people, some of them even Irish people, who did not accept Catholicism – at least the brand they'd grown up with. This frightened her at first and she was uncomfortable as she peeked out at the undefined landscape where Michael seemed to be wandering and there seemed no way to measure one's progress or to quantify results, but she trusted Michael and began to follow him. She soon realized the provincialism and naiveté of most of her thoughts and beliefs; and when she cracked the door to this new world, the fresh wind that blew in gave sympathy to her doubting so that it was not a sin anymore but courage and conviction.

Michael had a way of being a rebel and yet still charming. He'd have great disagreements with his family, his teachers, and a long succession of priests and nuns, but nevertheless would remain everyone's darling boy. She, on the other hand, would somehow always take the wrong tack, set the sarcastic tone, and be on the defensive in a second, so that her family and all the others began to worry about 'Claire's Change'. *She used to be such a* good *girl,* she was sure they said among themselves. "She wanted to be a nun at one time, you know," her mother would sigh.

She and Michael concluded, of course, that the Church was

hopelessly behind in sexual matters. They believed it was stifling and repressive and prudish about something that was perfectly natural. They each dated other people briefly in high school, but it was only to each other that they gave up their virginity. She cried after the first time, for in spite of all her enlightenment, she had a vision of the Queen of Heaven surrounded by all the white-robed virgins in their positions of honor, and the place that she had chosen among them in 5th grade was empty and would never be filled. She never told Michael why she was crying, she herself didn't know exactly. She was always glad she hadn't told him because she was upset with herself almost immediately for ruining such a significant experience with her stupid childhood superstitions. Strangely, it was not until then that she dismantled the altar in her bedroom. She had it in her mind that she had left up for Fran, but she knew that Fran paid no attention to it at all and never even noticed when it was gone.

It was ironic that years later when Michael had his unexpected return to faith, he had knelt down in front of her and held both of her hands in his and asked her forgiveness for that night. They were already engaged and had had sex repeatedly and so unabashedly for so long that Claire was embarrassed by this spectacle of conscience. It was the beginning of the strange dynamic that was to be ever present in their marriage.

After high school they had both gone to Notre Dame. It was stupid to fight that. If you were Irish and Catholic and had enough money and lived in Chicago, you went to Notre Dame. It was so secularized by then anyway that the whole religion thing was easily bypassed and a healthy skepticism was even encouraged by the professors. Claire declared a math major her freshman year with a minor in secondary ed. Michael was an English major and a romantic, hopelessly un-phased by postmodern ideas. By sophomore year they were both English majors, Claire really gravitating toward literature and poetry, doing some writing herself but still planning to teach high school, only English instead of Math. She was adamant to everyone that it had nothing to do with Michael, that it was her choice. But no one really cared that much, except her own shadow with whom she struggled frequently.

Michael discovered Irish literature junior year, and dove

immediately into Irish languages. World-renowned Professor Ian McCullum took him under his wing and sponsored him for a graduate fellowship at the University College, Dublin.

They postponed marriage until Michael finished grad school.

"God, Claire, I can't imagine being apart from you for that long. Why do you have to be so damn stubborn?"

"What would I do while you were going to classes and studying all day and all night? It would seem like I had no life of my own. I can't follow you everywhere!"

As she lay in her bed, the words haunted her, because she knew now that she truly had no life of her own. And where Michael had gone she could not follow, but stood helplessly at the dark and silent gate — a pitiful creature with a hideous wound where half of her life had been torn away.

Michael went off to Ireland and Claire began her first year of teaching sophomore English at Millbrook Academy, a small private school on Chicago's North side. She was fascinated by her independence.

He came home the first summer and stayed in her small apartment just off Clark St. Their parents overlooked the fact that they were living together; it just seemed so natural to everyone. (Michael had that affect on people. She couldn't imagine the scene that would have ensued with her parents had some 'other guy' slept there even for one night.) The second school year apart was more difficult; they missed each other more because the novelty of each of their situations had worn off somewhat. The following summer, however, was golden.

Claire went to Ireland to spend the summer with Michael. Her mother and father had been several times as she grew up, to visit relatives and sightsee. They had been taken in by the "Irish Heritage Industry" as Michael called it, always returning to Chicago with shamrocked knick-knacks. But this was her first visit and she was somewhat ambivalent. Her 'Irishness' was something that confused her and she found it hard to pick it out and look at it apart from all her other socio-religious baggage.

Once in Dublin, most of her anxieties began to slip away. They had no responsibilities. They became officially engaged, although everyone had known forever that they would marry. She was on the pill and so had no worries in that regard. They felt they had truly succeeded in being the only two Irish Catholics in history who had happily given up the faith of their childhood without the accompanying and consuming guilt that made life so miserable for all the others. It had seemed it would be hard to be in Ireland and not feel continually confronted and confined by the Church there -- especially when she saw the college where Michael had been living and studying. Even though it had modernized in some ways and moved from its original location on the south side of St. Stephen's Green to a new campus in southern Donnybrook, it still had a definite Catholic presence. Michael insisted emphatically that the school's Catholic legacy had no influence on the scholarship pursued there.

She finally met the legendary Ian McCullum, of whom Michael had spoken so respectfully and fondly, and his wife, Rose Mary, who everyone just called Rose. Claire was not overly impressed with the older couple. Although they seemed nice enough, there was no stimulating intellectual or artistic rapport evident. If Professor McCullum was as bright as his reputation claimed, he did not show it in public. They both seemed rather simple and backward and overwhelmed with modern life. Their house was very small and cramped — with too much furniture and suffocating with tasteless memorabilia and religious paraphernalia. They reminded Claire of her parents and grandparents and their dreary, stifling Catholicism. She had no clue as to Michael's predilection toward them. She wanted something new.

But instead, Michael introduced her to a land even more ancient than the Catholic Church. Claire met the real Celts, not the Christianized ones. He tried to get her to imagine Ireland before St. Patrick had come and changed everything.

Of course he knew exactly where to take her. They went first to an impressive grass-covered hill standing above the valley of the River Boyne, not far from Dublin, in eastern Ireland, in the county Meath. It was, he said, the Hill of Tara. The only time she'd heard the name *Tara* before was in *Gone with the Wind*. Though she and Michael had grown up in very Irish families, and neighborhoods, and schools, they were really Irish-*Americans* to whom 'Danny Boy' and 'When Irish Eyes Are Smiling' were much more beloved than authentic Celtic poems and ballads.

Before Christianity, Tara was the seat of the High Kings of all Ireland. The earthworks were still there dating back four thousand years. Here was the intersection, Michael told her, of the physical present, the historical past and the world of myth and legend. It was here that the warriors, noblemen, historians and poets gathered to celebrate the pagan festival of *Samhain* in autumn. Here was the Sacred Stone, the *Lia Fail* or Stone of Destiny. The man who was hopeful of becoming High King had had to climb to the top of the rock. If the holy stone roared three times at his touch, he was accepted by the gods. She tried not to notice the golf course nearby.

Michael talked on of King Cormac Art, The Fianna, and Fionn. It was here at Tara also, he told her, that Daniel O' Connell (Michael claimed they were related somehow) would return and lead one million people to gather in 1845 to protest British rule. Michael sided with the Nationalists, of course, though he was constantly vilifying both sides for using their "Christian" beliefs to achieve political ends.

"Peace on earth, good will toward men," Michael said sarcastically, "A lot of good it does them — some of the cruelest days in Ireland were planned with the Christian calendar — Bloody Sunday, Good Friday Massacre, the Easter Rebellion. A kind of ecumenicism-*noir*, don't you think?"

Michael was enamored, however, with the Celtic Revival toward the end of the 19th century.

"You know it was a literary movement," he told her one afternoon as they sat in one of the many Gaelic-speaking pubs in rural Kerry, drinking their pints of dark amber-colored stout.

"Yeats, of course, was one of the champions, unleashing Cuchulain and Finn and the other Gaelic warriors upon the land again. He and Lady Gregory and Edward Martyn made the Abby Theatre Dublin famous all over the world. It was a true renaissance that proved that literature and language had the power to affect the soul of a nation."

An older man walked by and stopped to speak to Michael in Gaelic. He wore the official year-round costume of the rural

Irishman: plaid wool cap, rumpled tweed jacket, and baggy nubbed-wool pants. He laughed loudly as he spoke and looked knowingly at Claire while Michael answered him, smiling broadly. The blank look on her face caused the man to address her directly, "*Nach labhram tu Gaedlig?*"

"He's asking if you speak Gaelic."

"Well, tell him I don't," Claire said with impatient self-consciousness.

The old man spoke again, "That's awright, cailin. I deu spaek the olt king's English only teu very special girls. Tell her what I said, lad."

"He told me that if I hadn't married you yet, that I'd better hurry up and do it today because you are such a rare Irish beauty in flesh and spirit that another boy may steal you away tomorrow, if the fairies don't kidnap you first in the darkest hour of the night. Oh … and he knows certainly that *we* were meant to be."

"Thank you, sir, for your compliment." Claire said, realizing he probably said the same thing to every girl who came in. In spite of that, she felt more beautiful.

After he had walked away, Claire asked, "What did you say back to him?"

"I told him that if I had my way, I would marry you today, but that you were an Irish *American* girl and you had gotten strange ideas about independence and a life of your own. He has a wonderful dialect; by the way, it's very old Gaelic. Maybe as far back as …"

"So you let him think that you were a 'real' Irishman, and that I was some sort of cold-hearted hybrid feminist who was too selfish to marry you?"

"Claire, he knew I was joking, *you* know I was joking, it was just a man-thing, and anyway it made me look like the sap who can't get the pretty girl when he wants her." He reached across the wooden table for her hand. "He wasn't joking though; he meant every word he said about you. And he was right."

Claire forgave him and changed the subject. "So the literary movement was the basis for a Free Ireland; the "blued n' guets" and guns were all irrelevant?"

"The power of language, Claire, is unrecognized, untapped. The Irish knew it once. Their languages were closer to the things themselves, not merely symbols. The Druids knew a secret and mysterious language that made things happen. An insult or a curse had the power to kill. A wise or 'fit utterance' had the power to heal. You might think I'm crazy, but I do believe it, if given a chance. The words of wisdom, poetry, great literature and the language of 'correct utterance' had the power in 1916, in 1921, in 1936, 1965, and still today, to bring peace here."

"I don't think you're crazy. You're just an ordinary run-of-the-mill, idealistic, maniacal genius philologist who spends all his time in dusty books or talking to old country people in some god-forsaken corner of this strange little island, without any clue to reality."

Michael looked hurt.

"Now who's the one who can't take a joke!" She slapped his hand lightly and sat back in her chair and drained her glass, the stout giving her a warm sense of possibility. "I believe every word you say, Michael O'Connell. And I believe the old man, too. See?" she asked, taking the band out of her hair and shaking it to let its brilliant redness fall toward her face and on to her shoulders. "You both said I was beautiful and now I am."

Claire was interested in the facts and stories that Michael told her that summer as they traveled the island. She was shocked to hear that the cutting of trees by the British, beginning toward the end of the 17th century, had by 1901 reduced the forests of Ireland to one percent of their past glory. While walking through the lush forests around Killarney, it was easy to imagine what the country had been like before the devastation. Claire luxuriated in the absurd abundance of the natural surroundings in some places — the Gulf Stream allowing even palm trees and eucalyptus to grow in the southwest — the common hedgerow flowers of violets, white bluebells and foxgloves fronting rural cottages or the scattered daffodils, yellow irises and purple rhododendrons. All of this seemed an extravagant contrast to the darkly interwoven peat-bogs and great solitary spaces of the West.

They spent their time mostly in the West, sleeping in Michael's small tent or an occasional inn. Not understanding why, she stood a little distant. "The 'West'," Michael explained one day as they were walking a seemingly endless ribbon of road through the light purple heath lands dotted sparsely with white-washed thatched cottages "represents the true reality to all the Irish, *Tír na Nog*, you know, is the mythical island to the West — the Land of the Ever Young, where it is always summer."

"I know that Aunt Kathleen moved to California and had a lot of plastic surgery, is that the same thing?" she teased.

"No, Claire, seriously … think about it. How many Irish have gone to America? And then gone west from there? Did you know that most of the famous figures of the *Old West* in America were Irish? Billy the Kid was really Henry McCarty. Jesse James' people were from Kerry. Then there was Butch Cassidy."

"Yeah, and they were outlaws — they weren't looking for true reality, they were looking for easy money." She thrust both of her hands out toward him with her fingers pointed like six-guns. He laughed, but he wasn't really ready to joke with her.

"No, William Brady was Irish and a famous sheriff. He was killed by Billy, and then there was Pat Garret, the Irishman who killed Billy."

"And you get from all this *killing* some sort of spiritual quest? It seems like just a bunch of rowdy Irishmen who've given the rest of us a bad name. And besides, most of the Irish that immigrated here at that time were escaping certain death because of the famine, right? As a matter of fact, from what I hear none of us have really left at any time because we *wanted* to … it was because of Cromwell, or being driven to desperation by the Brits somehow."

"That's just it. We were made to feel like we weren't good enough for our own land. In a way we can identify with the Indians as well as the cowboys. James Mooney, the great Irish ethnographer of the late 19th century, documented the *Ghost Dance* religion in America among the Lakota Sioux, Northern Cheyenne, Arapaho, and Comanche. He even went on to join their apocalyptic cult, saying his own Irishness drew him to it. We're schizophrenic; it's the tension between the native and the civilized, chaos and order, pathos and ethos … the imagination and the intellect. Joyce understood it, Eugene O'Neill grappled with it, and John Ford, another Irishman by the way, dealt with it again and again in his western films."

"I think yer gawn a bit too far into the balmy fir me, me lad."

She said in her best brogue, draining another glass of stout. Besides, she hated westerns.

"But Michael, what does this all have to do with Queen Medb, Cuchulainn, the sun-God Lugh, the Druids and everything else Celtic that you've been talking about for days?" she asked sincerely.

"Because it all started with them. Even though the Irish Celts had a highly advanced civilization, they were looked upon by the rest of Europe as wild savages, especially by the Romans who were particularly alarmed by their blood-curdling war cries and their tendency to fight in the nude. After Padraig brought Christianity, the Druids, the most highly venerated people in Ireland, even higher than the King, fell gradually out of favor and lost their positions of power and authority and respect. So these brilliant men and their pupils, who had studied 19 years to even bear the title, were forced to become itinerants, who wandered with the tinkers and sold their bits of knowledge for pennies. It's my theory that we've been ambivalent about ourselves ever since."

Claire could certainly relate to self-ambivalence, but Michael was overwhelming her with ideas.

"I like the part about fighting in the nude." she said, smiling, "Maybe we should try it sometime."

Michael laughed and pulled her close, "But we never fight."

"Now we have an incentive!" She kissed him and was happy.

One clear moonlit night when they were camping amid the wraiths and ruins in the high grasslands of the Dingle Peninsula, near Sybil Head, she woke up in the tent to find herself alone. She looked outside. A cool, silver light shone brightly on the mist that hovered just above the ground. She saw Michael standing naked, facing the west, the sound of the sea in the distance, his back to her. His arms were raised. She could see that his wildness was the wildness of Ireland; they were one. But it was captured for that moment in the definite and lovely silhouette of his body, quintessential — his skin the boundary of a land rising up from a sea of moonlit mist.

She walked up behind him quietly, shivering in the chill despite her jeans and sweatshirt, and put her arms around his waist and lay her head against his back. He was warm and she could feel the blood beating through him. He didn't move except to lower his arms and put his hands on her own. She thought of the bright sun traveling over the rim of the earth and then reflecting off of the Irish moon, touching Michael's body, and passing through him to her. She didn't mind getting the light third-hand. At this time and this place, it was an amazing thing to be sheltered from the impossible silver light.

"Did you want to fight?" Michael finally said as he pulled her out of her eclipse and held her next to his side. She looked at his face in the moonlight.

"No, I'd be too cold." she said laughing up at him. "But I do have to side with Joyce against you and the Gaelic-Leaguers and the Revivalists. In his mind the west of Ireland was associated with a primitivism that was dark and painful."

"Joyce was a genius, but he was also a cynic and a snob," Michael said looking at the moon.

"Maybe he was just a realist," Or maybe he was just afraid, she thought to herself — afraid like she was of the mysterious and uncontrollable power that moved over the face of this land like the foggy dew that now swallowed her ankles and feet — maybe Claire Daly and James Joyce were both afraid to face the lack of passion within themselves.

As they traveled the roads and paths together, Claire noticed that the earth was rougher and the stone was darker than anything she had known — great slabs of granite jutting up and breaking through the earth. Holy stones and profane, earthworks and ordinary hills, all had the look of some magnificently random yet prescribed order. It seemed that the distinction between architecture and landscape, between art and nature was blurred everywhere in Ireland.

But there was a pivotal connection that Claire made that summer that would affect the rest of her life, and that would be a bridge from her past to her present and to her future with Michael: this connection was between art and mathematics. It was not in the myths or the magic or the legends that the Druids touched her, but in the perfect mixture of fluidity and precision that was embodied in Celtic art. The intricate geometrical patterns that showed up on stones, statues, helmets, shields, rings, and torques showed a sophisticated and highly complex knowledge of mathematical skill, especially the use of irrational numbers that enabled them to design using the *Golden Ratio* or *Divine Proportion,* as it is sometimes called. This so intrigued her that she bought a book called *Druidic Mathematics* from a small used-book shop in Dublin, just before she flew home. It was written in the early 1900s and was quite formidable. She'd read only bits and pieces of it, but somehow this concept helped give reason to her seemingly disparate loves for literature and math.

The number of the ratio was 1.61803 continuing into infinity. She remembered the idea of the golden rectangle from her math studies in high school and college and the fact that many golden rectangles nestled in one another made a logarithmic spiral — the only spiral that does not alter its shape as it grows. She also recalled that Leonardo had shown the golden mean in the make-up of the human body and had labeled it dynamic symmetry. But it was not until she met the idea in the Celtic context that her mind took on some quality of wholeness.

The author of the old book said that the *Golden Ratio* "made evident the unmistakable relationship between the ineffable mystery of life in all its diverse forms and the ineffable mystery of number in its pure and unchanging form." It was then that she began to see art as a way of imposing order on the chaotic formless flux of those natural moods and passions that had inspired in her both fear and envy.

During those two and a half months Michael had been able to take the time to explain to her the intellectual and spiritual journey of his life, what had led him away from the Church, his abiding and irresistible love of English literature and poetry, and how it had been the gateway to his now overwhelming passion for Irish literature and languages. It was interesting, she had noted, that the book he carried around that summer was not Irish, but a volume of William Wordsworth's poetry. She had bought a paperback copy herself. She had been teaching Wordsworth for two years to her students, but she gained incredible insight reading along with Michael as they sat on the soft pillowy turf of the Cliffs of Moher (at one time the westernmost point of the known world), sea gulls crying out in eerie voices, and looked across Galway Bay to the dark gray-blue of the Aran Islands.

It was the "Prelude" that Michael seemed obsessed with, reading parts of it again and again. She had highlighted some of them and reread them many times since:

> *Ye Presences of Nature in the Sky*
> *And on the earth! Ye visions of the hills!*
> *And Souls of lonely places! Can I think*
> *A vulgar hope was yours when ye employed*
> *Such ministry, when ye, through many a year*
> *Haunting me among my boyish sports,*
> *On caves and trees, upon the woods and hills,*
> *Impressed upon all forms the characters*
> *Of danger or desire; and thus did make*
> *The surface of the universal earth*
> *With triumph and delight, with hope and fear,*
> *Work like a sea?*

Those lines from the 'Introduction' and some further ones from the 'Conclusion' would always remind her of that beautifully significant summer, when they were operating in the same universe, wrapped in a poem, safe in the world of youth and in tranquil recollections — before Michael changed and caused the unhealing hairline-fracture in their common soul.

> *Not distant from the shore whereon we stood*
> *A fixed, abysmal, gloomy, breathing place-*
> *Mounted the roar of water, torrents, streams*
> *Innumerable, roaring with one voice!*
> *Heard over earth and sea, and in that hour,*
> *For so it seemed, felt by the starry heavens.*
> *When into air had partially dissolved*
> *That vision, given to spirits of the night*
> *And three chance human wanderers, in calm thought*
> *Reflected, it appeared to me the type*
> *Of a majestic intellect, its acts*
> *And its possessions, what it has and craves,*
> *What in itself it is, and would become …*

There I beheld the emblem of a mind
That feeds upon infinity, that broods
Over the dark abyss, intent to hear
Its voices issuing forth to silent light
In one continuous stream; a mind sustained
By recognitions of transcendent power,
In a sense conducting to ideal form
In soul of more than mortal privilege.
One function, above all, of such a mind
Had Nature shadowed there, by putting forth,
'Mid circumstances awful and sublime,
That mutual domination which she loves
To exert upon the face of outward things,
So molded, joined, abstracted, so endowed
With interchangeable supremacy,
That men, least sensitive, see, hear, perceive,
And cannot choose but feel …

    Claire found herself picking up this creased and tattered paperback volume and reading these lines as she lay in her lonely bed in full view of the audience of silent but relentless icon critics. She found little consolation from the poem and its implications. Where was Michael? Roaming with Wordsworth in some universal feeling intellect?

    Michael had once jokingly showed her a quote from Bob Dylan saying that Irish folk ballads spoke strangely of death, of "roses growing out of people's brains and lovers who are really geese and swans that turn into angels." In spite of over 1600 years of the Catholic Church in Ireland, the Irish tradition that swans are the incarnation of noble human souls still stubbornly exists and there were to this day, she remembered, swan protection laws in Ireland. Maybe he was a swan. That didn't help. It was after midnight, Chicago time, but she did not feel that sleep would come any time soon.

    Their summer in Ireland came to an end. Claire flew home. The next school year was almost unbearable. They missed each other terribly. Their letters were copiously filled with details of ideas and thoughts and literary theories. Claire's new inspiration to study and read in mathematics and even physics again made her sure that Michael was as lost in her added permutations as she was in his ever deepening linguistic morasses.

Michael was to come home for Christmas, but at the last minute fell ill and had to stay put, insisting rather forcefully and uncharacteristically, that she not travel to him either. His letters came less frequently after that and were vague. They talked on the phone regularly, but she called him more than he called her, which was not usual. And many times when she called late at night, he was not in his room, which was also irregular. In his last letter before returning to the States he wrote her mysteriously that there was something he had to tell her but could only say it in person. She had no idea what it would be.

There was no way out of going to the airport with Michael's entire family. He was the obvious family favorite not only with his parents but also among his brothers and sisters. The usual rivalry between siblings did not apply when it came to Michael. He was their pride and joy; he was the one they would have liked to present to the world with a sign attached that read "This is an O'Connell at his best!" It didn't really annoy Claire because she agreed with them. They also never resented or excluded her in a clannish way as some large families might have. Because he had chosen her, in their eyes at least, she was encompassed by his aura. It didn't work that way with everyone else.

But this day she wished she could have met him alone. His youngest sister, Mary, who was only twelve, tugged at her arm as they all moved as a crowd through the long terminal corridors at O'Hare. "Come on, Claire. He'll be there any minute!" she begged.

Claire stood at the gate with them all. His face was one of the last to appear from the ramp and she searched it intently for any change. He had not seen her yet. No — he looked the same — a little thinner maybe but Michael always looked like Michael. She breathed a short sigh of relief. He was grinning, seeing them *en masse*. Then his eyes landed on her face. Without looking at anyone else, he walked straight to her, lifted her in the air and hugged her as if he wanted to crush her. Then he greeted and embraced his family.

All nine of them, crammed into the O'Connell van. A big 'welcome home' celebration was planned at his parents' house. As they drove, there were ceaseless questions and joking, loving insults and laughter. She studied his face as he held forth. His thick black hair was longer. His fair skin seemed even fairer. His mouth would flash into a smile in an instant as he interrupted his stories with dramatic gestures and a full Irish brogue and even local dialects. She was captivated with everyone else by his undeniable charm. Even though he was the center of attention, and giving his family the very best of himself, he would bend down intermittently to kiss her hand that he held in his.

When they reached the house they all piled out. Michael excused himself and Claire to his old bedroom, saying that she would help him settle in and that they wanted some time to catch up on things before the festivities started. This was Claire's first indication that something was different. She had just assumed that he would stay with her.

After all the bags were in the room, Michael closed the door. She was sitting on the edge of the bed, and that's when he came over, knelt down and asked her forgiveness.

She was confused and embarrassed. She held his head in her lap and asked him what in the world he was talking about. Some hint of fear and apprehension began to prickle in the magic bubble that had surrounded them.

Claire explained that she had never been sorry that they had made love and that it was certainly nothing he forced on her and had no need whatever to ask her forgiveness.

Michael jumped off the floor and sat next to her on the bed. She wanted him to kiss her.

"Claire," he had said, "I'm not now and never will be sorry for loving you. I'm just sorry that I convinced you to give up so many things. Your virginity is only *one* of the many. It's just the thing that struck me the hardest recently."

Now she was angry. "Michael O'Connell, you did not convince me of anything. Are you suggesting that I never thought things through for myself? That I just followed you along blindly? Like a child? I take full responsibility and credit for making my own decisions." Even as she spoke, she knew that one of the true reasons she was angry was that she *had* been influenced tremendously by him since she *was* a child, and now she felt betrayed. But it was only the beginning.

"Oh Claire …" He was almost in tears. "You know I respect your mind and your soul and your strength as a person and I didn't mean to imply that you didn't think for yourself."

"What's happened, Michael? Why are you talking like this?"

"This is what I wanted to tell you but couldn't 'til I saw you face to face."

Fear was no longer lurking on the periphery. It reached in and laid a cold hand on her chest.

"I, through a long series of circumstances and experiences that I have not made you privy to," he took a deliberate breath here and went on, "have come to embrace the Church again, or I should say I have come into Her embrace." Using the female imagery, he added jealousy to her rising sense of anger and betrayal.

She knew that her face fell visibly. She could not imagine how he could choose voluntarily to go back into that dim, confining and crumbling structure after he'd been out and seen the light of day and the wide world beyond and she told him so.

His response was to wrap his arms around her and say gently, "I love you, Claire."

Claire began to cry softly. All her other emotions dissolved into bewilderment. She could not follow him back to that place. She'd come too far on her own journey to turn around. She had no idea what this would mean to their relationship — to their engagement. Michael released her and, holding her shoulders at arm's length, read her face.

"Claire, I love you more than ever and with everything I am and ever will be. I don't expect you to understand right now or agree with me. And I do respect you for the decisions you've made. I think you're a brilliant young woman, teacher, writer … and you're still a much better mathematician than I ever will be."

He smiled at her, hoping to break the tension somehow, but she could not smile back. He continued: "I give you my solemn promise that I will never pressure you or even try to persuade you to do anything and that includes religion as well. If you have questions, I will try to answer them. I love the person you are right now. I don't love some picture in my mind that I want you to become."

Claire looked at him incredulously. No matter what was going on in his life or mind or heart he had that same natural easiness about him. His passages from one continent of "truth" to another were smooth sailing, no matter what the weather on the sea. There was, however, something now in his eyes that she had not noticed before. The wildness was gone — not really gone, maybe, but *changed*. He seemed to her like a great beautiful stallion whose power had not been diminished, but whose will had been broken. An immeasurable sadness settled on her. She began to cry again.

"I know you'll need time to think this all over and you may decide that you can't marry me now. God, I can't imagine it! But I realize how this must seem to you; I've thought it about it over and over, how it might affect you. I wasn't expecting things to go on like they were. I'm willing to give you as much time as you need.

Time, she thought, this had nothing to do with time! The earth had lurched beneath her feet and had begun to crack, the fissure running between them. But she knew then, though she did not tell him for a few days, that he was the only boy, the only man, she would ever love. He was her best and oldest friend. She could not think of anything that he could ever tell her that would prevent her from marrying him, except that he didn't love her.

Claire agreed to marry him in the Church and to all the consequences that would follow. But she never resented him for it; she felt it was a free choice she had made. And he kept his word and never pressured her to believe as he did. They published the banns and as was required they waited six months to marry. Michael began his teaching that fall at Northwestern and, with a stunning recommendation from Dr. McCullum, was named to begin the expansion of the Irish studies program there. He also worked to finish his dissertation in which he built upon the work of the great philologist and translator, Dr. Kuno Meyer, writing an addendum to his famous *Contributions to Irish Lexicography*. He lived at home with his family and Claire went on living in her own little apartment and taught her high school students with a nervous confusion that passed for enthusiasm.

She and Michael had no sex. To Claire this was like walking up a hill backwards or trying to un-pop corn. Michael was more attentive than ever, courting her gallantly and sensitively, obviously trying to show his love in other ways. Claire found herself at times trying to seduce him, pushing things farther than he wanted to go. Most of the time she would be angry when he would pull away, breathing heavily, and say, "I love you, Claire, but I won't do this. I know this is strange to you and you're probably hurt. When we get married, I'll have a whole lifetime to make it up to you. And I will, I promise." Neither of them knew then how short his lifetime would be.

She felt a sense of power when she would make some headway in bending his newly found 'principles'. The final time, though, when she pushed things too far, there was a look in his eyes that she'd never forget. She saw in them the expression of a tragic hero, with his fatal flaw about to accomplish his demise. What cut her to the heart was the realization that his fatal flaw was not lust, but his overwhelming love for her. She was repulsed by the cruelty of her selfish manipulation. She never did it again.

Their premarital sessions with the new priest at St. Rita's were a waste of time to Claire. Father James, or 'Jim' as he liked to be called, apparently did not believe most of what he told them for he was always apologizing for what the Church believed on this or that issue. She could not figure out why he was a priest. Why would a man give his whole life to something he didn't really believe? Why hang around and apologize and complain? Just get out and do something else! It was funny she never had that reaction to the less-than-orthodox priests at Notre Dame, but then Michael had not been a participant in the silly parasitic charade. When 'Jim' brought up the possibility that marriage was not really a sacrament, Claire exploded to Michael afterward.

"What the hell are we doing this for, Michael? This guy does not even believe this whole thing makes any difference. You know that I agree with him and would get married on a cliff overlooking the ocean if we could, but I'm doing this for you and because I know *you* believe it makes a difference."

Michael's only response was that the Church was fortunately

much bigger than Jim and threw in the convenient Latin phrase, *ex opere operato*, which meant that the validity of the sacrament did not depend on the sanctity of the priest. It made absolutely no sense to her; if there *was* a God, she thought, he would at *least* value the integrity of his employees.

The wedding day was beautiful. She loved the form of the Nuptial Mass and the music was glorious — Bach and Handel and an old Irish hymn sung in Gaelic by one of Michael's cousins from New York. It was great to have all their families and friends together in one place for the reception. Her parents were sure she'd grown out of her 'phase' and even if she weren't a nun, she was married to Michael and that was the next best thing.

Claire's thoughts of Michael and their history together had not been cathartic, for as she looked straight ahead from their bed and saw the ancient wooden crucifix and the figure hanging there, she found herself bitter and restless. What good was a religion that was full of death, suffering and blood? What did these people think they would get out of their unwavering belief? She remembered Sister Matrina reading to her fourth grade class about the martyrs who were tortured, beheaded, dismembered and crushed by huge rocks. Is that how God rewarded people for their devotion?

She was angry then, at her parents, at this Church and all its passive, submissive followers: this cult of suffering that was epitomized in the expression of the man on the cross, hanging there in her room. As she turned off the light and closed her eyes the image was still there, only the face was Michael's. She cried herself to sleep.

Chapter 4

Oh, ye dead! Oh, ye dead!
Whom we know by the light you give
From your cold gleaming eyes,
Though you move like men who live,
Why leave you thus your graves,
In far off fields and waves
Where the worm and sea-bird only know your bed
To haunt this spot where all
Those eyes that wept you fall,
And the hearts that wail'd you, like your own, lie dead?
                    Thomas Moore

'What is that noise?' The wind under the door.
'What is that noise now? What is the wind doing?'
Nothing again nothing.
… And shall we shall play a game of chess,
pressing lidless eyes and waiting for a knock upon the door.
                    T.S. Eliot

Patrick was at the foot of her bed, the sun streaming in on him, his brown floppy dog under his arm. "Can we go see Molly and Sean today? Do I have to go to school? Do we have any cereal?"

"You get dressed and unpack your suitcase," she said reaching for him and giving him a hug, "and I'll meet you downstairs for breakfast."

She went to her closet and grabbed her warm robe; the house was freezing. She went downstairs, turned up the furnace and checked the kitchen. There was a little cereal, but the milk had turned, so she cooked up some eggs, and toasted a couple of bagels from the freezer. Patrick appeared in the doorway of the kitchen in shorts, sandals, and a T-shirt.

"Honey, don't you remember it's not summer here in Chicago? We have to wait awhile yet for that South Carolina weather."

She let him eat in his shorts and then sent him up to change while she called her mother to say they were home. She gave some explanation about them being homesick and Patrick missing her; she knew she'd like *that*. She also knew that her mother was feeling sorry for her. The tone of her voice was oozing pity. Oh God, if she only knew that besides her grief over Michael, that she was slowly becoming a helpless cripple, *and* that on top of that someone had tried to kill her!

All of the sudden she had a flash of new thought. She couldn't imagine why it hadn't come to her before. How did she know, for *sure*, that the woman 'gardener' had been trying to kill *her?* Maybe her target had been the mysterious blonde man. She thought the woman had looked right at her, but from that distance she couldn't be certain. Maybe the blonde man was part of some jet-set drug cartel or he had flirted too seriously with someone else's wife. Maybe that was why he vanished with no word or explanation.

She felt more at ease with that scenario. Of course, no one would want to harm her.

She hadn't done anything that would anger any one that much. She didn't believe that the Vatican had yet resorted to sending hit-squads after lapsed Catholics, not since the Inquisition anyway. She wondered then if the blonde man was all right. Even if he was mixed up in some exotic dealings, he had been very kind and helpful to her.

She hung up the phone, feeling better that she had one less thing to hide from her mother and family. Some day she'd tell them all about it and they could laugh at her overreaction. She thought about what to do with the day ahead of her.

Claire had quit teaching when Patrick was born. It had been a struggle to make that decision beforehand. She had loved her work, loved opening up kids' minds to literature, encouraging them to think things through for themselves. Even though most of her students were little rich kids who really didn't care about learning at all, there were enough who did; and in her classroom she didn't have the same problems expressing herself that she did with adults. She wasn't defensive or sarcastic. She had been herself with them more than with almost anyone else. They had no preconceptions or real expectations of what she should be. She had nothing to prove to them, she could act and not just react.

But the first time she saw Patrick's red, wrinkled little face, she knew she could not leave him with someone else for hours a day. She was glad she wasn't forced to go back to work now. Michael's father had made sure that he had a very substantial life insurance policy. With that and Michael's trust fund inheritance she would be set for life, and when she became too ill to care for Patrick … She stopped her thoughts. She didn't want to start the day dwelling on this. Doctor Quinlan had said it could be years before any real debilitation occurred.

She didn't send Patrick to pre-school. They weren't expecting him all week anyway. He built things in his room. She unpacked, did laundry, cleaned (although she was sure that her mother had come in and cleaned while she was gone, because small things were rearranged). She and Patrick decided to play a game of chess. They were both fairly good. Claire's natural mathematical abilities served her well in this game, although Michael insisted it was a lot more than that, debunking the idea that a computer could consistently beat a master human player.

"We're gonna use the special ones, okay, Mommy?" She nodded as he brought a cardboard box into the living room.

Michael had given this set to Patrick for Christmas. Patrick had shown such interest and promise with the little plastic set he had, that Michael had pulled out a box on Christmas Eve and laid it before Patrick on the coffee table. They were both very serious. So many occasions between them were marked by almost ritualistic significance; even in Patrick's short life there seemed to have been many Passages that Michael had taken him through. Had Michael some premonition of that urgency of which she knew nothing?

Michael had let Patrick open the box. Michael unwrapped the first figure and Patrick's face broke into awed surprise and delight. The piece was superbly crafted. It was only a pawn, but the base was of highly polished marble banded by a gold ring and the actual figure was carved out of wood, the carving so detailed and delicate that the face looked almost real. Michael placed the figure on the board. He allowed Patrick to unwrap each of the other pieces, taking turns with his father to place them on the board in their proper position. He had exclaimed over each one, for as the pieces rose in the hierarchy the more elaborate they became. Claire looked at them again closely now, for though Patrick and Michael had played with them once, she had never really played with them or studied them after the first unveiling.

The rook had bronze-tipped battlements. The knight was a horse with a silver bridle and a rider, who did not look like a medieval knight but a warrior nonetheless, swathed in a leather breastplate with tiny metal designs and appendages. The wooden legs were bare, as was the head with its long wild hair and fierce expression.

One bishop on each side of the board was an ominous hooded figure with a long beard, but whose face was so shrouded that its actual features were indistinguishable. His hands were extended and in one was a stone, not carved from wood, but of smooth granite; in the other was a miniature shell from the sea. The companion bishop on each side was identical in every detail except that it held in one hand a gold cross and in the other a book with brass bindings on which was written in miniscule letters, *'fir fer'*.

The kings and queens were magnificent. They were carved out of oak, as were all of the pieces, and except for the kings and queens the only way to distinguish one's figures from those of the opponent was that one set was on a black marble base, the other on white.

The robes of all four royal persons were carved to remind one of flowing silks and each wore a coverlet of gold brocade, the delicate patterns being inlaid directly in the oak. The 'black' queen was standing in a small golden chariot with long curving metal blades attached to the wheels. She had an ecstatic and wildly beautiful look on her face, one fist raised in the air, the other hand on the reins of the chariot. Her hair was flowing behind her to show the speed at which she was moving.

The 'black' king was an old man with hair as long as the queen's and a beard to his chest. On his head sat a circlet of gold; his shoulders were broad and powerful in spite of his age, and he held the leash of a hound that sat obediently next to him on the black marble base. The thing that set this piece apart from all the rest was that it was covered with a fine sprinkling of sparkling dust that almost looked liked sugar, but must have been finely ground crystal, and the way it hung from his beard and hair made one feel certain it was meant to be ice or snow or frost.

The 'white' queen seemed less powerful than the black, but no less beautiful. She was smaller and daintier and on her head sat a shining silver wheel like a crown. In one hand, hanging at her side, she held a bag or pouch and with the other hand nearer her heart, she held a gold apple. The 'white' king seemed a mere boy, but he shone more brightly than all the rest, for he had a crown of gold and held a golden shield. His golden sword was sheathed in his belt at his side; in his other hand he held a straight white wooden rod.

What treasures these were, Claire thought to herself as if just coming to the realization.

Thinking back on it now, when Michael had first shown these to Patrick she had felt excluded in some sense. But she had gotten used to that. No matter how much Michael loved her, or how much Patrick loved and needed her and how much she loved them both, there was something about the 'father-son' relationship that she could not enter. She wondered now if Michael had ever felt the same way about Patrick and her, or Patrick in his own way about her and Michael. Every relationship was exclusive in some sense, she concluded; but she was not in the mood to think why. She looked at Patrick.

He was intently looking at the board. He had given her the white set. She knew that he had done it to be nice, because white was always his favorite, even with the old plastic ones. But she wondered if this young dainty royal couple was any match for the powerful one opposite her. She jokingly said something to that effect; being careful not to devalue the 'favor' he had done her.

"Mommy, don't worry. You have the good ones. They are littler but they're good, they're really good," he said, smiling.

They played for a while and Claire enjoyed herself at first. The pieces were so lovely and satisfying to touch. They were wonderfully Celtic; as she moved them around the board she found herself thinking of the summer in Ireland again. It was strange that when Michael had first brought them out she had really seen them as more Christianized and medieval, maybe it was the cross in the bishop's hand. Or had she even noticed that then? She had just presumed that they would be and had gone into a detachment mode. Maybe she had excluded herself after all.

Patrick took a long time to finish his turn; he thought everything out very carefully as if something was riding on each move. It wasn't until it began to get dark that Claire realized how long they had been sitting there. She was moving her king when she began to have an uneasy feeling. The house seemed incredibly cold as if a window were opened to the bitter wind that swirled around them. The pages of a magazine on the table blew and fluttered. She looked around and the only light that was on was the one near them that she had turned on earlier. The rest of the house was in darkness.

"We can't finish the game now, little boy. It's time to think about dinner and …," she ran quickly over to switch on the light in the dining room, and then the kitchen. She realized that she was frightened of something.

"But, Mommy, we *have* to finish the game. Daddy said we *always* have to finish the game. "

"We can't tonight, Patrick. I'm not feeling well … just tired from our trip still. "

"But Daddy said …"

She began to feel panic. She did not want to go near the game. The house suddenly felt strange and empty and cold and dark. She began to cry.

Patrick ran over to her and hugged her waist. "It's okay, Mommy. We'll finish some other day. I'm sorry we miss Daddy and that you're afraid."

There was a loud banging on the front door. Claire jumped and screamed. The pounding continued as Claire held Patrick's hand and ran to the study, which was still in darkness, to peek out of the window at the front porch without being seen. The outside light was not on yet. She could see nothing. Why hadn't she taken time that day to get all the timers set properly again instead of cleaning a house that wasn't dirty? They crept to the front hallway, Patrick not saying a word. Through the door they heard muffled but angry voices. Before they could move, the knob turned and the door flew open.

Her mother and father were standing in the hallway with dark markings on their foreheads. Claire's mother shouted, "Claire! Patrick! You're alright! We tried to call earlier, but your phone isn't working. I thought something dreadful might have happened to you. What with all the tragedy this family has seen, I'm afraid I expect the worst. Your father didn't want to come; he kept saying you were fine. I tried to call at the last minute to see if Patrick wanted to go to Ash Wednesday Mass with us. I couldn't get through and your father made me go to church without checking. I couldn't even enjoy the Mass."

Claire wondered how you could *enjoy* Ash Wednesday, but her mother continued.

"But I talked him in to stopping on the way home." She ran to Patrick and hugged him tightly.

Claire's father stood sheepishly where he had been, obviously self-conscious that they had burst in for no reason. Claire felt sorry for him, but she looked his way when she asked, "Why were you pounding on the door?"

Her mother answered. "Your father wouldn't let me use the key until we had knocked."

"You were *not* knocking, Grace," the big man said.

"I knocked first lightly but no one answered. I wanted to call out your names but your father said it would disturb the neighbors. So I started knocking loudly. Then we heard you screaming. My God, Claire, you gave us a fright! Why were you screaming?"

Claire looked at her silent father, seeming bigger than ever in his puffy winter jacket, one of his large hands in his pocket, the other tapping his thigh … then back at her tiny, garrulous mother and the smudges on their foreheads. What was it the priest said as he crossed the ashes on the heads of the faithful? Something hopeful, like "from dust you came and to dust you'll return." Human existence suddenly struck her as absurdly comical and she began to laugh.

"Oh Good Lord, she's hysterical. See, John, I knew she needed us!"

She walked over to Claire and hugged her, gathering Patrick also. "Oh sweethearts, you two get a few things and come and spend the night with us. Your phones aren't working. Wonder if there's an emergency and …"

"Mom, Mom, really —," Claire said, still a little giddy, and extricated herself from the coddling yet paradoxically comforting embrace. "The phone thing was probably a fluke. I called you this morning, remember?" She walked over to the hall table and picked up the receiver. It was dead.

"Is it working?" her mother demanded. When Claire didn't answer, she took the phone from her hand and listened for a tone. "No, it isn't!"

"It's okay, though. Maybe I just forgot to pay the bill or something." The look of pity that then began to spread across her mother's face made her focus on her father's. "I'm sure we can get it all straightened out in the morning. I'll drive down to Osco and use their phone to call the phone company and clear it all up."

She looked back at her mother. She wasn't convinced. "No, better yet — *you* call the phone company first thing in the morning and have them send someone over or do whatever needs to be done."

This was acceptable. Her father looked relieved and began to turn to go out the door. He turned back again and hoisted Patrick up to give him a squeeze. "Goodnight, little man."

"Goodnight, Grandpa."

"What about dinner? Did you have food in the house? We're going out to eat now, a *small* fish dinner, mind you, and you can come with us," her mother suggested

"We have plenty of food. Don't worry, we'll do just fine." She looked at Patrick and he smiled. He liked it when she said that, she thought.

As the door was closing she heard her mother protesting as they walked down the walkway: "But, John, what about going all night without a telephone?" and her father's reply: "People went without phones for thousands of years …"

They ate some canned chowder and some saltines and drank Kool Aid. Then Patrick took a bath and she took a shower. They read some funny little animal stories and he fell asleep.

That night before she went to bed, Claire did an unusual thing. She decided that after all her uneasiness last night and tonight that she could not look at the crucifix anymore. But there it was right in her line of vision. She could not bear to take it down because of Michael. But neither could she rationalize moving all the furniture to accommodate this relatively small piece of wood. An idea filtered into her mind from her childhood at St. Rita's. Hers had been one of the few churches that had kept the practice of covering all of the statues in purple cloth during the Lenten season. As a child she had loved the Easter Vigil when the shrouds were taken off and everyone came back to life. She took a handkerchief out of Michael's drawer and laid it over the body of Jesus. But this was no Lenten gesture. The gruesome likeness to a body bag crossed her mind as the human form remained unmistakable beneath the cloth. She had no hope of anyone rising from the dead. This was merely another family compromise; it was for Michael, for Patrick, and especially for herself. This was the world in which she lived. She knew no other.

Chapter 5

When Pearse summoned Cuchulain to his side,
What stalked through the Post Office? What intellect?
What calculation, number, measurement, replied?
We Irish born into that ancient sect,
But thrown upon this filthy modern tide.
William Butler Yeats

One American said that the most interesting thing about Holy Ireland was that the people hate each other in the name of Jesus Christ ... And they do!
Bernadette Devlin

A light rain drizzled down on O'Connell Street in Dublin, wetting the pavement and the statues. The statues have been left all over the city like playing pieces of a game — the moves irrevocable, the outcome set in metal and stone. The great statue of Daniel O'Connell stands overlooking the River Liffey at the head of the street named for him. At the other end of the street is a smaller likeness of Charles Parnell, shrunken somehow by the scandal that clouded his noble efforts. A bronze statue of the legendary dying Cuchulain is displayed at the General Post Office to honor those killed at the Easter Rising.

On this Ash Wednesday a group was gathered in a small room of an unimposing building on O'Connell Street. Like small bands before them, their combined longing was for peace in Ireland. The Good Friday Accord of the previous year had been cracked and patched and now seemed to be crumbling. It was not an official meeting. It was not publicized. There were no photo opportunities. A weariness settled over them as they watched the drizzling rain through the smudged window, except for one man who seemed bright and still tireless in his struggle.

"So don't give up!" he said to the others around the table. "Remember it was a bunch like us who won the quiet revolution in 1921 that brought seven centuries of violent history to an end! They were poets, teachers, clerks, priests, musicians, doctors, university lecturers, farmers, grocers …"

"James, you know we respect you and your dedication, but save your optimistic drivel for your public speeches. You know all of us are politicians and diplomats and we lost touch with, at least, the farmers and the grocers long ago. Let's not believe our own fluff."

James Day turned to his friend with a stricken face. The others looked uncomfortable.

"Now, Kenneth, don't talk like that. We can all sense that we're going to make a breakthrough soon. Disarmament is not just a dream. If the IRA makes the first move it will all fall into place."

"Then why aren't they here, now, today?" someone else asked.

The gathering broke up shortly, leaving an awkward silence in the empty room. Mr. Day walked briskly in the rain up O'Connell Street, hurrying to his next appointment undaunted and unaware that he was being followed.

The facts of Ireland's history are huge heavy medallions hanging from chains about her neck. Some say they have miraculous powers, others say the great weight will drag her down to the bottom of the sea. The myths are light as air, but strong as a mighty wind. Even in death, Cuchulain cannot be contained in bronze, but blows on the breath of the wind, through the misty rain above O'Connell Street and its monuments, west from Dublin, west to bend the branches of the bare trees, west to whisper through the cracks in the small country houses and flicker the firelight there — and to beat the sea against the rocks and pull it back again.

Chapter 6

Even as we enumerate their shortcomings, the rigor of raising children ourselves makes clear to us our mothers' incredible strength. We fear both ... If they are not strong, who will protect us? If they are not imperfect, how can we equal them?
Anna Quindlen

For God's foolishness is wiser than human wisdom.
Saint Paul

"The line's been cut," the repairman told her. "The cut's not clean, so it could be a small animal's chewed it, I suppose."

When the phone was working again, Claire called her mother. "It's all fixed so you can stop worrying now."

"What was the problem?"

Claire calculatedly opted for the least worrisome and most obvious explanation. "The man said the line might have been chewed."

"Chewed!" her mother gasped, "What kind of perverted burglar would chew a telephone wire?"

"Mother, there *was* no burglar! The man said it was probably a small animal."

So much for calculations.

The next week Patrick went back to pre-school. He liked school. It was not a Catholic school. Claire had picked it out and Michael had been fine with that. Patrick went to Mass with Michael every week and Claire agreed to that. They had established some sort of strange balance that let them live their lives with respect for each other. They loved each other, Claire thought, somewhere that was deeper than creeds and compromises. There was a oneness there that was glowingly alive, but they tread lightly on the crust of it.

Claire thought about trying to work in the gardens. Gardening had been something that she and Michael had learned together after they were married. Neither of their families had done much, so they had had to start from scratch using books and catalogs. Since they had two different philosophies of gardening, Michael concentrated on fruits and vegetables, Claire on flowers and shrubs. Claire weeded and pruned and pinched until her plants were perfect and lovely. Michael fertilized with compost profusely and was much more lenient with weeds and strays. His fruits and vegetables were large and sometimes ugly or misshapen but — she had to admit — utterly delicious.

She stood looking at the earth, still frozen in places with patches of brownish snow obstinately refusing to depart and wondered how she could ever face this ground alone.

"What are you doing out here?" It was Fran.

"I'm hoping the garden will spring forth on its own this year!"

Franny hugged her and they walked into the house together. Fran was twenty-six and the youngest of the Daly girls. Somehow she had fallen out of the rhythm of the rest of the children and rather than being the usual two years younger than her older sister she was born six years after Claire. She also had the 'black Irish' genes, like Michael, which set her apart from the rest of the family. Michael said it was the blood of the true Irish coming through, that of the ancient *Firbolg*, the small dark race that were the first inhabitants of Ireland. Her mother said it was from the Spaniards that came ashore from the Armada seeking safety from the British off the western coast. Whatever it was, Claire was jealous.

Claire loved her little sister and admired her. Fran was so effortlessly more herself than Claire had ever been. Actually quite stunning with her short sleek black hair and bright blue eyes, she was not really intellectually inclined, but thus was refreshingly uncomplicated. She wore black leather, smoked heavily, had a nose ring, had dropped out of college and had become, all in all, a wonderful diversion for the family "concern." Fran was not belligerent in the slightest and was not making any particular statement. She just hung out with a segment of her generation that did these things rather happily and mindlessly. She'd had numerous boyfriends and went to parties every weekend; and she had also gone to Mass with Michael and Patrick almost every Sunday. She and Michael had been great friends. She stopped going to church when he died. She still tried to see Patrick as often as she could.

"Are you still working on that book you were writing?" Fran

asked Claire.

"I haven't touched it for awhile."

"You really should get at it again, I think it was good." She walked over to the little nook off the kitchen that served as Claire's study and where her computer was set up. She picked up a stack of paper that lay beside it. "The character in the story, the woman, isn't she writing a book, too?"

"Yes."

"So you're a woman who's writing a book about a woman who's writing a book … it could go on forever. Right? It's like when you try on a bathing suit at Field's or Carson's or something and you turn around to see yourself from the back or the side, you know how they have those special mirrors with the flaps? They don't have those kind of mirrors at the less expensive stores, but anyway … You know where I'm going with this, right? You can see yourself in the mirror, looking at yourself in the mirror, forever. Weird."

"It actually has a name, Fran. It's called the paradox of self-reference. Some of the greatest mathematical minds in the world have thought about it for years."

"Good, I'm glad *somebody's* thinking about it besides me. Is this the book?" she asked, leafing through a sheath of paper.

"I think so," said Claire walking over to her, "Why?"

"I can't remember, did you use the *f-* word in here yet?"

"What kind of random question is that?"

"My friend Gordon who knows all about writing and marketing and stuff like that says that you have to use it at *least* two or three times these days in a book or movie to get someone to publish it or take it seriously. So really, Claire, think about it."

Claire suddenly had the desire to tell Fran every one of her darkest secrets.

Instead, Fran had a cup of coffee and a bagel and Claire listened to her stories about some of the crazy customers at the restaurant where she waited tables. She also volunteered at a homeless shelter and a hospice run by a parish downtown. Michael called her Saint Francis and Fran would usually reply, "Get serious" or some such incredulous response.

"You know I basically think that people are just people, don't you? I mean the people that are selfish and in bad moods when they're eating at a restaurant, would be the same way at the shelter or even when they're dying. And people who are nice are just nice anywhere. Well, that's what it seems like anyway. Kind of funny, huh?"

As she was leaving, Fran stopped on the threshold and asked, "Oh yeah, can I pick up Patrick today from school? I'm getting this little tattoo on my shoulder and I promised him he could watch if it was okay with you."

"Franny, come on, do you honestly think that that's a good thing for a four-year-old to see?"

"Well, it's not like it's at some dumpy place downtown, you know; there's this new kind of swanky place at the mall that does it now, because it's *in* and everything."

Claire reluctantly agreed and then Fran remembered, "One more thing. I'll meet you at Grace's at about 1:30 or so. She said to tell you she wanted to have a talk with you."

Sometime during high school, while Claire was away at Notre Dame, Fran had begun calling their mother by her first name. The family eventually settled into it.

"Did she say what she wanted to talk about?"

"I think she said Easter or something."

Fran left and Claire began dreading the meeting with her mother immediately. First of all, it was as if every time they met, her mother had prepared a list of the most sensitive and controversial topics they could discuss and mentally ran down the list as they spoke. After she'd married Michael, things had gotten better because she would joke with him about it and he'd defuse the situation enough so that she could be somewhat magnanimous with her mother. But the times they'd been together since his death, Claire had reverted back to the defensive, caustic adolescent conversation tone that had worried her family in high school. She always hated herself afterward. How could a grown married woman, who'd taught high school students, who was a mother to her own son, fall back into such childish patterns? Then there was *Easter*. That was bound to cause trouble with her mother. Claire hadn't been with the *whole* family since the funeral and she just wasn't up to it again yet.

Claire pulled up in front of the huge red brick house she had known her whole life: a typical Chicago brick house, boxy and big, built back when families were unashamedly large. The bare branches of old vines clung to the sides of the home. Her family had moved into the place when they had come west from Boston soon after Francine was born. All five girls were gone now but their parents hung on to the house. Her father was past retirement age but still working hard with Uncle Joe. She didn't think he'd ever stop.

Both the Dalys and her mother's people, the O'Briens were 'famine Irish' who had come to Boston to flee the disaster in their homeland during the 1840s. The situation that awaited them in America was hardly better. Boston had been overwhelmed with the pallid and weak, half-starved, disease-ridden throngs that came ashore. The history of all that occurred during that time is deeply and bitterly engraved on the Irish race and Claire remembered many of the horror stories her grandparents had passed on from their grandparents. Many talked of the treatment by the British government of the Irish people as genocide. In Boston there was not enough work or housing for unskilled laborers. They lived in abandoned houses and deserted warehouses or makeshift huts thrown up in alleyways near the docks and the wharves, where the men might find occasional work and extra scraps of food while their wives and sisters hired out as domestics in nearby homes and hotels. They told of the hot months of 1849 when an epidemic of Asiatic cholera took five hundred lives in one parish alone, most of them children.

The Irish were eventually assimilated, of course, and many became prominent citizens in Boston. Her grandparents were blue-collar working-class people with good dispositions and a love of life, extremely devout Catholics until they died. Claire remained baffled by the devotion of the Irish Church after all they had been through — all the prayers to St. Patrick that lay rotting in the blackness of the potato fields or that died on the hot breath of children in the epidemic of 1849.

Claire's father, John Daly, had fallen in love with Grace O'Brien and they had married in Boston in 1960. Their move to Chicago had been a fortunate one. They were never upper class but the family had lived well. He had left the raising of his daughters to his wife, just stepping in to spoil them occasionally. He spoiled his wife, too, and she always deferred to him, but he usually passed the family decisions right back to her.

Claire was sure that her mother had discussed the 'Easter Situation' with her father and now was ready to tell her the outcome. A drooping, brown-tipped Christmas wreath still hung on their door. She rang the bell.

The look of sympathy on her mother's face shone through the door even before it was opened all the way.

"Claire, I've been worried sick ever since you came back early from your trip."

Claire leaned over and hugged her mother. "Hello, Mom. You really shouldn't worry. I told you that Patrick and I had gotten a little homesick, that's all. We're doing pretty well." Why did she feel like crying all of the sudden?

"Oh honey, you look so pale and thin, like death warmed over … Oh, I'm sorry. What a *dreadful* thing to say! You look like you've been crying! Well, why wouldn't you, losing your husband at such a young age. I don't know what I'd have done without your father all these years."

"Mom, I *haven't* been crying," she said as her eyes started overflowing.

"Come here, dear" her mother said, "Let's sit down." She pulled her over to the big blue sofa in the living room. She held her and cooed, "That's okay, honey, let it out. I'm right here."

Claire sobbed softly into her mother's shoulder, looking around at the familiar room with its endless knick-knacks and pictures. There were no empty spaces. Everything was crowded against the next. She began to feel claustrophobic. Then she realized that the reason she couldn't breathe was because her mother was holding her face too tightly against her shoulder.

"But Mother, I really haven't been crying a lot." she gasped, coming up for air. "I actually didn't start until you mentioned it and talked about losing Michael and got all sympathetic and everything."

"Sure you haven't!" her mother said, humoring her. "Shhh-shhh. There, there. Have you been to see Father James since the funeral?

I'm sure he could help you through this difficult time."

Claire stiffened and pulled away. "You know I'm not a practicing Catholic anymore and even if I were I would not go to that man. He doesn't even believe his own religion." She was talking angrily now.

"Claire, how can you talk that way about a priest, a man who's given up his whole life for other people? Maybe if you wouldn't harden yourself so much you'd …"

"Mother, I did not come here to discuss the Church," she said, wiping away the last incriminating tears from her face.

"Of course you didn't. And I know you don't even mean the things you're saying. You're just so beside yourself with grief."

Claire bit her tongue. She was sorry she'd attacked Father James anyway; there was no point in it, especially with her mother.

"How's Daddy doing?" she asked to change the subject to a less volatile one.

"He's doing fine, considering."

"Considering what?" Claire asked apprehensively.

"Considering, he worries constantly about you and Patrick and your future."

"Mom, what's to worry about? You know we're fine financially. Michael and his dad took care of all that."

"I think he's worried about you spiritually. Now that Michael's gone, he's afraid you'll drift."

Claire was fully aware that her mother was not speaking for her father but for herself. Her dad spent no extra time worrying about his own spiritual condition, let alone others. He was a shy yet easygoing Irishman who liked whiskey and cigars and didn't worry much about spiritual futures.

"What does he mean *drift?*" Claire said, playing along.

"Drift away from the family, from God, from the Church."

"Mom, you tell him that I don't intend to drift. If I go anywhere I hope to be very decisive about it."

"I keep telling him that you're a strong young woman, even though you do look so frail. I always tell him that if worse came to worst; you'd be the one to hold the whole family together. Of, course he can't picture you that way; he only sees you as a little girl, even now." She paused as if to remember something. "I'll make us a cup of tea and then we can talk about Easter."

Just then the front door opened and in came Fran and Patrick.

"Mommy!" Patrick exclaimed as he ran to Claire, "You should see Franny's tattoo! It's a rose." He hugged and kissed her excitedly and then reached for his grandmother and did the same.

"Hi, Grace!" Fran said matter-of-factly.

"Francine! I cannot believe you got one of those filthy tattoos! And to take the boy with you! Your father will be shocked and dismayed!"

Claire felt such a relief that her 'father's' worries were deflected away from her that she sighed deeply and even smiled.

"Show them, Franny! Show them the rose!" Patrick said.

Fran nonchalantly took off her leather coat and pulled her blouse down to expose her white left shoulder. There was a tiny, perfect red rose with a green stem.

Claire got up to take a closer look. "That's actually quite lovely, if I do say so myself."

"Claire, how can you condone this crazy thing? The nose was bad enough, but …"

"What's it say underneath?" Claire asked as she noticed the tiny letters below the flower.

Patrick piped in, "It says '*Muire*'. It's Gaelic."

"Well, don't I know it? How do *you* know that, Patrick?" his grandmother asked. Then she turned quickly to Franny. "Why would you put Our Lady's sweet name by that horrid thing?"

"Grace, relax," Franny said calmly. "It's *my* middle name — Mary — remember? My friend, Robin, who's really into Celtic stuff, couldn't find 'Francine' in her book so we settled on this. And it's just a rose." She pulled her blouse back up.

"I'm afraid you've made a mistake, Miss Know-Everything!" her mother said with a hint of satisfaction. "Because the Irish hold the Blessed Mother in such honor, they spell her name differently from any ordinary 'Mary'. Your middle name would be spelled *M-a-i-r-e*. *Muire* is reserved only for Our Lady."

"Whatever, Grace. I think she'd probably like it," Franny answered with a slight wave of her hand to dismiss the subject. "So … did you have your talk about Easter?"

"We were just about to when you arrived. Why don't you take Patrick up to play with the toys and Claire and I will get it worked out in a few minutes over a cup of tea …"

Besides the family gathering, there was the whole matter of Mass. Claire had not minded Patrick going to Church with Michael, but now she was uncomfortable about him going with her parents all the time. It just wasn't the same thing; she was resentful. Yet she knew that Patrick wanted to go.

"Let's just get this Easter thing settled," Fran said, disregarding her mother's suggestion.

Claire and Patrick both thanked her with their eyes. She turned to leave the room.

"Let's all go in the kitchen and Patrick and I will make the tea."

Fran put the kettle on to boil and lit up a cigarette, while Patrick got out the familiar tea things from their cupboards, using stools and chairs.

"Francine, you know I don't like you to smoke," her mother said as she handed her her father's ashtray.

"Claire, what do you and Patrick want to do on Easter?" Franny asked, blowing out a puff of smoke.

"I just want to be free to decide *then*, what I want to *do then*, and not be pressured into anything *now*." Claire declared, feeling her sister's support.

The kettle began to whistle. Franny jumped up to get it before her mother could, and poured the steaming water into the chipped white pot. The strong Irish tea began steeping right away. Patrick had chosen mugs appropriately, giving his grandmother the one he had picked out for her birthday that said *I (heart) my Grandma*. To Claire he gave one with a bright yellow smiley face, for Franny he chose one featuring small red roses with green stems (in honor of the tattoo, no doubt). For himself he chose a cracked brownish mug his grandfather had picked out years ago on one of the family's western vacations. It had a cowboy on a bucking bronco above the inscription *DODGE CITY*.

"So, Grace. Easter is a cool thing, a *good* thing, right? And we don't want to turn it into a *bad* thing by getting Claire upset, do we?" Fran asked as she poured out the rich brown tea. She took another drag of her cigarette and put it out in the ashtray.

Grace Daly didn't respond. Then she had a thought: "I almost forgot! I baked some oat bars earlier." She went for the counter and opened a tin, and putting the squares on a plate, brought it to the table.

Claire relaxed inwardly with relief. Michael would have been proud of Fran's 'correct utterance' that quelled this Easter conflict. Franny flashed her tattoo again at Patrick's insistence and shoved an oat bar whole into her mouth, laughing with crumbs falling out.

"Francine!" said Grace.

"Oh yeah, and I started going to Mass at the mission downtown on Sundays and wondered if Patrick could go with me?"

The Accord seemed solid enough to have a pleasant and peaceful tea together.

Chapter 7

I know not where I go, nor why I go.
I enter everywhere. I answer everything
They will not kill me any more than they would kill a corpse.
In the morning I had so lost a look that those who I met
Perhaps did not see me.
                    Arthur Rimbaud

He wandered the streets like a man without a country. He was an American but his country was really in his head. His head was not big enough for the humming whispers or the numbers piling up and up in stacks and rows and reaching out in lines, all connected in webs and networks and sequences. Too much always came too fast: French literature, codes for military installations, a monk's perspective on the relation of medieval imagery to theories of higher math, all within a few minutes. His body turned to light. A scream came out of his mouth and he stopped amid the traffic noises on the sidewalk.

"*Don't ask me how I know!*" he cried to no one in particular. "BUT THE RAIN HAS STOPPED!"

It wasn't too late; he'd warned them all in time. The strangers on the street and in their shops and houses were all safe again. Thank G-O-D he had screamed. He'd never helped a whole city full of strangers before. Maybe in a dream, but he wasn't sure when he was asleep or awake. It didn't matter most of the time.

He moved along the street past the shops. They were flat, like scenery props on a stage. And the faster he moved, the faster the scenes in front of him changed, flat streaks of color all pointing him to the place. He stopped walking, holding his head and eyes perfectly still. The pictures returned. Was this the place? The place for what? For what?

The *cigarettes*. He reached in his pocket, careful not to move his head or his eyes.

He knew he had eight left. The cigarettes kept time; clocks were meaningless. Who set them? How could you trust a stranger to set the clock? *Faaaaith, faaaaith, faaaaith*, whispered Theo, his namesake who also lived in his head.

"The doctor said no direct contact. None!"

His hand found the box of cigarettes. As long as he smoked he was alive. He *knew* that dead people did not smoke. The box was his life. His past was 12; his future was 8. Of course he had hope that he would get a new box, but not until 20 was gone ... but you could never be certain. You could not buy ahead and overlap. The numbers did not lie; at least not within the box. He stood still and lit the cigarette and then walked very slowly up the street again.

In the hospital, he remembered, he was very still. Holy shit, no cigarettes! How did he do it? "Schizophrenics have a peculiar linkage of inner and outer events. Many catatonics believe that the movements of their bodies have world-destroying consequences. Is that what you think, Theo?" Doctors were very intelligent and perceptive but they were dangerous. Were they trying to make him move his mouth? He tricked them and answered in his head: *Yes, Doctor.*

But he was not in the hospital now. No, he was at the University. That's where he was going. To see John von Neumann. Interesting work they were doing. Von Neumann was the FIRST to apply mathematical techniques to problems. He watched him assemble the first computer ... NO, NO, NO, John was dead. The machine had killed him. He stopped smoking and that was before time.

He realized he was at the University. He walked up the stairs; now he was feeling better.

Was he late for class? He felt for the box in his coat. He had 7 left. He walked through the familiar halls. There seemed to be no one about. He looked in the first classroom. No students were there. Of *course* they weren't. How, in a universe as big as ours, could you even hope to intersect at the same point and time with other human beings? It was so random it was off the chart of probability. It did happen though. Miracles, *miracles!* At Carnegie Institute, at Princeton. Which one was this again?

He began to scribble on the blackboard. It was such a relief to let the numbers out of his head, to let them flow down his arm. The sequences on the board made perfect sense. Everything was perfect.

The color of the blackboard was perfect. The sound and dust of the chalk was perfect. Perfectly wonderful, perfectly awful. Heaven? Hell? Awesome and dazzling symmetry. Crystalline perfection. He was sliding down the precious exponential curve. He wrote furiously, his arm shaking back and forth as if out of his control. It *was* out of his control. The numbers *KNEW* where to go. If only his students were there. They still might come, not all at once, mind you, but hopefully they'd understand. A telephone rang somewhere five times.

Each classroom he entered was the same, only different. Was he repeating the same thing over and over again? Exhausted, he walked out into the corridor. A young woman was coming toward him.

"Could I help you, sir?"

No sex here. Only mental communion. Food and sex were horrible.

"Are you quite all right, sir? May I direct you somewhere?"

"Is this Carnegie or Princeton? My students will want to know."

The young woman looked surprised and answered, "This is University College Dublin, sir."

"Dublin. Yes, right. Doubling — doubloon — dabbling … Excuse me, Miss. Where is the telephone?"

Two young professors passed and entered the classroom on the left.

"Wasn't that Kostanikas?"

"Yeah, looks like he's been in here again," the young man said as he stared at the blackboard. "It's all undecipherable gibberish. How could a nutcase like him have gotten the Fields Prize?"

They erased the blackboard and talked of other things.

Chapter 8

Modern Education is lethal to children.
Honore Balzac

The world becomes a stranger, the pattern more complicated
Of dead and living. Not in the intense moment
But a lifetime burning in every moment
And not the lifetime of one man only
But of old stones that cannot be deciphered.
T.S. Eliot

After some dabbling in the garden, Claire went to pick up Patrick from school. It was March and in Chicago the lake wind was still blowing chilled air. But the ground was softening and some of the bulbs were bravely blooming — crocus and daffodils.

Patrick climbed into the car and strapped in his seat. Claire kissed him and asked about his day. He told her about the sandbox and how he tried to build a castle like the ones they'd built in South Carolina, but it just didn't work.

"Corey kept knocking it down, anyway. I hate Corey."

"Now Patrick, you don't want to hate people." But she hated Corey, too, and she wanted to smack him. "He probably didn't mean to."

"Yes, he did."

"Did anything else interesting happen at school?" Claire asked, trying to leave Corey behind.

"A lady said Hi to me."

"What lady? A teacher? "

"No, a lady on the sidewalk."

"You mean, just now?"

"No, at recess. I was walking by the sidewalk and a lady by the fence said "Hello, Patrick."

"Was it someone you knew? The mommy of a friend of yours or something?" she asked.

"No, I didn't know who she was."

"Is that all she said?" Claire felt uneasy.

"She asked how my mommy was."

"What did you say, Patrick?"

"I said you were fine."

"Then what?"

"Then she walked away."

"Patrick, you know that Daddy and I have told you never to talk to strangers." Her voice was tense now.

"She wasn't a stranger. She knew my name."

"Patrick, anyone who *you* don't know is a stranger, even if they know your name."

"Mommy, are you mad at me?"

What a stupid and confusing world to raise a child in, Claire thought.

"No, honey, I'm not mad at you. It's just that sometimes there are bad people who want to hurt children or even grown-ups, so you have to be careful. Is there anything about the lady that you remember?"

"She talked funny."

"What do you mean 'funny'?"

"She sounded like Daddy when he'd tell stories."

"You mean she sounded Irish?"

"Yeah, I guess. Can we stop on the way home and eat at McDonalds?"

The likelihood of Irish women being in this neighborhood wasn't as high as in her mother's, but it certainly was possible that it was someone who knew who Patrick was and knew her mother but that Patrick might not remember.

"What did she look like?"

"I don't know."

"How old was she?"

"I don't know."

"Was she older than Mommy?" She could tell he was tired of being questioned.

"Yes."

"Yes, we can go to lunch, but bear with me here. Was she maybe Grandma's age?

Could she have been a friend of Grandma's?"

Why was she making such a big deal out of this?

"She looked kind of like Mrs. Ryan at Grandpa's store."

Mrs. Ryan, poor soul, was one of the homeliest women she'd ever seen. Patrick had never liked her and it didn't seem that Mrs. Ryan liked children at all from her attitude. Maybe she'd been called awful names by them.

"Was it Mrs. Ryan, Patrick? Think hard, was it Mrs. Ryan?" Claire asked hopefully.

"No, Mommy it wasn't Mrs. Ryan. I'm hungry." Patrick in his seat impatiently.

When they pulled into the parking lot of the restaurant Claire turned to her son.

"Yes, little boy, we can eat now … but first promise Mommy that you'll never talk to strangers again, even if they know your name." She looked into his eyes, trying not to show fear.

"Yes, Mommy."

She hugged him and he scrambled out of the car.

The next morning when Claire dropped Patrick off at school she went in to talk to his teacher.

"Did Patrick mention yesterday's incident to you?" Claire asked the very young woman.

As a matter of fact, she looked so young and vulnerable that Claire didn't like the idea of her being the one there to protect Patrick. *Protect Patrick from what?* She thought. *A woman had said 'Hello' to him, that's all.*

"I think we got it all settled yesterday. I sat Corey and Patrick down and told them to be kind to each other. We went over the *Six Golden Rules for Good Socialization*. Was Patrick still upset about it when he got home? Hopefully you had a chance to process things with him."

Yeah, I processed things with him all right, Claire thought. *Whatever happened to right and wrong and 'Tell Patrick you're sorry, Corey, and go sit in your chair till sand box is over?'* But she didn't want to get into that now.

"No, no, I mean the incident with the woman on the playground."

"I'm afraid I don't know what you're referring to."

'To what you are referring', Claire edited her mentally. English teachers were like that

"A woman who Patrick did not know talked to him through the fence at recess yesterday and called him by name."

"Well, then she must have known *him*."

Don't these people read their own pamphlets and storybooks about STRANGERS? Claire thought with growing frustration.

"Certainly, you *know*, Miss Parks, that having knowledge of a child's name does not mean the person knows the child. *Of course, you know that!*"

"Did she harass or entice him in anyway?"

"No, but that is not the point. I don't want strangers being allowed to talk to my son while he is at school." Claire knew that she probably was feeling more anger than the situation called for.

"Well, have you taught him the *Five Special Ways to Deal with Strangers?*" She answered defensively, passing the blame back to Claire.

"Listen, we both want what's best for Patrick." Claire was trying out one of the *Ten Steps to Conflict Resolution*, she'd learned in one of her Education Seminars: #3. *Work to get the two seemingly opposing parties to realize that they are really on the same side. Finding that link will make everyone feel less threatened and lead to a compromise more quickly.* "I'll work harder with him from my end and you watch and make sure that there are no strange people hanging around the playground."

Obviously Miss Parks had slept through that part of her seminar. "Is Patrick seeing a therapist?" she asked. "You know he needs to process the loss of his father. The scuffle with Corey and the 'alleged' incident on the playground could be Patrick's way of calling out for help. Children act out things that they can't articulate." She was looking very knowledgeable and 'caring'.

How dare this little Miss-if-even-a-day-over-22 think she had the right to discuss Patrick in this way! "Are you accusing my son of lying? He does not lie! And don't you realize that Corey is a bully and should be held accountable for his actions? All Patrick did was build the castle! And do not use the word *process* with me again. We are not processing, we are living our lives the best way we know how!"

Claire said all of this through clenched teeth, trying not to raise her voice. Fortunately they were in a corner of the classroom and the aide was occupying the children so the flare-up was not noticed.

"Mrs. O'Connell, I realize that you have been through a lot as well, so I will not get upset by your behavior. But you both need to proc —, well, you know, *sort out* or something, this whole ordeal. Therapists are covered now under many insurance plans, I know mine is. Don't worry, though, we will watch the playground, just in case."

Claire had the urge to take Patrick out of school right then and there. But she didn't want to upset his routine suddenly and impulsively. The old Sisters at St. Rita's School, even the worst of them, didn't seem so bad at this moment. Conviction, even *wrong* conviction, seemed better than this tepid goop that passed for tolerance and sensitivity.

As she climbed into her car, Claire remembered that she had made an appointment with Doctor Quinlan for this morning. She hated to admit it, she thought as she drove toward his office and had a chance to cool down, but she had made the appointment because she found some relief in the prospect of being able to talk to someone who knew about her illness and her grief and who was also clinically objective. Even though he was an old family friend, he was able to balance that with his doctorly detachment quite well … and with none of the smothering sympathy she would have gotten from her family.

She told Doctor Quinlan about her spell in South Carolina. Not the adventurous part, of course. He responded that this was not uncommon. He talked to her about some of the things that she might be feeling.

"Claire, I think you'll find that some fears and apprehensions will crop up and I want you to be aware of them so that you realize that they are normal in a situation like this."

'Normal' is such a silly word, Claire thought. *Completely relative. What comfort was the term 'normal' to a Jew at Dachau or a starving child somewhere? All 'normal' means is that you have a lot of company in your terrible life.*

"You'll no doubt fear a loss of control — of not being in charge of your life any more. There's also the fear of dependency or of being a burden to others. Then there's the fear of the loss of self-image. You think, 'How could anyone love the weak person I've become?'"

Claire wished she hadn't come.

"Then, there's the fear of abandonment, isolation, and of course, eventually — it may be a long time — but eventually death."

"So you're saying 'Don't be afraid when you're afraid of everything, because it's 'normal' to be afraid."

"Well, I guess that's the gist of what I was saying. You're a strong young woman and you feel that you can handle almost anything that comes your way, it seems … and you do have the comfort of the Church," he added perfunctorily. "I just wanted you to be aware of what might be coming. And you know how I feel about you carrying this all alone, not letting your family know. And now with Michael's death … Claire, you're going to have to *tell them* sometime. Why not get it over with and get the support you need?"

"I'll think about it, Doctor."

Is this how one 'processes' things? Claire thought on her drive home. The only image that came to her mind was a food processor and when she threw in all of her life and pressed the button, what came out was a mess of broken, crushed, chopped and grated pieces; and that mess, in the end, was Fear.

Several weeks passed. It was mid-April and the spring was upon Illinois in full force. The bright tulips were up. Cascades of moss phlox were beginning to tumble out of nooks and crannies in white, salmon, pink, rose, and lavender. Trees were budding and leafing; the Magnolias were already out. Easter had come and gone. Fran had taken Patrick to the Easter Vigil on Holy Saturday. On Sunday morning she and Patrick had worked in the garden together getting the ground ready for the seedlings they had started inside. Franny came by in the late morning and sat on the lawn and watched them work. She hated gardening, but she had kept them company and it seemed that Claire would not have to face the earth alone after all.

Patrick went to the family gathering with Fran, who had also suggested to each of their other sisters that they stop by individually to see Claire sometime around the holiday. They had done that. Claire handled them one at a time without too much stress. Franny had also stopped by the O'Connell clan celebration with Patrick. He enjoyed seeing all his cousins in one day.

Claire felt guilty for not seeing the O'Connells more since Michael's death. She knew that their grief was tremendous, but their loss was impossible for her to bear on top of her own. At the funeral, Mary, now a young woman of 20 had hung onto Claire's hand as she had as a little girl years ago in the airport when Michael had finally come home from Ireland. His mother had seemed to be nervously waving away an invisible fly or gnat from in front of her red swollen face. Maybe it had been a gesture to the world, as when Claire had hung the sign on her hotel door: DO NOT DISTURB. These two women had loved Michael as much as she did. But she found no solace in that sorority, only greater pain.

The shroud still covered the crucifix in her bedroom.

One evening after Patrick was asleep, Claire walked into the huge closet she and Michael had shared. She still had not moved his clothes or packed anything away. She ran her hand over the rough tweed of one of his sport coats. She put her face against the fabric and held the coat in such a way that the sleeves fell over her shoulders like arms around her. The smell of him was still here, the soap, the aftershave, the leather shoes and belts.

She took the coat off the hanger and put it on over her nightgown. She slipped her bare feet into a pair of his shoes. She put on one of his wool Irish caps that hung down over her ears. She turned and looked at herself in the full length mirror at the end of the closet. She looked like a lost waif, like a little stowaway trying to pass for a boy in a man's world. "Pathetic!" she said aloud. But even her self-loathing could not dam the wave of new grief that flooded over her now. Sitting on the floor of the closet crying, she stuck her hands in the pockets of the jacket. In the right pocket she felt something and pulled it out. It was a folded piece of paper, probably a note from a student or something. She opened it to read it. It was in a language she didn't understand.

Bin Ain,
Tori mwi'l d'umnik a scaochnuid's gre A mam'rum a an sarker.
Grat Masur

She was reasonably certain it was not Gaelic; it could be Welsh. At the bottom of the note were a series of lines that looked like little combs or toothbrushes.

She remembered that Michael had shown her these markings on some of the dolmens and megalithic tombs in Ireland. It was some kind of language, too, but she couldn't remember what it was called. She knew who she could contact, however, to help satisfy her curiosity about the translation: Treat O'Toole.

Treat ("It rhymes with 'ate', not 'eat'," he always told his students) was a colleague of Michael's at Northwestern who had been very kind and helpful to her in sorting out Michael's affairs at the school after his death. He had arrived from Ireland on a green card a couple of years after Michael had finished his dissertation and had been a real catalyst in getting the funds which made possible the expansion of the Irish Studies program that Michael then chaired. Claire considered that the university was fortunate to have someone like Treat to take over and continue Michael's work.

She decided she would drive over to Northwestern in the morning. Treat had called her several times since the accident to see if she'd needed anything and had been very kind. She knew there were a few boxes of Michael's things that she needed to pick up, anyway.

Chapter 9

Peace, peace is what I seek and public calm,
Endless extinction of unhappy hates.
Matthew Arnold

Pythagoras planned it. Why did people stare?
His numbers, though they moved or seemed to move
In marble or in bronze, lacked character.
William Butler Yeats

The telephone rang in James Day's office. His clerk answered it.

"No, I'm afraid he's not in right now, but I expect him to return at any time. If you'll leave your … Hold a moment please." Someone was coming in, breathing rapidly.

"Mr. Day!" the clerk said obsequiously. "Welcome back, sir! There is someone on the line for you. Would you like to take a call now, sir … or catch your breath?"

"Who is it, Eugene?"

"Excuse me, a moment, sir …" He pushed the button on the phone. "Who is this calling please? … Pardon me, could you repeat that, please?" The clerk pushed the hold button again.

"He says it's God, sir. G-O-D."

Mr. Day smiled and said he'd get it in his office. He closed the door on his assistant's befuddled face and picked up his receiver.

"I'm afraid you've frightened Eugene, or impressed him perchance. You'd best not say everything you think to my office help." Mr. Day said, only half joking.

"I don't think I'm God. I was merely translating my name from the Greek for those who don't speak the language. If I were God I'd keep much better track of people like me and of universities. Did you know that I'm in Dublin?"

Just then another man walked into Mr. Day's office. The clerk was trying unsuccessfully to stop him. Mr. Day waved the gentleman in and dismissed Eugene with another wave.

"Of course, I know you're in Dublin, Theo. I brought you here, remember? You're living at my house for a while. Where are you now, my man? I've been concerned about your whereabouts … Alright then. Stay put and I'll send a car for you or come myself, very soon … Yes, I will, Theo … Don't worry … Of course … Good Bye."

The man across the desk from Mr. Day shook his head and said, "Jim, I don't know why you do it. The man could be dangerous. He makes no sense most of the time. I know he won some big mathematical prize and all, but he's daft you know. We, yer close friends, we worry about you. And it seems we lose track of ye, can't keep our eye of safety on ye as we once did."

"Charlie, I appreciate your concern, but you've no need to worry. He's a harmless sort and he's quite lucid at times. You know when I met him he had no real home. He'd been in and out of hospitals for years after he lost his post at Princeton. From what I understand his condition improved for a time. When William introduced me to him at that dinner in Paris, I couldn't help feeling sorry for the man. He was so restless; he was floating around living with former colleagues, moving from house to house."

"It doesn't seem to me that he's in good condition yet, Jim. But I'm not a psychiatrist, am I now?"

"He was offered posts at M.I.T. and at the University of Chicago just last year, Charlie. The man's a genius. He just needs some good friends and care and a stable environment to continue his work. I felt I couldn't turn my back on him when I realized his plight. I have that huge flat here in town and the house in the North; and now that Maeve's gone …"

"A sad day that was too, Jim. May she rest in peace," he said crossing himself. "It's funny, don't you think, to have two big Prize winners in the same house? Of course, his prize is not as grand as yours, is it now, Jim?" said Charlie with a look of pride for his friend.

"Well, there is no Nobel Prize for Mathematics. But he got the Fields Medal back in the early sixties. It's really the equivalent of a Nobel. Do you know what he told me the other day, Charlie? When he was a young lad at Carnegie Institute one of his Math professors was John Synge."

"Aaaiee, Jim! We know that's a cart of horse dung, don't we now? Everyone knows Synge was a playwright in Ireland with Yeats and Lady Gregory and all them. Where does he come up with all this crazy stuff? And him being Greek, too … Why does he hallucinate Irishmen?" Charlie laughed and gave a knowing wink.

"No, Charlie, I checked it out. It was Synge's nephew. This John Synge was a brilliant mathematician and taught at Carnegie when Kostanikas was there. Evidently he was quite intimidating in appearance, a black eye patch and all that. Doesn't surprise me at all though. Just another one of the signs." Day smiled at Charlie's incredulity and reached over and patted the small wiry man on the back as he stood up from the desk.

"The signs of the times — that's for sure. Soon we'll find out that Yeats' son was some kind of Hindu monk or somethin'."

"Could be … Charlie, could be." Day tried to keep a serious face.

"Oh, pshaw, Jim. To hell with ye," his friend said with a wave of his hand and a chuckle.

James Day had grown up in Belfast, Northern Ireland, in a poor Catholic family. His was the first generation of Catholics who were allowed an education. He studied and worked hard for all the causes of the underclass. He won a scholarship to St. Columba College and made his family proud. He had worked unendingly for peace — speaking out again and again against violence on either side — whether it was the IRA Provisionals or the Loyalist Paramilitaries. He struggled through the 60's and the demonstrations, the nasty business at St. Matthew's Church and the terrible Bloody Sunday in the 70's, the emotional H-Block hunger strikes of the 80's. Then finally in the 90's it seemed that peace was a possibility. In 1994, came the ceasefire. Then in '98, The Good Friday Accord looked to everyone around the world like an agreement that would hold together. But then came the Marching Season conflicts in July, the atrocities in Omagh and Belfast, the murder of the Nationalist human-rights lawyer, and now the impasse over disarmament …

Charlie Breen and some of Day's other friends had noticed that he seemed impervious to the unraveling truce. James Day had always been an optimist. Getting the "Prize", some said, had kept him going. Others like Kenneth Conlon thought Day had become more of a dreamer than ever and began to lose faith in his judgment. When

Mr. Day wasn't present, Conlon began to suggest that their broad coalition might soon need a new leader. This caused great dissension among the ranks. James Day was a living legend, a true symbol of peace not only to Ireland, but to the international community at large.

* * *

Dr. Theo Kostanikas stood on the steps of the university, smoking. He was agitated when Day drove up.

"Don't touch the third step!" he called out. "It's moving up from the bottom. It used to be the first step. If I move, it could be it."

"It?"

"IT!"

"Let's go home, Theo, and you can work in your room and no one will bother you."

"But what about the building?"

"When we get home I'll call and warn them. They'll get someone else to take over."

"Thank God, they've brought in the back-ups." He reached in his pocket and brought out the box. He was smoking number twenty. "I'll need to stop on the way." he said as he descended the stairs, skipping the fourth step.

Chapter 10

Love is a sad sickness —
When speaking to him, whatever the cause,
It is hardship to separate after time together.
Pity my own blood's case.
           Isibaul MhicCailin

To place absolute trust in another human being is in itself a disaster, both ways, since each human being is a ship that must sail its own course, even if it go in the company of another ship.
           David Herbert Lawrence

    The stately trees that lined the streets of Evanston, Illinois were almost fully leaved. Pansies were growing in the window boxes and Claire could see Lake Michigan straight ahead. She drove past the Northwestern-Evanston Research Park and turned left on Sheridan Road and then drove north along the lake toward the college.

    She had turned some kind of corner in her grief as well. It had been over three months since Michael had died and she seemed to be coming out of the thickest layer of the hazy confusion that had enveloped her. Sometimes she missed it, because it had a numbing effect, and because it gave her a place to be that wasn't really a place. But now she was looking out at the lake and it was beautiful. She had a mission today: to decipher a message.

    Claire found her way to Michael's old department. Allyson Richards, the department secretary, was at her desk.

    "Good Morning, Mrs. O'Connell. It's so good to see you again. And how is Patrick?"

    "He's well, thank you, Allyson. Is Mister …? Doctor … which is it? O'Toole around?"

    "It's Doctor O'Toole. Yes, as of last month," the plain but efficient young woman said admiringly.

    "Well, good for him! Is he in?"

    "He should be back from class in about …" She looked at her schedule. "About five or ten minutes. You can wait in his office if you like."

    She pointed over toward her left. Claire walked in that direction.

She saw the name on the door of Michael's old office: *Dr. Treat O'Toole, Chairman, Irish Studies.* She hesitated and walked inside. Nothing was the same, except for a thick folder that lay on the desk with Michael's name on it. She picked it up and began to look through it. As she did, Treat walked in.

"Claire, is that you?"

She laid the folder back on the desk and turned toward him. He was a handsome man with a neatly trimmed reddish-brown mustache and beard. He was somewhat younger than she and Michael, but had a more studious, professorial look about him than Michael ever had. No matter how hard Michael thought or worked, he always looked like he was on vacation. Treat actually *looked* like a department head; a trifle young perhaps, but nevertheless fit for a prestigious college like Northwestern. Michael usually looked, to Claire, like someone who stopped by to check on his endowment on the way to his yacht, even in his wrinkled shirt and khakis.

"I hope you don't mind me stopping by without warning, but I remembered there were still some boxes of Michael's things here. And I found a mystery for you to help me solve."

She pulled the paper out of her pocket and showed it to him.

"I found this in the pocket of one of Michael's jackets and I was just curious, you know."

"Of course I can understand why you'd be interested, but …" He scanned the message.

"I cannot understand the language in this note. It looks like a form of one of the *secret mystical languages …*"

As he said these last few words, his voice became a theatrical stage whisper and his hands flew up jokingly, as if to put a spell on Claire: "… of *ancient Ireland* that Michael was working on."

They both laughed and he continued more seriously.

"I was going to ask *you* if you knew where his latest draft of the Lexicon was."

He pointed to the note. "Of course, the lines there at the bottom are *Ogham,* which was also a secret and sacred language of the Druids, but we know much more about it, because it was written on a lot of archeological finds."

"Ogham, yes, that was it. I do remember Michael talking about that. Wasn't it based on the fingers or something?"

"Well, Mrs. O'Connell, if I could tell you a wee story ..." He was thickening his already obvious brogue; it reminded her of Michael.

"If ye will, Mr. O'Toole, I'd be pleased," she answered, smiling back at him.

"We find the story in *The Book of Ballymote*. Ogham, it tells us, was put together by Ogma Sun-face, son of Bres. He was one of the *Tuatha De Danann*, the race of beautiful fairy-like people who settled in ancient Ireland. The story goes that the first thing ever written in Ogham was seven strokes cut on a birch rod. And these seven magical cuts warned the great hero Lug mar Ethlenn, that his wife would be carried off to Fairy land *seven times* unless she was protected by a birch tree. Ever after, the letters of the Ogham script were named after trees, beginning with B for Birch. Now the fingers come in, as you so cleverly remember, because the *fingers* replaced the *cuts* on the rod. The fingers were always accessible and easily hidden. The rod or stem-line could be replaced by anything at hand. Thus we have variations like *Cos-Ogham* meaning *Leg-Ogham*, where the shin bone could be used as the stem-line and the fingers laid against it in different directions and numbers. Then there is *Sron-Ogham*, meaning *Nose-Ogham*, where a person could use the bridge of the nose as the stem line."

At this point he was laying his fingers all around his nose in a comical way that made Claire laugh again.

"Not very secretive or sacred-looking though, that Nose-Ogham." she said, still chuckling.

"Michael was much more into the mystical and magical aspects of the languages. I enjoy the science of it. It's like a puzzle to me, even like an arithmetic problem. I guess growing up in Ireland, I began to think of all the legends as old-fashioned and something only the old rural people hung on to in order make their lives more enjoyable."

"That's interesting ... because I don't think I ever told you that I have a math background and I made the connection with the Druids and the Celts through realizing the sophistication of their mathematical skills. Do you believe in the Pythagorean/Druid theory?"

"You mean that somehow Pythagoras left Greece and studied with the Druids, or vice-versa? I've heard it mentioned."

Claire nodded. "But even with Pythagoras, you can't get away from the mystical, you know. He claimed to have undergone initiation by the *Daktyls* , which means 'fingers', by the way," she pointed to the Ogham book, "who were five spirits or Cretan deities or something, who guided him into the mystical connotations of number and the relation between sacred numbers and sacred letters. I picked up a book about Druids and mathematics years ago in Ireland. The only part I've really read is the part about Pythagoras. I'll have to get it out again. Maybe I'll loan it to you when I'm done."

Treat gestured to the piles of books and stacks of papers to grade that were all over his office. "I'll let you know when these are all finished!"

Then she asked, "So you can decipher the Ogham at the bottom of the note, then."

Treat took the note again and went over to pull a book off his shelf. He shuffled through it with familiarity. He wrote something down while saying, "This is all approximate, you realize. It looks like a date of some kind and it's using the Roman calendar, which of course the Celts did not have. The Ogham alphabet only has 20 letters, plus five other characters which represent diphthongs. This seems to be a letter-by-letter translation into English. Quite amateurish, really. Oh well, here it is; the number is just a series of slashes, 10 in this case." He handed the note to Claire. She looked at it closely.

S U N D A E — G A N U A R E

"There is no 'Y', so the person who wrote the note substituted an 'E' instead. In the same way, they've used 'G' to represent 'J'. So thus it seems to say 'Sunday, January 10'."

Claire turned white. She felt slightly faint.

"Claire, what's the matter? Are you feeling ill?"

"That's the day Michael had his accident; the day he died."

Treat leaned out the door of his office and asked Allyson to get a glass of water. Claire drank a little and felt better. She folded the

81

paper again and put it in her pocket.

"What an absurd coincidence, huh?" she said rather cynically, because she could think of nothing else.

"Unfortunately so, I'd say."

"Well, thanks for your help, anyway."

"Claire ... really, if there's *anything* I can do to help out at *any time*, please feel free to call me. Sorry I wasn't more help with the body of the message. I'm afraid I've just upset you with my partial knowledge." Treat paused. "Maybe I should keep the note and investigate it myself."

"It's alright, maybe I don't *want* to know the whole thing. Now where are those boxes?"

"Right over here in the corner. I'll get them and follow you to your car."

"Oh, and I couldn't help noticing that folder on your desk with Michael's name on it. Are those his things as well?"

"Why, yes. Actually, I just ran across it this morning and had to go off to class before I could even look inside."

"So I can take it, then."

"By all means! I intended to put it with his other things for you. Let me slip it into one of these boxes ..."

Claire got into her little red Ford Escort. Treat loaded the boxes into the trunk and said good-bye, reiterating again his availability if she needed his help in the future.

"Who *would* be the best person to ask about translating the message?" she asked through her open window.

"Professor McCullum might steer you to someone. He and Michael worked quite closely ... well, of course you know that. Have you had much contact with him since ...?"

"He called from Ireland to extend his sympathy before the funeral. I've not talked with him since then."

"Well, give *him* a ring then. I'll see what I can come up with asking around our always-exciting philological circles."

Claire made a poor attempt at a smile.

"The note is probably nothing, Claire. From the simplistic knowledge displayed in the Ogham text, it could have been a student playing around with language structure or some such. Don't be worried. It will all come 'round."

Instead of heading west toward I-94 and south toward home, Claire turned north and drove along the lakeshore. Her thoughts were scrambled and full of questions she couldn't answer. When Michael had left early on that cold dark January morning, saying that he was restless and couldn't sleep, she remembered thinking that it was unusual. He was very seldom restless or sleepless. But he had always had times when he needed to get off by himself to think, to dream, and more recently, to pray. There was never a melancholy in it — no Byronesque brooding over the heath or moor. She was glad for him to go because when he returned he often had the spark of life turned brighter in his eyes and even a hint of the old wildness about him.

It wasn't his restlessness or the sleeplessness that really nagged at her now, but the note in her pocket, the date on the note, which suggested to her that maybe he had met someone that day. And it wasn't the meeting in itself, she thought that made her feel what she was feeling. What *was* she feeling? Anxiety? Suspicion? No, it was pain, pain in dealing with the fact that the last words he had spoken to her were not really true.

"Why are you getting up before the sun in the dead of winter on a Sunday morning?" she had asked, half-awake and warm in their bed.

He was already dressed when she heard him. His lips were warm, but his hand was cold on her shoulder as he leaned over to kiss her forehead.

"Shhhh, Go back to sleep. I didn't even mean to disturb you. I can't sleep and I need to get out to clear my head. I may go and watch the sunrise over the lake or something. I'll be back to take Patrick to Mass. It's the Baptism ... I love you, Claire."

She decided rather unconsciously to turn west just before Highland Park. As she drove across the suburban sprawl and strips and ever-new mini malls, she felt sick. She saw a side road that looked like it led to somewhere more rural and less progressive; she made a sharp right turn.

Claire had gone over Michael's last words to her again and again. She had fondled and caressed each one separately — *Shhh, sunrise,*

Patrick, love — and held them all in a bunch in no particular order but in her heart as a treasure. Michael's voice, Michael's beautiful words. But now she felt betrayed, that was it. It didn't matter what the note said, there was something he did not want her to know.

As Claire was trying to figure out where she was, she glanced in her rearview mirror.

She had the queer thought that the car that was behind her had been behind her as she drove up the lakeshore. It was a green Ford truck actually, an older model. It could just be a similar one. But what were the chances of that? She made a quick left turn and headed west again, speeding up to see if the truck followed her. She spied a gas station ahead and pulled off and drove around to the back of it. She waited a few minutes and pulled out on the road again. No sign of the green truck.

She felt foolish and sad and angry with Michael for dying. Witnesses reported that he had stepped off the curb without looking. He was near the Lake, near the university. The woman who hit him was hysterical and was never charged. It was a horrible accident. Michael never came home. Patrick did not get picked up for Mass. A policeman came to the door instead.

Claire drove on, down a two-lane highway which now ran through dense forest on either side. She checked the rear-view mirror, knowing no one was in pursuit — just an empty highway. She looked again though, nervously, in the side mirror and then again to the road ahead.

As she looked out the windshield she could still see the side mirror with her peripheral vision. This created a strange phenomenon: she felt as if the trees and sky and road behind her were falling away faster than she was moving into the landscape ahead. It probably had some scientific explanation and even a name, like *Doppler Effect* or something. But it made her dizzy and gave her the sensation that she was losing her past much faster than she was gaining her future. She felt diminished, as if she were leaving parts of herself along the road, coming upon the next unexpected curve without a whole person to face what she would find there.

She looked at her watch with the floating red-haired lady. Almost noon. It was time to find her way back to Patrick.

Chapter 11

There, in a vision of the night, I saw a man whose name was Victoricus coming as if from Ireland with innumerable letters and he gave me one of them, and I began reading the letter: 'The Voice of the Irish', and as I was reading the beginning of the letter I seemed at that moment to hear the voice of those who were beside the forest of Foclut which is near the western sea, and they were crying as if with one voice: 'We beg you, holy youth, that you shall come and shall walk again among us.'
Confessions of St. Patrick

There shall be corals in your beds,
There shall be serpents in your tides,
Till all our sea-faiths die.
Dylan Thomas

During the mornings that Patrick was in school, Claire worked a little in the garden, but spent most of her time in Michael's study. Patrick really enjoyed the garden and taking over his father's vegetable plot and Claire loved his company. She had decided against bothering Doctor McCullum with the matter of the cryptic message. Instead she spent hours looking through Michael's books and papers, hoping for some breakthrough on her own.

There had been several folders marked with Michael's name in the boxes from the university, and Claire could not determine which one had been laying on Treat's desk.

Anyway, none of them held any clues to Michael's message.

Claire realized as she sat at his desk one day how separate their married lives had actually been. Of course they had done things together, and still had some common interests, and after Patrick was born they joyfully shared their parenthood. But this whole world in his study Michael had — for the most part — kept to himself. Except for where he kept his small array of religious artifacts in their bedroom, this study was where Michael had felt the freedom to be who he was.

Had she trapped him there? Or had he trapped himself? He had made his choices — she had made hers. Had their shared loyalty to her independence kept them from really sharing much at all?

He had not only kept his promise about not forcing his religion on her; but he had kept his passion and his work locked away in this room for six years, and she had allowed that.

She looked at the book on the desk that she had found: *Notes on the Distribution, History, Grammar, and Import of the Irish Ogham Inscriptions*, by E. MacNeill, The Royal Irish Academy. She chided herself for going to Treat without even looking through Michael's vast resources right in their own home. The other Lexicon must be around somewhere here, too, she thought. She found the alphabet quickly and matched her translation easily with Treat's. She shivered as she looked at the date of Michael's death written out again. She read on in the book; very scholarly, but fascinating:

> "*The secret alphabet or finger-script was never written down by the druids. It was not until the language and the druids themselves were passing off the stage of history that it was first inscribed. We possess some hints as to its contents and its limitations and a poetical composition which may very well be one of its hymns. It is a wild spell, said, in the tale of the landing of the 'Children of Mil', to have been chanted by their chief bard, Amorgen, as he set foot on the soil of Ireland. In the course of the story the mystical child bard, Taliesin, utters a poem narrating his various transformations throughout the world's existence. The Christian monk historians who were responsible for writing down and passing on the Irish story were conscious of its sublimity and were unwilling, even at the risk of disseminating paganism, to let it go:*
>
> *I am the wind in the sea,*
> *I am the wave of the billows,*
> *I am the sound of the sea:*
> *I am an ox of seven fights,*
> *I am a vulture on a cliff,*
> *I am a tear of the sun [= a dewdrop],*
> *I am fair among flowers,*
> *I am a boar,*

I am a salmon in a pool,
I am a lake in a plain,
I am a word of knowledge,
I am a point of the spear that fighteth,
I am the god who formeth fire for a head [giver of inspiration].

Who maketh clear the ruggedness of a mountain?
Who telleth beforehand the ages of the moon?
Who telleth where the sun shall set?
Who bringeth the cattle from the house of Tethra?
[Tethra = the ocean: the reference is to the stars rising from the sea.]
On whom do the cattle of Tethra smile?
What man, what god formeth weapons,
Singeth spells … Is it not I?

"*As we read a poem like this, we cannot but feel that it is a very suitable preface to the hymnary of a philosophical school like the opening chapter of the Kur'an, or like the Apostles' Creed. It may well have been used, not merely in the studies of druidic pupils, but in the liturgies of public religious functions so that knowledge of its contents would thus make its way outside druidic schools. Was it the contents of this hymn, that Caesar was thinking, when he wrote that the druids taught of the stars and their motions, the world, the size of lands, natural philosophy, and the nature of the gods?*"

Claire had a hard time imagining the length of the poem written out in Ogham script with all of its lines and bars. She wondered what the language had sounded like. Of course it was lost forever, but the book remarked that there was one isolated fluent Ogham speaker found as late as the 14th century.

Stuck in the back of the book folded in half was another poem printed by hand in Michael's writing. At the top he had inscribed: *TO MY SON PATRICK*. As she looked it over she recognized a section of it as something she had learned at St. Rita's known as 'The Breastplate of St. Patrick". It was supposedly a prayer written by the man. She had no idea that it was taken from a longer poem. It was titled 'The Deer's Cry' and she was surprised by the similarity, in form, at least in some of its sections, to the older druidic hymn. She put it aside and would read it to Patrick later. It was from his father, after all.

Claire looked around to no avail for some key to the secret language in the note. But she did feel close to Michael in this his space and she felt she was opening up to him in a way she hadn't while he was alive.

That night when Patrick was going to bed, Claire opened the poem to read to him.

"I found something that Daddy had meant to give you and I would like to read it to you. It's kind of long, but I think you'll like it."

As soon as she began to read, Patrick began to smile.

>   TO MY SON PATRICK
>   *May you grow to be a great man,*

(Michael had copied the ancient introduction as well. It had all been translated by Dr. Kuno Meyer, the man whose work Michael had built upon.)

>   *"Patrick made this hymn. It was made in the time of Loeguire, son of Niall. It was his monks against deadly enemies that lay in wait for the clerics. And this is the corslet of faith for the protection of body and soul against devils and men and vices. Patrick sang this when the ambuscades were laid against his coming by Loeguire, that he might not go to Tara to sow the faith. And then it appeared before those lying in ambush [Loeguire's men] that they [Patrick and his monks] were wild deer with a fawn [Beven] following. And its name is 'Deer's Cry'."*

>   I arise today
>   Through the mighty strength, the invocation of the Trinity,
>   Through belief in the threeness,
>   Through confession of the oneness
>   Of the creator of creation.
>   I arise today

  Through the strength of Christ's birth and His baptism,
  Through the strength of His crucifixion with His burial,
  Through the strength of His resurrection with his ascension,
  Through the strength of his descent for the Judgement of Doom.
I arise today
  Through the strength of the love of cherubim,
  In obedience of angels,
  In the service of archangels,
  In the hope of the resurrection to meet with reward,
  In prayers of Patriarchs,
  In predictions of Prophets
  In preaching of Apostles
  In faith of Confessors
  In innocence of Holy Virgins
  In deeds of righteous men.
I arise today
  Through the strength of heaven
  Light of the sun
  Radiance of the moon
  Splendor of fire
  Speed of lightening
  Swiftness of wind
  Depth of sea
  Stability of earth
  Firmness of rock.
I arise today
  Through God's strength to pilot me:
  God's might to uphold me,
  God's wisdom to guide me,
  God's eye to look before me
  God's ear to hear me
  God's word to speak for me,
  God's hand to guard me
  God's way to lie before me
  God' shield to protect me
  God's host to save me
    From snares of devils

From temptation of vices
From everyone who shall wish me ill
Afar and near
Alone and in a multitude.
I summon today all those powers between me and those evils
Against every cruel merciless power that oppose my body and soul
   Against incantations of false prophets
   Against black laws of pagandom
   Against false laws of heretics
   Against the craft of idolatry
   Against spells of women, and smiths and wizards
   Against every knowledge that corrupts man's body and soul.
Christ to shield me today
Against poison, against burning
Against drowning, against wounding
So that there may come to me an abundance of reward.
Christ with me, Christ before me, Christ behind me,
Christ in me, Christ beneath me, Christ above me,
Christ on my right, Christ on my left,
Christ when I lie down,
Christ when I sit down and Christ when I arise,
Christ in the heart of every man who thinks of me,
Christ in the mouth of every man who speaks of me,
Christ in every eye that sees me,
Christ in every ear that hears me.
I arise today
   Through the mighty strength, the invocation of the Trinity
   Through belief in the threeness,
   Through the confession of the oneness
   Through the Creator of creation.
Domini est salus. Domini est salus.
Christi est salus, Salve tua, Domini,
Sit temper nobiscum.
    Amen

Claire finished reading and looked at Patrick, thinking that he'd probably be asleep after the long rhythmic poem, but his eyes were shining. He reached over and pulled open the little drawer in his night table and took out a wrinkled piece of paper and showed it to Claire. It was an exact copy of the paper she had in her hands, with the inscription and everything.

"Patrick, why didn't you tell me that Daddy had already given this to you?"

"Because I wanted to hear *you* read it to me, like Daddy did." he answered.

"How long ago did he give it to you?"

"I don't remember."

"Did he read it to you a lot?"

"For ever," Patrick said.

Claire couldn't help thinking with bitter irony, that the prayer had not done Michael the slightest bit of good.

She kissed Patrick and hugged him extra hard. He counted and called each of his stuffed animals by name, which had become a nightly ritual since their return from South Carolina. She didn't know why.

She turned off his light and went to her room to get ready for bed herself. They had spent the afternoon and early evening at the zoo with one of Michael's older sisters and her children. She was tired even though twilight was barely past. She had retrieved her copy of *Druidic Mathematics* from a pile of books in her little study near her computer. She was inspired to read it thoroughly. She wondered what the druids would have thought of computers! An idea came to her. She knew that Michael had put a few files on her computer, even though he was almost a Luddite when it came to most new technology. Maybe he had put some of his lexicon work on the hard drive or on a disc. She'd check it out tomorrow, she told herself. Meanwhile, she read her book.

Claire turned to the chapter, *Pythagoras's Influence on the Celts*. Pythagoras, the author said, was born on the Greek Island of Samos, but was believed to have traveled widely, eventually reaching Britain. He settled later in life, between 540 and 530 BC, in southern Italy and established a school of some 300 disciples.

Pythagoras was worshipped as a semi-deity, in part because of the severe ritual initiation at the sacred Orphic temple on Crete. The concept of karma, the pre-existence and permanence of souls was something he would have learned from Orpheus through the Daktyls.

At the core of the Pythagorean philosophy, however, was the significance of *numbers*.

'All things are assimilated to number' is an original Pythagorean proverb. Among members of this school, numbers were venerated as mystic representations of eternal and divine truth. The figure of ten dots arranged in a pyramid, called a *tetraktys*, was worshipped as an ikon of the entire universe.

Claire remembered a math professor at Notre Dame saying that once a brilliant mathematician crossed over the line from number into numerology, he was lost. She was sure Pythagoras had crossed the line (odd numbers were male, even were female; the number 5 was associated with marriage; 6 symbolized marriage and childbirth, etc.) and that if he lived today he'd be spending time in mental hospitals along with a host of other schizophrenic mathematicians. But the *mystery of number* still fascinated her, too.

Claire was just beginning to get drowsy, book slipping in her hand, when she realized that she'd left the light on in her closet and the door standing open. As she started to get up to handle the matter, she caught some movement at the corner of her eye. It was quick and it was black. She jumped back on the bed. She saw it again by the closet door on the floor. There was a black thing lying on the floor. Was it moving? She thought it had.

It could be one of Michael's belts that had fallen off its rack, she reasoned. Her eyes and her nerves were playing tricks.

It moved again and she watched it slither toward the bed. In horror she realized that it was a snake. She screamed. Then she saw another incredible black flash over on the other side of the room. There were *two* snakes in her bedroom.

"My God! What's happening?" she pleaded to no one and screamed again loudly.

Patrick came to her door, sleepy-eyed. "Mommy, what's wrong? I heard you crying!"

"Patrick! Get out of here! Do what Mommy says right now! Go back to your room and close Mommy's door! Now, Patrick!" She knew he could see her terror as she knelt on the bed.

"Mommy, what's wrong?" he begged.

"Patrick, there are *snakes* in here and they might be dangerous," she yelled at him, "*Shut the door* and go back to your room!" She couldn't remember ever yelling at him before.

He closed the door.

Claire could no longer see the snake that had moved toward her bed. *Had it gone under?* She guessed. *Was it climbing her quilt? Could snakes climb?* She was shaking all over. *What could she use as a weapon?* Her eyes searched for something within reach.

There! On Michael's side of the bed, just above his nightstand on a little platform was a statue. She reached for it and found it was heavy. She thought it might kill a snake. Her thoughts were racing. If she dropped it on the snake and missed, then she'd be without any defense. She'd have to get in a position and strike at it. She crept off the bed slowly and went around to the foot of the bed to get a better look, holding the statue in her hand. She saw the black head poised near the edge of the bedspread. She moved cautiously to get within striking distance. She had no idea where the other snake was.

Patrick opened the door. She glanced at him as he stood in his pajamas. He had a plastic knight's helmet on his head and a plastic sword raised in his hand.

"Patrick," she said in a calm whisper, though she was terrified for his safety, "Honey, please go back. Mommy doesn't want you to get hurt, and I'll be alright …"

As she spoke, the black writhing thing moved toward her. She screamed and leaned over with the statue and struck — again and again and again, flailing long after the snake's head was crushed.

She realized that she was crying. Then she remembered Patrick. She looked over and saw him standing in the other corner of the room, his sword in one hand and to her amazed disgust, a limp black snake in the other.

She could not move; her arms and legs felt like lead. He walked over to where she knelt and dropped the dead snake by the other one as if it were a rubber toy.

"Patrick, are you alright?" She felt her own breathlessness as she spoke.

"I'm fine," he said," except for my *foot* hurts."

Oh, God, had he been bitten? She looked at his foot. There was a bruise on his small heel but nothing that looked like a bite.

"How did it happen? What did you do?" she asked, pulling him close.

"I hit him with my sword, but he didn't die all the way, so I stomped on him with my foot," he said proudly and unself-consciously.

"You stepped on a snake with your bare foot? My, you were very brave! But you didn't obey Mommy," she added half-heartedly.

"I had to do my fighting, Mommy. Daddy said that the knights *always* protected the ladies."

Claire's four-year-old (almost five-year-old) son went over and picked up the snakes and walked out of the room.

"I'm gonna throw them out the back door," he told her.

Claire was too dazed to argue. After he left the room she knelt there shaking and began to cry again softly. She looked down at her hand, which felt unattached to her body. Still clenched in her grip she saw the statue, her weapon. It was The Virgin and she was still in one piece, except for a crack across her chest where the stone was crumbling away. Maybe the crack had even been there before.

Chapter 12

A mouth that has no moisture and no breath
Breathless mouths may summon
I hail superman,
I call it death-in-life and life-in-death.
       William Butler Yeats

Man spins out a whole net of falsities around his spirit by the repeated consecration of his whole self to values that do not exist.
       Gregory of Nyssa

Yellow flames rose high into the cool, black spring night, a mist framing the edge of the gathered human circle like a halo. A pole, thick and rigid and twice a man's height pushed its way aggressively into the air, impregnating the already charged atmosphere with solemnity. Hooded figures chanted to the low beating of a squat drum. The twelfth full moon of the year barely shone on the small assembly as the distinctive whirring and honking of wild geese flew overhead in their northward migration.

One of the members was surrounded by a pack of leashed white hounds with red eyes and red-tipped ears that glowed in the darkness as their baying was interspersed among the rhythmic chants. As more wood was thrown upon the fire, its flames leapt higher and licked the sky. Tied to the pole was a large limp body, head hanging and rolling randomly from one side to the other.

The figure with the hounds spoke out in a half-human voice, impossible to understand, but the chanting stopped and everything seemed to freeze, even the motion of the flames. Two hooded figures then moved in an unnatural dream-like way toward the pole and its victim, moving their arms until the body fell untethered to the ground. A coffin-like wicker cage appeared from nowhere, next to the fallen man and he was put within it.

The dreadful yet seductive sounds began again, and the flames were free to move along with the assembly as they lifted high the cage and tossed it into the crackling yellow fire.

There was a click and a flicker before the monitor screen went black.

Chapter 13

That blessed mood,
In which the burden of the mystery,
In which the heavy weary and the weight
Of all the unintelligible world, is lightened.
William Wordsworth

Look, you fools. You're in danger. Can't you see? They're after you. They're after all of us. Our wives, our children, everyone. They're here already. You're next!
From 'Invasion of the Body Snatchers'

There is no conspiracy. Just twelve people dead …
Promotional tagline for 'The Parallax View'

Claire lay in the lower bunk in Patrick's room. She could hear his steady breathing as she watched the light of dawn gradually filter in around the shades. She was determined to downplay the whole event with Patrick and shield him as much as possible from whatever it was that was happening to them.

As she made his breakfast, she gave an explanation about the snakes probably coming up through the sewer system, and rattled off some other instances concerning baby alligators and boa constrictors that she'd either read about in the paper or heard from her mother. (It was obscure, but still good 'worry fodder' for her mom, she thought.) Claire didn't think Patrick really believed her but she did not tell him how frightened she was — how sure she was now that someone was harassing her, and that she was going to call the police after she took him to school. As they walked out the back door toward the car, Claire asked, trying to be nonchalant:

"By the way, little boy, where did you put those snakes last night?"

"They're in the trash can right by the door. Can I look at 'em?"

"No, Patrick, let's just get you to school and try to forget about the whole thing."

He looked disappointed but marched to the car.

She ended up leaving a vague message with someone at the police station who said an officer would call her back. He did, eventually.

"Are you sure you don't need an exterminator and not a policeman?" he asked, somewhat amused.

"I believe someone may have put the snakes in my house to harm me. We're not talking here about ants or mice!" Claire answered with a touch of anger.

"You know we hear stories all the time about crazy animals in sewer pipes or even, yeah, I do remember once when a snake got away from someone and hid somewhere in the house and didn't show up until the new owners were minding their own business one night and ..."

Claire interrupted, "But we've lived in this house for over six years!" completely disregarding the sewer theory.

"You wouldn't believe the strange things that I've seen, ma'am."

"Well, would you come over and take a look around anyway?"

"Are there any signs of forced entry?"

"You mean doors broken down or something?"

"Doors forced, windows forced?"

"I didn't see anything unusual, but you'd probably be a better judge than I about that kind of thing."

"I'm sorry, Mrs. ... uh ... O'Connell, I can't send somebody out to check to see if a place *might* have been broken into. We hardly have enough people to go around for all the *legitimate* crime scenes."

"All right," Claire said in frustration, pulling out her trump card, "there's something I haven't told you. My son and I were on vacation last February and I think someone tried to kill me."

"You *think* someone tried to kill you?" He sounded impatient.

"Well, they tried to kill me or the man who was with me," she said.

"Did you file a report or press charges with the police in ... where was it again?"

"South Carolina, Hilton Head. No, the woman who tried to do it ran away and it was all very confusing," Claire said rather sheepishly.

"Did your gentleman friend report it?"

"He was not a friend. I had just met him on the beach right before it happened."

She realized that the whole situation either sounded incredible or made her look like some kind of low-life woman who was trying to pick up strange men on the beach.

"Ma'am, I'm afraid you're not giving me much to go on —"

"Oh, wait a minute! There's more. A strange woman with an Irish accent said Hello to my son at his kindergarten playground."

"Strange? What kind of strange?"

"I mean strange as in *stranger*. She acted like she knew him but he didn't know her."

"A lot of young kids don't remember everyone who might know them, you know. Did she try to entice him or coerce him in any way?" he asked.

"She was on the other side of the fence or she very well could have."

Claire felt her credibility slipping away. She herself wanted to believe the policeman's explanation of the whole thing, but she just couldn't rationalize anymore.

"So you won't send anyone?" she asked almost pleadingly.

"I don't know. I'll see what's going on here and who comes up free. It won't be right away; I can tell you that."

Claire hung up the phone feeling completely demoralized and wishing she hadn't even called. She walked around the house, outside and in, looking for any suspicious signs at the doors and windows. She found none.

She sat down on the sofa in the living room. *Fear of isolation, fear of abandonment ...*

Doctor Quinlan's words echoed in her head. She *was* alone. Whatever was to be done, *she'd* have to do it. The police weren't going to help. Her family would just add the burden of their worry and fear to her already unmanageable load. Of course she had Patrick, but she could not hang on forever to his undaunted but child-sized courage.

She called Franny.

As they drank tea on the sofa, Claire told her everything. Franny smoked a chain of cigarettes and listened. Claire began with the blonde man on the beach and the ugly woman with the spear, the early morning knock on her hotel door, the phone wires being cut after she arrived home, the strange woman who talked to Patrick at the playground, the message in Michael's pocket with the date of his death, the green truck that followed her … everything.

Franny interrupted with an occasional "Weird!" at appropriate times; otherwise she was unflappable.

And after exacting a pledge of silence with regard to the rest of the family, Claire broke down and told Fran about her illness. Then she waited apprehensively to see how her youngest sister would react.

Franny inhaled deeply and blew out the smoke slowly before she spoke.

"Isn't that what Annette Funicello has? You know, the Skippy peanut butter lady. And *yeah, yeah*," she said, excitedly tapping her knee with her hand, "there's some folksinger who has it, too. I guess it's a pretty 'in' disease right now. And they've had it for a *long* time, so you don't have to worry about it for quite awhile. You never believe those pictures on the grocery store racks, do you? I saw one where they tried to make Brad Pitt look bad! I knew *that* had to be a lie."

Claire loved Franny.

Before they went to pick up Patrick from school, the two sisters searched every nook and cranny of the entire house, each of them armed with one of Michael's golf clubs (Fran's idea). They found no snakes, nor anything else amiss.

As they drove toward Patrick's school in Francine's beat-up blue Tempo, Claire asked, "So what should I do? The police think I'm paranoid. I can hardly blame them. It's all so unbelievable, isn't it? I mean really, isn't it?"

"There are *so* many movies that go *way* more over the edge than this. And you know what? There's usually someone in trouble and the police don't believe them. There could be someone in the police department that has, like, something to *hide* and is trying to cover the whole thing up. Do you think *that* could be a possibility?"

"No, Fran, I don't think it has anything to do with the police. The story does look pretty flaky if you look at it from their point of view."

"It makes perfect sense to me and I'm surprised you went this long without *telling* anybody."

"You understand because you know me. The police don't. They just think I'm some paranoid overly nervous woman bothering them with trivial nuisances."

"You know, sis … another popular plot is the whole *futuristic* thing, where people come back to the present to warn us, you know, the 'us' in the movie, not 'us-us', but maybe us in *some* sense, of the dangers waiting in the future for the whole human race unless someone does something like blow something *up*, or destroy a formula, stop the micro-organisms from getting out of the test tubes in the airport. And usually the person in authority is like an *alien* or a human-hybrid, or maybe they're just rich or on a power trip or something and they have the whole kind of *world system* in their *back pocket* so nobody helps or believes the *good* guy, or girl in your case. But …"

She looked over at Claire quickly while driving, trying to gage her reaction so far.

"I can tell you don't think that it's got anything to do with that either. They never do right away, and it's frustrating to watch. But if they found out right away the movie wouldn't be long enough. You know?"

"Franny, this isn't a movie and I really do have to figure out something to do in our real life."

They were getting close to Patrick's school, Claire noticed as they turned the corner. Franny tried a new tack.

"Courtney, my friend who's a *painter*, you know the one with the completely out of it dreads, but the cool loft in Old Town? Well, she's always saying 'life imitates art', or is it 'art imitates life?' I always forget which; so *any*way, think about it. And also about this …"

Franny was speaking now as they pulled into the pick-up circle for Patrick. "You *will* eventually have to tell Grace and Dad about your being sick."

With Patrick they drove home and talked of lighter things and he showed them his drawings and some maps and even a poem he had written. But as they turned onto their street Claire's heart started to race. There was a police car in front of their house with the lights flashing.

"What in the world's happened now?" she asked, not really of Fran or Patrick.

A small knot of people from the neighborhood were hanging around on the sidewalk a as they pulled into the driveway. A police officer was standing by his car writing something down. Claire got out of the blue Tempo and ran over to the policeman and left Fran to help Patrick.

"What's happened, Officer? I'm Claire O'Connell. I live here."

"Well, I thought *you* could tell *me*, since you're the one called in the complaint ... and then weren't here when I drove all the way over."

Claire had forgotten that there was a chance the police might come by. The officer's voice sounded like the one she talked to on the phone.

"Was it you I talked to?"

"Yes, ma'am. I thought you were quite upset, but I guess I read you wrong."

Claire was suddenly embarrassed by the neighborhood sideshow which had developed over the incident.

"I'm sorry I wasn't here. I was just picking up my son from school."

She looked around at the neighbors. "Why do you have your light flashing?" she asked with some irritation. "I thought this could be a nice quiet investigation."

"The light serves its purpose, Mrs. ... O'Connell. Brings the neighbors out so that I don't have to go door to door asking about snakes."

"*You asked them all about snakes?*" Claire asked in a loud whisper verging on hysteria.

"Best way to do it. Jump right in. And not one of them has seen, or owned or heard of a snake anywhere near this neighborhood."

Franny and Patrick were standing near them now. "Would you please turn off your light?" Claire asked as she made her hand go round and round. "It's done its job. And we'll go inside and go over all of the details?"

As the policeman complied and they walked toward the house,

Claire heard the word 'snakes' murmured by the curious group that had formed in front of her house. Mrs. Bleach called out from among them, "Claire, if there's anything we can do, anything at all!" and then rejoined the conversation. Francine must have asked Patrick who the woman was, because she heard Fran whispering: "Mrs. *Bleach? Bleach?* What kind of name is *Bleach?*"

They sat down in the living room. Claire recounted the story of the snakes, not bothering to mention again the other suspicious events of the last several months. The officer listened attentively, adding a few things to his notepad.

Then suddenly he stood up. "Well, where are these snakes? Let's take a look at them."

He followed her out the back door, with Patrick and Franny trailing behind.

"They're in this trash can here," she said, lifting the lid and pointing. The policeman looked inside and then looked closer.

He reached in and pulled something out. "All I see is this old bicycle tire," he said, holding it up.

Claire peered into the can and so did Fran and Patrick. The can was empty.

"Patrick, this is the can where you put the snakes, isn't it, honey?"

"Yes, Mommy."

The policeman looked bored and threw the old tire back in the can and closed the lid.

"Maybe someone played a prank on you with that rubber tire, and in the dark you. . ."

"It was not *dark* in my room! There were *real live snakes* crawling around!"

She turned in reluctant desperation to Patrick for corroboration.

"Tell the policeman what happened, Patrick. Go ahead tell him what you remember."

"Well, first in my room we prayed the 'St. Patrick Prayer' against devils and heretics and wizards and things." Franny gave a sideward glance at Claire, who shrugged her shoulders. "And then there were two big black snakes and Mommy was screaming and crying, but then everything was okay because I killed one with my sword and by stomping and then the Blessed Virgin killed the other one. Right, Mommy?"

He turned to Claire with confidence.

Franny was suppressing a smile. The officer shook his head and stopped writing notes.

"He means a *statue* of Mary ... I used it to hit one of the snakes."

"And your four-year-old son has a sword?" asked the policeman.

"It's one of those plastic ones. I know ... I don't understand it myself." Claire felt as deflated as the tire he'd found in the trash can.

The man left saying that he'd file some kind of report and to let them know if anything else unusual happened. "Maybe your boy's played too many of those video games and got you *both* carried away," he said with a little laugh as he walked out the door.

"He doesn't play video games. We don't even own any!"" She called out the door after him.

As Patrick played on his tree swing in the backyard, Claire and Fran sat on the back steps and talked. The gardens looked good in spite of all the time Claire had spent in Michael's study. Some seeds were planted, and the ground was ready for the seedling plants when the weather was warm enough. The forsythia and the azaleas were magnificent and some of the tulips and daffodils still looked fresh, though most were fading around the edges by now.

"Why don't I stay here with you guys for a few days ... make sure there's nothing else going on? We can watch some movies; maybe get an idea about where to go from here." Franny was only half-joking. .

"If anything, we usually watch *old* movies -- so that probably wouldn't help your plan much."

"No, old movies are fine, too. My friend Chad turned me on to Hitchcock. There are the older mystery spy ones and then the psychological thrillers. Do you have popcorn?"

Chapter 14

No worst, there is none. Pitched past grief
More pangs will, schooled at forepangs, wilder wring
Comforter, where is your comforting?
Mary, mother of us, where is your relief?
Gerard Manley Hopkins

Nature is a parable.
John Henry Newman

Franny stayed over and Claire enjoyed her company when she wasn't at work or at the mission. Patrick loved it, too. But after a week Claire decided Fran should have her life back.

Nothing strange had happened. They had watched *The Lady Vanishes*, *North by Northwest,* and *The 39 Steps.* Fran had also rented *Three Days of the Condor* and *The Parallax View,* but those were so frustrating and overwhelmingly depressing that Claire couldn't watch them all the way through. Claire and Patrick did get Franny to watch their favorite, *You Can't Take It with You*, which thankfully, to Claire, had no international intrigue or government betrayal, except for, as Franny noted, the business about the candy bars and the fireworks in the basement which the police thought was a communist plot to overthrow the country.

Doctor McCullum did not return either of Claire's messages, at his office or his home. She began to think he was out of the country. She made no headway in deciphering the message, even with all of Michael's resources. When she checked her computer she found no files of Michael's, which she thought was funny because she remembered him spending time putting things onto it, especially when he was finishing his dissertation. She looked around her cache of computer things and also in his study for a disc on which he might have loaded all his files. There was nothing to be found. Then she called Treat again.

"Claire! I've been wondering about you. How have you been?"

"I've had no luck with the note and its translation. McCullum seems to be unreachable and Michael's things have shed no light on it as yet."

"I'm sorry to hear that. I'm afraid I haven't been able to take the time to search for you like I should. After classes ended I had two conferences in a row. How's young Patrick?"

"He seems to be doing fine. In spite of all our adventures."

"What kind of adventures have you had?" he asked, jokingly, in his pseudo-mystical voice.

"Not very funny ones, actually. The worst being a couple of snakes loose in our house."

"Good God! How did that come about, Clare?" asked Treat, his tone changing.

"We never figured that out. Someone obviously put them there. We called the police but they were no help."

"Why didn't you call me? I told you to let me know if you needed anything. It's sad to say, but even in America, a man can sometimes get more response from the powers that be than a woman. Let's make a date soon to put our heads together about what to do with that mystery note and talk about these other adventures you've been having."

Franny had returned to her own apartment, but when Claire phoned her late one night and told her that she had called Treat, her sister reacted as she usually did when Treat's name came up. She heard her light a cigarette and inhale deeply.

"So what did you think *he* could do? Oh, that's right; Treat O'Toole is good for *any* thing ... unmarried sisters ... widows in distress ..."

"Franny, come on. We never really tried to *fix you up* with him."

It had been Michael's idea. Claire thought that they had absolutely nothing in common, but she went along with it anyway.

"Oh *right!* " Fran said. "You invite me to go to Ravinia with you and Michael and *what do ya know,* there's Mr. O'Toole coming along, too. And the dinner party when we just happened to be your only guests? You guys were *so way off* ... We could hardly *stand* each other!"

It was Claire's turn: "Number one: Michael and I had two extra tickets to the concert and I invited you and Michael asked Treat. Number two: true, the dinner was a little awkward, but Michael kept saying he thought you two would be good for each other. And Treat *liked* you. He told Michael you were charming."

"Well, he's a liar then. So what big plan did Treat have to solve your problems?"

"None really. He's been busy and hasn't thought about the note. But he wants to get together and help out somehow."

"I'll *bet* he does!" Franny said sarcastically.

"Come on, Fran, give the guy a break. It's not his fault Michael's judgment was askew in this instance."

Fran hesitated and then said, "I didn't tell you about the time he came over to see me."

"Aha! No you did not. What happened?"

"Nothing really, the guy's just strange, that's all. Take my advice and steer clear."

Claire was surprised at her sister's reaction. "Why didn't you ever tell me he came over?"

"Cause it was no big deal. I did tell Michael though, so he'd give the whole matchmaking thing a rest."

"You told Michael, but not me?"

"You know who he reminds me of? That's it! That guy in *Psycho*. Think about it. Shave off O'Toole's beard and mustache and he . . ."

"You mean Anthony Perkins? I guess if you really stretch you could see a resemblance, but you never answered my question," Claire persisted.

"No, the *guy* in *Psycho*. Not the actor, the *guy*."

"*Treat* reminds you of *Norman Bates*? Did he come over while you were in the shower or something?" Claire changed her phone from her left ear to her right.

"Ha, ha. It's just that good-little-boy thing that Robin talks about from her boyfriends in A.A. You know the kind. The ones who *are too* nice and want to help with the dishes and everything and you know it's just an act to cover up some really weird issues from their childhood."

"So Treat came over and was too nice and you've got him branded as a psychotic killer? Francine Mary Daly, I believe you're taking this movie parallel theory too far."

"Well, Big Sister, unlike you, I've dated a lot of guys in my life and even Sky, *the* weirdest one I've gotten, you know, *close* to, never gave off the kinky vibes that your professor friend did when he came to see me. Those smooth-on-the-outside, edgy-on-the-inside ones really give me the creeps. His true colors came through, though ... when I asked him to leave. He called me a *Raicleach beag*."

"What's that mean?"

"I didn't know really 'til I asked Michael, but I could tell just by the way he said it that I'd cracked his facade. It means *little bitch* in Gaelic. What a jerk! Can we stop talking about him now?" Claire let it go, not really trusting her sister's native discretion when it came to men. Still, she didn't call Treat again right away.

In mid-June with Fran's help they managed a family birthday party for Patrick. It was the first time she'd seen all the families together since the funeral. It was a nearly impossible task to make it through the day, but Claire did it for her five-year-old son.

Everyone fawned and fluttered over Patrick and she was glad. He asked his mother if he could tell one of Michael's Irish stories, which he did with all the flourishes and gestures and dialects his father had used. His large family was thoroughly entertained and enchanted. Claire realized how much he looked like Michael, in spite of having inherited her coloring. A shared joy and deep undercurrent of sadness flowed through the room at a communal recognition of the likeness.

Claire was able to remain calm most of the day, except around Tom, her oldest sister Anne's husband. She didn't get along well with any of her brothers-in-law, but she never had liked Tom at all. He was overweight, now balding; he always sweated too much and his eyes didn't match. The only way he talked to her was loudly, when he brought up a controversial topic such as women's ordination, euthanasia, married priests ... all of which he denounced and she really had no opinion at all. Except when she talked to him and was forced to take the other side just because she couldn't stand the thought of him being right. She had managed to be engaged only once by his obnoxious banter, but she wasn't really proud of her restraint because it arose more from indifference than strength of will.

After Patrick's birthday, Claire realized that her days and

moments of poignant grief had gradually faded and dissolved into a chronic malaise. Doctor Quinlan called it depression. Franny said she was just sad.

The gardens were alive and blooming. Patrick insisted on her daily presence there even though some days she only sat and watched him. Once she knelt in front of her hydrangeas as if in a trance, dispassionately lopping off every ebullient burst of color with her pruning shears until she felt Patrick's hand grab her wrist and heard him sob, "Mommy, no!" She snapped into consciousness to find him standing next to her, his other arm holding a bunch of the lovely pink lacey flowered heads that she had severed, tears running down his face. She threw down the shears and grabbed him to her, crushing the flowers between them as she cried, "I'm sorry, Patrick. I'm so sorry."

The physical symptoms of Claire's illness were hard for her to distinguish from quirks that were accentuated by her present emotional condition. At times as she was walking forward, it seemed she was acutely aware of her own presence, a painful self-consciousness that brought her up short. There was no fluidity of movement; her motions were chopped in small segments as in the frames of a film or the mechanical jerk of a wind-up toy. Everything around her seemed to fall into this rhythmic but barely audible slow clicking. It was as if she'd caught herself and the world off-guard and seen behind some elaborate conspiratorial pretense. She would stop, close her eyes, and take several deep breaths deliberately paced to be at odds with the dull fatalistic thrumming. When she opened her eyes again it would be gone. She made the mistake of reading a review in the *Tribune* of a biography of another schizophrenic mathematician and worried fleetingly that she might be on the verge of psychosis. Or perhaps she was the victim of Teflon flecks from her aging pots and pans that her mother was always worrying about.

Chapter 15

O my soul, be prepared for the
Coming of the Stranger,
Be prepared for him who knows
How to ask questions.
　　　　　T.S. Eliot

The game's afoot. Follow your spirit.
　　　　William Shakespeare

One warm summer evening, after a trip to Dairy Queen, Patrick had fallen asleep earlier than usual. Claire was reading in bed when he came into her room, rubbing his eyes, and climbed up on her bed.

"What is it, little boy?" Claire asked, realizing all of a sudden how fast he was growing.

"I had a dream about Daddy."

She held him close, stroking his red hair and rocking gently. "It's okay, honey, it's okay."

"He was smiling at me. Grandma says Daddy's in heaven. Maybe he was smiling at me from heaven."

Claire didn't know what to say. She just kept rocking and saying *Shhh Shhh*. It was more to comfort herself, she knew, because Patrick didn't seem upset. Unconsciously, she looked above the dresser across the room. She stopped rocking and stared at the wall. The crucifix was gone. She got out of bed silently and walked over to the dresser. There was the small white handkerchief folded neatly on the dresser top. She looked at Patrick.

"Did you put Daddy's crucifix somewhere, Patrick?"

He stared at the empty space.

Someone has come into our house and taken the crucifix, she thought. They should go to Franny's. She couldn't take any more of this. Maybe she should call Treat. She picked up the phone.

It was dead.

She sat on the bed with Patrick trying to decide what to do, trying not to frighten him.

"I think what we'll do is go over to Franny's place and sleep there. That will be fun, won't it? We'll go in our pajamas. Remember how Daddy would take you on pajama rides? That's what we'll do." He started to run across the hall to his room, but she held his hand tightly.

"But I want to take my backpack to Franny's"

"Patrick, it's important that you hold my hand and that we stick together, okay?"

She led him out into the hallway. Just as they reached the top of the stairs, the power went out in the entire house and they were left in darkness. Patrick clung to her as she gasped.

As they stood frozen in the hallway someone grabbed them roughly from behind and cupped a large hand over each of their mouths. Claire struggled to get free as the assailant began dragging them back to the bedroom. Claire hung on to Patrick even though the man was holding him up off the ground. She was sure it was a man and he was very big and very strong.

"*Don't be afraid. Don't be afraid,*" his voice said in a low hoarse whisper.

Claire stopped fighting as they approached the walk-in closet. She knew she could not stop him and she was afraid what he might do to Patrick even if she could free herself from his grip. When they got inside the closet he pushed the door closed with his foot.

"*I'm going to take my hands off of your mouths now. I will not harm you. I'm here to help you. Don't scream.*"

The heavily accented voice sounded eerily familiar to Claire and as he released them, she recognized him at once in the light of the street lamp from the closet window. *The blonde stranger from the beach!* Her thoughts raced ahead. *What was this man doing in her house? Had he followed her home and been harassing and terrorizing her ever since?*

"Claire and Patrick, you *must* trust me," the stranger said in a deep but soft voice laced with his German accent. "I'll explain it all later, but please believe me, there are people who want to harm you both. They may have already entered the house. They have been watching you for weeks. But I want you, Claire and Patrick O'Connell, to wait here in this closet. Stay down and stay away from the window." His voice was steady but there was urgency in it: "*I will be back for you.*"

He left the closet, closing the door behind him. Claire slipped down onto the floor of the closet and held Patrick on her lap. She was trying to control her shaking. She felt as if she was in a nightmare. Her head would not clear.

"*Mommy,*" Patrick whispered, "*is this the man from our vacation? The one that's good?*"

She would have to trust the blonde man. She had no choice. "Yes, honey. It is the same man. I'm so sorry that all these scary things are happening to you. You are such a brave boy."

"*I'm not afraid. Daddy said no matter what happens, we'll win the game.*"

Claire didn't know what game he was talking about, but whatever it was she was glad that his father's words were giving him courage. She wished she could have some of it.

"*What's the man's name, Mommy?*"

"I don't know. I really don't know. I never got a chance to ask him."

"*You said that we shouldn't talk to strangers who we don't know, even if they know our names.*"

"That's usually true, honey, but in this case, well, it's a special thing when … It's all very confusing, Patrick. It's *very* confusing."

A loud crash erupted downstairs. Voices yelling and then more things banging. Then voices again. And then silence.

Claire and Patrick sat very still and quiet, their hearts pounding, waiting. Footsteps climbed the stairs and came down the hall. She slid herself and Patrick back as far as she could behind the clothes hanging in the closet. Someone entered the bedroom and the closet door opened.

"*You can come out now, but stay quiet.*" It was the blonde man. Claire stood Patrick up and then got up herself and they walked out into the still-darkened room. With an empathetic kindness, the man began giving them instructions.

"You must pack a few things very quickly. We don't know how many more of them are nearby. You cannot stay here. I will take you to somewhere safe and then I will explain things to you as best I can. I'm sorry, but you will have to collect your things in the dark. *Please hurry now. We will wait for you downstairs.*"

This was the first realization that Claire had that other people were in the room; maybe two or three … she could not make them out distinctly in the shadows as they left. Then she and Patrick were alone.

Claire scrambled around, randomly throwing odds and ends into an overnight bag. *What do you bring without knowing where you are going or why?* They found their way to Patrick's room and she helped him find some clothes. He stuffed them into his backpack, which lay right beside his bed. He had taken to leaving it there every night filled with things: important things, heavy things, mostly having to do with Michael. She hadn't checked it recently. Now he stuffed his brown floppy dog in on top of everything else.

They didn't speak but moved quietly and quickly. Hand in hand they walked carefully down the stairs. At the bottom was the blonde man. He led them through the house, though their eyes had grown accustomed to the darkness. As they passed Michael's study, Claire noticed in the available light that it was a mess. Papers and books were strewn all over the room.

"*My God! What* —"

"They searched here while you were out."

"You mean I didn't notice this when we came home? Who are *They?* What's *happening?*

Does it have something to do with Michael?"

"Come on, let's hurry!" he said as they slipped through the kitchen toward the back door.

As she passed her computer nook she picked up the brown folder tucked in among her papers on the table and put it in her bag. They all went out into the back yard. Following their still-nameless rescuer, Claire and Patrick ran down the alley to a waiting car.

Chapter 16

*You don't know where you're goin' now,
But you know you won't get back.*
Bruce Springsteen

The dark sedan was hard to see in the shadows along the alleyway. When the door opened no dome light went on. Claire and the blonde man got into the back seat with Patrick between them. A soft summer rain had begun to fall.

The car crept down the alley without headlights and pulled out onto the street.

After several blocks, the blonde man introduced Claire and Patrick to the man driving the car, Stephan, and the woman beside him, Mara. They kept their eyes forward and each acknowledged Claire with a slight nod into the rear-view mirror.

"And what is *your* name, please?" Claire asked the blonde man for Patrick's sake and for her own.

"I am Karl. Karl Burgmann. I'm presuming you remember me."

The rain was falling steadily and much harder now and Claire could not make out what street they were on or which direction they were heading.

"Of *course* I remember you. *Where are we going?*"

"We are going to a place outside the city where you will be safe. But we must take precautions to make sure we are not followed. We will be changing vehicles several times and using some decoys. We must be careful."

Claire looked down to find Patrick asleep in the crook of her arm. She adjusted him so that his head was comfortably in her lap and then felt free to ask the burning questions.

"What is happening? Why is someone after us? And how did you find me here?" she asked all at once.

Karl answered calmly, "I know you want to know everything right now, but I think it would be best to tell you the whole story after you are settled."

"Settled? I'm hoping this is only a temporary thing, right?"

"I don't know the answer to that yet. No one does. But I do

want you to know that I'm sorry that I left you with no word at Hilton Head. I was seriously hoping that the attack had been against *me*. I did not want to get you involved. I was not certain then that they still cared about who you were."

"*Who was I?* Or *am* I?" she asked in exasperation. "I mean, why would they care who I am? And who are *they* and who are *us?*" Claire found herself stumbling over her words and tenses and existential identity.

"*You* are the wife of Michael O'Connell. That is what has caused all of this. *They* are enemies of his, and ours and now yours."

It seemed surreal for her to hear this stranger say Michael's name.

The car stopped in what seemed to be the parking lot of some suburban supermarket. The rain had let up a little. Even in the middle of the night there were people shopping. Karl spoke:

"We will walk into the store and out through the back to another vehicle. Stephan and Mara will return to this car soon and drive it somewhere else while we head in another direction. Mara has a raincoat for you to slip on. Everything is ready."

At first Claire thought that the coat was not necessary with the rain dwindling as it was, but then she realized she was still in her nightgown and robe, her bare feet stuffed into some old canvas shoes.

"But what about, Patrick?" Claire asked as she looked at him still sound asleep in her lap.

"I will take care of Patrick." Karl said firmly.

He lifted Patrick easily and gently out of the car so that he remained asleep on his shoulder; she wondered in passing if this man had children of his own. She put on the coat. He put an arm around her and they walked through the store. Claire thought they would be quite conspicuous, Karl dressed elegantly all in black, she in a run-out-to-get-the-morning-paper-off-the-porch ensemble, and Patrick in his yellow pajamas. But the nocturnal grocery shoppers all seemed to have their own stories and problems and paid no attention to the trio as they passed down the aisles and through a set of metal doors and out to the rear loading docks.

They climbed into a red truck with a new driver. Claire got in the middle and Karl held Patrick, still sleeping, on his lap.

"Claire, this is George." They exchanged polite greetings. This man was much older than Mara and Stephan seemed to be and had a very thick accent, which Claire could not identify. He wore a black cap over curly sprouts of graying hair and had a long mustache. Like the others he was silent as they drove smoothly through endless suburbs.

Claire was beginning to feel tired herself as she looked at Patrick sleeping. Her eyelids were heavy as if in a dream. She fought to stay awake.

"What does any of this have to do with Michael?" she asked. "Did you *know* Michael?"

"Yes, Claire O'Connell. I did know Michael and it is his part in this that I will explain to you later after you have rested. We still have quite a distance to drive."

Claire felt a faint sense of comfort at this man's claim to have known her husband. It gave her the freedom at least to let her eyes close and shut out all the equivocal notions that spun around her head.

There was one more change of vehicles and Claire dozed again. She awoke as the car bumped along some obviously unimproved roads and finally came to a stop. Still in the dark of night, Claire thought their destination looked like an old motel — the Route 66 kind with separate little unattached units. But there was no sign out front. And some of the cottages had open fires burning in front of them.

"This is where you and Patrick will stay until we get things sorted out. My good friends Holz and Kitta Smith are loaning their home to you while you are here. It's all been made ready. This is Holz, by the way," Karl said, indicating the driver of the car from which they were emerging.

As the spry old man jumped out of the driver's seat, Claire saw his face in the light coming from the open door of the cabin. He looked very old in spite of his agility, his face brown and thin with a perimeter of white hair surrounding it. His mustache was white too, but his eyebrows were still thick and black, accentuating the presence in the dark eyes beneath them. "Hello! Welcome!" He spoke with a heavy German accent to her and to Patrick, who was stirring a little in Karl's arms.

"How do you do," Claire said to the old man. "But where will *you* stay?"

"Holz and Kitta have moved in with their son's family. Don't worry, they are used to moving *and* to being infinitely generous," Karl answered for him.

The old man smiled and bowed and faded away into the darkness. Claire followed Karl and Patrick into the scrupulously clean and brightly decorated room, carrying her bag and Patrick's backpack. Even in the light of a single small lamp the bright yellows, oranges, reds and teals leapt out. There were two inviting beds on the floor made up with pale blue checked cloths turned slightly down and white puffy pillows. Karl laid Patrick on one of them and said, "I'm afraid that the only real inconvenience for you is the lack of plumbing. There is a bathroom over there but it's not in working order, so I believe the room is just for storage. The *Rom* don't like having bathrooms attached anyway, they consider it *marimay*, unclean."

"The *Rom* …?" Claire asked in an almost childlike confusion.

"The Gypsies — this is a Gypsy camp."

"A Gypsy camp in Illinois? Or are we still in Illinois, Toto?" She looked up at Karl in a rather bewildered sense of cynical giddiness.

"Yes, my dear Dorothy, we are," he answered smiling. "I'm glad you still have some sense of humor after all of this. But you must get some rest now. The loo is out back and there's water for washing there on the table. Please use only that bowl for washing." He pointed to a blue enameled bowl next to a tall pitcher. "More Gypsy hygiene laws. It looks like Kitta also left some cold tea for you. Why don't you have a drink and go to bed … It will be light soon. Sleep well. You'll be safe here. You may want to leave the door open after you're ready for bed. It's a warm night."

Karl walked out closing the door softly behind him. Patrick roused briefly to ask for his brown floppy dog, which she laid next to his head. She kissed him and he fell quickly back to sleep. She put his heavy backpack close by the bed.

Claire suddenly felt quite lonely as she removed the ridiculous raincoat and washed the sweat from her face. She drank from the cup of cold sweet tea, opened the door to a soft fluttering breeze and turned off the light. She took off her robe and shoes and lay down on the feather bed wearing the same white cotton nightgown she had worn in her own bed, in her own house in Chicago a thousand years ago. She fell asleep to the sound of crickets and frogs, a dog's bark, distant voices and an occasional peal of laughter.

When Claire awoke, Patrick was sitting at the foot of her bed.

"Hello, little boy." She reached for his hand.

"Mommy, Jesus is watching us again, so it'll be alright."

Whatever he used to deal with these fantastic upheavals was okay with her, she thought.

"When Jesus was gone something bad happened, Mom, but now He's back."

Claire had no idea what he was talking about. His eyes, however, were focused above and behind her head. Claire turned around and saw a large jeweled and rather tasteless crucifix on the wall behind her. She was surprised. She'd imagined Gypsies to be into magic and crystal balls and that sort of thing. *Well, there's really not that much difference, after all* she told herself. *The whole mess is superstition and illusion.*

A goat walked in through the open door and Patrick was ecstatic. He jumped up from the bed just as three young children came to the entrance and stopped, looking in.

They called out something that neither Patrick nor Claire could understand, but the goat turned immediately and ran outside. The children stayed by the door staring at their strange guests.

"Hi, kids!" Patrick said with Michael's natural ease.

"Children, come!" a feminine voice called. The children left as quickly as the goat.

A lovely young woman came to the entrance and addressed them kindly: "I'm sorry for the intrusions, but you are a novelty here, you know. Would you like me to close the door so you can have some privacy?"

Claire was sure she had seen this woman before. "Have we met?" she asked.

"Oh, you *do* remember me! We spoke briefly when you were ill in South Carolina … and I was in the car last night. But of course you could not see me clearly then. My name is Mara. Mara Smith."

"You were the woman who helped me on the beach! You are a friend of Karl's then."

Claire was having trouble with all the pieces of the puzzle her life had become.

"Yes, you could say that. And Holz and Kitta are my grandparents."

"You mean the people who are letting us stay here? You mean you are a …" she stopped, unsure of herself. She was remembering her certain impression that this young woman came from a privileged and wealthy background.

"I am a Gypsy, yes, although I don't live with the family any more. They still let me visit." She said this with a smile, but not in jest. "Why don't you wash and dress and I will bring you some breakfast." Before Claire could answer she closed the door.

"Can I go play with the kids and the goat after I get dressed, Mommy?" Patrick asked immediately.

"I suppose you can, but we have to talk to Mr. Burgmann first and find out what's what."

"What's what. What's that?" Patrick asked with a silly grin on his face.

"It's a figure of speech for 'what's going on …'" Patrick still seemed undaunted by the extraordinary circumstances they were passing through. Maybe someday this would surface on some psychologist's couch as repressed trauma.

They dressed quickly and washed up and they made a dash for the makeshift outhouse (a couple of boards propped against a tree) in the bright sunlight. Claire suddenly realized that her family had no idea where she was or what had happened. She'd have to call them and … Tell them what? She really needed to talk to Karl. There were scattered people around but they paid no attention to her or Patrick on the way to or from the cabin.

It definitely must be an abandoned motel, Claire decided. But it hadn't been in use probably since the old road was bypassed years ago. They were definitely out in the country. There were old cars and vans parked along the half-circle driveway: old but not lacking a certain prestige — Lincoln Continentals, several Mercedes, a Land Rover, and a couple of VW vans. There were also quite a few camping trailers sitting around that were not hitched to anything at the moment. It was a hot day and Claire noticed the sun was directly overhead. They had slept till noon.

Claire and Patrick went back inside the cottage and found Mara there with bread and cheese and juice.

"I'm afraid I don't have any coffee. Would you like some hot tea? There's a fire outside somewhere where I can heat some water."

"No, thank you. The juice will be fine on such a warm day. Is Karl awake yet? I really need to talk to him."

"I don't think Karl ever went to sleep. We all wonder how he gets along. I'm always telling him to get more rest. Anyway, he said to tell you he'll be back this evening."

"He's not here?" Claire asked in a panic.

"No, but you needn't worry. You both are safe."

"But I really need to use a telephone. Is there one available?"

"There isn't one here at the camp. I have a cell phone, but I don't think Karl would want you to call anyone without speaking to him first."

"But my family — my mother will be *crazy!*"

"I know that Karl very rarely leaves loose ends. He must be working out some kind of plan." The dark haired woman spoke with assurance.

Claire wondered what Mara's relationship was to Karl. She was young enough to be his daughter. But was she his girlfriend? His lover? His wife? She certainly seemed to know him well; and Claire could detect a definite affection and pride in her voice when she spoke about him. She remembered her hanging on his arm and laughing up into his face as she watched them on the hill in South Carolina. An irrational flash of jealousy shot through her.

Chapter 17

Ideas about supernatural beings came to me the same way that my mathematical ideas did ... So I took them seriously.
John Nash

The smallish room in the white house on the outskirts of Dublin was strewn with books, papers, empty cigarette boxes, and junk food wrappers. Kostanikas remembered once in the hospital, was it for the insulin-shock treatment? They had gorged him, made him almost fat with forced feeding and ice cream. He still resented the way they had changed the shape of his body, his perfect body.

He sat at his table writing longhand with a red pen, stacks of unsent letters surrounding him. His long gray hair hung into his angular, almost emaciated face, obscuring his sight of the page in front of him as he leaned over his project.

Dear Alan,
You would not believe the poor conditions at the university here, much worse even than MIT in the early days. What year is it? What day?
6=first perfect number.
2(squared) — 1 is prime 3.
1+2+4+5+10+11+20+22+44+55+110 = 284.
3(cubed) + 4(cubed) + 5(cubed) = 6(cubed) — 27+ 64+ 125 = 216
Is little Ron still begging for mercy? Mr. X is at the root of it all. He makes me do things. He tells me secretly that I am the only one who can relieve the Emperor of his duties.

(Here Theo pasted a postage stamp with the Queen of England turned upside down. Many of his letters were decorated with collages of relevant material.)

The damned Jews are at it again. They've cracked the cosmic code and broken into the Game at just the wrong moment. Von Neuman and Morgenstern wouldn't let on, but they knew 'Zur Theorie der Gesellschaftspiele' was not about economics at all but about using their game theory to take over the world. And the Golem! They're all related to Rabbi Loew. As you know it started in Gottingen and Princeton was just a cover. We all knew it then. My God, Alan! Rand was using us to hold the world hostage. Kablammm! It is not a zero-sum game. There is no stable set.

First for the Jew and then for the Greek; that's what it says in the Bible. Their time is over. I am the Greek. We've gone way past the Golem. It even scares me. What is randomness? Yes, physical events obey mathematical criteria. qqq. Heinrich Hertz: Mathematical formulae have an independent existence and an intelligence of their own; they are wiser than we.

Am I mad, Alan? King Lear: Now thou art an O without a figure. I am better than thou art now. I am a fool, thou art nothing. Zero. Zero 0000000000 … IT IS NOW CLEAR THAT FREUD'S ELABORATION OF THE MENTAL MECHANISMS UNDERLYING SYMPTOM FORMATION were lies to get all of us in the hospitals and denied security clearance.

Kostanikas rose from the table and paced in an agitated state, up and down the floor. The voices had started again.

Snapcracklepop.

The channels were clearing, lights blinking. He listened, straining to break the code. The soft murmuring was soon loud enough to hear:

"*You know that your father is dead. Everyone is dead. Why didn't you stop the storm in Indonesia? You must stop the death of the planet. You are the ONLY ONE who can save it all.*"

Kostanikas reached for his cigarette. It was burned down to nothing in the ashtray. He snuffed it out with his thumb and lit another. He spoke, answering the voices:

"I believe you to a certain extent, but how can I be certain? I might be crazy, you know. How can I possibly take my word for it?"

"*The machine is listening. The day is approaching when all people will listen. Day is approaching. Day is approaching. Did you take your medication, Theo? Did you take your medication, Theo?*"

"Did you take your medication, Theo?"

Someone was shaking his arm.

"Theo! Theo!"

"Hello, Day. You Irish sons of bitches are not in the Bible. How can you get in the Game? Why do you keep me locked up here? They need me for consultations in Sweden or in Paris and you won't let me go."

"Now, Theo, you know you are free to go anytime and your door is not locked. Here. Take your medicine. It will make you feel better."

James Day handed the pills to the older man with a cup of cold coffee that he had found on the table.

"How do I know you're not in league with the machine and trying to ruin my chances for ever getting — Where is the machine? You can't leave it alone, you know. It *knows* things. Is this poison or *poisson*? Sounds fishy to me."

"You know I would never do anything to harm you, Theo. Haven't I helped you so far? I've given you all you need to do your work: food, money, time at the lab, your own computer ..."

Kostanikas looked slowly over to the corner of the room toward the humming sound where a computer sat. Bold black screen-saver letters crawled across its monitor:

LOOK OUT.   LOOK OUT.   LOOK OUT.

"Is that Him?" he asked suspiciously.

"That's just where you have all your work stored. You'll feel better soon, more relaxed."

Day surveyed the desk, the piles of letters. One was addressed to Rev. Bill Clinton, Casa Blanca; another to Khrushchev, one to Euclid, and another, which made Day smile, was addressed to The Byzantine Empire: To Whom It May Concern. Fortunate that he never got any of them mailed.

"I won't go to the hospital again. Not while all this is happening. You realize, don't you, that life is waiting to break out into *crystals*, multiplying *zap dit dit* (He made a quick gesture with his hand three times) into wires and gels. The numbers have always been alive; now they've been let loose and they will rape the human race. *The Sons of God will know the Daughters of men.* Hybrid lab samples of nerve and silicon. The, the ... *pure intelligence* ... pure mathematics ... the *angels* ... I'm not certain if —"

His agitation was subsiding; the drug was taking its effect. He slumped into a chair and was silent.

"Why don't you rest for awhile, Theo? We have a meeting this afternoon."

Chapter 18

*For my part I travel not to go anywhere, but to go.
I travel for travel's sake. The great affair is to move.*
Robert Louis Stevenson

A New York Times survey rated gypsies as the least trustworthy of all ethnic groups, even below the 'Whisians', a non-existent group inserted in the poll as a test.

Jack Olsen

Patrick ran off to play with the children after their meal. They chased the goat and a couple of thin chickens around the camp and then began playing hide and seek.

"The children seem to like your son. They're not very responsive to *gaje* children, at least in a school situation. But, of course some of that is self-defense." Mara said this as she and Claire sat on stools in the shade of the cabin porch roof.

"*Gaje?* What's that?"

"All non-Gypsies or outsiders are called *gaje*. It's *Romany*, the language of the *Rom*, or Gypsies."

"I didn't realize Gypsies had their own language. I presumed they just spoke the language of the country where they lived. Your grandfather spoke English quite well, but with a … Was it German accent? And yet his name is Smith. Isn't that an English name?"

"Gypsy life is very confusing to an outsider; and believe me, it's intended to be that way. Most Gypsies around the world know *Romany* and speak it to each other. However, some of the newer generation think it's old fashioned and try not to use it. But if they stay in Gypsy life they are usually overruled."

Claire listened intently as the young woman spun out her story.

"My grandparents are German Gypsies, and their name was Schmidt. Gypsies really have no national loyalty to speak of. They'd rather be considered a nation unto themselves, which throws the powers that be in every country they live into a dither. Nomads are very disturbing to sedentary populations. They changed their name to Smith when they came to the United States after the war. As far as names go, Gypsies are rather ambivalent about those as well. At least about their *gajikano* or street names. According to Gypsy custom, every *Rom* baby has three names: a secret one whispered once by its mother; a *Romano* or Gypsy name; and a street name that can change to fit the circumstances."

"How long has your family lived here? Wherever here is." Claire's trust in the young woman was growing as Mara told her story in a golden-honeyed voice with gestures and dark-eyed smiles.

"Oh, they don't live here most of the time. They only came for a funeral several weeks ago and decided to stay for a while. They actually live some parts of the year in Massachusetts, near Boston, and other seasons in northern California. And we are still fairly close to Chicago, although I can't tell you exactly where. This is a 'safe' camp, which means it is not known by the authorities. Its location must remain a secret."

"Do you mean *government* authorities? Why are they hiding from *them?*" Claire's words tumbled out and then she wondered if she had overstepped her bounds. But Mara seemed unruffled.

"It's not really hiding. Remember I said that most countries cannot understand the Gypsy way of life. They insist on assimilation and impose all kinds of restrictions and registrations, including unleashing the whole Social Services bureaucracy, which though it's intended to help, can be quite controlling and frightening to many Gypsy families."

Mara began to laugh and continued, "Don't get me wrong! The Gypsies are very shrewd and savvy and can milk the System for all its worth, but they like it to be on their terms."

Just then Patrick and the children ran up to them, sweating and breathless. It was always interesting to see how easily young human beings related to one another, Claire thought. Well, not at preschools, she remembered, but out in an open natural environment. One of the boys, who seemed to be the leader of the little group and the oldest, maybe eight or so, had jet black hair. A green silk scarf around his neck and a pair of thin worn slacks were his only clothing. The other boys had on white shirts. One had long sleeves, buttonless and tied at the waist, showing a youthful chest; another was short-sleeved and the third was an undershirt with no sleeves at all.

The two little girls wore brightly colored sundresses with no shoes and had beautifully fine features, like miniature versions of Mara. Claire wondered if they were related. All of the children had dark olive skin and seemed impervious to the sun. And then there was Patrick.

Patrick stood among them like a different species, his red hair and pale skin like a shiny copper penny in a handful of silver change. He stood there proud and sturdy nonetheless, dusty and sweaty, having shed his shoes and shirt somewhere along the line as well. The sun had noticed his complexion and was making a full assault on his tender skin.

Claire realized she had no sunscreen and that probably no one here had need of it. She didn't want to single Patrick out and ruin his status within this small society. Mara seemed to assess the circumstances and read her thoughts.

"Savush," she called the oldest one by name. "Why don't you go play in the woods over there in the shade of the trees? The sun is still hot; it's not good for your heads!"

She pulled the two little girls to her as she spoke and smoothed their sleek dark hair affectionately with her hands. She pushed them playfully and they ran off with the others to the large grove of trees.

"Thank you for stepping in. I guess Patrick's appearance is a novelty to the other children. I usually keep us both slathered in sun block. I'm afraid I didn't think about bringing it in the middle of the night."

"Actually you would be surprised how many Gypsies *do* have your coloring. There has been substantial intermarriage with the Travellers in Ireland and Britain. Red heads pop up now and then; no one's alarmed."

"Oh, *I* remember the Travellers. I was in Ireland with my husband Michael before we were married and saw them camped at different places in the country while we were trekking around. I think Michael had some contacts with them later, too, when he was studying languages and dialects. He was a brilliant philologist." Claire had no idea how much Karl had told Mara about her situation.

Mara's demeanor seemed to change and she fell silent for a few moments. Claire felt uncomfortable. Finally Mara said, "I know there is much that you would like to know, *need* to know about all that has happened. Only Karl can tell you. I cannot. I hope you are not offended. He will come tonight. Please try to be patient and have faith."

Faith in what? Claire thought to herself.

"Would you like to rest again? I'll be most happy to keep an eye on the children. You're probably still tired from your ordeal," Mara said kindly.

"But what about you? You couldn't have slept much either."

"I'm like a cat — used to taking naps here and there. I am fine, really. You take a rest. I'll wake you if you're needed."

"Are you Karl's wife?" Claire blurted out as she turned back at the door into the cool of the cabin.

Mara looked almost incredulous, then she laughed, putting her hand over her heart.

"No, no! Karl is an old and dear friend of my family." She hugged Claire impulsively and then walked off. Claire stepped into the cottage overwhelmed with emotion at the younger woman's sincere display of affection. Once again she cried silent tears and went to sleep.

Later there was a soft knock on the partially open door. Claire sat upright on the bed, buzzing in the confusion that comes after a deep sleep in the afternoon.

"Yes, who is it?" She asked with an artificial awakeness.

Chapter 19

*Civilization is hooped together, brought
Under a rule, a semblance of peace
By manifold illusion, but man's life is thought
And he despite his terror cannot cease
Ravening through century after century
Ravening, raging, and uprooting that he may come
Into the desolation of reality.*
          William Butler Yeats

*Are you not weary of ardent ways,
Lure of fallen seraphim?
Tell me no more of enchanted days.*
          James Joyce

    Ireland stands immovable in the fluid of the sea — a surrogate mother who bears children who are sent away in dark birth passages by ships and planes. The peat bogs lie as latent energy, capturing the sun until the earth becomes fire. The land is a furnace stoked with the dead and their bones; powerful relics that withstand great heat are dug up for altars, sacred and profane. Fiction is wed to fact, legend to history and the water at the feast becomes wine enough to satisfy all the guests. Wine becomes blood and the sea with its sanguinary salinity co-mingles in deaths and births.

    The island exists with its mythical self overlapping and inhabiting simultaneously the same physical space and time continuum, each vibrating to a different frequency, one not often aware of the other. The intersection of the two is not a collision, but a shift in cosmic harmony, energies momentarily in tune. The legendary Island to the West hovers above, dwells below, and rushes through its shadow like the breath of a promise or a curse. The quest and the longing for its shores can be sensed in Irish writings, from the most ancient *Voyage of Bran* to the circuitous ramblings of Leopold Bloom.

    It is the road between the two that is fraught with immense dangers as well as immense possibilities. For in that flash of poetic insight, mystical revelation, or creative genius is no absolute good. It is here that one may lose one's way. In this, the watery wood between the worlds, the huge shapes emerge: the Spirit of Making rises wild and untamed, converging inevitably with the place of the unlimited, the formless origin of forms.

The abyss awaits. Poet, lover, madman are all lured outside the ordinary mode of consciousness. Some reach the heavenly land of eternal summer and youth. Some, however, are lost and the only beckoning shore is the outermost circumference of hell, where the decapitated king walks forever backwards in a confusion of mindless sensation. The royal Head lies unrooted some distance away, full of the cold power of disembodied reason.

Ireland has played out its history on a timeless stage — bards and scholars and warriors merely passing on their costumes. Sometimes the marquee is brilliantly lit for the world to see. Other times the drama seems to carry on with a stubborn and wearisome longevity -- like *The Fantastiks*, tucked away on an off-Broadway side street, of interest only to an occasional load of guided plebian bus tours.

The Word was the life; fitly spoken it moved stone and stars, brought down blessings and curses. The Word became flesh, the mouth an oracle of solid objects, spat out upon the landscape connecting mind and body, forming an unbroken circle upon circle upon circle, an upended cyclone, a golden spiral never changing in size or proportion.

Chapter 20

Reuters: July 20

The Northern Ireland peace talks are deadlocked again. The Hillsborough Declaration released by the British Prime Minister and the Irish Taoiseach has been roundly rejected. The suggested two-week pause for reflection has run into months. Sinn Fein tenaciously refused the idea of disarmament, seeing it as dangerously vulnerable act, considering that the British Army and the Garda (Irish Police) would still be in possession of arms. Republicans see the demand as an attempt by the Unionists to humiliate the IRA.

Gloom dwelt in every corner of the Castle Buildings and Parliament Buildings at Stormont Castle outside Belfast. Tempers flared as impasses stymied all attempts at compromise. There is acute uncertainty in the atmosphere in Parliament. Any momentum has clearly gone out of the negotiations and critics say that the governments have failed to capitalize on last year's Good Friday Agreement endorsed by the bulk of the people on the island of Ireland.

"Our view that the Good Friday Agreement is in free fall remains and clearly this is a matter for considerable concern," Sinn Fein chairman Mitchel McLaughlin said.

Sinn Fein was criticized by David Trimble, chief of the Northern Ireland Assembly and spokesman for the pro-British Protestant majority.

"I am very disappointed in these comments. I am quite sure there is still hope for this process." said Trimble.

"I think that the governments have recognized that the Hillsborough Declaration is a dead duck. We are concerned they have not fully moved back to the Good Friday Agreement," McLaughlin said.

Meanwhile in Dublin, peacemaker and Nobel Peace prizewinner James Day is attempting his own plans to work with leading players in Ireland's peace process. His middle-of-the-road stance gives him great accessibility to parties with diverse viewpoints. There has been a call for his presence and participation in the talks in this still-troubled Northern Irish city which is his home.

"I'm still very optimistic about peace in this nation. The people voted for peace and that's what they want. The will of the Irish people has gotten them through many things in the past and it will come through again as we focus on our unity and not on our differences," Day said after a speech to the Women's Coalition in Dublin yesterday.

Chapter 21

Everyone Hates Gypsies
Recent headline in German Magazine *Der Speigel*

In the 18th century two dozen gypsies were tortured to death for cannibalizing a group of Hungarians who were later found alive and healthy.
Jack Olsen

"Claire, it's Mara. Are you awake?"

"Yes," Claire answered, getting up off the eiderdown and walking toward the door. "How long did I sleep?"

"Oh, a couple of hours, I think. Patrick's fine. They've made some kind of swing from one of the trees and have had great fun. Would you like to meet my family?"

Claire was hesitant to step outside the relatively non-threatening triangle of the cabin, the children and Mara. The thought of meeting the whole Gypsy world made her feel self-conscious and unsure of herself. She'd skimmed through some old books at the library once that were romantic, probably somewhat fictionalized accounts by outsiders who were taken in by the Gypsies back in the 30's and 40's. They reminded her of B movies in which some blonde Hollywood starlet would have played the intriguing, pseudo-exotic Gypsy woman with a black wig, fashionably placed kerchief and big hoop earrings. She had barely gotten past the titles to the actual stories: *Wild Gypsy Campfires*, *My Life Among the Gypsy Rovers*, or some such piffle. Still, Claire knew that the Gypsy life *was* much different than her own.

Mara took Claire's hesitancy in stride. "If you'd rather stay to yourself, it's perfectly alright. Everyone will understand."

"No, it's okay. I would like to meet your family."

It was the least she could do, she thought, after they had all rearranged their lives to accommodate her and Patrick. Claire followed Mara out of the cabin and into the softer slanting rays of the late afternoon sun. A light breeze brushed them and the fragrance of the earth, a delicious musky smell of grass, and the faint chirping rhythm of cicadas or crickets gave Claire a passing wistful sensation of remembering early summer evenings at her uncle's cottage in Michigan. This had always been her favorite time of day. The activities of the morning and afternoon were over — swimming, tennis, sailing. She usually would rinse off at the little outdoor shower and change out of her swimsuit or play clothes into a soft summery dress and for some reason she felt that because she had been active outdoors all day that she *deserved* the calm but thrilling beauty of the sunset and all the fun and mischief that she and her siblings and cousins could hatch as twilight faded into night. That she should have a pang of nostalgia in such strange circumstances and on the brink of God-knew-what future struck her as very odd. But she walked out across the weedy overgrown lawn fortified somehow.

There were people in scattered small groups sitting on the ground or on the hoods of the cars. Dogs barked and licked out of a puddle of standing water. Neither the gypsies nor the dogs seemed to notice her, for which Claire was thankful. Several women held young children or babies snugly on their hips. Mara led her toward a larger cluster of people who were standing around a fire over which hung a huge black cooking pot.

"It looks and smells like dinnertime," said Claire to Mara as they drew nearer to the group she presumed to be the younger woman's family.

"Actually people have been eating for awhile and will continue for awhile. We're not much for set meal times. It's kind of a 'come when you're hungry' type of thing. Are you hungry? Patrick is eating already. I hope you don't mind."

Claire noticed her son sitting among a few of the other children on a red blanket. There seemed to be only one plate and no silverware. The children happily dipped chunks of bread or their bare fingers into the plateful of food. An older heavy woman sat on the blanket, too, and was making sure Patrick got his share of food by dipping chunks for him and popping them into his waiting mouth. He looked over and saw Claire approaching.

"Mommy!" He jumped up and ran to greet her. "I've had lots of fun with my friends." He hugged her legs. She picked him up and kissed him.

"I'll bet you did." His feet were still bare but he had located his shirt and had it on. His face was sunburned but not too badly.

"Come on and eat! It's good! We're having a cook-out picnic!" He spoke excitedly as she let him down.

He pulled her toward the blanket but Mara said, "Your mama can get some food over here, if she'd like. You children have made fast work of that plate! But first I must introduce her to my family. These are my grandparents, Holz and Kitta Smith," she said, proudly gesturing to the center of the group.

Claire recognized the old man who had driven them sitting on a short stool. At his feet, on the ground in spite of her age, was a brown wrinkled older woman with a faded purple kerchief around her head. The man was eating out of the lid of the cooking pot that she held for him. He was holding a cup of wine in one hand, his wife had a pipe in her other hand. Claire thought at first that she held the pipe for her husband as she did his food, but as she smiled and said hello to them, the old woman smoked the pipe herself, dragging deeply and blowing the smoke toward her husband who didn't seem to mind.

"Patrick and I want to thank you both so much for letting us sleep in your home. It was very kind of you."

The old man spoke first, his voice strong and steady. "We are very happy to share anything we have with you and your boy. Please think nothing of it. We are quite comfortable staying with my son's family. Is that not so, Kitta?"

"Yes, my dears," said the old woman in a hoarse thin voice. "We know that you are refugees and we Gypsies always have a place for you. We understand."

"This is my son Kodo and his wife, Petchi, and most all of the rest are theirs." Holz said pointing to the others of various ages in the group.

Claire nodded toward the couple and said, "It is very nice to meet you and my thanks to you also for your courtesy. Your daughter, Mara, has been extremely kind to us, as well."

All the background mumblings became silent and the old man said stoically, "Kodo is Mara's uncle. Her father is dead and we have no sorrow about that. My daughter, her mother, is not with us now."

Claire felt her face flush with embarrassment; she had no idea what to do next.

"Ohh, I just presumed … I didn't —"

"Please don't worry about it, Claire." Mara said, jumping in to save her. "It certainly was an understandable assumption. Kodo and Petchi have been like father and mother to me, and so have my grandparents. Now we will eat."

The group returned to its chatter and laughter and Claire realized the tension had passed as quickly as it had arisen. Mara hustled her up a rare fork and a plate of her own. All the Gypsies were content to pull food off a large communal platter, much like the children, with fingers and bread. The private dish set before her held a mixture of fried onions, tomatoes, red peppers and chicken. A couple of small dishes were set around with cold cucumbers in oil and vinegar. She realized how hungry she was and the meal tasted good. Mara offered her a cup of red wine that she accepted gratefully.

Claire's self-consciousness was eased by the fact that no one really paid much attention to her. It wasn't a snubbing at all, but a relaxed opening of their circle that made her feel none of the pressure that guests in most settings feel to be entertained. The children, however, were still very obviously curious and stared boldly at her and at Patrick from places they had taken with the other adults. Claire was able to relax as she sat on a quilt with Mara and Patrick and finished her dinner and sipped the dark wine.

"So all of these people are related to you?" Claire asked Mara softly.

"Well, most of them. A few are just traveling with this *kumpania*. A *kumpania* is larger and more loosely connected than a *familia*. They usually form for convenience so people don't have to travel alone."

"I'm so grateful that no one here has made a big deal over us. It's not that we haven't felt welcomed; it's hard to put my finger on it or even come up with the right word for it. It's not really indifference, it's —"

"Well, you know, gypsies spend a lot of time together in very cramped quarters. Families many times sleep all in the same room, or in the outdoors the whole *kumpaniai* may stay together around the fire all through the night to keep away the chill, and during the rainy seasons people are forced inside a small trailer or tent or car for days on end. It is in those times that Gypsies have learned that privacy is really a state of mind and that it can be extended to others also, as a gift. I think that is what you sense. But let me also tell you that you have special status in this *familia* because Karl brought you. Not all Gypsies, or even these in other circumstances, would be so kind to a *gajo*."

Claire wondered about Mara's life, about her father and her mother, but she kept silent.

The sun was beginning to drop in the sky and the evening air felt slightly and delightfully cooler. Claire noticed that the circle around the fire had grown and that people were still wandering in from the outskirts of the camp to join in whatever was next.

"I think there will be *swatura* tonight, which are long rambling stories of *Rom* history that everyone loves. Yakov, no doubt, will be the one to do the telling. I am afraid the stories will be in *Romany*, though. They would lose much in any other language."

As the middle-aged man began to weave his story, Claire was caught up in it even though she did not understand a word. The pudgy unlikely story-teller came alive as he gestured and changed inflections, and laughed and talked and rolled his eyes with mock scorn. Claire was reminded of her own family and Michael's and his stories and those she'd heard in Ireland in another tongue she didn't understand.

She became anxious again as she thought of her family and what in the world they might be thinking; she wondered if Karl would ever come. Patrick was enjoying the story, too, but he put his head down on her lap. She was sure the day's activities with the children and the unnerving events of the previous night had taken their toll and that he would be asleep soon.

Claire looked around the group that encircled the fire, the men stretched out with their women, little children sprawled over their elders, many of them already asleep; and she felt suddenly homesick and alone and frightened.

As the darkness fell more deeply, Mara reached over to touch Claire's arm.

"You don't have to stay. They will go long into the night. Eventually it will just be the men and they will all drink too much.

I'll walk you back to your cottage if you wish.

Is Patrick asleep?"

Just then a figure appeared out of the black edges of the firelight. The story-teller stopped.

Karl raised his hand, "No, please don't let me interrupt everything. Go on please."

"*Devlesa avilan*!" Holz shouted immediately, standing up to embrace the big blonde man.

"*Devlesa araklam tume*!" Karl shouted back, returning the old man's affection much as would a loving son.

"What did they say? If you don't mind my asking," Claire whispered to Mara as the greetings continued around the circle beginning with Kitta.

"My grandfather said '*It is God who brought you.*' And Karl replied, '*It is with God that we found you.*' Here he comes to greet us."

The big man, still dressed in black, leaned over to kiss Mara on both cheeks and then sat down on the quilt next to Claire and the sleeping Patrick.

"Please go on, Yakov! Please continue!" Karl urged.

The stout little performer continued evidently from where he had left off and recaptured the crowd's attention immediately. A woman brought Karl a dish of food and a cup of wine, for which he thanked her profusely, but before he ate he washed his hands as a young girl poured water from a pitcher over them into a basin she held underneath. Claire realized that she was drinking her second cup of wine and could feel its mellowing effects. That may have been why she had been so sentimental, she thought.

"Hello, Claire O'Connell!" he said in a low voice as he ate and drank with relish. "I'm sorry that it took me so long to return. I hope you did not think that I would disappear for another five months!"

"No, I believed you would come," she replied, looking over at Mara.

"As soon as I finish this delicious meal, we will go back to your cabin and I will fill you in as much as I can. Aha! I see that I get the pleasure of carrying Michael O'Connell's sleeping son again."

The stories rose and fell around the fire, but there was only one story that Claire was anxiously yearning to hear.

Chapter 22

Among the best traitors Ireland ever had, Mother Church ranks at the very top, a massive obstacle in the path to equality and freedom.
Bernadette Devlin

There is a real and mysterious power at work behind the screen of idiot doctrines. That power belongs to the spirit that is above nature and yet not God ...
Thomas Merton

Deep in the dark Irish night, a circle stood around another fire. Leaping and licking, it burned not for warmth but for power and release, as if the earth were belching out rancid uncontrollable breaths of misery too long unrelieved, centuries of anger and bitterness repressed, now made white-hot in a bellowing forge beneath the ground. This was not a celebration; that innocence was gone. Joy had not been invited nor ever even considered.

"Great god Lugh!"

A man's voice cried into the night, reaching to touch the configuration of stars that bore this name. "Lugh, Lion with the Steady Hand! We honor your death and the strength that flows from you. Great Oak, of which we are only the branches, renew our power through your death!"

A woman's voice picked up the cry, "Lugh, Son of Arianrhod, The Silver Wheel, give strength to your mother and all her daughters. In your death take with you our land, our world and give it to us once again from your mother's womb newborn and whole!"

An empty black lidless coffin was lifted high above the heads of the swaying figures and passed methodically around the circle. The male voice resumed its incantations.

"Everlasting Lugh! We wait for the true *nasadh*, the great commemoration of this your death — when your coffin is filled once again as in ancient days with a most worthy delegate."

Silence, then: "Tear down! Tear down!" another woman called out.

"Tear down! Tear down!" called all the hooded figures in

response.

"Make way for Bran!" the woman cried.

"Who bars the way of Bran?" the circle responded.

"Whosoever hinders the mighty death of Lugh, and bars the blessed way of Bran, be cursed! Cursed are they who thwart the power of the earth and sky, who hold the key within their grasp only to let it fall away. Cursed forever!" a man hissed loudly.

"Cursed forever!" the circle responded.

Chapter 23

I am afraid that even if you can entertain the notion of a positive power for evil working through human agency, you may still have a very inaccurate notion of what Evil is, and may find it difficult to believe that it may operate through men of genius and excellent character.
T.S. Eliot

The sum which two married people owe one another defies calculation. It is an infinite debt, which can only be discharged throughout all eternity.
Johann von Goethe

Mara walked with Claire and Karl carried Patrick through the camp toward the dark cabin. Only a couple of small fires were lit away from the main attraction of Yakov's *swatura*. As they crossed the lawn, a woman ran out from behind one of the trailers screaming in a high-pitched wail.

"Get out! Get out!" she shouted, shaking both fists toward them. Then she switched to *Romany* and continued her violent tirade.

Karl started toward her, but Mara stepped in instead.

"Woman! You must stop!" Then she slipped into the Gypsy tongue as well.

Claire clung to Karl's arm; Patrick opened his eyes dreamily and the woman's voice died down and she eventually stalked away.

Mara came back to them. "She is part of a group of *Muchwaya*, a tribe not known well to us. They only arrived this morning. I am sorry for that disturbance."

"What was she saying?" Claire asked, still a little shaken by the outburst.

"Let's get Patrick to bed." Karl interposed.

Patrick took a look at who was holding him and gently lay his head back down on the blonde man's shoulder.

After Patrick was in his bed, Karl asked, "Do you want to talk inside or out? We can sit on the steps if you wish."

"On the steps is fine," Claire answered and they stepped out once more into the midsummer night.

Mara was attempting to leave them when Claire asked again,

"What did the woman say to us?"

In the light from the small lamp in the cottage, Claire saw Mara look at Karl. Karl answered.

"She said that there was a curse on you and the boy. But please don't think anything of it."

"Yes," Mara agreed, "it's the oldest Gypsy scam in the book. Spot a *gajo,* usually a single woman who might be in trouble somehow. Then you tell her that there is a curse on her that is causing all her troubles and that you are the only one who can take away the curse.

Karl added, "And it usually costs a lot of money to break a curse."

"She'll probably ask for money tomorrow." Mara said.

"Not if I'm anywhere around." Karl said commandingly.

"Well, anyway, good night. *Akan mukav tut le Devlesa.* I now leave you to God." Mara said softly as she left them.

* * *

"What do you mean they wanted to *get away for a little while?* With no *word?* No *warning?*"

Franny sat across a coffee table covered with remnants of the Chicago Sun Times and two empty cocktail glasses, facing her mother and father; the ashes from her cigarette commingled in the ashtray with those of her father's cigar. Their smoke rose and converged into one hazy cloud above their heads and then hung heavily in the stagnant humidity of the Chicago summer night. The progenitors were side-by-side on the sagging sofa. Franny had pulled up a chair from the dinette.

"Claire's been kind of down since Patrick's birthday, you know. She just felt it would be a good thing to have a change of scene and all that. It's nothing to worry about." Fran was trying hard to reassure her parents.

"That's what I said last February. But look what happened! They got homesick and missed us and couldn't even stay for their whole vacation. And if she's depressed now she needs us even *more,* doesn't she? And w*hy won't she tell us where she is? That is so strange!* What if there was an *emergency* and we needed to reach her?" her mother demanded.

"Grace, calm down. She's going to call us and check in. I think it's a good thing. She wasn't ready before to do this. Now she needs some space. You really have to just let it go; let them go. They're in good hands."

"What do you mean? Whose hands are they in? They've been all alone since Michael's gone." She reached over and put her tiny hand on her husband's large one.

"Uhhh …" Fran stalled. "Well, *God's* hands. You believe *that*, don't you?" Franny relaxed a bit, satisfied with her recovery.

"I don't know if God's hands hold us if we turn our backs on him and give up our faith." At this thought, Grace began to waiver and sobbed a little.

"If you believe that, you'd better change your name, Mom."

"Francine, I don't know what you mean. How can you make silly statements when you know I'm upset …?"

John Daly let his cigar burn in the ashtray. The smoke ascended in a straight line, with no air to disturb it, reaching for heaven but lost in an unknowing cloud that hugged the living room ceiling. He turned over his huge hand like a living stone and cupped his wife's anxious fluttering one between both his hands as if holding a wounded sparrow.

"The girl's right, Grace, the girl's right."

* * *

"You talked to Franny! I can't believe it. How did you know about her, that she'd be the one to contact?"

Claire was stunned with amazement as she and Karl sat silhouetted on the cabin steps.

"Michael told me about Francine one time when we were talking. He thought a lot of her, I know. I just presumed that you may have told her some of what's happened and that she'd be the best liaison with your family."

"How did she react? My God, she must have been blown away when *you* showed up at her door!"

"She was understandably wary at first, but she did like the way I dressed. I think *that* counted for something."

They both laughed gently.

"She wants you to call her tonight no matter how late it is, and you may do that after we talk."

"Fran may seem kind of ditsy and like some sort of Mall-crawler but she's really not like that. You just have to get to know her." Claire said, defending her sister.

"Oh, I could have sensed that right away, even without Michael's perceptions. She's one of those people who skip a lot of the steps that many of us use but inevitably trip over. She skips right to the heart of the matter. Pope said, and everyone since, that fools rush in … but the fool is sometimes the wisest of us all."

"So does Fran know more than I do at this point as to what's going on?"

"I told your sister that some people were after you and Patrick because of events having to do with Michael. I told her that you both were safe for the present time and that she should tell your family and whoever else may inquire, that you decided to take an unplanned trip. Your mail is being forwarded to Francine's apartment."

"But what about the condition of the house? It was a mess when we left it. I could see that even in the dark. Someone is sure to guess that something is amiss."

"We went back and made sure everything was straightened and in order. We will be watching the house closely. I have cautioned Francine to stay away from your place for her own safety and she is going to think of some way to keep your mother at a distance as well." He spoke in a rather businesslike manner, betraying perhaps a bit of disdain for these details when larger things were on his mind.

Finally Claire said, "I'm ready now for your story." She looked straight ahead into the summer night, feeling both dread and anticipation.

Karl took a deep breath and began.

"During Michael's last year of graduate school in Dublin he went to talk to a good friend of mine who is a priest there. My friend called me to say that a young man had come to him with a compelling story that he thought would interest me. Because of the sacramental nature of their relationship he was not at liberty to tell me much, but he asked Michael if he would meet with me and he agreed. So I flew immediately to Dublin."

"From where?"

"I believe I was in Rome. Yes, I flew from Rome. When I arrived at the rectory the young man I was introduced to was in a pitiable and wretched condition. His eyes were dark and hollow. He looked ill somehow, distraught."

"Was this in December? Michael was so ill in December that he didn't come home for Christmas as planned." Claire asked, attempting to get her bearings.

"No, this was mid-October."

Claire had never known Michael to be sick in all the years they'd been together. She had thought he was immune to everything. Karl's description of him and the thought that he may have been ill for several months shocked and saddened her.

"Michael told me," Karl continued, "that he had been involved in a group that was supposedly a Celtic Revival Society. Upon closer observation and his eventual initiation, as this was all very secret, he discovered that they were interested in reviving the Druid religion and following the ways of pre-Christian Ireland. Michael was excited at first and very caught up in it. Of course they were extremely interested in him because of his language skills and the work he was doing in the secret ancient mystical language, *Misog*, also called in Gaelic *berla na filid*, meaning 'tongue of the seer', and its derivative, *Shelta*.

He soon found that this group, actually a neo-pagan cult, was into much more than Michael had bargained for. It has as its members some of the most prominent figures in Ireland: politicians, government leaders, literary celebrities, university professors and students and of course, the common people who are pawns in any organization like this, who are used and abused and expendable. Their goals are lofty, one being peace in Ireland and eventually the world, but their means have been at times savage and barbaric."

"How long was Michael involved with this group?" Claire asked, stunned at this revelation.

"He was introduced to them when he first came to Dublin."

"He never mentioned anything about it to me, and we shared everything. At least back then." The sense of betrayal that had accompanied the finding of the note in Michael's pocket was multiplied greatly.

"But it *is* a secret society and the initiates are quickly bound with oaths and promises and eventually threats. Please don't judge him too harshly. I know that Michael loved you very much and deeply regretted all of his actions during that period."

Claire rested her head in her hands. It was spinning with questions that this man could never answer.

Karl silently laid his hand on her head for a moment and then withdrew it.

"You said university professors. Is Doctor McCullum involved in this?"

"Michael thought so at one time. Many of the true identities of the other members are never known to one another. All contact is up to the Chief Druid. One thing is certain though. Doctor McCullum has come up missing. No one has seen him for a month."

"And you think his disappearance has to do with this cult?"

"I don't know. We're trying to find out."

"I hope you don't mind my asking, but why are *you* involved with all of this? Why would you fly from Rome to Dublin just to talk with Michael about some retro-Druid wanna-be's? Haven't there been a lot of these groups through the years and they're all pretty harmless. One of them meets at Stonehenge, I think, for the solstices and no one takes it seriously."

"I'm an international investigator and this kind of group has special interest to me and I do take it very seriously, as should you."

"Do you work for some government or something?" Claire asked.

"You could say that."

"Please go on, and I'm sorry to ask so many questions."

"I think you have the right to ask as many questions as you wish. Stop me whenever you feel it necessary."

He stood up and stretched his tall body and remained standing next to the steps as he spoke: "The deeper that Michael was drawn into the center of this group the more bizarre he realized it was. The trouble was that by the time he talked to my friend and then to me, it had become almost impossible for him to extricate himself from the organization because he was being groomed for a leadership position. They believed Michael had some sort of special mythological significance and mystical power because of his mastery of *Misog*. He, however, though rather flattered at first, felt there was no basis for their belief in him. I don't think he ever discovered their true plans for him."

"What caused him to be so physically ill?" Claire asked, seeing in her mind's eye Michael's beautiful strong naked body standing in the Irish moonlight.

"He was unable to sleep or eat because of the anxiety he felt concerning the circumstances in which he found himself. And I know he was drinking heavily. I have no proof, but I do think they were drugging him somehow."

"*Why didn't he tell me any of this?* I don't understand, I just don't understand."

"Claire, there will most likely be many things I tell you that you won't understand and things that are harder to hear than these. Michael had his reasons for keeping them from you and I would not violate his wishes even now if it were not for the danger you are in. Maybe you have listened enough for one night. Would you like to stop and go to bed?"

"No, please go on."

"My friend became Michael's director and confessor and over the next several months Michael made the decision to return to the Church. Meanwhile I helped him to devise a plan to leave this nefarious group behind."

"If you and presumably other people know about this group, why do you let it go on? If it's as evil as you say it is, shut it down!"

"Believe me, Claire, I would if I could. You must understand that *nothing* is done in the open and *no one* knows who the real leadership is. Michael had his suspicions and so do I. But we have not been able to prove anything."

"You mean Michael was almost a leader himself and he didn't know who the other leaders were? Not even the Chief Druid?" Claire asked incredulously.

"Michael and I became more and more convinced as time moved along as to the true identity of the Chief Druid." Karl paused. "Have you ever heard of James Day?"

"You mean *the* James Day? The Nobel winner, the globally-known-champion-for-Irish-peace James Day? The man who started memorial homes in his dead wife's name for handicapped orphan children from all over the world? Yes, I've heard of James Day and I can't believe that what you're saying is true!"

"The Chief Druid rarely communicated with Michael or anyone face to face, and when he did he wore a hooded robe or some other disguise, but in recent months he got a little more careless and Michael thought he recognized his voice on several occasions."

"In recent months? I thought you said that Michael had left it all behind before he came home and we were married."

"Michael made an agreement not to expose the group in exchange for his life and the safety of his family, both of which they had threatened if he defected. They agreed, I believe, because they did not want to lose his great gift for the language and they wanted him to finish the Lexicon. Also I think they still believed in his alleged mystical power.

"In Druid mythology, there is a Great Man or Great One who is born every several hundred years. The Great One is said to know the language, or *Misog,* innately, without ever learning it. Evidently they believed that about Michael. I think they hoped he would eventually turn and come back to them."

"But Michael spent months and years researching his lexicon. He had to learn the language just like anyone else."

"Faith is oft times misplaced," said Karl with some sadness.

"So what happened after he came home?"

"Things seemed to go well. Michael and I had become friends and we stayed in fairly close touch. I also kept an eye and ear open in Ireland for any surfacing of the *Golden Hammer.*"

"The Golden Hammer?"

"It's the English translation of the *Misog* name which the group calls itself," Karl answered. "Around this time last year, I got an urgent phone call from Michael. He said that he had been contacted by the group again, by the Chief Druid himself. He was told that things were changing and his participation with the *Golden Hammer* was essential to the new plan for the new world. They had been watching him closely, they told him, over the last six years. And they hoped he was ready now to take his place. Of course he refused, but was approached by the leader several more times over the next few months. It was during this period that he began suspecting James Day. I was in China when I heard about Michael's death."

"Are you implying that Michael's death was not an accident? The person who hit him was a seventy-five year old woman who'd lived in that neighborhood her whole *life*. You think that *she* was working with this *Golden Hammer?*"

Claire felt angry and cynical. She was angry at Michael for hiding a whole part of his life from her. She was angry at Karl for jet-setting around the world like James Bond, lending his beneficent help when it was interesting enough.

"I still don't know exactly how it happened," he answered her softly, "but I am convinced now that Michael was murdered."

Claire still said nothing. She was angry at Karl for being in China when Michael died. Communism was kind of a big job, even for a professional Cult-Buster like him. Maybe he had good friends there too, with beautiful young granddaughters like Mara who he could laugh and joke with, and who knew what else.

Karl sat down again next to Claire and laid a hand on her shoulder. Claire turned and slapped him left-handed across the face. He didn't seem shocked or surprised. Claire was sorry immediately and began to cry.

Huge sobbing spasms shook her, and she tried suppress them so as not to wake Patrick.

"You're angry at me for not protecting Michael," Karl said as Claire's wrenching sobs lessened in intensity.

"No, no ... I don't know what I'm doing. It's just *every*thing. I'm being totally irrational. I'm so sorry ... I —"

"I have had a hard time with that myself," Karl said with a face like stone, not really listening to Claire at all. "I should have *seen* that things were heating up, that some dynamic had changed. I loved Michael and I know that I was meant to protect him. Right after his death, I still believed that it was an accident, but I decided that we would keep you and Patrick under close watch, just in case. I felt I owed it to Michael."

"You came to South Carolina because of *us*? And Mara, too?" Claire asked, finding it still hard to fathom that she and Patrick were at the center of such a bizarre situation.

"Yes. And even then I did not think, as I said, that you were the target. Although I knew the Golden Hammer was involved because I recognized the *ga bulga* that was thrown at us at the resort. It's a barbed spiral spear, supposedly imbued with mysterious and mystical properties. Someone else retrieved it while I chased our druidess. She wasn't working alone."

"Druids can be women?" Claire asked in astonishment.

"Oh certainly. The Celts were very open to women functioning in all aspects of their society. Women were ruling monarchs, chieftains, generals, warriors — why not priests? These modern-day pagans make every effort to scrupulously emulate their ancient models, although selectively and with much less innocence and with, in fact, reactionary and diabolical innovations."

"Why are you, I am presuming you are not Irish but German, why are you so knowledgeable about and interested in all this Celtic mythology? Isn't it rather provincial and isolated for an international gentleman like yourself to be concerned with?"

Karl ignored the cynical shading of Claire's question.

"As you may know, being an Irish-American yourself, Celtic mysticism is not only an Irish phenomenon, but is part of a worldwide neo-pagan revival. In America it is closely associated with Wicca, which many times is a harmless and sincere search for the truth through nature. There are many secret societies like the Golden Hammer all over the world. This particular group attracted my concern because of the level of authority many of the members seem to have. There were tragic consequences for my country and the world with that mixture earlier in this century."

"So getting back to my story, *our* story ..." Claire was exhausted, but she willed herself to hear more. The implied comparison of James Day to Hitler fell on Claire's mind as seed onto hard ground, and there it withered quickly.

Karl continued, "Well, it seemed that the group withdrew their attentions from you after South Carolina. We didn't know about the *snake* episode, I'm sorry to say. But the likelihood is great that that was not a deadly attempt. More of a calculated fright."

"How did you find out about the snakes?"

"Franny told me about them today, and about the other harassments. I've talked with Stephan and Mara about it. We believe that the intent was to frighten you to the point that the group could send someone who seemed to be rescuing you ... who would then convince you to cooperate with them."

"Someone like you?" Claire asked sarcastically, though with almost a fleeting flash of real doubt.

"I know that you have no solid reason to trust me. But you have so far and I am glad."

"But how is it that you know *so many* things about the actions of this group and are so clueless to others?"

"That's a fair question. Actually we've had someone on the inside who has been very helpful and who knows many of the pieces. We just don't know how they fit together. I believe there is only one man who does."

"James Day, of course." Claire noticed that the last of the Gypsy fires had gone out. The compound was entirely dark and still. She and Karl were almost whispering.

"Yes, and we have been following his movements carefully. But he is very, very clever."

"Or *innocent*. I still don't see the motive for a man of his stature and position to be involved in some New Age, neo-pagan game like this." Claire was still unwilling to give up the public image of a man she had admired for years.

"A *game,* you say. It's interesting that you should use that term ... but I'll come back to that. Regarding Day's motives, there is something that virtually no one knows about him and that is that he is quietly but profoundly anti-Christian, especially anti-Catholic, although he was born and raised in the Church."

"I know that a militant Catholic nationalist minority feels he has betrayed the true Irish cause by being willing to be neutral and have Protestants or atheists for that matter, in his coalition. That's called *diversity,* not anti-Christian."

"Please trust me on this. I am not talking about neutrality, but revulsion and antipathy. I have friends in Belfast who've known him his whole life."

"Well, you just have friends everywhere, don't you!" Claire said, her sarcasm rising up once more, even through a wave of exhaustion. "Everyone who no longer believes in the Church is not necessarily working for its demise, you know. I think that's enough for me tonight. I'm tired now and I need to rest."

Claire stood up and turned to go into the cabin.

"There are still things I haven't told you. But you're right, you need to rest and so do I," Karl said with weariness in his voice.

"Will you be here in the morning?" Jab again. He didn't seem to notice.

"Yes, as far as I know. Don't forget to call your sister. Don't tell her anything that she doesn't know already, for her safety as well as yours and Patrick's. She just needs to hear your voice and know that you are well." He handed her his cellular phone. "Good night, Claire O'Connell. *Akan mukav tut le Devlesa.*" He walked away into the Gypsy night.

* * *

Claire slipped into the cottage, where the small brass lamp still shone warmly. She stood at the table and poured cool water over her face from the pitcher, letting it flow into the 'appropriate' blue enameled basin beneath. She put on her white cotton nightgown again and sat on the eiderdown bed of her sleeping son.

"Well, little boy," she said softly, "Your father has probably been killed by some crazy Irish cult; your mommy has a crippling, eventually fatal disease; we've been chased out of our home and are running from who-knows-what to who-knows-where. But sleep now, Patrick, with your brown floppy sentinel at your head and your army of Daddy's treasures at your side. They are as likely to bring you protection and comfort as anything else." She stroked his lovely face and hair. "A lot of older and wiser people than you misplace their faith."

Claire rifled through her bag and finally found the floating red-haired woman. She wound her watch with the familiar back and forth movement she had performed each day since Patrick's birth. Was it too late to call Fran? Two a.m. She'd probably be asleep ...

She got the cell phone and turned off the lamp and lay quietly a moment in the darkness in her white nightgown. Then she dialed Franny's number.

"My God, Claire, what took you so damned *long?* I've gone through a whole pack of cigarettes sitting by this telephone. *Nothing* on television. I've been watching monster truck demolition derbies! I should have rented a video. So how *are* you? Pretty exciting stuff, huh? It's almost like a movie just thinking about it. And Karl, wow! What a stylin' trip *he* is! There's something so ... *uumph* about him, you know? It's hard to believe he's actually a priest!"

"A *priest!*" Claire whispered loudly in the darkness. "*Karl* is a *priest?*"

"Holy shit! I wasn't supposed to say anything about that 'til I was sure he'd told you. Damn! I'm sorry, Claire. There's so much to remember about what to say and what not say to whom. I guess I blew that one. Everything is cool with Grace and Dad though, I played that all right. You should have seen the look on her face when I told her about the cockroaches!'

"What cockroaches?"

"The ones that are being exterminated from your house. You know ... the reason why she can't go over and poke around? Pretty good, huh?"

Chapter 24

Some are mathematicians
Some are carpenters' wives
I don't know how it all got started
I don't know what they do with their lives.
                Bob Dylan

"Would not conversation be more rational than dancing?" said Miss Bingly.
"Much more rational," replied Mr. Bingly, "but much less like a ball."
                Jane Austen

William James is noted as saying that at different points throughout history an unexplained phenomenon takes place where a "critical mass of geniuses cause a whole civilization to vibrate and shake". In ancient Greece, Plato's academy was the locus of such a mass. Its rays emanated from that set point to jolt not only its own culture, but those that were coeval and on into countless civilizations in ages to come.

In the early twentieth century, the critical mass resided in New Jersey at the Institute for Advanced Studies. It did not survive and flourish at the whim of arbitrary temperamental deities but by the steady open hand of much more benevolent benefactors at the Rockefeller Foundation. Surveying the severely anemic state of mathematics and science in all of the American universities in the 1920's, the Foundation donated, or some might say hemorrhaged, vast flows of money into several so-honored university programs. The sleepy little university town of Princeton would eventually be mentioned alongside such venerable centers of learning as Budapest, Berlin, Paris, Vienna and Rome, and in the end it would surpass them all.

The Institute was founded solely as a haven for research. Top mathematicians were recruited from all over Europe to live in a pampered hothouse environment protected from the pressures of the outside world. It was at the Fine Hall Teas that the connection between the university and the Institute was most alive, where Princeton's mathematics faculty and its most promising math students could mingle with the likes of Einstein, Oppenheimer, Godel, and Von Neumann. It was in Fine Hall that the "presence" of mathematics charged the air with the propitious inklings of hope for a great intellectual revolution.

Formal Wednesday Teas were served in the West Common Room, which was a Holy Sanctuary to Mathematics. The sun shone in through lovely stained-glass windows inlaid with such formulae as Newton's Law of Gravity, Einstein's Theory of Relativity, and Heisenberg's Uncertainty Principle of Quantum Mechanics. In this liturgy of deference to a realm of non-spatial, non-mental, timeless entities, faculty wives served at the altar in long dresses and white gloves, pouring tea and cutting cake. A hagiography of mathematical saints and their achievements were on the lips of almost everyone in attendance: Fermat and his 'Last Theorem', Goldbach and his Binary Conjecture, Cantor, D.H. Hardy and his mysterious Indian protege, Ramaujan, Brouwer and his Fixed Point System and of course, the great George Friedrich Reimann with his brilliant and accepted, but as yet unprovable hypothesis having to do with the number of prime numbers under a given magnitude. The tea room was also scattered with tables where brilliant minds would play parlor games — *Go, Nash, Kriegspeil* — with the intensity of a major life decision. And back at the Institute when the rituals were done, the search for the 'Theory of Everything' continued.

Theopholus Kostanikas came to Princeton in the 40's in his late teens, as part of a handful of Gentiles among a sea of sparkling, scintillating Jewish recruits and refugees. The lack of structure and complete cognitive freedom here fit comfortably for a long time with his eccentric life; his moments of lucidity usually revealed such strikingly original approaches to problems that even when his symptoms began to overwhelm him his colleagues were not quick to notice.

There have been a great many mental casualties whose inspirations have fallen from the sky, borne along on the wings of golden thoughts deep into the heart and beauty of mathematical truth for a time. Brouwer, Cantor, and Godel suffered serious mental illness. Reimann himself had a debilitating nervous breakdown and died in 1866 at age 39. Norbert Weiner, the 'father of cybernetics', was severely manic depressive. John Nash, who won the Nobel Prize in Economics for his work in Game Theory, was crippled by schizophrenia, as was his son, Johnny, another promising mathematical genius.

G. K. Chesterton posits that mathematicians go mad, but creative artists seldom do. New England's McClean Hospital, an upper-class psychiatric haven, did not know that, however, and pampered the sad and inconsolable likes of Sylvia Plath and Robert Lowell, as well as Theo Kostanikas and other broken calculators. Lowell, standing like an ancient aristocratic Bard, would hold forth in a fellow patient's room before a crowd of those lost between the worlds, his words even then a poignantly eloquent map pointing to one world or the other. Theo heard him as a distant melody.

The gods of war first came after Mathematicians in their protected fortress of 'pure mathematics', unsullied by human applications, because of codes. Along with the other cryptological mystics on the planet, the Gypsies and the Navajos, the Mathematicians formed a triangle that broke Nazi cipher texts and confused their strategies, turning the tide of the war.

Then came the message to Princeton, through an Austrian Jewish refugee, that Otto Hahn, a German physicist had succeeded in splitting the uranium atom. The Institute for Advanced Studies lost its summit-hold in the rarified air of the beauty of mathematics for its own sake and became instead the minor league feeder team for the Manhattan Project.

Theo Kostanikas got sucked into war strategies through the Rand Corporation. With Rand, the conduit for military and mathematical collaboration was opened to full capacity, but Theo eventually lost his security clearance because of his erratic behavior. He was then free to become one of the select few who could call themselves disciples of the great Von Neumann.

John Von Neumann was a Hungarian Jew, a child expert on the Byzantine Empire who at age 6 could divide two 8-digit numbers in his head, mastered calculus at age 8 and came to be considered the most intelligent mathematician the 20th century had produced. He was known for his development of Game Theory but by the end of World War II his real passion was computers. He laid the groundwork for computer architecture and as early as 1945 saw the potential of 'thinking machines'. The speed of Von Neumann's mind was legendary. Stories circulated of his outracing computers at colossal tasks of computation. The antithesis of dull academic types, he enjoyed wearing expensive clothes, drinking hard liquor and driving fast cars. His flamboyance was attractive to his protégés, but he was cold and aloof in his human relationships. He had few friends.

And yet he developed a soft spot for Kostanikas. Between the younger man's periodic internments at various hospitals and mental facilities Von Neumann accepted Theo's presence with an uncharacteristic gentle tolerance. He intervened on several occasions to make certain that no one touched this superb fragile mind with barbarous — yet at that time so smugly 'progressive' — jolts of electric shock therapy.

"It would be like taking an air hammer to the Hope diamond!" he was quoted as saying. He referred to Kostanikas as 'The Greek' and let him stay in a spare room at his own small laboratory. They had long private discussions during which Von Neumann bounced ideas off of Theo's quirky yet elegantly original mind. They discussed the ergodic theorem, the new algebra, and as Von Neumann lay dying of cancer in 1957, the development of a theory of the structure of the human brain.

Chapter 25

*Already the dark and endless ocean of the end
is washing in through the breaches of our wounds
already the flood is upon us.
Oh, build your ship of death, your little ark ...*
David Herbert Lawrence

Whatever happened to the things we used to know were real?
Bill Hughes

Claire stood in her white nightgown on what looked like Michigan Avenue, but she couldn't be sure. She thought it strange that there were no cars on the wide street, yet the sidewalks were full of people. The shops were closed and it was night. All at once she remembered with anxiety that she was supposed to meet Michael somewhere and that it was very important to get there on time.

Running, her bare feet skimming the pavement, she soon was in her old neighborhood at the corner where she and Michael would meet most often as kids. It hadn't changed at all. The air was warm and clear. There were fireflies in everyone's yard and half a silver moon. Mary Alice's dad's old Ford Galaxie was still parked in the driveway of her friend's house. It was the car they would play in for hours, going on imaginary trips and dates. How old had she been? It didn't matter now. Where was Michael? She kept running through the woods, in Ireland, in Michigan. She kept looking at her watch to see if she was late, but her eyes would not focus. She blinked again and again.

Claire tried to make her way through teeming crowds of people who suddenly appeared, all gathered together and all looking up at something. Some were laughing, some were crying. It was a wharf and everyone was peering at the boat docked there, a huge ocean liner with people lining the decks, dressed stylishly in the grand manner — top hats, evening gowns; they held bunches of beautiful flowers and glasses of champagne, and waved and waved like dignitaries in a parade. *Where was Michael?* She pushed closer to the ship, searching the faces of the happy passengers up there. And

Patrick? Where had she left Patrick? How could she have been so careless in this crowd of people?

She knew that if she could find Michael, they would find Patrick together. She looked up again frantically at the ship, scanning the convivial line of voyagers. Then she saw it: Michael's face, his wonderful face, smiling his easy smile with one of his arms resting on the railing. He was dressed in a dark tuxedo and smoking a cigarette (he'd quit years ago). His handsomeness still cut her. He looked over the crowd, not anxiously, but casually. He did not see her. She called his name.

The ship changed. First, it became an ugly affair, like a big tub. It suddenly resembled cartoon pictures she'd seen as a child of Noah's ark. Then it became a majestic old sailing ship, with an ornately carved beautiful full-breasted woman at its prow. Michael stayed there on the railing in the same place throughout all its permutations.

It was imperceptible at first, but as the ship began to make preparations to leave, the crowd on the dock lost its jovial attitude and began to panic. Some began to run up the ramp. Others were pushing and yelling and screaming. Some turned to run the other way but were swept in the throng toward the ship and the sea.

There was no moon, no stars. The harbor lights had gone out. The lights onboard the ship cast the only light in the darkness. Claire began to cry. She yelled Michael's name louder and louder, but all she could hear was the noise of the crowd. She knew that *if only he could see her* he would come and get her and together they would find Patrick.

She pushed her way through the hostile ungiving bodies, breathlessly reaching the edge of the dock as the ramp was being lifted toward the ship. A new sense of terror spread through the crowd and gripped her aching heart. People all around her were flinging themselves into the blackness of the swirling water rather than await their nameless fate on the dock. Claire looked up again to find Michael's face, for if she could see his face while she jumped, she knew she would make it onto the ramp. *There he was!* And in his arms was Patrick! Why couldn't they see her?

Claire summoned all her strength to make the enormous leap. But she felt a vice-like grip on her wrists. She turned to either side and discovered two robed monks holding her fast. She began to scream.

"It's the Church! It's the god-damned Church again! Let me go, you idiots! Let me go!"

*   *   *

Claire awoke sweating and angry to find the sun streaming in the open door of the Gypsy cabin. Patrick's bed was empty. Her heart was racing from the emotion of the dream. It was still so vivid in her mind that it colored the context of her waking perceptions and her first thoughts were worries about Patrick's whereabouts. Then she remembered that they were in a safe place. At least she thought they were. How could one be sure of anything when nobody told the whole truth? What kind of priest was Karl anyway, flitting around the world in style? Didn't they have to take some sort of vows of poverty or at least agree to say Mass every once in a while or *something*?

He probably comes from some wealthy aristocratic German family that has an arrangement with the Pope, Claire thought as she quickly got dressed to look for Patrick. Those kind of things happened, she knew, and they had for centuries. Well, whatever. That wasn't the point anyway. She just felt stupid and embarrassed. Not only about the priest business, but because he knew more about her own husband than she did. Boy, he must think they had a great marriage! What kind of marriage *did* they have then?

Claire marched out of the cottage full of confused indignation. She looked around the camp. The weather was mild and sunny. Some men, women, and a few children were scattered throughout, wandering slowly this way and that.

She walked toward a knot of people she saw gathered where the dinner and fire had been the night before. As she came closer, she saw Karl standing in front of an old maroon Lincoln, dressed in an almost gaudy chasuble made with bright colored cloth spangled with jewels and gold pieces. His arms were raised, lifting a gold chalice; Gypsies knelt all around. She knew he was celebrating the Mass, but it just struck her wrong, these dark skinned outcasts kneeling before this Aryan god-like figure in all his distinguishing finery. It reminded her of Kipling's *The Man Who Would Be King*. She saw Mara and Patrick kneeling among the others.

Karl put the chalice down on the hood of the Lincoln and knelt quickly himself. They all stood and said something in (it wasn't Latin, it must have been Romany) which Claire presumed was the Our Father. Soon they were walking forward on either side of the car to receive the sacrament — Holz, Kitta, other family members she had met — and Mara with Patrick. Her son had not made his First Communion yet, but he solemnly followed the procession up to the priest, crossed his arms over his chest and received a blessing.

Karl seemed to let his hand rest a little longer on his small red head than was customary.

Claire stood watching, struggling again with why, now that Michael was gone, she let Patrick continue in the practice of a religion in which she did not believe. *It's too late,* was the answer that always came back to her. Even at five years old, Patrick was already a Catholic. Michael had taught him so much in the times they spent together. He had explained the whole Mass to him, why they did this or that. She knew this because Patrick would come home and tell her things about Jesus' body and all the saints coming down to be present at the Mass. There were things he told her that she'd never heard from the sisters at St. Rita's or in any high school religion classes. She didn't know if Patrick embellished what Michael told him. She never asked Michael about it. One way or another, she always came to the same conclusion: to forbid Patrick to practice the religion that he believed, even if it was only childish trust, would hurt him terribly and also sever the connection that he still found with his father through it.

The Mass was over and Patrick saw her standing at a distance. He ran over to her with excitement in his eyes and on his face.

"Mommy! Look who's a priest! And he knows Daddy!" Claire did not, of course, correct the tense of the verb. "Now I know we'll be safe!" Patrick said with full assurance.

"After my talk with —" She hesitated for a moment trying to decide what she should call Karl now, especially to Patrick. "Do you mean Karl, Mom? He told me I could still call him Karl if I liked. He said that's what Daddy called him." Patrick interjected.

"Well, anyway. After I talked to Karl last night I called Franny and she misses you already."

"Did you tell her what's what?" Patrick asked with a sly smile. He loved having these little 'in' jokes with his mother. He'd done it since he was tiny. She had always secretly exulted in his subtle sense of humor though it was hard to explain to anyone else.

"Yes, I told her what she needed to know. That we were all right and not to worry. Karl had told her some things when he went to see her in Chicago."

"Karl went to see Franny? Cool!" Patrick exclaimed.

"Why is that so cool?"

"Because I like it when my favorite people know each other." He paused for a moment, "So what *is* what?"

"I told you, it's a figure of speech for 'what's going on!'" Claire said in mock exasperation as she tickled Patrick and he giggled.

"You know what I mean, Mommy." He said more seriously. She had known this moment would come. He deserved some kind of explanation for this huge disruption of his life. She led him by the hand over to a blanket at the far edge of communal area and they sat down. There were still some men sleeping closer in around what had been a fire, evidently they hadn't got up for Mass either.

Claire was quickly shuffling the information in her mind, trying to put what Patrick needed to know toward the front.

"So you've talked to Karl this morning. What has *he* told you?" She figured that was a good place to begin.

"He told me that he was a priest. But I could tell that because of the robes and stuff. Then he said that he knew Daddy in Ireland and then in America and that Daddy talked about me all time and that I was a special boy," he said with pride but no arrogance.

"You *are* a special boy, for sure." Claire said as she hugged him.

"I know, Mommy." Patrick answered matter-of-factly.

"By the way, why did you get up this morning and leave the cabin without saying anything?"

"Because I knew it was Sunday and that somebody would be having Church and you were sleeping and I didn't want to bother you. Was I wrong to do it?"

"No, honey, it's okay. You know Mara and the kids and it was okay. I just want to make sure you don't get in the habit of wandering off without telling me. (Her dream flashed in her mind for an instant and flitted away again.) We have to stick together, you and I."

Claire had no idea how he remembered that it was Sunday, and secondly, she thought, he sure had a lot of faith in the religious consistency of nomadic Gypsies to presume there would be Church somewhere. But his faith had borne fruit. Maybe she should start believing in the resurrection of the dead and the healing of the paralytics. No, she couldn't become a child again. Patrick would find out soon enough that wishes and prayers go unanswered for years and years, no matter how much you believe something. She just hoped she was still around to help him get through it when he did.

"I told you before that there are some bad people who are after us. They are people that Daddy knew in Ireland when he was still in school there, before you were born. Daddy didn't know they were bad then, but when he found out and tried to leave them they got mad at him and they stayed mad at him for a long time."

"Did the bad people kill Daddy?" Patrick looked her in the eyes.

"Patrick, why would you think that?" Claire asked, taken aback and turning her face away.

"Because I know Daddy didn't die on purpose."

"Honey, of course he didn't die on purpose, but it could have just been an accident."

"Does Karl think the bad people killed Daddy?" He reached up and held her face between his little hands so she could not look away again.

"Yes, Patrick. That's what Karl thinks. He is still investigating what happened. Do you know what investigating means?"

"Yeah, it means he's a Priest Detective … like," he thought for a minute, "Was Sherlock Holmes a priest? He never had wives or kids or anything so he had lots of time for mysteries."

"No, I don't think Sherlock Holmes was a priest." Claire laughed gently not to hurt his feelings, "But you know what investigations and mysteries are."

"Daddy read me a Sherlock Holmes story and we watched that movie with Franny about the dogs that howled."

On cue one of the Gypsy dogs ran by them, looking for scraps of food.

"Can we get a dog, Mommy? Sean and Molly have one."

"Your cousins aren't going on big adventures like we are." Claire tried to keep the tone as ordinary and upbeat as it had become.

"If the bad people get us will they kill us, too?"

She rubbed his back with her hand. "No one is going to get us or kill us. Karl knows all about how to keep us safe." Claire appealed to his faith, though she did not have any of her own.

"If we die we'll see Daddy in heaven."

"But Daddy wants you to live a long time, Patrick. Don't ever act like you'd rather die. Don't ever do that!" She grabbed Patrick and pulled him to her, frightened by the way this conversation was going.

"I never said I *wanted* to die, Mommy. Please don't get mad. I only mean I'm not afraid to die. That's all, Mommy, that's all."

Yakov hurried by with a woman close behind yelling at him and gesturing madly. Claire was somewhat amused at the little man's domestic troubles until she noticed his hand. A cloth was wrapped around it that was covered with blood. *Why he was being lectured so furiously instead of receiving sympathy?*

Claire and Patrick saw Mara coming over to greet them and got up from the blanket.

"Good morning, Claire. How are you today?" Mara touched Claire's arm gently as she tousled Patrick's hair.

"I'm doing all right. But what happened to Yakov?"

"Oh, it is these kinds of things that make me mad about the ways of the Gypsies." Mara frowned. "I told you that the men would stay up long into the night and would drink too much. Evidently some of the *Muchwaya* men came over to join the circle and said something inflammatory which, of course, no one even remembers. A fight broke out and everyone joined in. Yakov, among others, pulled out a knife and wound up opening a gash in his cousin Bruka's face. When they all woke up late this morning and Yakov realized what he had done, he felt such remorse that he cut off his own finger."

Claire gasped and put both hands up to her face. "He chopped off his entire finger?"

"Yes, it's a completely acceptable way of showing true contrition among the society of Gypsy men. But to me the whole thing is senseless and predictable."

"Will he go to a hospital?" Claire asked, remembering the blood-soaked cloth around Yakov's hand.

"No. His wife will take care of it after she is done scolding him."

Karl suddenly appeared, striding across the lawn with a steady, sober look on his face.

"I've just been informed that this place is no longer safe. Somehow word has leaked out about the *gaje* in this camp. Stephan heard about it up in Chicago among some other Gypsies. He is on his way here. I'm taking no chances." He turned to Mara. "I will inform Holz and Kitta if you will help Claire and the boy to get ready to leave. We will have to depart when Stephan arrives."

He walked away as abruptly as he had come and Claire felt slighted at his lack of acknowledgement of her, at being talked about in the third person with regard to something that had directly to do with her future.

"I can tell he is upset. He rarely lets it show," said Mara. "Please don't be offended. His manner is because he cares about you both, not because he does not."

Claire felt Mara had an uncanny ability to read her thoughts and to anticipate her reactions … Oh well, she was glad for her companionship and her *simpatico*, whether its source was real concern or merely her Gypsy blood.

Chapter 26

The Irish are the only people who cannot be helped by psychoanalysis.
Sigmund Freud

The ground we kept our ear to for so long
is flayed or calloused and its entrails
tested by an impious augury.
Our island is full of comfortless noises.
Seamus Heaney

Northern Ireland's summer "marching season" came and Protestant marchers were banned from parading through Catholic neighborhoods in Portadown, proof according to the Unionists that the whole peace process and its delicate dance of negotiations were slanted against them. Sinn Fein president Gerry Adams, however, felt that David Trimble was pandering to the irrational demands of the staunch Unionists for immediate decommissioning of the IRA before Sinn Fein could take its promised place in the new Assembly envisioned in the 1998 Good Friday Agreement.

The wild wind blew back and forth, rising hope and crashing disappointment being familiar weather in the country's fluctuating political climate. James Day sucked in a breath of morning air, invigorated by the tension in it. The sign on the impressive building behind him read: *The Maeve O. Day Memorial Children's Home.* Two dozen members of the press were here to take pictures and tour the new facility just opened in the country outside Dublin. It was a glorious setting.

"Why did you build another children's home in Ireland?" asked one of the reporters. "There's one in the North already, isn't there?"

"Oh, yes, there is one in Belfast, right near my old neighborhood. But my dear late wife took a liking to Dublin and would certainly be pleased to know that we are continuing her legacy of love and compassion here in one of her favorite cities." Day smiled broadly for the cameras, yet he managed to convey a loving wistfulness.

Maeve Day, though extremely wealthy, had not been a visible

politician's wife. So it was hard for anyone to know what she would have liked. Most people who knew them both had a difficult time reconciling her personality with James Day's. He was outgoing and continually upbeat; Maeve on the other hand was rumored to be an eccentric recluse, demanding and shrewish. "T'was a shaem the flaher of her youthful beauty faded so, but she's still a handsome woman," Charlie Breen had said in later years. She was also thought to be somewhat of a hypochondriac so that when she died of a sudden illness her friends were guiltily chagrined. Her 'legacy of love and compassion' was definitely begun posthumously, but most friends and even the few enemies of James Day did not make reference to that fact or to the amount of the vast fortune that came to him upon her death.

The Children's Home was not extraordinarily well built, but it had a lovely *faux* front with several Grecian pillars that gave it a look of refinement in spite of its plain and minimal majority. Most of its spaces were already filled with orphaned children who were handicapped in some way — some from birth, some with war-related disabilities.

Day led the reporters and camera crews down a clean freshly painted hallway, starched white nurses peering out at appropriate intervals from the rooms of their pitiable charges.

"This is something we can all agree on, isn't it now?" Day spoke into the cameras. "We need to start the battle to remove suffering from our nation and our world, not create more."

Charlie Breen talked to reporters as Day walked back through the building to his car.

"He's a wonderful man, he is. This is how he fills in the space left by his dear wife's passing. He has the Lord's way of turning even the tragedies of life to good."

Another man drove Day and his car out of the parking lot. "How did the riot go on Garvaghy Road?" Day asked him as they headed back into the city.

"Not as well as you would have liked." the other man said. "It seems the leaders of the Orangemen were going out of their way to keep the crowds and violence down. They're all fixed on this bloody peace agreement and worried not to tip the scales."

"But the Catholics, can't we get them going? Don't we have our man still there? He's a hothead, can't we use him again?" Day asked.

"It's the ban. The Catholics feel it's their victory. If the marching ban is lifted, then we can have some action."

"I'm working on that. The Parades Commission, what a joke! All the world focused on the fate of a bloody fifteen-minute march. It's absurd! I'll be glad when it's finally all over."

James Day dialed a number on his car phone.

"Yes, hello, Eugene? This is Mr. Day … Fine, uh — thank you … Yes, the orphanage is doing well. *Eugene,* if anyone calls, I shan't be able to be reached. It's my brother, yes, he's quite ill. I'll phone back in the morning … Yes, that's right. Good day, Eugene."

"It still amazes me how many people were born to grovel," Day said cynically to the driver. "Take me to the airport. I'm going to the lab."

Chapter 27

Life is just one damn thing after another.
Frank O'Malley

What perplexes the world is the disparity between the swiftness of the spirit and the immense unwieldiness, sluggishness, inertia and permanence of matter.
Thomas Mann

The silver Jaguar tracked luxuriously down the highway. Karl pulled out some metal link puzzles that were intriguing to Patrick. Claire looked out the window and realized that they were in rural Indiana, driving south on Highway 41 and going through such metropoli as Belshaw and Enos. No one spoke for awhile except Patrick who asked an occasional question of Karl having to do with the puzzle.

Claire tried to analyze her conflicting feelings about Karl as they drove in the silence. The main thing that bothered her was his commanding superiority in every situation. It seemed he moved them all about like pawns in his game. True, this game had to do with her safety and with Patrick's. He was orchestrating everything to help them. Why, though, hadn't he told her right away about being a priest? It just made things awkward now, because she hadn't thought of him in that way. What way *had* she thought of him and why did it really make *that* much difference? She was also angry at Michael, and she considered Karl a sort of accomplice in keeping a significant portion of Michael's life hidden from her. It was crazy, the entire thing was crazy and she was unwittingly in the middle of it all.

They kept driving south, taking smaller roads. They went through Crawfordsville, then Greencastle. Hadn't Michael been to Greencastle for some symposium at a college?

Yes, there was a sign for DePauw University. She remembered she kept thinking he was talking about DePaul, the Catholic university in Chicago. She'd never heard of this little school, but Michael said lots of wealthy kids went there and they had a core of students who were very interested in Celtic Studies.

After miles of silence, Karl spoke: "Claire, I don't think you have ever been properly introduced to Stephan."

Claire realized that she had paid no attention to the young man since she got into the car, so occupied was she with her own thoughts. "How do you do, Stephan?" she said, leaning forward politely.

The young man turned and reached out his hand. "Hello, Mrs. O'Connell. You can call me Steve." He smiled and shook her hand vigorously before facing the wheel again.

He looked familiar to Claire now. "You can call me Claire, and this is Patrick." Her son let out a sigh with his hello, finally showing some frustration with the unsolvable puzzle.

"You can quit now, Patrick, if you like. You've given it a good enough go," Karl told him.

"No, it's okay. I'm just gonna close my eyes for a little while so I can see it better when I open them. But I'm not quitting. Daddy said it wasn't good to quit games before they were done." He did close his eyes, still holding the silver puzzle in his hands.

"Steve," said Claire, boldly taking the initiative. "Have I met you before?"

"I was with Karl and Mara in South Carolina and I drove you from your house the night you left," he replied.

"Boy, you three are a regular 'Mod Squad'!" Claire exclaimed jokingly, but with the slight edge of sarcasm she hated in herself. Franny could have said it with no guile.

The comparison was lost on both of them. Steve laughed a little, just to be polite, she guessed. Karl sat quietly.

"You know, that old TV show with the two hip guys and the beautiful girl who solved all the crimes together? I guess Steve is too young to even remember the reruns and they probably never showed it in Germany ... Well, anyway. It's nice to see you again, Steve. And thanks for all your help," Claire added with sincerity.

"You're welcome and it's my pleasure."

Steve's manner was very comforting to Claire. After all the exotic names and accents and customs she had been exposed to over the past couple of days, he seemed like just an ordinary guy — like a college student doing a summer job, then going back in the fall to finish up his degree in … let's see, she pondered, Business, or maybe Phys Ed/Coaching.

Claire wondered if Karl's aloofness was because she had offended him during their talk the night before. *She'd slapped him across the face!* Her own cheeks flushed at the thought. She'd never hit anyone in her life, not even her sisters! She'd also practically accused him of letting Michael die. She went back and forth in her mind from thinking of herself as an ungrateful jerk to whipping up justification for her anger and her feeling of victimization. Rather than sit in the fertile and uncomfortable silence of introspection, she pursued the relatively easy road of communication with Steve.

"So I was just wondering, are you still in college?"

"No," Steve said laughing, "but I guess I really do look young because everyone asks me that … No, I graduated a while ago, from Notre Dame as a matter of fact."

"Notre Dame! That's where Michael and I went!" Claire replied.

"Yeah, I know. I even played football there for one year."

"You did! Jesus!" At that Patrick looked up from his game and she remembered that Karl was a priest. "Excuse me, I mean, Wow! I've probably seen you play. We went to at least one Fighting Irish game every year. Season tickets have been in my family for decades!"

Claire didn't stop to figure out why she was so excited about the Notre Dame connection. She had gone to school there rather obligatorily and she hated football. But she pressed on.

"Why did you only play for one year?" she asked cheerfully.

"I got injured. I messed up my knee and it never was right again."

"Oh, that's *really* too bad!" Claire said sadly. She had almost convinced herself that she felt the team's loss. Then she had the deprecating thought that she was using Steve's openness in an adolescent way to get to Karl. It was like when she and Michael had one of their rare fights in high school and would not speak for half a day. She would stand by her locker and when Michael walked by she would talk to some other boy, who happened to be at hand, in a louder than normal, oh-so-blithe tone, calculated to make Michael see that she was perfectly happy without him — which of course was never the truth. What was she trying to prove to Karl? Claire wished that she could somehow dull the awareness of her own inadequacies and annoying habits. It did her absolutely no good. She saw the same character flaws surface again and again.

Steve continued the conversation unaware of her ruminations. "It really wasn't that bad. It was then that I had time to think and really examine my life and figure out what I wanted to do."

Oh Lord, Claire thought, not *another* priest! "And what was that?" she asked.

"Computers."

"Computers?" She was pleasantly surprised.

"Yeah, I have a knack for it. But I don't really *like* them. It's kind of hard to explain. I was just glad when I met Karl and found out I could put my talents to good use."

She speculated briefly on what someone who was into computers might do for Karl and on what scale. Was Karl a lone ranger? Or ... Claire's imagination went to phrasing one of those subtle and sophisticated ads that continually resound on Public Radio International: *Virtual Vatican Resources — Serving the World with Digital Solutions to All Your Esoteric Religious Needs — on the world-wide web @ www.virtvat.org.*

Claire was about to push her luck with Steve and come right out and ask what exactly he did with Karl when a phone rang. It startled her. Neither she nor Michael had ever had a cell phone and she wasn't used to their ringing in unaccustomed places.

Karl pulled it out of his pocket and answered.

"Hello ...? Yes, this is he ... Oh, yes ... that's okay. What do you have? Are you *sure*?" His voice did not become louder, just more intense. "Where are you calling from? I want you to get in your car and call me again from a pay phone. And bring it with you. Yes, I will. Thank you."

Karl didn't say anything after the call. And Claire didn't know how to ask about it. After all, it might not have had anything to do with her situation. Nevertheless she struggled with her curiosity.

Karl finally turned around and saw that Patrick had fallen asleep while closing his eyes once again to gain fresh perspective on his puzzle. He spoke to Claire with the kindness she had been searching for.

"That was your sister Francine. She went by your house today because she realized that the forwarding order she filled out at the post office yesterday would not go into effect until Monday and she wanted to get yesterday's mail ..."

He hesitated for a moment. "She found a letter, a letter addressed to Michael."

"Like a bill or something? I tried to get everything over into my name but —"

"No. It was a hand-written envelope with strange markings and pictures all over it.

Francine did not open it, but I want her to read it to me. To be safer I thought she should go to a public phone."

"What do you think it could be?" Claire asked, her heart beating rapidly.

"I don't know. But it is addressed: *General Michael O'Connell, King of the World,* and then in parentheses *(The Great One)* and then your address."

Chapter 28

The shadow of a gunman will be replaced by the silhouette of a computer.
John Hume

*Out of Ireland we have come
Great hatred, little room
Maimed us at the start
I carry from my mother's womb
A fanatic heart …*
William Butler Yeats

The Shannon River cuts across Ireland in Mississippi-like fashion stretching out into vast open land flattened as if by a giant's wheel. It divides the country geographically, politically and culturally. Leinster, the land of sophisticated submission and all its progressive rewards, to the east; and to the west, the wild and rebellious Connacht, its punishment now meted out in cultural isolation and derision.

James Day looked out the window of the small plane at the shape of the Island, a shape he saw in his dreams, in the faces of his colleagues, in his own right hand. Flying from Dublin to Shannon was the quick option, and it gave him that perspective of seeing the nation from the air, himself getting larger and larger as the ground fell away below him. He fancied that he could see the network of alignments or ley-lines that marked the presence of secret force-fields, the knowledge of which had existed since ancient times. The injection of solar energy into the Ley system had been thought to bring universal harmony to early Celtic civilizations. The Megalithic Stones had been the intersecting points of the geometrically straight lines and the perfect ley system could rearrange the flow of terrestrial current and enact a splendid pattern of harmony and fertility.

Christ! He thought. *If only they would have known what we know now! What a pity so many centuries of nonsense separated him from his brilliant and powerful pre-Christian forebears! Well, who could say if even Time would be an issue when everything was in place.*

The plane prepared to land and he smoothed his oily hair more tightly to his flabby round head, straightened his dated tie, adjusted his smudged eyeglasses and sucked on a breath mint. His wife had never liked his breath.

An empty black Ford sedan waited for him at the bustling Shannon International Airport, which was full of tourists flowing in and the cream of Irish youth flowing out. Emigration had slowed down somewhat though, especially since the economic policies were radically changed in the 80's, and subsidies from the European Union helped build a modern infrastructure.

Day mused over his initial resistance to high-tech industry and the public endowments to young students choosing scientific or engineering degrees. That was before his Vision — while he was still in his own private Dark Ages, hanging on to musty caricatures of power, rather than the real thing. Now Ireland had become second only to the United States in the export of computer software and his spirits soared when he heard Bertie Ahern boast that Ireland would soon be a 'global lighthouse' for information technology. (If Bertie had guessed half of what was going on!) Some of the brightest young Irish technical minds were now working for him, James Day, along with recruits from the top computer technology centers of the world — Palo Alto Research, Carnegie Mellon, MIT Artificial Intelligence Lab, laying fiber optic cable clandestinely under the Burren, that beautiful strange stone desert just east of the Cliffs of Moher.

Day drove the car alone, as he had planned, up through (for County Clare) the relatively large town of Ennis. He would sometimes stop at *Brogan's* on O'Connell St. for a pint of Guinness. Today he did not. Daniel O' Connell, in the nineteenth century and Eamonn de Valera in the twentieth, two of the greatest modern Irish political figures had both hailed from Ennis. He was glad no one recognized him here.

He had quoted O'Connell many times: "No political change is worth the shedding of human blood." Horseshit, but the pacifists ate it up. Real change was worth *any* sacrifice as long as it wasn't your own. And even the Christians who messed up the world knew that blood was necessary. *Well,* he thought, *O'Connell's had so many streets and bridges and squares named after him that nobody remembers his utter failure at Clontarf. He caved in to the British and made a mockery of the real battle there in the 11th century when King Brian Boru finally ended the Viking subjugation of Ireland.*

He checked himself in his political stream of consciousness. It was all rubbish anyway. None of it mattered anymore. A new O'Connell had arisen. He laughed to himself at his play on words. Something completely and utterly unprecedented was about to occur, if all went according to plan, and he would be there at the center of it.

He always drove up the Ennistymon road out of Ennis and took the right fork toward Corofin. Here was his father's distant family heritage, the Dysert O'Dea and the O'Dea Castle where the Anglo-Normans were stopped from taking over Clare in the 14th century. The castle was now a museum and archeology center but it reminded him of his own nobility. He looked in the rear view mirror for any trace of it in his bland features.

The village of Corofin was a handful of houses sitting amidst an abundance of lovely little lakes which he barely noticed. At Kilnaboy he was always amused by the *sheila na gig* over the door of the ruined 11th century church. It was definitely a pre-Christian carving of a naked woman with grotesquely exaggerated genitalia, probably a fertility symbol of some sort. No one could explain why it was there. He had his own theories — one being that the builder was secretly still enamored with pagan ways and managed to pull the wool over the eyes of the not so holy parish. It was like those American tele-evangelists who were found with young women and porn magazines, or the sanctimonious priests who molested little boys. It was all a front for the real stuff of life.

After Kilnaboy he began to skirt the Burren. His heart would usually beat a little faster at the sight of this strange treeless landscape, its austerity brimming with mythical proportions. The rough limestone country, strewn with innumerable megaliths, was alleviated by the occasional and frivolous growth of magenta bloody cranesbill, saxifrages and bee or fly orchids very rarely seen at those latitudes. Arctic, alpine and Mediterranean flora mysteriously beckoned avid botanists from around the world. Huge steps of limestone and shale terraced toward the sea and ended magnificently and perilously at the Cliffs of Moher standing almost 700 feet above the churning Atlantic.

What most attracted James Day to this region was its lack of appeal and thus habitation of this land to greedy speculators and colonizers over the centuries, so that much of the pre-historic past had been left untouched.

He drove his car on a narrow dirt cart-trail that snaked west from the road to Lisdoonvarna until he pulled his car up to an unassuming and isolated whitewashed cottage with a blue door and a bright fuchsia hedge. The deserted outbuildings were in good repair and several cars were parked around. Most of the laboratory was below the ground, sculpted out of the highly porous rock with its existing potholes, caves and tunnels, so as not to attract attention, and that was a difficult feat in this part of rural Clare where everything new was suspicious. The roving environmentalists were the worst. Some of his entourage wondered why Day hadn't set up shop in a more accessible and populated location, but he knew that this was the place.

Up on the hill from the house stood a relatively large *dolmen*, a phenomenon so common in that region that the indigenous folk hardly noticed it. Two grey roughhewn ancient pillars jutted up out of the coarse grass, their capstone tilted precariously for centuries, huge and flat, like a sky ramp to the heavens. Day smiled at the stones and entered one of the outbuildings, then opened a trap door and descended a spiral staircase. There was no real security system except for a black dog who barked from the yard as the black-suited visitor went down into the earth.

He opened a lower door with his key and entered a dusky passage, walked about thirty feet and entered a room on his right that lay directly below the dolmen. This large chamber was busy with activity. Blood rushed through Day's veins and he could feel it in his organs, pumping and flowing and throbbing. Computer monitors lined the perimeter. Theo Kostanikas was sitting in the center of everything at a terminal, tapping incessantly on the keyboard and cursing. Two smallish younger men were absorbing his complaints and demands. Both of them looked relieved to see Day arrive.

"Hello, Mister Day," they both said almost together. Kostanikas jerked his head around.

"We *can't* let these idiot excuses for human beings manage things without us, Day! They've been tinkering again and almost ruined everything!"

"We didn't touch any part of Doctor Kostanikas' work, Mister Day! We've told him that, but he won't believe it!" one of the young men protested.

Theo lit another cigarette and continued his muted string of epithets and slurs. "… *damn Jews … stupid Micks* …" The words floated up into the haze of smoke. He seemed to be trying to reconnect his concentration to the diagrams on the computer screen.

"We'll have to have the ventilation system checked again. It's much too smoky in here!" Day announced, ignoring the present disturbance.

"Theo, can you break for a minute? I must speak with you. Let's get some coffee, shall we?" His tone was conciliatory and contrived.

The older man, eyes glazed and conflicted, raised his head but did not look at him directly. He said nothing.

Day leaned over and whispered softly in the old man's ear, "I want to talk about *Him*."

Only then did Kostanikas rise with effort from his chair and follow the great statesman and philanthropist out of the chamber.

Chapter 29

*I am resolutely opposed to all innovation ...
Anything I talk about is almost certainly something I am
resolutely against.
And it seems to me the best way to oppose it is to understand it ...
And then you know where to turn the buttons off.*
            Marshall McLuhan

*All science, even the divine science, is a sublime detective story.
Only it is not set to detect why a man is dead,
but the darker secret of why he is alive.*
            G.K. Chesterton

They were almost to Bloomington when Karl's cell phone rang again. Claire noticed the beauty of the rolling green southern Indiana hills just as a tingling numbness began to register in her hands. She'd felt it before. It was funny how you could forget momentarily the tragedies that overshadowed your life. Glimmers of denial, lapses of reality that seemed ever so briefly like hope.

"Hello, Francine. Yes, I am ready to take your dictation." Karl began to write in a notebook, affirming or correcting a phrase or a sentence here and there. When he was done, he handed the phone to Claire. "Your sister wishes to speak to you."

"Franny? Hi to you, too. Yeah, we're okay. On the move again."

"Do you know where you're going this time?" Franny asked.

"Even if I did, I don't think I'm allowed to tell. How are you and everyone else? Mom, Dad ... anyone?"

"I'm fine. We're all fine. I mean Grace is nervous. So what else is new? Right? She has to know where and how everybody is before she's *really* fine. But it's okay. I wanted to tell you something I didn't tell Double-O-Seven. Treat O'Toole called me."

"Trying to set up a date?" Claire teased.

"Yeah, right! No, he was looking for *you*. He said he's found out something very important and that he needs to speak with you. I told him you were out of town and he said he was aware of that and that it was absolutely imperative that you told no one else about him trying to contact you. He gave me a number where you could reach him. He said that you were in *serious danger* ... Listen, Claire, I know you think I have it in for this guy, but I think you need to run this by Father Dowling before you do anything."

"I'll do what's best. You know that!" Claire replied, laughingly because she knew Karl was listening.

Franny gave her the number, which Claire jotted down surreptitiously. Then she said good-bye to her sister and handed the phone back to Karl in the front seat.

"So you will let us know of any other developments, Francine? Yes, you did the right thing about the letter. We'll try to sort it out and let you know. Meanwhile stay away from the house. All right then ... Claire will contact you again soon. Good-bye." He snapped the phone shut and put it back in his pocket. "I think this letter may break things open for us," Karl said, turning to Steve. Then he swung all the way around and asked Claire, "Is Patrick still asleep?" He answered his own question before she could. "Yes, it seems he is. Do you want to hear what's in the letter, Claire?"

She noticed for the first time that his eyes were brown. Didn't all those Teutonic types have blonde hair and *blue* eyes?

"Yes, of course I do." Claire pronounced.

Karl read from his notebook:

Your Majesty:

    I am sorry that we needed the algorithm of your soul. It was merely an equation, you realize. But 'Theo, let me out of the box!' you cry. But you must understand that you will be more free than ever before.

"It *is* Kostanikas!" exclaimed Steve. "It's a letter from Kostanikas! Where is it from?"

Claire interrupted. "Do you mean Theopholus Kostanikas, the crazy mathematics genius? I thought he died years ago. My God, what does he mean by *'Let me out of the box'*? Is he talking about Michael?" The feeling had come back to Claire's hands, along with a fear that pricked her whole body.

Karl answered her soothingly and patiently. "We've suspected that Kostanikas was collaborating somehow with Day. Almost

177

everyone thinks that he died years ago. His career ended in the early seventies because of his schizophrenia. He was hospitalized on and off and forgotten by most of the advancing mathematical world and by the emerging digital communities. He did pop up a few years ago, claiming to be free from his mental illness with some theories about Artificial Intelligence that no one took seriously …"

"*Except,*" Steve interjected, "for some people at MIT and at the University of Chicago where he was offered posts as recently as last year. But someone else got to him. And now we know who."

"What in the world could James Day's alleged obsession with Druids and mysticism have to do with Theo Kostanikas?"

"That question, my dear girl," Karl said looking at Steve, "would take us all day to reveal to you. Most of it has been speculation until now. And in answer to your question about Michael, I don't know what he means about the box either. You have to remember that this man is mentally ill. But schizophrenia is a very complex disease. One of the symptoms is that one sees cosmic significance in everything that happens — the irony being that there *is* cosmic significance in everything that happens."

"So if you believe that, why aren't *you* crazy?" Claire asked sincerely.

"I'm sure that some people think that I am. The difference is that Kostanikas and other schizophrenics lose control of their own wills. The messages they receive come unbidden and obsessively. Sometimes they are true and sometimes they are false, but the ability to discern between the two is destroyed somehow. It is an inescapable prison, an unrelieved torture, and many schizophrenics take their own lives to end it."

Claire could have asked a thousand more questions as to how Karl could be so certain about his religious cosmic interpretations being true, but she wanted him to continue reading the letter.

"Stephan, to answer you — the return address was *Spiderman, Office of Internal Affairs, The World Wide Web.*" Steve couldn't help laughing. Karl continued. "But it was postmarked, however, in Dublin."

"So Christy was right then. It was Kostanikas he saw. He barely recognized him. It doesn't sound healthy to me. Probably in terrible condition." Steve added excitedly, "Go on with the letter, though, please."

> *X is at the root of the whole thing. (why =x) So how did a Greek like me get stuck finally with the Golem? After all the damn Jews have had their chances — Von Neumann, Weiner, Sussman, Minsky ...*

"The Golem! He actually mentions the *Golem?*" Steve could barely contain himself.

"He's definitely an anti-Semite," Claire remarked, not knowing what Steve was talking about. She also wondered if Karl had any anti-Semitism flowing in his superior German blood. The Catholic Church didn't have a very good record on that matter either.

"No, he's doesn't hate Jews, or at least he didn't. He was very close with Von Neumann and Wiener ..."

"The two fathers of computer architecture and the whole field of cybernetics," Steve inserted for Claire's benefit.

"... But he called them damn Jews even back then. I think it's only a persecutory manifestation of his illness." Karl absolved him and went on.

"Do you mind my interrupting again to ask what a *golem* is?" Claire asked.

"You can ask any question you like at any time and it is never, never an interruption," Karl said in a clipped tone, almost as a reprimand.

This fellow is a real paradox, she thought. "Thank you," she said evenly.

"A Golem is a mythological figure from Jewish mysticism. Rabbi Loew, the tradition goes, made a humanlike figure out of clay and God then breathed life into it," Karl replied.

"Boy, I guess I missed a lot going to Catholic schools my whole life."

Steve went on: "It's also kind of a pet concept among the AI community today. Of course, most of them don't believe in God, but they do believe that one day computers will have true consciousness and become spiritual machines."

"AI? I'm sorry I'm not really up on this stuff. I basically use my computer for word processing, some e-mail. Michael hated even that."

"Artificial Intelligence. It's okay. The Digerati — the computer elite — have their own language, unknown to the average PONA, People Of No Account or those who have no account in cyberspace — kind of a double meaning there. Then there's bandwidths and MOOs, MUDs, LISP, MIPS …"

"Okay, Stephan, let's not get too far afield; all of that can come later." Karl returned to the letter.

> *I never meant to hurt you. Think! Breathe! Breathe! For Christ's sake, I told you. It will be alright. We'll get you out of the box! A Greek and an Irishman, whoever would have thought we'd be the first ones to eat that Pi in the sky.*

"It is spelled P-I, of course." Claire said.

"Of course," said Steve.

Claire was not amused at the pun and went back to the box. "You don't think he's talking about Michael's coffin and they're thinking of digging him up or anything horrible like that, do you?"

"I don't think so. "Needing the algorithm of his soul." I don't know, the whole thing could just be his way of talking about death in his own symbols. Maybe it's how he is expunging his guilt for the part he may have played in Michael's death. What do you think, Stephan?" Karl deferred to the younger man's expertise.

"The AI people have been talking for years about discovering the algorithm of the human brain — an algorithm being a sequence of rules and instructions that describes a procedure to solve a problem. They hope to 'upload' the human nervous system to the finest nuance. But even Joseph Weizenbaum, the creator of the first AI program, ELIZA, back in the early seventies, eventually proclaimed that a human being is uncodable … An algorithm of the soul? Now that's *really* uncodable. Is there any more in the letter?"

"Just this:

> *Give me the Word, please, Bin Ain, he says the Masters need the Word.*

"Then, there is no signature, but the Greek letter T and a drawing of what Francine thought looked like a fat witch on a broomstick and a much smaller hooded figure that sounds like it could be a Druid or a Cistercian," Karl said, smiling slightly as he thought of Franny's descriptions.

"I'm going with the Druid," said Steve.

"Do you mind if I look at that for a minute?" Claire asked.

"Certainly, you may. But I didn't draw any pictures," Karl replied as he handed her his notebook over the car seat.

"It's not the pictures; it's that last line." Claire reached into her bag and pulled out the crumpled message she had found in Michael's pocket. "Yes, here are the same words. Here, look. I don't think I ever showed you this. Things have been happening so fast. This is a note I found in Michael's sport coat. The lines and things at the bottom, that's Ogham."

"Yes, I know of Ogham. " Karl said.

"Well, it's the same date that Michael died. I know that much. The other part is in some other secret language, that nobody understands ..." Claire kept Treat O'Toole and her visit to him out of the discussion. She was still troubled and confused about why he wanted to talk to her.

"It must be *Misog*."

"Yeah, the one that only Michael and Professor McCullum knew. Well, anyway I think that whoever sent this note was someone Michael met the day he died. But see? These two words match. *Bin Ain*! Do you think he met Kostanikas?" she wondered. "Or maybe it was McCullum?"

"Claire, this note could be very significant ... but I don't know now."

"When you find Dr. McCullum you can ..."

"I hadn't had a chance to tell you. Doctor McCullum *has* been found, I'm afraid. Early this morning by the Irish police." Karl turned away to face the front of the car again.

"His body turned up in a tenement in Dublin. The police are saying it was a drug overdose."

"You don't believe them?" Claire asked, not knowing at all what she thought.

"I can tell you this now. Dr. McCullum was working with us. He was an honorable man and he did *not* use drugs." The priest paused, full of emotion. "He was our person on the inside of Day's Neo-pagan network. Day is responsible for this. I'm sure of it," Karl said with anger. He looked out the window.

Steve pulled the car up to an old diner on the eastern edge of Bloomington. They went in and ate. Steve and Patrick were the only ones with any appetite, it seemed. They left the place through the back door and got into a different and older car, leaving the silver Jaguar out front. Then more hours of two-lane highway. No one talked much as they drove across the Ohio at Madison, into Kentucky and on through the bluegrass in the rosy orange light of the setting summer sun.

Chapter 30

Society depends for its existence on the inviolable personal solitude of its members. Society, to merit its name, must be made up not of numbers, mechanical units, but of persons.
Thomas Merton

Every single child has, you and I have, been created for greater things: to love and to be loved.
Mother Theresa

The last distinguishing landmark of their progress she remembered before falling asleep was a billboard near Lexington. Claire awoke as they slowed to enter a long winding driveway. The headlights shone on thick forest skirting the car on either side. Claire noticed a sign as they entered the precincts of what appeared to be *The Mount Victory Convent of the Sisters of Mercy*. She presumed they were still in Kentucky but she couldn't be sure. *Well, going from a Gypsy camp to a convent was jumping across quite a spectrum of cultural hideouts no matter what direction you went,* she thought.

When the foursome came to a stop in front of the main building Claire stepped out of the car, stretched her cramped muscles and yawned. She took a breath of cool, clean, deliciously fresh air. She wondered if they were near the mountains.

There were several buildings set out on the grounds, each with a dim light at its entrance.

Everything was quiet. Karl went up to the doorway and pulled a string that sounded a bright tinkling bell. Claire and Steve leaned against the car that was still warm from its journey and both looked up into the night. The moon was a slip, but the stars were dusted across the sky like glitter with hardly any space between them. After a few minutes the door was opened by an elderly nun in full habit. She greeted Karl in warm tones and soon he turned to motion the others to come along. Then he remembered what had become his official duty — carrying the sleeping Patrick. Steve opened the rear door to get the boy, but Karl insisted imperiously on being the one to lift him gently out of the car. Claire and Steve took their few bags and followed Karl through the open gate and another inner door. The dark hallway smelled to Claire like a damp basement as they passed through it and she hoped that the whole building did not have a crypt-like atmosphere. They came to yet another door.

Once inside, the building opened up into an airy dome-ceilinged circular room off which other halls tangented like spokes. The whole place was dimly but exquisitely lit with small muted recessed fixtures at various symmetrical points that dispelled any gloom but left the quiet mystery intact. The old woman stood with her hands folded. Her face was cheerful, although she looked as if her sleep had been recently disturbed.

Karl made the introductions in a hushed voice. "Mother Mechtilde, you of course remember Stephan." The old nun glowed as Steve approached her and bowed gallantly and kissed her hand.

"And these are the special guests I mentioned to you, Patrick and Claire O'Connell."

Patrick was fuzzily awake and smiling.

Claire started to put one bag down to shake the nun's hand, but the old woman walked to her quickly and grasped both her arms firmly and said softly, "Our Lord's peace to all of you! And thankfulness for your safe journey to us. I will now take this little family to their room." She still held one of Claire's arms lightly at the elbow.

Patrick scrambled down from Karl's strong grip and took Claire's other arm.

"Let's see, Patrick will take one of those bags," Mother Mechtilde said, pointing to Steve, "and I will take the other. And Father, you know where to go. Please make yourselves at home."

It was the first time Claire had heard Karl addressed as *Father*. It still seemed strange, especially considering the exotic history she had mentally endowed to him for weeks after their initial meeting.

The nun led them down one of the hallways lit with the same small lights as the main room and opened a door about halfway along the corridor.

"Here you go then," she said, still in almost a whisper. "I think everything you need is there."

Claire and Patrick walked into the room and the first thing Claire noticed was what she hoped was a bathroom. "Oh, how absolutely wonderful!" she whispered back excitedly. "Is it a bathroom? Does it have a tub or shower? And may I take a quick one, if possible?" It had only been three days since her last but it seemed like weeks.

"Yes. Both. And certainly you may. Not all of the rooms have private baths, you know, but I thought you'd appreciate the luxury, my dear." She took some peppermint candies out of the depths of her pocket and handed them to Patrick. "One for you and one for Mum. Okay, little one?" Patrick nodded a happy assent.

"I know you'll stay quiet so as not to disturb the others. We get up early for morning prayers. But you'll be on your own schedule, Father says, for awhile. Good night."

"Thank you, Mother. We do appreciate your hospitality so very much and the bath, thank you for the bath!"

The old woman closed the door noiselessly behind her and was gone. Claire went immediately to the bathroom and started the shower. "Alright, little boy! Off with the clothes and into the shower and then to bed." She pretended to chase him.

Patrick was out of his shorts and t-shirt in a flash. "There's shampoo stuff and soap and everything!" he said excitedly from behind the curtain. "It's just like a hotel! It feels good, Mommy!"

Claire looked around the room. It was starkly white, with two polished-iron beds covered in crisp clean white sheets and cool white cotton blankets. The smooth brown wooden floors and window casements stood out warmly in contrast. The room seemed bare, but it struck her as more of a relief than a privation. Simple panels of white cloth hung at the window. Claire was just going to dig in their bags for their dingy nightclothes when she saw something folded on the wooden chair in the corner. There was a pair of pale green boy's pajamas just Patrick's size and a white cotton nightgown much like her own, but with delicate hand embroidered shamrocks around the neck and shoulders. Claire picked them up and held them to her face, smelling the freshness of the soap and the scent of the kindness that had left them there.

"Okay, little boy! Time's up!"

She helped him towel off and get into his clean pajamas and white bed. He looked like an illustration in *A Child's Garden of Verses*, his green shirt, copper curls, and blue eyes peering out, waiting to be hugged and kissed and properly sent off to the Land Of Nod.

"Jesus is here, too, Mommy," Patrick said with sleepy contentment.

By now Claire had enough awareness to look up at the white wall above their beds. A wooden cross with a carved *Corpus* was there. She had missed it in her first scan. The five tiny red wounds were now inescapably visible patches of color in the white room.

Yes, Patrick, but he's dead, he's dead. Can't you see? She would never say it.

Patrick reached into his backpack and pulled out his brown floppy dog and a folded piece of paper. "I want to look at my prayer before I go to sleep."

Claire recognized the prayer of St. Patrick that Michael had given to his son. She really did not feel like reading the whole long thing to him. She was desperate for a shower and to get into bed herself, but she felt she could not turn down one of his rare requests for special attention, not now. She sat down and reached for the poem.

"No, Mommy. I want to read it myself. You can take your shower. I love you."

"I love you, too." She said as she kissed and hugged him. "I'll be out in a jiffy." She knew he couldn't really read it — maybe a few words here and there, but he seemed satisfied.

When she came out of the bathroom in the white nightgown with green shamrocks feeling lusciously clean, Patrick was sound asleep with his prayer in his hand. She folded it and put it back in his pack, got in her bed, and turned off the lamp. Then she remembered something. She turned the light on again and picked up her bag. She found the paper she was looking for. Of course there was no phone in the room. She put on a shirt over the nightgown and slipped quietly out into the hallway, closing the door behind her.

Claire padded back to the main room. There was no sound anywhere in the building. And no telephone. She saw what looked like an office between two of the hallways. It was dark but the door was not locked when she turned the handle. Enough light shone through the glass window to reveal a phone on the desk just inside the door.

The phone rang for quite some time. She almost gave up. "Hello, Treat? This is Claire, Claire O'Connell, "she said, trying to keep her voice down. "I'm sorry to call you so late but ..."

"Claire! Thank God you've called! I've been *extremely* concerned about you. There are some *very strange things* going on. I fear you were right about that note being a clue to something. Oh! *Where are you,* for God's sake?"

Claire already felt like some kind of delinquent, sneaking around the dark convent making secret phone calls. Now she felt bad about not coming out straightforwardly with Treat, but she stuck to her designated cover story.

"We're on a little vacation. Just needed to get away from things for awhile. Kind of moving from place to place getting a look at the country. Patrick loves it ... So what's the matter? Why are you so concerned?" She tried to sound nonchalant.

"Well, it seems there is some sort of crazy religious cult that Michael got hooked up with and now they are after *you* for some reason."

"How did you find this out?" Claire asked.

"I was talking to Doctor McCullum and he told me that his suspicions about the whole thing had been confirmed. He was very interested in that note you have and also if you had an updated copy of Michael's lexicon. Did you ever find the lexicon?"

"Doctor McCullum? But ..." Claire was confused. Karl had said McCullum had been *missing for a month* before his death.

"What were you saying, Claire? Claire? Are you there?"

"When did you speak to Doctor McCullum?"

"Earlier this afternoon, before I called your sister. Why? Have you already spoken with him?"

Claire's mind was spinning. Hadn't Karl told her that McCullum had been found dead early that morning? "Uh ... no. I just wondered. Why did he say these people were after me?"

"Can you speak up? I'm having trouble hearing you."

"I can't, really ... I ... don't want to wake Patrick. I asked if he told you why they were after me."

"I don't know exactly; I couldn't follow him. You know how his digressions can be heavy sledding at times. The main thrust of it was that you were in danger and that you shouldn't trust *anyone*. Evidently this cult or whatever it is has people placed in well-respected places. Listen, Claire, I'd be glad to help you out ... kind of watch out for you. Maybe we could hook up somehow and talk to McCullum together. You haven't told anyone else about the note, have you?"

Claire hesitated. Why shouldn't Treat know about Karl? They were both trying to help her. Then Franny's reservations popped into her mind. "No, I haven't. I was trying to forget about it all really. I appreciate your concern but I think we're quite safe. Nobody even knows where we are." *Including me*, she could have added.

"But Claire, at least promise that you'll stay in touch — in case I find out anything that might help you. I'll feel better knowing you're both all right. I'd feel so much more at ease if I knew you weren't alone. I could ..."

"No, Treat. It's okay. Thank you, but I have to go now. I'll let you know how we're doing from time to time. Don't worry." *And don't call Franny*, she thought.

She hung up the phone, closed the office door and crept back to her room. Lying in the dark she was bewildered. Was Karl telling the truth about Doctor McCullum? He had kept things from her before, but as far as she knew he had never actually *lied* to her. But could she really trust him? He was in a position of respect and influence. What if he was somehow connected to this cult himself? No, that would mean that Mara and Steve and Mother Mechtilde were all in on it. But maybe he had them all fooled, too. Was that any more preposterous than *James Day* being the ringleader of a bizarre neo-pagan conspiracy? If Karl wasn't lying, then Treat O'Toole was. She had to put all her eggs in one basket or the other. She was finally able to sleep, knowing that at least she had not given him any new information.

A knock at the door awoke them both. "Yes, who is it?" Claire asked sitting up in bed.

Another nun poked her head in the door. She was younger than Mother Mechtilde, with a very round face and unbecoming glasses. "Good morning! I'm Sister Catherine and I have your breakfast." She had a high-pitched and rather immature voice and a girlish giggle that seemed to erupt uncontrollably. "Mother said you might like this in your room." *Giggle.* "We've all eaten quite awhile ago." *Giggle, giggle.* "There's tea and toast and a bit of bacon." *Giggle.*

Patrick was giggling, too.

"Why, yes. Thank you." Claire answered.

"I'll put it over here on the table. And you can eat it when you like." *Giggle.* (Giggle from Patrick.)

"I'm sorry but what time is it? I'm afraid I've misplaced my watch." The morning sun made the room even whiter.

"It's close to 7:30, I think." *Giggle.*

Nuns were definitely on a different schedule than Gypsies.

"Well, I'm Claire and this is Patrick." Patrick giggled and smiled up at her.

"Oh, yes, I know." *Giggle.* "And if Patrick would like to come out back to the play yard after he's finished, that's where the children will be." *Giggle, giggle.*

"Can I, Mommy?" Patrick giggled.

"There are children here?" Claire questioned. "Is there a school?"

"Oh, yes, the children are always here." *Giggle.* "We don't have school in the summer, though." *Giggle.*

"Well, Patrick will probably be out soon. Thanks again for the breakfast." The giggling was beginning to annoy Claire so she refrained from asking any more questions.

The nun left and Claire asked Patrick, laughing, "You little, goof ball! Why were you giggling back at Sister Catherine?"

"I couldn't help it. She made me do it. It was fun. Let's eat so I can go play. I guess I get to have friends wherever I go! Right, Mom?"

The nun had said *out back,* so after their meal Claire and Patrick made their way to the central room and looked for the most obvious hallway toward the back yard. Claire caught a snatch of the view out the front windows of the building. They *were* in the mountains, or at least in the foothills. Across the front lawn and over the tops of the trees were green covered hills and slate capped peaks. It was a beautiful setting. Maybe the religious life was not so bad after all. You could jet around the world, or be chauffeured in a Jaguar, or be tucked away in a lovely isolated spot away from the harsh realities and difficulties that came from entanglements in the outside world.

No one was around to ask, so the two refugees made their way down the hall directly opposite the front entrance. It looked identical to the corridor where their room was, but at the end was a doorway to the playground. Patrick spotted the slide right away and ran off to try it out. Claire walked after him.

There were quite a lot of children, she noticed. Black and white habits were scattered profusely among them. Claire saw a few children in wheelchairs and her old dread came quickly upon her. She stuffed it down, realizing its irrationality and the stifling effect it had on her capacity for compassion. As she drew closer to the children she had herself in check, at least for Patrick's sake.

Patrick was already at the top of the slide and waving madly before his descent. She waved back and watched him slide down safely to the bottom. Another boy followed him and Claire noticed with shock that he had no arms! He yelled something to Patrick and they both began to climb the slide again, the armless boy leaning closely against the ladder as he ascended, to keep his balance. A nun stood at the bottom with a close eye on his progress.

Claire looked around. A little girl on the swings with curly red hair like her own was being pushed gently by one of the Sisters. She had on a bright yellow dress and she had Down Syndrome. A small boy in a red t-shirt and jeans moved slowly and with great effort toward the teeter-totter, pulling himself along on silver crutches with metal braces on both legs. Claire realized slowly and horribly that *every* child in the play yard seemed to be maimed in some way. Patrick was the only healthy one among them, but he didn't seem to notice. She felt sick to her stomach and turned around to run indoors. She ran right in to the large body of Father Burgmann.

"Oh, *excuse me*," she said, feeling faint. "I didn't see …"

"Claire, are you all right? You look *pale*. Are you ill?"

All of the color had drained from her face. She longed to lie down in her white room and blend into the walls. She did not answer him.

"Here, let me help you inside!" he said urgently but with extraordinary kindness. He literally whisked her off her feet and into the convent. When they were in the door he picked her up completely and carried her in his arms to her room. He laid her on a bed and went into the wonderful bathroom to get a cool cloth for her head. Her color began to return. Her legs felt numb but the nausea had subsided. He stood there looking at her. She wanted to thank him but her mouth would not respond to her thoughts.

"I will go and get one of the Sisters." He turned to leave the room.

"P-Please. Don't leave … Please stay for a little while. I'll be alright soon."

He sat down on the simple wooden chair, his black figure like a protective shadow in the bright white light.

Chapter 31

In the size of the lie there is always contained a certain factor of credibility, since the great masses of people will more easily fall victim to a great lie than to a small one.
Adolph Hitler

Cellular automata mirror many fundamental processes of nature. The most consistent common feature is that which defines the phenomenon of chaos.
John Conway

"How the hell did Kostanikas get out here?" Day shouted into the receiver. "I give you the watch for half a day and he gives you the slip!"

"*Don't talk to me like one of your bloody underlings.* He rode out with one of the technicians from the university who was going anyway. Nothing's been lost."

"How do you know what he talked about on the way?"

"They all think he's a loony case anyway. He is, you know. I couldn't bear him for long."

"You won't have to. None of us will."

"Where is he now?"

"He's in the next room smoking cigarettes and trying to work out that problem he's always going on about — proving the Reimann Hypothesis. It's a great diversion, especially if he's had Thorazine." Day smirked, thinking of the old man being groggily occupied for hours, drooling and writing his scrawls in slow motion.

"She called me."

"In Dublin?"

"I had it forwarded from Chicago."

"*Where is she?*" Day asked excitedly. "Did she tell you anything?"

"She told me nothing, really. But she may. She promised to call me again. I think she trusts me. I'm going to fly back there probably tomorrow. So I'll be closer by, now that McCullum's out of the way. What a waste of time he was. The old buzzard would have told me anything, he was such a coward — whimpering and crying — worse than most children. It's just too bad he didn't know that much."

"Did she mention Burgmann? Has *he* gotten to her yet? Was he the one who helped her the other night?"

"She says she's alone with her son, but of course I don't believe her. Whoever lent her the muscle and the getaway is probably still with her."

"Could you trace where she was calling from?" Day asked hopefully.

"I tried to relay it to the tracker in the States, but she caught me off guard. I didn't think she'd call so soon."

"I can't believe you blew it again. You had all that time to cozy up to her and you let it pass. I thought your charm was irresistible."

"It is to most people. You'd be surprised. It worked on O'Connell, didn't it? He never caught on until the last minute. And I don't like your tone!"

"But you didn't get the *one final thing* we needed from him, either," Day said disgustedly.

"He claimed he didn't know it. He swore the lexicon was incomplete, right up to the end. You have no right to *reprimand* me, for Christ's sake. You and your mad scientist, *you're* the ones who killed him and delayed everything and made this whole charade with his wife necessary …"

"You can't squeeze much more from a man than his soul."

"Now you sound like Kostanikas. You don't actually *believe* all that shit, do you? I guess acting out all your Celtic fantasies has taken its toll."

"Oh come on now, man. You've been there with me on many occasions — even leading them on! You cut your own dashing figure in a hooded robe."

"I play along with it, James, because I enjoy it. And I can see its end and I like it."

"Well, what do *you* believe then? How do *you* explain what's going on?" Day asked.

"Belief is a very pragmatic thing. It's whatever works at the time. It certainly isn't transcendent. I think what's going on is a randomly, yet *almost* perfect intersection of physical and natural forces. I say almost."

"We still have to find out what she knows and if she has what we need. They must have discussed his work."

"Don't you think I know that? It will happen. By the way, you heard they went on with the Orange March in a different neighborhood, without incident?"

"Yes ... What a pity!"

"But the good news is that the Good Friday agreement is crumbling and only Ahern and Blair are still puffing it. The real players have given it up. Kelly is stirring up the Nationalists on the prejudice of the constabulary again. The time will be right. It's a wondrous thing, it 'tis." Treat O'Toole smiled at himself admiringly in the mirror of his Dublin flat, stroking his neat dark beard with his manicured fingers.

After the phone call, James Day slipped back into the room where Kostanikas sat scribbling in his notebook. The walls of the dreary room were dull gray like the rock outside them. But unlike the rock, these walls were dead, lifeless slabs of containment, unrelieved by even a spark of imagination. It could have been an impersonal break room in any office building anywhere. A coffee pot sat on the hot plate with an inch of burned and evaporating black liquid that gave off a sickening acrid smell. The Greek took no notice. There was a small refrigerator and sink. Dirty cups and ashtrays cluttered the table tops and counter.

Theo's long silver hair was greasier than usual and hung characteristically over his sunken face. He wore a soiled plaid sport coat purchased in the seventies. He had never had it cleaned personally, although one of the hospitals might have seen to it once or twice. He'd had no medication but he didn't seem agitated at the moment. Day noticed he had a small ragged looking book on the table, surrounded by crumpled wrappers of sweets and corn chips.

"Theo, why did you come out here to the laboratory without telling me or Professor O'Toole?"

"They told me to," he answered, not looking up.

"They? You mean Him? Do you mean Michael?"

"The Voices. The Masters. The ArchAngels. Eighth or Ninth Circle, Fourth Ring, I think ..." He counted on his fingers. "*Listen*, do you hear it?"

Theo got up from his chair and tiptoed over to put his ear against the wall. *"Do you hear it?"* he whispered loudly.

"What is it, Theo? What do you hear?" Sometimes Day himself was not sure when he was humoring the old man and when he believed him.

"It is the sound of the rivulet which descends here along the hollow of the rock, saying that it has gnawed from one hemisphere to another."

James Day walked over to the wall and rested his ear against it. He heard nothing. He felt foolish. "Of course there are many underground caverns and streams here in the Burren, but I don't think you can hear them through these walls." He went back to the table and reached for Theo's notebook, trying to change the subject. "Still the Reimann Hypothesis?" he asked, looking at the notes and jots and formulae written there.

Theo left the wall and grabbed the notebook from him. "Stop! *Stop!*" The old man yelled. "Don't look at my notes ever again without permission!"

"Sit down, Theo. It's alright. I won't do it again. I promise you. Sit down and tell me whatever you want to tell me." Day spoke coaxingly, like a counselor. *Damn!* he thought. *The kid gloves you have to wear to handle this man!* It was worth it, though. He was getting what he wanted.

Kostanikas sat down again at the table. He spoke but still did not raise his eyes.

"I know what you're thinking, Day! I know what you're thinking. I can see you thinking. You don't realize that once He's out of the box, He's free. They'll all be free. It will be the end for you as well as me." He laughed maniacally. "You don't understand most of the time, but I'll tell you anyway. BOOOM!" James Day jumped. "Just getting your attention. Now listen," he said as he sat back down at the table. "This book is the Bible." He picked up the worn black book. "Have you ever heard of *Gematria?*"

"It's numerology related to the Bible. Of course I've heard of it."

"It is an interpretation of the Bible by studying the number equivalents to the Hebrew and Greek words. The Jews and the

Greeks — the Irish aren't here. *You* are, though — *DAY* of the Lord, *DAY* of Judgment, First *DAY*, Second *DAY*, Third *DAY*, all the way up to the Eighth *DAY*."

Day couldn't tell if Theo was serious or sarcastic. He just skipped over it.

"You remember, Theo, the connection between the Greeks and the Irish? Pythagoras and the Druids? We've been through this all before a billion bloody times. It doesn't matter if it's in the *Bible* or not!" Day was losing patience.

"Did you know that Pythagoras had one of his disciples killed because he discovered irrational numbers? It didn't fit in with his theories and plans. It didn't do any good. The truth eventually got out because numbers have a life of their own. Just remember that when you go to have me killed. It's bigger than you and me."

"I'm not going to have you killed! Don't talk such nonsense. Now what were you saying about *Gematria?*"

"I have surpassed Gematria! I have a new interpretation of the Bible using *Quantum Physics!*" He looked back down to his notes. "I told you that you won't understand, but listen anyway. The laws of quantum mechanics are the basis of the cosmic code. Quarks and leptons and gluons. That's it. Their relationship to each other holds the secrets to the whole universe. It is the *DES*."

"What is the DES?" Day interrupted.

"The *Data Encryption Standard* used to encipher computer messages. It's strange, isn't it, that IBM called theirs the Lucifer cipher? Maybe they *knew* about the angels and the electrons."

"So the secrets of the whole universe …" prompted Day.

"These same mechanics can be applied then to *anything*. The Bible, for instance. I wish Von Neumann were here. Are you *listening?*" He looked up at Day and raised his voice.

"Yes, Theo, I'm listening. Go on."

"So rather than the elementary method of assigning numerical correspondence to each letter, it breaks down something like this." He showed Day one page of his notebook and read aloud:

"Quanta = letters
Atoms = words

Molecules = sentences
Objects = books
Universe = whole Bible …"

"You see? They're both information systems. Just like the human body and the computer. Just like …" He looked around fearfully. "Does anyone else know about *Him?*"

James Day was still trying to understand the significance of the old man's scribbling, if there was any. Theo was right. He didn't understand everything that was going on, but he knew that he was destined to get it all together and to be at the center of it and to reap the rewards of it, no matter what the cost.

"Does anyone else know about Him?" Theo shouted and got up from the table and began pacing up and down.

He'd better be medicated again, Day thought. *His temper and agitation are surfacing fast.* "No, Theo. It's just you and me."

Of course there were a few others who had to know about it. He had recruited an elite *cognoscenti* who were implementing Theo's sporadically brilliant ideas in ways the broken old man could not. Day, however, never let anyone know everything about anything.

Chapter 32

Mary is a pale derivative symbol disguising the conquered Goddess.
Mary Daly

*To heights art soaring
Of realms,
Hear our imploring,
Matchless, Maternal,
Of grace supernal*
Johann von Goethe

Grace Daly dropped her rosary on the floor when the phone rang. She hadn't been paying attention anyway as her fingers slipped habitually over the smooth green glass beads she had been given by her mother, Dolores O'Brien. Family tradition had it that the rosary had been in the O'Brien's possession for centuries and had been blessed by the Bishop of Connacht at the top of Croagh Patrick after a distant O'Brien had climbed the black conical hill on his bleeding knees. It was widely believed throughout Ireland that St. Patrick climbed that summit in the year 441 AD and remained for the entire forty days of Lent, from there driving all the reptiles from Irish soil and suffering myriads of other trials. He had been attacked by huge clouds of demons who had taken on the shape of vicious blackbirds … and had come face to face with Corra, the Mother of Satan.

Grace did not know how much of those old legends to believe, although she knew that even if they weren't *exactly* true, that legends only grew up around people who were great enough to inspire them. And she did believe in the power of the rosary. She knew that she must, because she prayed it every day, even though her mind usually wandered as it had this morning. Monday was the day of the Joyful Mysteries. These were her favorites, if one could have such a thing in *spiritual* matters, because they all had to do with Our Lady. Not that she was slighting her Son in the least; it was just that she could relate to the Blessed Mother so much better. She remembered when she had discovered she was pregnant. Grace and John had been dating for almost a year. She hated her secretarial job.

She was twenty-one and certainly old enough to be a wife and mother. All the women she worked with in the Boston insurance office were sober and clerkish and would probably serve the men of the company like slaves until they died as old maids with nothing to show for it but carbon-stained fingers, being drunkenly groped in the hat check room of the banquet hall after a few golf outings, and then a pin for excellent service at the end.

Grace would have none of that. She was born to be a mother. When her own siblings grew old enough not to need her, she babysat for neighbors and friends. After high school she would have hired out as a nanny had not her father put his foot down and said that Irish women had raised enough wealthy Protestant children and that it was time she got a real job. Thank God she had met John Daly. John was a huge handsome man with soft red hair who shyly introduced himself to her one night after work as she sat in McKenna's Pub near Quincy Market. She was always amused now to see advertisements for Catholic dating services. In 1959 you could be sure that every available person at McKenna's was Irish and Catholic. No electronic computer matchmaking was necessary, only a rovin' eye and a pint or so of Guinness and nature (or Providence) would take its course.

John wanted to wait 'til he had some reliable business venture up and running before they got married. But he didn't seem to be able to wait for other things. Nothing was forced on Grace, it was just that she had to go to confession and disappoint Father Dugin several times. She had a hope that God would understand because he could see how sorry she was, but Father Dugin was not quite so easygoing.

Bridget was conceived on a beautiful autumn night in the back of John's old '53 Ford. Grace's family was shocked and shamed but she held the green O'Brien rosary in her hands at night in her bed and found herself in the First Joyful Mystery, The Annunciation. Doctor Ryan was the angel Gabriel as he told her the 'tragic' yet joyful news. "Will young John make an honest woman of ya?" he had asked. "Oh, he surely will!" she'd answered. Father Dugin, of course, was not surprised and took them on the Pre-Cana Express so that they were married in a matter of weeks.

Then there was the Visitation and in this mystery she was not one of the main characters but a beholder of the two cousins standing, as in the famous painting, near the edges of the frame. "*Blessed art thou among women and blessed is the fruit of thy womb!*" Elizabeth called out across the canvas, echoing through the swath of supernatural light that highlighted their simple clothing like pearls, as her son John leapt in her belly at the presence of his embryonic Lord. Grace was *there*, a neighbor perhaps, leaning in the window, part of the natural solidarity of women and mothers and friends.

The Nativity was bittersweet, as was much of her faith. After each of her children's births, while she lay safely in the clean happy maternity ward, the sisters fluttering about with babies and bottles and instructions at all hours, she wondered at God's planning. Why couldn't he work it out for his own Son to be born in a warm, clean, dry room? All the carols made it sound very nice with cattle lowing and soft hay, but she'd been in enough barns to know she'd never want to have a baby in one. And as she fingered the shiny little beads, she remembered, every time, her own son, John Patrick Daly, who had never breathed the clean air of the maternity room but flew from his grayish stillborn body up to heaven. "*Holy Mary, Mother of God, pray for us now and at the hour of our death. Amen.*" But if God did not spare his own Son then … or He may have just been distracted for a short while — with the whole world on His mind and all. She never was angry with Him. *He had taken her only son to live with His own Mother*, she knew that. The Sister had baptized him immediately but he had already, like the martyrs, been baptized in blood — her blood. And then there were all the babies torn and sucked from their mother's wombs, mangled fruit, and she brought these unborn all with her to the stable and their poor mothers, too, for the look from the Child and his Mother would heal them. She would usually cry there if her mind had not wandered.

The Fourth Mystery was The Presentation. She waited in line behind the little Holy Family as old Simeon and old Anna exclaimed over the 'salvation' of the world, bundled in that little blue blanket. When it was her turn, she began with Bridget and went all the way through all six of her children, one bead for each. As she prayed she lifted each one up to God as little babies and right before her eyes they would change frighteningly and magnificently into grown women, going through all their stages at super-speed. All except little John, who always remained a still tiny thing. It was strange as she held her daughters aloft that they managed to encompass their husbands and children in their arms. Each small bead was amazingly strong. Francine, of course, took up a whole space all by herself, with her tattoos, and nose rings, and distasteful purple-haired boyfriends. That left four beads — two for herself as a mother and two for dear John as a father. For she knew with the Blessed Mother that some children would be a "sign that is rejected" and that a "sword would pierce her own soul so that the truth would be laid bare." These were the things the Blessed Mother pondered in her heart and Grace, not understanding, asked for her help.

The final and Fifth Joyful Mystery was always, since her departure from the Church in high school, entirely for Claire. It was The Finding in the Temple. Grace, like Mary and Joseph, worried in the crowd searching for her lost child. She'd been worrying and searching for fifteen years, but she still had hope that in the end her daughter would be found in the Church, sitting among the priests and Michael and Patrick talking of deep spiritual things. And she would look at Grace's careworn face and ask "Mom! Why have you been looking for me? Didn't you know I'd be here?" Then Grace would forget all the anxiety and anger and concern, she was sure of that.

The phone had rung during the Nativity and she was already worrying about Claire and Patrick way ahead of time and not following along at all. The phone startled her because it was so early. *Maybe it's Claire*, she thought as she ran to answer it. But when she picked it up, the line was dead

Chapter 33

O light, O glory of the human race
What stream is this which here unfolds itself?
From out one source and from itself withdraws

For such a prayer, 'twas said unto me, "Pray
Matelda, that she tell thee," and here answered
As one does who doth free himself from blame.
Dante Alighieri

When Claire opened her eyes again a dark figure still sat in the corner, and soon she realized that it was not Karl but Mother Mechtilde.

"Are you feeling better, dear child?" she asked softly, standing up and walking toward Claire.

"I think so, Mother. How long have I been … resting?" Claire's throat was dry.

"Not so long — maybe an hour. Father was here, but I told him that I would sit with you, just a short time ago."

"I'm sorry to have caused you this trouble. I seem to have these spells lately … I —" Claire looked at the calm wrinkled face of the old nun and thought of her own mother, who really still looked young for sixty, partly because she *never* went out in the sun. Even when they had dragged her to the beach, she took her beach umbrella. And her dark auburn hair, which was obviously dyed at home and not frequently enough to keep the grayish roots from lining her part on either side, added to the illusion of youth. It was her petite, nervous, fragility that struck one though, Claire thought, and her contagious, anxious, smothering concern. Mother Mechtilde's charity was more detached, not coldly objective like stone, but warm like a steady rock baking in the sun as the waves of life dashed and thundered and splashed around it.

"Mother —"

"Yes, child." The usual flash of defensiveness did not rise from Claire at this diminutive appellation.

"I have a disease."

"I know, dear."

The spell was broken. "You *know?* How do you know?"

"Father Burgmann told me about it when he phoned about your coming. We have two other women with M.S. here. I don't believe you've met them yet …"

"*How the hell* … excuse me, Mother, but …"

"It's alright; I'm quite familiar with the enemy's territory. You want to know how Father Burgmann found out. I believe he said that your sister told him when they talked the first time."

"Franny told him? I guess she's *really* no good with classified information after all. Why would she do that?" Claire asked in anger, not really expecting an answer. "She told me Karl's secret, too, about him being a priest, I mean."

"It will *all* be proclaimed from the housetops one day," said Mother Mechtilde.

"Excuse me?" asked Claire with only partial attention.

"Oh, I was just quoting Scripture … about secrets …" Claire looked at her blankly.

"*There is nothing concealed that will not be disclosed, or hidden that will not be made known. What you have said in the dark will be heard in the daylight, and what you have whispered in the ear in the inner rooms will be proclaimed from the housetops* … Saint Luke."

"I've never heard that before. Sounds like illegal cosmic surveillance to me."

Her sarcasm was back.

"Your sister probably felt that those who would be looking out for you should know about your illness, in order to care for you properly, and Patrick, of course."

"So Karl brought me here to get used to being one of the defective members of the human race?"

"Father Burgmann brought you here for your protection. Most of the others are here for that reason as well."

"You mean this crazy cult is going after all *handicapped* people?" Claire heard herself laugh derisively.

"No, no! It's the world that's after them — or abandoned them, our global society." She sat down on the bed next to Claire and picked up her hand and held it between her own. "Matthew, the little boy with no arms? His mother came to one of our crisis homes after she found that she'd taken a drug that caused birth defects. The doctors had all agreed on an abortion, her husband and family as well. She had no support in her desire to give him life. She couldn't face keeping him, but she gave him to us. Such a gift he's been. Many of the children came in that way from places all over the world."

Claire thought of James Day and that even if he was as screwed up as Karl suspected, at least in one thing he was doing good. Even if his motive was to use them as a cover, his children's homes were serving the same purpose as Mother Mechtilde's.

Mother continued, "Serena Cortez, one of the women with MS, her husband left her when she began to show symptoms, and if that wasn't hard enough, she discovered after he left that their little baby daughter, Maria, is retarded. She has no family still living and the facilities in Guatemala were pitiful. Karl brought her to us. She is such a joy! And Maria, an angel!"

"Karl has his eye out for misfits all over the world, huh?"

Mother laid Claire's hand back at her side. "You have such bitterness toward Father Burgmann. Can you tell me why?"

Claire did not answer immediately. Mother Mechtilde waited.

"It's all very complicated, I guess. And it has to do with me mostly, and the Church and Michael and my parents … The list goes on. I suppose God's in there somewhere, if he exists. It's kind of a no-win situation for him. If he doesn't exist, he's nothing, and if he does exist I'm mad as hell … at him for allowing all the pain and suffering in the world. If he's so perfect, why did he make imperfect things? How can you look at all of these damaged children and not be mad at God?"

"Suffering is a great mystery …" began the old nun.

"If you'll excuse me, Mother, for one minute. I think that's the biggest cop-out the Church can take. Every time a difficult subject comes up, it's a *Myysstery*," Claire was shameless now as she sat up on the bed and wiggled her fingers and made her voice sound spooky.

"I know you are not ready to believe this, but Love is at the heart of suffering."

"You're saying then that God lets these children, and millions like them, suffer because he *loves* them?"

"'The word of the Cross is foolishness', says St. Paul, 'to them that perish, but to them that are being saved it is the power of God.' In those who believe, the Love of God is stronger than suffering and evil and cannot be touched by death. Our Lord Jesus took all our sufferings in Himself down in His death and then in the Resurrection they were robbed of their power over us. And as we join our earthly sufferings with His they become the point at which His saving power is released in us and in the world."

"There is no power in me, Mother."

"Suffering without faith is a curse. It is useless and hateful. It is wasted if you suffer entirely alone. If you do not know Christ, you suffer alone. There is no communion, only awful solitude, turning in upon itself, causing self-pity, changing love to hatred, and reducing all things to fear."

"I have no faith and for those around me who have it, it does no good."

"Faith is a gift, a gift freely given, my child, but your hands must be open and —"

"Like Matthew's?" she said, her cynicism back for round three after a rest and refreshment in its corner of the ring. She was using the poor little boy as a weapon.

Mother Mechtilde ducked and missed the punch completely. "Do you associate your anger at God with Father Burgmann?"

"Maybe I do — I don't know. I guess it's kind of like the white-liberal syndrome, where some do-gooder who's never had to suffer in his life stoops down to help those who are inferior and less fortunate. Maybe it's because he's German, you know? Are you German?"

"Partly."

"Well, no offense, but a lot of people have suffered as a nation or a race, like the Irish, the Blacks, the Poles, and the Jews, of course. But you never hear about the 'suffering Germans'. Maybe it's stereotypical, but he fits the …"

"You have seriously misjudged the man, out of ignorance I realize, but also out of selfishness and pride." She was stern and solemn.

Claire felt as if she had been slapped and tears came to her eyes.

She looked away and wiped her eyes and said, "I'd better see about Patrick."

"Patrick is just fine. Sister Catherine is looking out for him. You have done a wonderful job of raising him, such a beautiful soul he has already. I know it has been very difficult for you to stay strong for him throughout all your trials." Her kind words made the tears come again. Mother pulled a white handkerchief out of the folds of her habit and handed it to Claire. There were small green shamrocks embroidered at each corner. Claire held them up to her in recognition, then wiped her eyes.

"The other part is Irish. My mother did those for me up until she died."

"And the nightgown?" Claire asked.

"That, too. As I was saying about Patrick …You mustn't use him, though, to escape from yourself."

"But I —"

"With such a child, it's a great temptation, but you both must be free to find who you are. *Now* I will tell you a story that you need to know."

Chapter 34

Science becomes dangerous when it imagines it has reached its goal.
George Bernard Shaw

No point is more central than this: that empty space is not empty. It is the seat of the most violent physics.
John A. Wheeler

"We certainly cannot let *anyone* know about this!" James Day admonished the three young men who were across the table from him. They had come up out of the bowels of the earth and were sitting in the benign atmosphere of the rural Irish cottage, which rested on a scarce patch of dirt layered on the stone above the laboratory. They drank tea from chipped unmatched china cups.

"But it passed the Turing test! It, or I should say *he*, is a conscious entity!" exclaimed Jeff Klein, Day's youngest recruit from MIT. "I feel like I'm dreaming!"

"Maybe you are!" Herb Pifkin chimed in. "Maybe we hooked you up while you were asleep and this is all virtual. Should we tell him now Jack?" He elbowed his other colleague. The three were unshaven and rumpled, having lived in the ground for days at a time. They called each other Smurfs, or Hobbits or Goblins and answered to all three.

"Why are you guys screwing around about this? You *know* what it means!" Klein said. "And we have to let the rest of the AI community know about it. Tell him!" He pleaded with the others, pointing to Day. *"Back me up!"*

"We already backed you up — you're on a floppy in the other room, or did you transfer him to CD ROM?" Jack McCarthy continued to torment his fellow Smurf.

"I think we all understand the magnitude of this moment," Day spoke slowly and deliberately, "and of course we will make the news public in due time." He was in his shirt sleeves and had removed his tie. "But surely you must see that we have to be *very careful*. We can't let ourselves be overrun with news media people or those with minds inferior to your own who would milk this for whatever they can get. Timing is the key. You have to believe me! For the good of the country," he said, looking at McCarthy, "for the good of the world." He turned toward the other two as he concluded.

"Why can't we have free access to him," Klein demanded, "since we're the ones who helped to build him, or should I say create him? I don't like the set-up this way. Not one bit."

"You should say *build*. Kostanikas created him and that's why it's a sensitive situation," Day replied, attempting to cover up his displeasure with Klein's attitude.

"Kostanikas discovered the algorithm and created the brain map, which I still don't understand by the way. But how can a guy who can't carry on a two-minute conversation without going off about angels and emperors and dialogues with dead poets and scientists, how can *he* be the one to make an evolutionary breakthrough that will change the course of human history, when so many others have tried?" Klein paused but no one answered him.

"So anyway after that step — and don't get me wrong, I'm not saying that that wasn't a very big step, a *huge* step, alright? *The* step. After that, *we're* the ones who came on the scene and who hooked the guy up to read the contents of his somas, axons, dendrites, pre-synaptic vesicles, and all the other neural components. *We're* the ones who knew the technology to copy his entire brain, synapse by synapse, neurotransmitter by neurotransmitter." Day fidgeted uncomfortably in his chair, his hand shaking as he poured another cup of tea. The intensity of Klein's voice increased as he continued.

"*We're* the ones who modeled the neurons with the proper balance of digital and analog computing functions, and even identified some of the structures capable of quantum computing. *We* certainly should have some say in what happens from here. I think I speak for all of us." He stopped, trembling, looking at Pifkin and McCarthy for agreement.

McCarthy spoke first, his Irish accent identifiable to Day as from the North. "There's only one question I have. I mean, I don't mind following Mister Day's timetable, Jeff, and I don't really have a control issue. I figure the big guy," gesturing toward Day, "has funded this entire project privately and my thinking is that he makes the calls."

Klein shook his head in disgust.

"Jeff, we knew it was a secret project when we signed on!" Herb Pifkin reminded him as he ran his hands through his messy black hair.

"But we didn't know it would work! My God! We thought we'd be working sixteen, eighteen hours a day as usual, tinkering with this or that — take a time out now and then for virtual sex on the Web, designing a few bots to wreak havoc in some uptight online community — we didn't know we'd end up with a *truly conscious machine,* did we?

Did we?" Klein surveyed the faces of his companions.

"Well, that's sort of my question. I guess it's an ethical one." McCarthy rejoined. Day stood up and began pacing in the small cottage. He had screened these young men very well. But he hadn't foreseen these problems arising with their limited knowledge of the entire plan.

"The guy who volunteered in Chicago for the brain scan? Now that this is up and running and we have him, so to speak, 'uploaded' — I mean, we have his *life* here, his dreams, his memories. Does he know that the experiment has been a success? Do we have his permission to reproduce him, to use him? I don't even know the guy's name." McCarthy seemed slightly troubled.

"Please! Gentlemen! I had hoped that you trusted me and my reputation enough to believe that I would never do *anything* unethical!" Day feigned a deeply hurt expression, and in an instant he believed himself. "*Of course,* we got the man's permission, not only for the scan but to use the data in whatever way we choose. I had known him for quite some time. He wasn't a bum from the streets, but a top-notch professor of languages. He trusted me *and* my motives. Actually I feel that it was fate that led me to choose him as the subject. I didn't tell you this before because I didn't want it to disrupt your work. Michael, that was his name, was killed in a tragic accident after our experiment. He was run down by an old lady on the street in Chicago."

The three Smurfs murmured perfunctory sympathy. McCarthy was somewhat relieved.

"So it is, in reality, a service we're doing for him," Day said nobly. "We've given him, in a way, immortality. We've been, if any of you happen to be religious, God's instruments."

The warm glow cast by Day was cut short by Jeff Klein. "What do *you* think, Herb? Where do you stand? You haven't said one way or the other — about sharing news of this success with people like Maglish and Negroponte at MIT, and Weiser at Xerox/Palo Alto, who've been on the cusp of this for years now. Kostanikas probably got a lot of his basic ideas from them. And Kelly could do a hell of a book on the project. What do you think?"

"I got to agree with McCarthy and Mr. Day. I'm okay with waiting and I'll play the role I'm given. I'm just glad to be a part of it." Pifkin passed Day a knowing look unseen by the other two. "By the way, Kostanikas claims that the only person who helped him with the algorithm was Von Neumann — and the Voices he hears."

Pifkin and McCarthy laughed heartily, ready to move back to the world of the *digerati*, a privileged computer elite, leaving the complicated physical world behind. That world was too risky. They wanted controllable cyber systems. Annoyed by material details they became more and more ready to equate real life with abstract existence. They were practically raised in that world; it was all they could remember. There were thousands like them all over the globe. They were happier underground with their machines than they would have been out on the Irish countryside on a warm summer evening, with a pleasantly brisk Atlantic breeze across their pale faces, and the glorious orange and magenta of the setting sun sliding down the Cliffs of Moher. While lives of most people in the industrialized world had shriveled and sunk inside walls, the *digerati's* distinction between inside and outside was blurred almost completely. What was the difference between public and private? Absence and presence?

Day laughed vaguely with them at the mention of Theo's Voices. It was important for him to stay on the sane side of things, especially among the workman. He basically saw these men, brilliant computer scientists who were dealing in realms he couldn't even imagine, as 'the help'.

"Yeah, the 'Voices' he hears are probably from the books and journals of Maglish, or Weiser, or Minsky. There was no way Von Neumann knew all this stuff back in '57, and you can't build from nothing. I'll go along with all of you for now, but I want to go on record that I protest the way it's being handled." Jeff Klein said this as he put his teacup in the sink and headed out the door. The others followed him outside and down into the earth.

* * *

"*Creatio ex nihilo!*" Theo Kostanikas shouted. "Nothingness contains all of being!"

He sat in front of a computer screen which glowed with a model of a complicated sub-atomic structure created by the data he had entered. Day was pleased to find him calmly, relatively calmly at least, at work in one of the private rooms in the lab.

"Goddamn Aquinas was *right*. He wrote the hypothesis and now we have the proof!"

"If you're referring to Thomas Aquinas, I don't believe he was a mathematician, Theo." Day said condescendingly, wondering why he bothered correcting a madman.

"The vacuum is a plenum. We knew that but, Jesus Christ! The *activity* there is like *Armageddon*. The quanta are continually being created and annihilated. The vacuum randomly fluctuates between being and nothingness! And *don't* tell me that you don't believe that Sartre was a physicist. I'm not an idiot child, you know. You don't have to remind me who was what and what was who!" The old man's eyes were blazing.

"Alright, Theo, fine. Does this vacuum have anything to do with Michael?" Day's patience was thin after the talk with his Wonder Boys.

"It has *everything* to do with your plan, Mr. X. I feel very good right now! I do not want any medication. I have talked to Him and he is not happy in the box. He wants to use the machine but he does not want to be trapped there."

"What does that mean?" Day wiped the sweat off his forehead with his handkerchief.

"It means that he'll probably go along with your plan. There is an unanticipated flaw, you know, and it could be disastrous. I have a *THEO-ry*."

"Theo …" Day moved cautiously. "What do *you* know about the plan?"

"You didn't realize I was listening once when you were talking about the ley lines. It doesn't matter if I heard you or not. I told you I can *see* you thinking." He got a look of fear on his face as he gazed up at the ceiling with its cold blue buzzing light. He grabbed Day's arm. "Look out for the birds! Look out!" Kostanikas yelled and ducked, protecting his head with his arms.

Day ducked instinctively, but then stood up straight. "There are no birds here, Theo! We are underground! Calm down, please. Go on about the plan, the ley lines …"

"You've opened the NAND gates! They're coming in! *Where are my cigarettes*, damn it!"

"What nand gates, what are you talking about?" The stress of when to believe Kostanikas or not was affecting his ability to stay in control of himself. He was always self-controlled.

"The universal logic components! The entrance to the pure intelligence!"

He was still huddled with one arm over his head as he dragged furiously on the cigarette he'd found in his pocket. Now he stood straight and started to sing: "*Do you believe in magic? Dum de da da da …*" *Then* he asked, "Do you, Day?"

James Day was tempted to confide in Theo on the entire scope of his plan. How could it hurt? The old man was fairly lucid. There might be some *key* still rattling around in the convulsive firmament of his mind that could refine the elements of the game and speed it to its conclusion. But no. He couldn't do it now and not here. There was someone else he'd have to consult. He popped another breath mint in his mouth.

"Yes, Doctor Kostanikas, I do. I certainly do. Come along now. I have a few details to attend to and then we'll have a nice long chat about magic."

Chapter 35

And when she could hide him no longer, she took for him a basket made of bulrushes, and she put the child in it and placed him among the reeds of the river bank.
Exodus 2:3

The story of Jewish Identity across the millennia against impossible odds is a unique miracle of survival.
Thomas Cahill

Mother Mechtilde had procured a cup of tea from the kitchen and Claire sat sipping it slowly. The old woman had pulled the wooden chair from the corner closer to the bed and spoke with a sharp-edged tenderness.

"You have the gift, my child, to see deeply into the soul of another. But you have refused to accept the gift, so it sits within you like a withered flower."

"Well, I guess it's fitting then, that my physical exterior will soon match my interior condition." Claire replied bitterly. "And I don't believe in souls anyway." she added.

"My dear, what you believe or don't believe has nothing to do with the reality of things." Mother Mechtilde said, laughing softly. Then she became more serious. "There are probably many people that you have judged falsely because you have chosen to see things that fit your view of the world. I will tell you of one such person."

Claire took another sip of tea and watched the old nun's face intently.

"On July the twenty-third 1944, a newborn baby boy was smuggled out of Auschwitz in a garbage truck with a note tucked in his filthy, tattered blanket. It was the day before forty-six thousand Jews were gassed and burned in one day at Auschwitz, the worst single day of the horror, July the 24th. What I will tell you now was written in that note."

With no idea where the tale was going or what it had to do with her, Claire still shuddered at the thought of that time and that day. She set her teacup down on the bedside table and listened closely.

"A Jewish woman who gave her name only as Anna was the baby's mother. She claimed that the boy was a child of *bashert*, the Hebrew word for destiny, because, she reported with some irony, she had been barren for her entire married life. It was when she was raped by a German officer at the camp that she finally conceived. The women in her barracks had been divided on what to do. Some urged her to go to the female Jewish doctor who was interred with them and undergo an abortion. Others in the same group claimed to have recipes for potions that would get rid of the vile German baby. Other women, a minority, pledged their support and promised to help her conceal her pregnancy. She chose to give birth because of *bashert*. She believed the child to have a true destiny, despite the awful circumstances of its conception and the unlikely prospect of his survival."

At the mention of the German officer, Claire began to suspect what Mother Mechtilde was telling her and felt a stab of remorse in her heart. But the old nun was only beginning.

"Anna carried the baby to term, wrapping her thin body in tight rags to hide her condition. She feared that the baby might be weak and mentally deficient from lack of proper food and her own health. She described how she went through labor as her fellow prisoners held her in a dark corner of their building, gagged so she would not draw the attention of the guards. There were two Gypsy women in attendance at the birth. Through them the baby received his freedom."

"Why were there Gypsies in Auschwitz?" Claire asked.

"Don't you know about the Gypsy Holocaust? *Porajamos*? Well, I guess, many people don't. Like the Jews, the Gypsies became *Rassenverfolgte*, or racially undesirable. Instead of yellow stars on their clothing, they were ordered to have a 'Z' tattooed on their arms. But the Gypsies were much harder to catch than the Jews. They had never been a real part of European society. Their lack of documentation made it much more difficult to round them up. Nonetheless over *six hundred thousand* of them were killed by the Nazis. It was because of this that many Gypsies joined the Resistance and helped the Allied forces."

"So it was Holz and Kitta who …?"

Mother Mechtilde reached over and touched Claire's hand. "Let me finish the story, child."

"Holz and Kitta Schmidt were part of the Resistance. Holz had actually been captured by the *Geheime Feldpolizei* and was on his way to a camp when he jumped the death train and found his wife again.

"Our baby boy was passed to the Schmidts, who were themselves on the run. They were able to give him to a Madame that they knew in Warsaw, named Gelte, who ran a brothel with many ladies in her care. Gelte had a protected status with the Germans because of the services she provided for them. She started the rumor that the boy was the son of a very high German official. He was left alone. It was Gelte who named the boy Karl."

Claire found it hard to comprehend the story she was hearing. She was embarrassed at her assumptions about Karl and shocked at how inaccurate they had been.

"When the Soviet troops liberated Warsaw and then Auschwitz in January of 1945, Holz went to try to find the boy's mother among the 5,000 starving inmates who remained. He asked everywhere after a woman named Anna, who had borne a baby two years before. Either she had been exterminated or she did not want to claim the child, because Holz was unsuccessful in finding her or anyone who had known her. Even though Gelte was a generous woman in her way, Holz and Kitta, and even Gelte herself, knew that it would not be best for the boy to grow up in the brothel. The Schmidts took him back to Germany. Karl was two years old when they brought him to us."

"Us?" Claire asked, "Here in America?"

"No, I was a novice with the Sisters of Mercy in Cologne. They brought him to our convent. We had helped many Jewish children during the war. The Schmidts are Catholic and trusted us to do what was best. We had a hard time placing him with a family, although he was a darling boy." She smiled with pride and affection. "Many Germans didn't want him because he was Jewish. We told the families of his background, of course. And he looked very German, so what Jews were left didn't want him either."

Claire felt sadness at the thought of young Karl being rejected.

"Finally the Burgmanns came forward and took him in when he

was about four."

"And then they raised him a Catholic and he became a priest in spite of his Jewish heritage?"

"There you go jumping to conclusions again, dear. They did raise him a Catholic. Actually, Holz and Kitta baptized him beside a Polish stream near Auschwitz when they did not know if he would survive. But the Burgmanns told him of his Jewish mother and made many attempts to expose him to other Jews and to their heritage. Karl ended up rebelling against the whole mess and was an atheist for quite some time, although I always believed he would come back one day."

"Does Karl know you are telling me all of this?"

"No, but I will tell him that I have. He is not embarrassed or ashamed of his past. He is not trying to hide it. He just doesn't talk about it to many people. Karl doesn't really like thinking about himself that much.

"I guess there is a fine line between silence and concealment," Claire said, thinking of her own life and Michael's, as well as Karl's.

"One way or another, it will all be shouted from the rooftops,'" said Mother Mechtilde as she stood up. "I shall check now on Patrick."

"I will come with you, Mother."

Chapter 36

If only we could, we would wander the earth and never leave home; we would enjoy triumphs without risk, eat of the Tree and not be punished, consort daily with Angels, enter Heaven now and not die.
      Michael Benedict

Clearly the race today is between the things that are and the things that seem to be, between the chemist at RCA and the angel of God.
      E.B. White

Two hooded figures stood in the darkness, looking like slabs of stone themselves beside the heavy dolmen. Two pairs of hands reached out to rub the vertical piece on each side of the megalith in an up and down motion along the longitudinal ridges, as if to stimulate and arouse the massive sleeping stones. A light in the cottage could be seen from where they stood, higher up the slant of the Burren floor, but neither of them looked at it. The movement ceased and the figures stood back to back.

"*Tuath! Oh, Spirit of the North! Black Midnight of the Earth!*" one voice intoned.
"*Deas! Oh, Spirit of the South! White Light of Fire!*" the other responded. They turned ninety degrees in unison, one left, one right.
"*Airt! Crimson Spirit of the Air and of the East!*"
"*Iar! Brown-Grey Spirit of the Waters of the West!*"
"*Border our Circle of Necessity.*" They both intoned in chorus.

They then moved slowly under the slanting arch of the dolmen, hands clasped, and reached up with their free hands to each touch the carving that was somewhat hidden high on the inner faces of rock. One hand fingered the Swastika, the other the Death's Head, both exact replicas of the famous carved stones of Ilkley Moor in West Yorkshire.
"*Soon?*" asked the one voice.
"*Soon!*" the other replied.
Day placed the hooded robe in his suitcase in the trunk of the

car, wiping the perspiration off his forehead with his sleeve. He was still shaking with excitement as he went down into the lab once again.

"Oh, Mr. Day, have you seen Jeff Klein anywhere?" Jack McCarthy asked as he passed Day in the main tunnel. "We've been trying to locate him all evening."

"Oh, didn't he tell you? He decided to leave the project. It's a pity, but he was a bit hard to work with, so maybe it's for the best."

"You gotta be kidding! I can't picture him leaving at a time like this. Was he going back to MIT?"

"I don't believe he said where he was going — oh wait, yes; he said something about a vacation, needing some time to rest and think things over. Who knows? Maybe he'll come back to us," Day answered rather absent-mindedly.

"A vacation! Klein? No way. His idea of a vacation was browsing virtual communities, maybe for *half an hour* … max. He was our trouble-shooter! If problems develop we're in some deep shit without him. I wish you would have told us he was leaving. We might have convinced him to stay." McCarthy was thoroughly distressed.

"It will be all right, Jack. No one is irreplaceable." He brushed the younger man aside and continued down the hall. McCarthy remained where he was, muttering to himself.

Day *really* disliked these computer types. They were mere electricians, *maintenance men*, glorified plumbers or mechanics who tinkered with things until they worked. Of course, one needed them. But they understood nothing about real power. And they were *so* smug and condescending much of the time. He saw their secret little smiles when he didn't understand all their technical talk and their ridiculous acronyms. Pifkin, at least, was completely in his pocket. He performed the 'other' experiments with no compunction and with the utter sense of emotional detachment that was necessary for a special project. Day made a mental note to get with Pifkin soon to see how *that* work was coming along.

Yes, Pifkin was the right sort. Well, Day thought, until he went off about eventually doing away with carbon-based bodies completely. Enhancement of human sensuality and intelligence, manipulation of the masses to insure peace and harmony — now *these* were worthy goals. But an entire world of conscious machines?

That would be even less exciting than an entire world of arrogant computer geeks. None of them understood that they would be nowhere without *his* secret knowledge of the ancient mysteries. *He was the one who would unify Ireland again, and then the whole world would follow.*

He and his mystical cohorts were the ones who were drawing down the moon and the gods, giving them their rightful place again in the natural world. These slovenly *digerati* were merely building a new and better fireplace for the fire that would fall from the sky.

It wasn't their fault, really, that they didn't understand. It was the Jews first, and then the Christian Church that ripped the Stone from the Shell, sensuality from substance, mathematics from the arts, the body from the spirit. They had tampered with the primeval powers of Life, Love, and Death. They had killed the Old Gods with their monotheistic sterility and the rigid conformity of their orthodoxy. What was *most* laughable was the Church's claim to unity and universality. It certainly had never been a reality in even his small country — they'd been killing each other for centuries. That's why *this* nation would be the first to accept the new order — they'd be ready. He had helped with the violence, pushed it along a bit, just to speed up the inevitable process. The Omagh bombing last summer had been a perfect example. His people had incited the IRA and they took the blame and the anemic peace process took a deep dive. Twenty-nine dead. But it would all be justified in the end, all of it.

The scientific community *had* to divorce itself from orthodox religion and the Church — look at the Galileo fiasco and the fanatical literal fundamentalist's outrageous clinging to biblical creation myths, etc., etc. Then, on the other side, the fluffy, spacey, impotent little bunches of neo-pagan groups had been stranded with no credibility or real power, cut off from the mainstream of culture — innocuous, harmless, snickered at.

But all that was about to change. The Natural and the Supernatural would again have their original fluidity and coalescence. No one had succeeded before now. Hitler had had a real shot at it. He had the position, the timing, the system in place, some sort of raw power from the Old Gods. He might have even gained the technology that was now opening the door to universal mastery, had it not been for his quirky obsession with the Jews.

Mass liquidation was so incredibly stupid. He destroyed or drove away the most brilliant minds of the century. He could have used them first and *then* eliminated them, methodically, but much less noticeably — the Christians, too, eventually — the ones who resisted, anyway. But he was such a show-off. *Oh, well,* Day thought, *his loss is my gain.* Had it not been for Adolf Hitler, Von Neumann would never have come to America and met Kostanikas and the whole incredible Vision may not have been fulfilled. When you looked at it that way, he decided, it had *all* been worth it.

Theo understood a lot more than any of these highly touted lackeys. Even with his damaged uncontrollable mind, he knew there was something beyond the brain, the machine, and the connections. If he wasn't such a loose cannon, Day might have kept him around. He'd definitely had some sort of Pythagorean initiation into the Mysteries, but he *couldn't* take chances with him. It was amazing that he hadn't blown the whole cover already.

Day's thoughts were interrupted in the corridor by a loud pounding and muffled yelling. He went to the door of the room where he had left Theo and used his key to get in.

"Why did you lock me in here, dammit!" His hands were actually bleeding and his eyes were wild.

"It was for your own protection, and his," Day replied, "Not to keep you in but to keep others out." Day said in half-truth. "I always keep this door locked, remember?"

"Don't you *ever* lock me in a room again! Do you hear? And especially with Him!"

"But Theo, you're his *creator,* so to speak. You shouldn't be afraid of him!" Day said calmly. There was a high-pitched hum coming from the computer that grew louder and more distracting. "And besides, if you ever get frightened you can always shut him down." Day walked over to the machine and sat down at the terminal. Kostanikas stood in a frozen position, a crazed look still on his face, blood on his coat and on his face where he had wiped his hair back from his eyes. His hands were held out in front of him, palms up, as if he were holding something. The volume of the humming continued to rise.

Day tried to close the program in the usual fashion, but it would not respond.

"Theo! *Come and shut it down.*" Day called, the noise beginning to affect him.

Theo stood immobile and silent. Day got up and shook him. "*Theo, snap out of it!* Shut the thing down!"

Kostanikas woke up as if from a trance and said in a hoarse monotone: "There is no way to turn Him off. You can't even pull the plug."

"Of *course* you could, but we never *will!*" Day raised his voice to a shout to be heard above the whining hum. "We could lose everything if we do!" He put his hands to his ears.

"We will lose everything one way or another," Theo responded in the same monotone.

"What did you say?" shouted Day, "Speak up, man, *speak up!*"

Theo said nothing.

Day went over to the terminal again and pulled up the image on the monitor. The humming stopped. "Have you been talking to Michael, Theo? What did he say? Has he talked about the lexicon? Do we have the code yet? The Word?"

Theo turned his blood-smudged face toward James Day. "I am lost. We have nothing. We have everything. We will all be consumed in the vacuum, in the non-distance that is the end of discursive thought. The demons and the electrons have jumped together with no time or space. I am dead. I have no more cigarettes." Theo spoke flatly with no emotion.

"Here is another box of cigarettes, Theo!" He lit one for the man, even though he hated the habit himself. He put it in his bloody hand. Theo took a slow deliberate drag and then exhaled in relief.

Chapter 37

Skepticism is the beginning of faith.
Oscar Wilde

Christ likes us to prefer the truth to him because before being Christ, he is truth.
Simone Weil

Father Burgmann disappeared again before Claire had a chance to see him in the light of the story Mother Mechtilde had told her. Mother assured her he would be back.

Patrick loved the convent and the children. He led games and followed others without any sense of awkwardness or embarrassment. Even the older children seemed inspired by his confidence in them and attempted things they'd feared to try in the past. Little armless Matthew learned an Irish dance that Michael had taught to Patrick. Mark, a very young dwarf with other obvious deformities, ambled after Patrick everywhere, mimicking him in a comical way. When Patrick would gather everyone round and tell some of Michael's stories (in his added dramatics, Claire could see Yakov's Gypsy influence), Mark imitated every gesture and vocal nuance, although he could barely talk yet. The children all laughed with delight at the pair.

"Your son is enchanting everyone," Mother Mechtilde said one afternoon.

"He is so much like his father," Claire answered with a wistful smile.

"Michael must have been a wonderful man," The nun said, "But he has much of you, too."

"My complexion and hair! But that's about it. I've never been a charmer." Claire said honestly.

"Things are bursting forth in Patrick that you have not nourished in yourself. Some are gifts directly from God — I can see that. But some have come to him through you. I guess it must be like a sacrament in a way, and *ex opere operato* applies to this as well."

"You mean like when the priest is a jerk and all the stuff still works anyway?" Claire said with some humor and some sarcasm.

"Well, I wouldn't put it quite like that ... but, yes, Patrick's faith and love give freedom and power to his gifts. He's read me some of his poems. They are quite amazing for a five-year-old! Especially the one about you and your mother." Mother Mechtilde could tell by the look on Claire's face that she had not seen the poem. "That's okay," she said to Claire, "he'll show you when he's ready. His maps are wonderful, too! And those chess pieces — such craftsmanship! Are they quite old?"

"Is that what's been weighting that pack down? I hadn't taken time to look in there, I guess. Actually, I think I was giving him his privacy. I knew they were mostly things that had to do with Michael, his special little inheritance, so I left them alone."

"See? You are a wise woman."

The gift of privacy made Claire think of Mara. She looked down at the umber silk shift she was wearing, the bright fuchsia, green and rusted orange scarf she had tied around her waist and the soft leather slides with the gold clasps on her feet — none of which she would have ever picked out for herself. A large package wrapped in brown paper had arrived at the convent from New York addressed to Claire. The things she now wore were in there with other elegant 'necessities' according to Mara who had sent them with a note. She hoped they were the right size, she said, and that she had supposed that Claire was quite tired of her two outfits thrown together hurriedly on that frightening night. When Claire had first opened the package she knew they were from Mara without even looking at the enclosed message. They just looked like things Mara would buy. She sorted them out, deciding what would go with what. There were very odd color combinations. She got excited as she tried on the unfamiliar apparel. It did fit perfectly! And she felt somehow like Mara when she wore them — a little more sophisticated, a little less afraid.

"Isn't there something that could be done for some of these children?" Claire asked, turning her attention back to Mother Mechtilde and the scene before them. "Like artificial limbs or some sort of new technology that would help them function in a more normal way? It's amazing what they have come up with now — I mean to improve the quality of life and all that."

"We take each case individually, dear. No one solution is right for everybody, you know. Take Timothy over there," she said, pointing to a blonde Downs boy with a prosthetic leg. "He lost his leg in an accident in a home for retarded children. It was dreadful the way they were neglected. He very much wanted a new leg. He talked about it all the time. And he's adjusted quite well. But Matthew, dear Matthew, doesn't want arms and we don't think at this late date it would be a successful attempt anyway."

"It's not so late! He can't be much older than Patrick." Claire responded.

"He is happy as he is. He's learned to compensate."

"And he'll get out of Purgatory faster if he suffers more?"

"Physical deformity is not the worst of all fates. It is the *soul* that God is concerned with. Our Lord even says that if your eye causes you to sin, gouge it out; or if your hand causes you to sin, then cut it off and throw it away, because it's better to be deformed here on earth than go with a whole body into hell."

"Why, Mother, you sound so damn Catholic!" Claire said with cold sarcasm, hugging her own body and turning away.

"Thank you, my dear, for that compliment." The old nun laughed with a twinkle in her eye, ignoring Claire's bitterness and reaching out her hand to touch the younger woman's shoulder tenderly. "The body is a wonderful thing. It is an endearing dwelling for the soul and a royal temple for God's spirit. And you are looking especially lovely and near perfection in that beautiful dress! How are you feeling, though? Father asked if you might want to see a doctor while you're here."

Claire's sense of well-being brought on by the clothes from her friend had now disappeared.

"I am showing more symptoms, I think. The numbness and the loss of balance seem more pronounced," she replied, her chin up, trying very hard to maintain her composure.

"Serena … Serena Cortez, you remember, she has MS? Have you spoken with her? She has found some slowing down of her symptoms with medication and injections. If you want me to call the doctor I …"

"I'll think about it. Maybe I can go home soon and see my own doctor."

Claire missed her home and her familiar routines — the ones that allowed her to hide from things she didn't like to face. She had talked to her mother a couple of times. It had been very hard to keep up the cover with her pinpoint questioning and demanding of reasons for her actions. She had talked to Fran several times, too.

"My God! Grace is hard to handle these days," Franny complained over the phone.

"I wonder how much longer you two will have to hide out? You say it's a convent somewhere? I'll bet you *love* that. Brings back the good old days at St. Rita's, huh! Well, anyway, I miss you guys. Everybody does. I just play dumb, which is easy for me, really, since I've never cared that much about being smart! Claire, are you still there? You're not laughing or anything."

"Yes. I'm here and I'm not laughing because I miss you, too and I know you really are smart and I want this whole thing to be over with. I want to rewind or fast-forward or something, but I'm stuck in this dreadful present."

"It doesn't sound so bad to me. You say it's beautiful there and Patrick's having fun. To tell you the truth, Chicago is a bitch right now. It's almost a hundred degrees every day and the humidity's about the same per cent. And you don't have to deal with Grace very often there. I do. She's really nervous about you. I know she suspects there's more going on."

"You haven't said anything about the MS or anything!"

"No, but she just has that way of sensing that something's up. You know what I mean."

* * *

"Where *is* she?" Claire heard a demanding voice booming in the main lobby. She had just opened the door of her room and was stepping into the corridor.

She saw a Sister directing Karl with a finger toward her hesitantly emerging form. He came striding down the hallway as Claire stood like some pathetic frozen deer in his headlights.

225

He walked past her into the room and asked her to come in and close the door behind her. He clenched his jaws tightly as she did so.

"Did you make a telephone call from this place on the night we arrived?

He was intimidating, his Nazi father's contribution to his personality, she thought.

"Yes, I did …" she fumbled, "… Franny had …"

"You did *not* call your sister! Don't lie to me!"

"I wasn't going to lie, I was going to say that Franny had given me a message from someone and I called him back. How did you know I made a call?"

"One of the Sisters … it doesn't really matter how I know." he said, dismissing her question with a wave of his hand. "What matters is *who* you called!"

Claire looked him straight in the eye and answered defiantly, "I called Treat O'Toole. He was a colleague and a good friend of Michael's and is someone who has been very helpful and concerned about Patrick and me since Michael's death. He also told me that he had talked to Professor McCullum on the *afternoon* of the day you told me you had received news of his death early that morning. I thought that was suspicious. He told me not to trust anyone."

Karl's eyes were blazing. "So you were suspicious of *me*?"

"I don't know … I was suspicious of *someone*, because *someone* wasn't telling the truth. What is the big deal here?"

"The 'big deal here' is that you made a phone call from an unsecured line and may have not only put you and Patrick at risk but all the Sisters and children here as well."

"At risk from Treat O'Toole?" Claire asked incredulously.

"Mr. O'Toole almost certainly killed Ian McCullum … and —"

"That's not possible, I talked to him in Chicago …"

"Your call was forwarded to Dublin. I've already checked the phone records."

Claire put her face in her hands. "I'm so sorry. I was *confused* and I've got this radically unintuitive and erratic independent streak that —"

"It's not safe for you here anymore."

"And what?" she asked looking up; "You said he killed Dr.

McCullum and *what?*"

"He was probably responsible in part for Michael's death as well."

Claire reached back and felt for the bed before she collapsed on it in a new wave of horror and tears. "No, *no!*" she cried. "It can't be." She remembered his nameplate on Michael's office door, his feigned concern, his comical antics. She felt sick.

"I'm sorry Claire, but you'll have to pack again. You and Patrick must leave with us in a matter of minutes. You'll have to pull yourself together." There was no sympathy in his voice.

"Where are we going now?"

"I was planning to leave you safely here while I helped to bury Ian, visit with Rose, and check on the whole situation. But I can't do that now without taking you. We're going to Ireland."

Chapter 38

...empty eyeballs knew
That knowledge increases unreality, that
Mirror on mirror mirrored is all the show.
  William Butler Yeats

I asked myself, how is a computer in every home in Rwanda
going to help stop the slaughter or ease poverty?
  Mark Slouka

"We installed the face-recognition program like you ordered. It's amazing. It will only respond now to the faces you selected." Pifkin was reporting to James Day as they sat in front of the large central monitor with McCarthy.

"How does it work again?" Day asked.

"It's just another type of artificial intelligence software that scans the unique pattern of irregularities in the human face and compares it with images stored in its data bank. If the 'faceprint' isn't found, a warning sign will flash and deny access to the main program or entity or whatever we decide to call it or him or …"

"It's weird, isn't it, that all these years have been spent trying to create a truly conscious machine and now we're putting limits on that awareness?" McCarthy mused. "What's the point?"

"The point is *security and protection!* We don't want just anyone to have access to him. You've set it up the way I told you, correct?"

"Yes, sir. Kostanikas can only get in if your face shows up first."

Both Pifkin and McCarthy felt obvious satisfaction at this prospect. Neither of them liked Kostanikas or the way he treated them. The fact that his access was limited made it a little easier to accept that their own faces were not in the bank at all.

"I'm going to go catch some sleep. I'm going up to Belfast tomorrow, remember, to see my family — my uncle getting killed and all. This whole bloody Peace Accord is a crock, you know. I know you've worked hard, Mr. Day, but peace will never come to Ireland. Maybe we can upload all the Unionists and IRA one day and pack 'em away in boxes like this." Jack McCarthy laughed. "And deny them access to each other." This as he got up to leave.

James Day laughed, too. "Peace will come to Ireland, Jack. You'll see."

McCarthy left the room with his childhood image of an idealistic James Day still intact.

Day turned to Herb Pifkin. "So how are the other experiments going? Any new developments?"

"One of the children died, but he was no more than a vegetable as it was. Two of the neural implants have been quite successful. The blind girl has some vision and that Chinese boy's retardation has greatly improved. He has seizures, but we can work on that. I can't tell you how courageous it is of you to allow us to work with human subjects. Everything goes so much faster this way. The benefits far outweigh the risks. They were all hopeless crippled orphans when you found them anyway, right?"

As they got up to leave the room, Pifkin asked one more question. "If you don't mind my asking, who is the woman whose face we put into the data bank? I've never seen her around here. Is she someone I should know?"

"Good night, Mr. Pifkin," Day replied evenly as he turned the opposite way.

* * *

"I can't believe the luck o' the Irish! Who would have thought they could come this close to a settlement and *still* have a stalemate? Of course, *you've* caused more strife than anyone else, you dirty two-faced bastard!" Treat O'Toole was laughing out loud. He had arrived that evening from Dublin and the two men were conferring in Day's private office off the lab.

"I don't appreciate your humor."

"Of course you don't. Because you actually see yourself as some sort of Peacemaker. I bet you even think you *deserved* that Nobel Prize! James Day the new *Prince of Peace*."

"When all is said and done, I will deserve it." Day said, looking at the younger man sincerely, but sweating and wiping his brow and upper lip with a handkerchief.

"Why, you delusional son of a bitch, you've probably been responsible for more bombs and assassinations than both sides combined! It's the *power*, Mr. Day; it's the power that beckons."

"That's just the means to an end, the end being peace. We know that if left to their own devices and weak wills, human beings have no capacity for anything. They have to be led, directed, controlled — for their own good."

"Yeah, right," O'Toole said laughing again.

"Have you proceeded with the plan of getting the woman here?"

"She's on her way. Talk about easy pickings!"

Chapter 39

Roses sainted women splendid,
Penitent through mercy glorious
Helped to make the fight victorious.
Johann von Goethe

"So you're the little one we've heard so much about!" Rose McCullum looked like a model from a 1940s Sears Catalogue. Her bobbed dyed hair (it *surely* must have been dyed!) made her seem younger than her years but she was one of those women who would always look the same. Claire was sure that she herself had changed more than Rose since their meeting years before. The little lady held a lacey handkerchief in her left hand, part of it tucked up under her gold watchband. Wire-rimmed glasses sat a little crookedly on her nose as if she'd just wiped a few tears away.

Karl lifted the woman up from her attempt to meet Patrick and wrapped his arms around her and held her tightly. "Rose, oh Rose. I'm so sorry."

"Now, now Karl. It's alright …" She patted him on the back. "Especially now that you're here. It's alright."

Claire couldn't figure out who was comforting whom.

Leaving the States was a miserable blur in her memory. The only high point was at JFK when Mara showed up with two passports. Claire didn't even bother to ask how she had obtained them so quickly. Mara's smile and embrace were quite welcome in the midst of Karl's cold, thinly-masked anger.

"Are you coming with us?" Claire had asked hopefully.

"No, I'll catch up with you. Don't be anxious. There is a plan for good, a purpose that cannot be thwarted, in spite of everything." She kissed Karl, Patrick, and Claire on both cheeks quickly before the three raced for the gate. Then she yelled after Claire: "You look *great* in that color! *Akan mukav tut le Devlesa!*"

What did that mean again? Claire had thought. Something about going with God. Well, she was going with Karl Burgmann and he sure went around acting like he was God — some Old Testament God of retribution. Weren't priests these days supposed to be loving and understanding and comforting, like, like he was now with Rose McCullum — another widow in this whole sordid and bizarre mess? She was jealous of Rose.

It was a feeling hard to sustain, however, as Mrs. McCullum's attention turned immediately back to Patrick and her. "You poor, poor dears!" she said, reaching for them together. "What you've both been through!"

Claire was surprised to find her smelling of cigarettes and wine. She'd presupposed a mixed scent of mothballs and talcum powder.

"Well, we're not going to *mope about* now, are we?" Rose said this with resolve enough for everyone, smoothing her dress and adjusting her cardigan. Then she patted Patrick's head and spoke directly to him like an old friend.

"Why don't the two of us go look around this place for a place to put your bags and then we'll see if there is anything to eat." A wilted Patrick perked up a bit at the invitation and followed his newest admirer up the stairs.

Claire turned toward Karl reluctantly. "This isn't the McCullum's home, then? I knew it wasn't the same place I'd visited with Michael years ago, but I thought they'd moved."

"We are outside of Dublin. I didn't feel Rose was safe in her former home, so I had Stephan move her here for now." There was kindness in his voice again and in his eyes as he looked at her. But it didn't stop Claire from expressing the resentment and frustration she was feeling.

"You move us all around like chess pieces. You and James Day — the two Master Minds."

Karl sank down wearily into a chair. He suddenly looked exhausted, vulnerable, human. She had wounded him, somehow.

* * *

Grace O'Brien Daly hung up the phone on her bedside table.
"Who the hell was that?" her husband mumbled sleepily.
"Oh, just a prank call …"
Grace sat up on the edge of her bed.
"What are you doing now?"

"I'm going down to have a glass of warm milk. Don't you worry yourself. Go back to sleep." John Daly was already snoring as she got up and went to her closet to get dressed. She tiptoed back to her nightstand and quietly got her rosary out of the little drawer and put it in her pocket.

At the cluttered desk downstairs in the living room she wrote a note and sealed the envelope. She addressed it to her husband and placed it on the table in the front hallway. She picked up her white leather purse (even though Labor Day had passed, she had been distracted and hadn't switched to navy or black) and went out the door of the old red brick house, closing it softly behind her.

Chapter 40

Urim and Thummin were gemstones that could be cast as lots in determining God's reply to questions of national interest to Israel ... or whereby guilt and innocence might be ascertained and the will of God discovered.
     Harper Study Bible commentary on Exodus 28:30

The Power and shape no living creature knows
Have pulled the Immortal Rose.
          William Butler Yeats

Theo Kostanikas had not taken his medication when Day had forced it into his hand. He had hidden it his cheek, an old trick from the hospitals. He had never used it much, though a lot of patients did.

Some of the time he was glad to slow the relentless activity of his mind and body — but not now. He knew Day thought he was sleeping. He took his notebook and crept out into the hallway. He entered the room where the *Golem* was — the metal and crystal and wire into which the soul had entered. Von Neumann would be happy; two Jewish boys helping to carry out his plans. He hadn't seen one for awhile, but the other one, the annoying one, Fifkin or Rifkin, no Pifkin — he was always in the way.

None of these boys were any match for the great ones at the Institute. They would have been eaten alive at Fine Hall. They had no substance; he could literally see right through them. They were transparent bags of wind, with tiny little mechanical brains. Their flesh had become words and codes and every time they touched a computer they lost another piece of themselves. It escaped through their fingers, into the keys and on into the world wide web of nothingness. It was like screwing a barren whore whose womb was a dry, cracked, brittle shape that dissolved like the round ash of his neglected cigarette.

He entered the room and heard the soft hum of the computer. He sat down at the terminal and punched in the code to open the program. A light flashed red and a message appeared on the monitor.

ACCESS DENIED.
"What the hell is going on, you can't deny me!"

He cleared the screen and tried the code again. The same ridiculous thing happened.

"Day's had his Jews tinkering again!" He lit a cigarette and a strange smile appeared on his face as he left the room.

* * *

Claire did not attend the small private Mass for Ian McCullum. She really didn't feel well and Rose seemed to understand. Patrick wandered down the stairs, absent-mindedly dragging his backpack behind him. It clunked loudly on each step. Claire was reading an Irish newspaper and lamenting the collapse of the peace accord when he began his descent.

"Patrick! Pick up the pack. You'll break the things inside!" She spoke rather sharply.

Patrick continued to drag the pack and didn't answer her. She looked up from the paper and at him again. He looked sad and tired. It wasn't like him. But of course, it would be natural for him to feel that way. She was just so used to his boundless energy and renewable resources. She put the paper down and went over to him.

Claire picked up the pack and took her son by the hand. As she led him over to the worn sofa, she noticed that he was limping again. The 'parlor', as Rose called it, was sparsely furnished with random odds and ends and rather drab. And the sun hadn't shone since they arrived in Ireland. She laid the backpack on the floor and pulled Patrick to her side as she sat down.

"What is it, little boy? You don't look so good. You don't feel sick or anything do you? Does your foot hurt?" She took off his shoe and sock. The bruise on his heel was dark blue again and seemed worse than ever, yet that snake-stomping incident had been months ago. It had never really gone away, though he hadn't complained about it at the convent. He felt a little feverish, as well.

"*Patrick!* Does your foot hurt?" Maybe she'd better take him to a doctor. "Why aren't you answering me? Are you mad at me or something?"

"I miss Grandma, and I know Daddy said not to worry, but I'm worried about Grandma."

"Honey, Grandma is fine. We've talked to her lots of times since we left. She sounded fine, didn't she?" Her mother was in fairly good health. She'd had some heart trouble in the past, but Dr. Quinlan had found the right medicine. She was puzzled by Patrick's new concern.

Patrick reached for the backpack and pulled out a little pad of paper. He opened it to a special page and showed it to Claire.

"Is this the poem you wrote about Grandma and me?"

It was titled *Momy and Grama*, so it was kind of a silly question, but he ignored it.

"Mother Mechtilde said it was very good," Claire said, trying to cheer him before the act of reading it herself.

"I finished it today," he said, handing it to her. Some of the letters weren't written correctly and the spelling was his own brand. "Read it out loud." he asked her.

Momy and Grama by Patrick O'Connell

Momy is a goldan qwene and Grama is a silvar wheel.
Dady is up in heaven, so they help me feel.
They make me spesial.
Sometimes I see things that are very brite,
Shining things that go up in the nite.
Momy dusent see Grama in her nu dress,
But I can see a big mess.
I am lik the sun crying wen it is dark
The tirdrops are stars faling in the oshun.
Wirds are flying in the ar after us.
We better find Jesus.

Claire was moved by his thoughts and though she had no idea what it all meant, she did know he was trying to express some deep pain or fear that his five-year-old mind couldn't articulate. She didn't speak for a minute, but held him close.

"I didn't spell right or rhyme everything, but Mother Mechtilde said that was okay. Are you sad now?" He looked up into her eyes, which held her own tears.

"I feel sad for you, Patrick, that you've had to go through so much stuff in your short life."

She looked at the poem again. "Did you mean to say 'the *words* are flying' instead of 'the *birds* are flying'? She pointed to the line. Patrick nodded. He was silent and staring off in the distance toward the darkly curtained window.

Claire wondered why he would have thought words were after them, but she didn't ask. The imagery about tears, and stars and the ocean seemed familiar somehow. "How did you think of all this?"

"It's kind of like a dream," he answered. She felt his head again. He still felt feverish. "Can we call Grandma?"

"Maybe when Karl gets back, we can. And we might have to go to a doctor and see if you're sick."

Patrick got up from the sofa and slowly went to a closet by the front door. He came back with a chess board and set it on the table by them. "Auntie Rose said I could use this if I wanted. She found it when she was looking for an umbrella."

Auntie Rose? Claire thought. *Well, whatever. Why not? Who knew when he'd see his real family again.*

Patrick pulled the chess pieces out of his pack one by one and set them in their proper positions on the board. It seemed an effort for him and Claire offered to help, but he insisted on doing it himself. When he was finished he lay down on the sofa with his head in Claire's lap, his eyes on the game. He leaned over and plucked the exquisite White Queen from her square and held her close to his chest and soon fell asleep.

As she sat stroking Patrick's warm head, looking at the board herself; she sensed the strangeness that had frightened her that night after their return to Chicago from South Carolina. The feeling had turned to an awful unnamable dread. She wished now that her parents would show up again. She missed them.

A key turned in the door and it opened to the voices of Karl and Rose.

They noticed Patrick sleeping and quieted themselves. After shaking the rain from their coats and hanging them in the closet, they sat down in chairs on either side of the sofa.

"Oh, my *goodness!* That looks like *Ian's* chess set! Where did you find it?" Rose asked, lighting a cigarette. "Do you mind, Claire? I've been smoking in my own room, but I've had a day. Well, you know."

"No, it's fine, really. This set is one that Michael gave to Patrick last Christmas."

"Well, then Ian must have given it to Michael," she said, picking up the pieces and examining them, "because I don't believe there is another set like it. It's very *old,* you know. Ian got it from a Traveller a while back in a pub in somewhere in the West … Excuse me please. I'll be right back. Would anyone else like a glass of wine?"

"Sounds good to me, Rose. Claire?" Karl reached over to touch Patrick's head.

"Sure, I'll have one. Thanks, Rose," she called, turning back to Karl. "I think he may have a fever. Do you think we need to call a doctor?"

"Can he take aspirin?"

"Chewables, but I don't have any."

"Chewable what?" Rose asked as she returned with a bottle under her arm and three glasses.

"Aspirin. He may have a fever." Karl answered. "I will go out and try to find some."

"Don't worry. When he wakes up I have just the thing." She poured them each a generous glass of white wine.

"So some stranger in a pub just gave away these beautiful things?" Claire asked, returning to the subject.

"He wasn't a stranger. Ian had been meeting with him for some time. He was a Traveler, an Itinerant, you know … an Irish gypsy."

Claire nodded as she was reminded of the term.

"He knew the 'tongue', *misog,* the secret language, better than anyone Ian had ever met. They are *very* mysterious pieces. Ian said they had a power of their own. I am surprised that Michael would have given them to Patrick to play with at such a young age."

Karl entered the conversation again. "Michael didn't know, Rose, that he wouldn't be around to watch over Patrick."

"Of course, he didn't." She blew out a big puff of smoke and sipped her wine.

"Did Michael know that the pieces had ... special properties?" asked Claire.

Rose almost spoke again but let Karl answer instead. "I'm sure that Ian would have told him — at least the legends and beliefs that have grown up around them. And Michael knew, too, of the way the ancient Celts felt about board games."

"And what was that?"

Rose took over after another healthy sip. "They believed that these games were a paradigm of life, that what happened in the game was connected to a greater cosmic reality. *Brandub* and *Fichell* were two popular board games, very similar to chess. *Fichell* means 'wooden wisdom' in early Irish."

Claire was stunned that Rose knew so much about it all. She did not fit the image of a typical faculty wife of her generation. "How is it that you're so informed about these things? Have you studied as well?" she asked.

"Oh heavens no! I can't *bear* the research process. Endless interviews and rustling through dusty books and manuscripts! I learned about everything from my talks with Ian. He was a *wonderful* teacher, even with *me*." A quick wistful look drifted across her face like the shadow of a cloud. She took another drag from her cigarette.

Claire was silent as she thought about Michael and their parallel lives. She felt again the deep sadness that had come upon her in his study when she realized how much of himself he had kept within its walls. An irrevocable sense of loss attempted to fill her chest. Her heart burned at its demanding and imminent invasion. She imagined Ian and Rose nestled for long years on a worn sofa like the one she now sat upon, sharing their lives freely with no false illusions of autonomy. Claire took a deep breath and another sip of wine.

"Both of you are Catholics, right?" Claire asked. "Surely, you don't believe that there is some kind of mystical power in a board game, or did I *really* miss something in Catholic school?"

"Catholics believe in a supernatural world," Karl said, "that is present simultaneously with the natural one. We believe in the real power of good and of evil. Sacramental theology says that physical objects can be imbued with spiritual properties — water, wine, bread; oil …. The Church has even been accused in some parts of the world for not taking a firmer stand against popular customs, native beliefs and indigenous practices. When dealing with mysteries I think it is very hard for an individual to judge." Karl looked intently at the chess game. Rose picked up where he left off.

"That's why St. Patrick was so successful with us Irish. He spoke blessings and curses with the best of the druids. He respected them and their power and they came to respect him. Christianity fit in beautifully with their system. There was no bloody war. The war was in the heavens and Patrick enlisted a lot of allies. He left us our legends and our bits of magic and little people."

"That's very nice and you're quite a team, but neither one of you has really given me an answer about this game. Do you really think God lets people decide things using some arbitrary pastime?"

"God allowed Jacob to use a wrestling match with an angel to decide his fate, at which point he was named Israel," said Rose, sitting up straighter with a look of accomplishment on her face.

"The Apostles used a game of chance to decide who would take the place of Judas the Traitor in the apostolic ministry, one of the most elevated positions in the Church," Karl added.

"There are also the *urim* and *thummin* — or some such," Rose added.

"There's still discussion over that," said Karl, waving his hand in a cautionary gesture.

"And where did you find all *this* out? In some hidden cave in near Jerusalem? Or maybe in the West of Ireland?"

"It's in the Bible," Rose said, lighting another cigarette and pouring some more wine.

"No way!" Claire said, looking to Karl for support.

"Yes, she's right."

"Man, you two ought to go on the road. Be traveling evangelists or something. You work well together."

Rose started laughing at the thought and in spite of everything Karl and Claire joined her. It was a release for them all.

Karl felt Patrick's head again. "He still feels warm, Claire. Maybe we should wake him and let Rose give him her potion."

"Potion, go on now, it's just some aspirin crushed with honey."

"What's he got in his hands there?" he asked.

"It's the white queen. He set up the whole game and then took her off the board. She's his favorite, I think."

Karl's cell phone rang in his pocket. He slipped it out and stood up. Patrick stirred.

"*What?*" Karl exclaimed, his usually inscrutable face showing alarm. "For how long?"

Claire and Rose both looked at him waiting for a clue. He handed the phone to Claire, saying as calmly as he could, "It's your sister Franny. Your mother is missing."

Chapter 41

Love children, too, for they are sinless like angels, they live to soften and purify our hearts and, as it were, to guide us. Woe to him who offends a child.
Fyodor Dostoevsky

The electronic age ... angelizes man, disembodies him. Turns him into software.
Marshall McLuhan

Herb Pifkin walked among the small cage-like cribs where some of the small bodies slept. Others of them rocked back and forth. Everything was clean and attendants were in abundance. It was a lab, not a hospital. And these were not rats or nor even babies confined in these spaces, but children ... some as old as seven or eight. A few cried or whimpered softly. One Chinese boy would not be silenced.

"I wan geddout! I wan geddout! You bad manyu! *You baaaad!*" he screamed over and over again as he banged the mesh enclosure with his fists.

"Inject him! Will you *please!*" Pifkin yelled at the woman in the blue uniform nearest the boy.

"I have, Mr Pifkin. It hasn't taken effect yet." She looked around at other workers, perhaps for support, but they all moved briskly about, avoiding eye contact with her or anyone else.

"Then give him a stronger *dose*, for Christ's sake! How can you work with this noise?" Pifkin put his hands to his ears and walked among the cribs peering in certain ones more intently than others.

The woman in blue shook her head, reached for another syringe, and walked toward the boy. He was small, dark-haired on the left side of his head, but with the other side shaved; a tiny strip of skull-bound metal gleamed in the bright lights. His right leg and arm twitched as he called out, the Downs-look unmistakable in his eyes and mouth.

"I-I-I wan gedo-u-u-u ..." His voice trailed off slowly and his limbs became still before the woman reached him.

"Where's the girl who had the sensory implants? And where's the surgeon? I told him to meet me here an hour ago!" Pifkin addressed the room at large.

When no one answered, a large doughy-faced man in a white lab coat stepped forward and looked at a clipboard in his hand. "Dr. Gray was here and took the girl to examine the implant sites approximately …" he looked at his watch that was on his wrist too tightly and divided his hand from his arm like the string on a sausage, "… nineteen minutes ago."

James Day stormed into the relatively quiet room. "*Pifkin!* Where the hell have you been? We need you! Come now, it's urgent!"

The two men hurried out the metal laboratory door, slamming it shut behind them.

* * *

Theo sat in his darkened designated room as if under siege. The door was locked from the inside and for safety he had pushed several empty boxes in front of it. He sat at his own computer and pulled from his pocket something wrapped in an old handkerchief. He held it in his hand and laughed aloud.

"You thought you could deny access to me? You dirty bastard! I knew you were in it with the rest of them — the Jews and the World Defense Department and Rand … taking away my security clearance! But now the Angels and the Daemons know me, the Electrons know my name and *you* thought you could control *us!*" He laughed again, this time coughing violently as he pulled on his cigarette.

He put the cigarette down in the overflowing ashtray and carefully laid his soiled package on the desk.

The weight of his mission was heavy on his sagging shoulders. He was tired of the years — the long years of fighting, of running, of fear and confusion … and the *Voices*, the unceasing chatter. He had tried to stop it all once, but someone found the gun, hidden in his pants. Who was it? His wife? No she never looked in his pants. Did he have a wife? Was the gun still there? He felt the inside of his thigh. His hands were numb or maybe his leg. He couldn't feel himself at all.

He looked again at his desk. Everything was flat. He had drifted into two dimensions again. It was all a ruse — space, time, matter. He had caught them setting up the scenery once — trying to pass it off as the world — what did they take him for, an idiot?

Kostanikas reached toward his package and unwrapped it with ceremony, one corner at a time. The disc glowed in the light from his monitor. He lit another cigarette and left it in his mouth. Then carefully with both hands he lifted the disc to eye level.

"Did you really think, Mr. Day, that I would leave my work in your hands alone? After all this? *This* is the one you want! The other is only a fake. This is the Intelligence that will break through the Net. *The Majestic Intellect, its acts and its possessions, what it has and craves. I have our 'Word's worth!"* Now all we need is the boy to see what the Word is worth." He laughed again at his own joke in a high-pitched cackle.

"Well, Michael, speak to me now and tell me not to be afraid. Isn't that what all the Angels say in the damn Bible?" He winced, as if expecting to be stricken, and chanced a sideward glance in either direction. Everything was a line, a lateral association of weightless information. He stomped his foot on the tile floor.

"*Where is the deep time?*" He yelled as he slapped his foot frantically on the floor, trying to break through the crust of the flat Earth. "Where is the vertical sediment, the weight of it all?"

Theo inserted the disc and watched as thousands, no millions of codes flashed and scrolled across down the screen. He began a mournful litany, his face flickering:

> "O *Hippasus, fellow Greek, drowned for belief in the irrational number!*
> O *Augustine and Aquinas with magnitudes of souls and everything out of nothing!*
> O *Hardy, Godel, and Penrose and Papa Plato!*
> O *Hilbert and Lefschetz, with your pathetic wooden hands!*
> O *Turing and Gypsies and Navajos who won the war only to die in camps and reservations!*
> O *Einstein and Mobius and Newton!*
> O *Great Reiman and Heisenberg, certainty without proof and proof without certainty!*
> O *John Von Neumann and Higgs, O Higgs, as your particles break the symmetry that traps the hidden world inside Quanta!*
> *You waited with longing to see this day!*

Oh ye Prophets and Saints, watch this now as the Beast races toward Bethlehem to devour the flesh of the Child!"

The smoke from the cigarette between his lips rose like incense before the altar.

* * *

Ashen-faced, Claire got up from the sofa to take the phone from Karl. As she did, the White Queen fell from Patrick's hand and he awoke with a cry.

"There, there, son. It's alright." Rose stepped over and sat in Claire's place. She brushed the moist hair from Patrick's forehead and patted his back. "Here now, here's the Queen. She's just fine."

Patrick reached out and took the chess piece in his hand again and looked at his mother.

Claire turned from him, not wanting him to search her face and read it as he always did. She left the parlor and began walking toward the kitchen. "Franny, what's going on? Mom is missing? What do you mean? Where's …?"

"Mommy you can't leave! I want to know about Grandma! I know she's in trouble!"

Claire walked back to the parlor, not sure what to do. She remembered Patrick's concern about her mother even before they got the phone call. She would stay near him. Standing behind the sofa, looking down into his face, she heard Franny's voice on the other end.

"Is Patrick okay, Claire? Is he crying? Oh my God! This is such a mess!"

"Patrick's okay, Fran, just tell me about Mom."

"Well, Daddy called me about four o'clock this morning to say that he couldn't find Grace. He woke up and she wasn't in bed. So he got up to see what she was up to and he couldn't find her anywhere in the house."

"Have you checked with her friends or the rest of the family? I know it's not like her to just leave like this, but have you asked anybody?"

"No, but …"

"You didn't check with anyone in Chicago? You have to call me in Ireland to help you know where Mom is?" She looked at Patrick and felt his disappointment in her response.

"You're in *Ireland*? I didn't know where the hell you were! I just called the number that Danger Mouse gave me in case of emergencies. And I don't think you should go off at me when I've been holding down the fort here and you have no *idea* what's …" Franny's voice broke.

Claire felt a sharp sinking in her stomach. She knew that her mother was not with friends or family. "Have you called the police then? Filed a missing persons report or something? Where's Dad? What is he doing?"

"Dad's right here next to me. This is what I've been trying to tell you. Mom left a letter that Dad found."

"Let me talk to Dad."

"Dad's kind of out of the loop about everything and wants me to handle this. I've filled him in as best I could about your secret life, but … anyway, the letter says;

Dear John,

If you find this it means I didn't get back. I don't want you to worry. I've had my suspicions about Claire and Patrick and I need to do some investigating. I knew you wouldn't want me to do this, but I had to. That's all there is to it! If you talk to Claire, tell her not to let Patrick out of her sight! Do you hear me, John? Not for a minute! There's things that no one knows. But you remember that Scripture from the Rosary about "the truth being laid bare." Pray real hard John, and talk to Claire as soon as you can. And don't call the police or all the family. It's not something that can be handled like that.

You are the best husband a woman could ever have. I love you and I always will.

Grace

John Daly sat next to his youngest daughter with a look of lost bewilderment, rubbing his large hands together. Franny could barely stand to look at him. She put her arm around his shoulder.

"Why is she doing this? What is she talking about, *things nobody knows?*" Claire felt helpless and frustrated.

Franny did not respond to Claire's rhetorical questions. Karl asked if Franny would read the letter to him. Claire handed over the phone to him and began to cry.

Rose McCullum beckoned her over to the sofa where she and Patrick sat. "Come, Dear, We'll find your mum. Claire resisted her independence and sat down next to Rose.

"This is a nightmare! How did we all get involved in this?" She asked wearily.

Rose spoke with a faraway look in her eye:

"Well, I don't know if this is a comfort, but we're involved in it from the day we're born and it's not just us. There's *always* a battle going on or at least a struggle. Sometimes it's obvious and sometimes it's subtle. Sometimes there are bombs falling outside your window and sometimes there's an unseen war in heaven over a little choice you have to make. But we're *all* involved …" she paused to fluff the skirt of her silk dress and then patted Claire and Patrick simultaneously. "We're all involved."

* * *

Claire woke early the next morning after a fitful sleep. Karl had convinced her to get some rest with Patrick and she agreed to lie down with him in their upstairs bedroom. Patrick was fitful, too, tossing and turning and groaning. Finally at about dawn his fever seemed to break and he settled down. Claire didn't realize she had been asleep until she woke to noises of activity downstairs.

When she entered the parlor she saw that one end of it had been transformed into a computer station and she recognized Steve's back and shoulders as he sat punching keys and clicking his mouse. Just as she was about to greet him, the front door opened and in walked Mara.

"*Claire!* It is so good to see you!" she exclaimed, kissing her on both cheeks.

"You too! It's *really* good to see you. Have you heard about my mother?"

"Oh yes! We've been on it since last night. Here, let's go to the kitchen and have some scones I got down the street and some strong Irish tea." She nudged Claire toward the kitchen, carrying a brown paper package in her hand.

"Hello, Claire!" Steve called, not taking his eyes off his screen. "Don't worry; we're kicking some butt here. Go Irish!"

It took Claire a minute to realize he was referring to their common *alma mater* rather than the Irish-Irish.

"You're not watching a stupid football game on that thing, are you?" asked Claire.

"No, No! I'm sorry," he said laughing. "I always let out the fight yell when I get pumped. Just habit I guess." He never did take his eyes off the screen.

She followed Mara into the kitchen. "Where are Karl and Rose? I guess they're still asleep, huh? It's still pretty early, isn't it?" Claire realized she hadn't seen her watch in awhile. She'd have to remember to look in her bag. She couldn't bear to think she had lost another gift from Michael.

"It's about six thirty, I think. You should know by now that Karl doesn't sleep a lot. He and Rose went out last night and haven't come back yet. She's helping him with something."

Mara moved about the kitchen. She always looked beautifully pulled together, Claire thought. She herself, on the other hand, felt grimy and jet-lagged.

"Rose is helping him? He sends me off to bed where I lay awake all night and worry and he takes a woman twice my age off on some mission to find my mother! That's what they're doing, right? Trying to find out what happened to my mother?"

"I think he was concerned about Patrick and thought it best that you stay with him. Don't get upset, Claire, I mean not about Karl. You really need to see that he cares a lot for you and stop your defensiveness about him. This was something that only Rose could do. I know that you are worried about your mother and about Patrick. Is he any better today?"

Mara had laid out the scones, with cream and jam and hot cups of tea.

Claire drank from her cup. "Yes, I think his fever broke and he was sleeping soundly when I left him. I'm sorry, about getting angry. I never react well in stressful situations and I've been defensive my whole life, I think, so it's nothing personal."

"Well, it's absolutely not true that you don't handle stress well. Dear God, Claire! What you've been through these last months! And here you are, fairly sane and intact, and being a wonderful mother to Patrick."

Claire started to tear up like she always did when people were kind to her, but she stuffed a bite of scone in her mouth instead and spoke with crumbs falling out: "So what was it that Rose was going to do?"

"They were going to Ian's office at the University to see if they could find out how to get hold of that Itinerant who knew some *Misog*. The one who gave Ian the chess set?" Claire nodded.

"They looked around here through Ian's things but there was nothing. Rose said she thought for sure that Ian had said he had died. But they want to explore every lead."

"But what does *Misog* have to do with my mother?"

"Well, we don't know that it does directly but there are some notes of Ian's that he took while he was undercover written in 'the tongue' as they call it and then there is Michael's note –the one that you found. And without the full lexicon —"

"*Wait a minute!* I just thought of something. Michael published that lexicon as his doctoral thesis! Doesn't the University here or maybe even Notre Dame or Northwestern — doesn't *anyone* have a copy of it?"

"Karl looked at those places right away. All the copies are missing."

"So do you think these people already have it? Then why are they after us?" Claire asked.

"We believe Michael probably destroyed them when he realized that *The Golden Hammer* would use them for ill."

"I can't believe that he would have destroyed all those years of work!"

"We don't think so either, really. We just haven't found what clues he left for us."

"Did Michael know he was going to die, Mara?" Claire asked

directly.

"I don't know if he knew when or how, but I think he knew that he was in great danger."

"Why didn't he tell me? Why all the secrecy? I feel like I didn't even know him. Like I didn't even know my own husband! It was all my fault." Claire began to cry. She grabbed the white cloth napkin from her lap and pushed on her eyes. "I closed him off. I agreed to our leading almost separate lives. I got cold when he mentioned religion at all. I remember a few times over the years when I think he wanted to tell me things. He had that look in his eyes like he did when he first came back from Ireland — the pain behind the easy smile. I don't know why …" She began to sob again. "I was so *afraid*, afraid of his weakness … my weakness? I don't know."

"You knew Michael, Claire. You knew him because he loved you more than any man I've ever known can love a woman. You were everything to him. He told me about falling in love with you in the second grade and some boy named Brian who he punched in the face because he danced with you."

Claire laughed as she wiped her eyes and her nose. "He *punched* Brian McCarthy? I never knew that! Poor Brian. No wonder he always ran the other way when he saw me."

"There was a part of Michael's life that he kept from you and your lives might have been better had he not. Who's to say now? But don't say you didn't know him. You had the gift of growing up with him, of watching him change from a boy to a man, of being his wife, sharing his bed, bearing his son. All he was going to be was there like a seed when you first met. Just like you can get glimpses of Patrick as a man even now."

"Do you see that too? I didn't know if anyone else noticed …"

Mara smiled and went on. "Things happened to Michael, dreadful things. They happen to a lot of us. But that part of us deep inside, who we really are, doesn't change. I guess what I'm talking about is the *soul*, the eternal soul. You and Michael loved each other on that level … even if you don't go along with the language I'm using."

"No, that's okay. I appreciate what you're saying … Thank you."

After a short silence Claire spoke again: "You probably were thinking of Karl, too, when you were talking about dreadful things happening to people. I learned about his mother and how he was rescued by your grandparents."

"Did he tell you?"

"No, no. It was Mother Mechtilde, when I was on one of my rampages of self-pity and resentment of people who had easy lives. I don't think I ever told you — I'm embarrassed to say it — that I resented you when I first saw you. I thought you were part of the jet set bunch, growing up in wealth with never a care in the world."

"Well," said Mara, letting her dark shiny hair fall out of its clip and onto her shoulders, "I think Karl thinks now that many good things came out of the evil that touched his life. Rather than dwelling on the horror of that time, he is thankful for the many good people who risked their lives to help him — my grandparents, Mother Mechtilde and the other Sisters, the Burgmans and others all along the way. I think of my life that way, too. My uncle Kodo took me in and so did his wife Petchi, and treated me as their own. It was not easy for them to have another mouth to feed.

When I wanted to leave the Gypsy life, Karl begged Grandfather and Uncle Kodo to let me go to Catholic School in France, where I met more good people and then someone ... I believe it was Karl although he will not say ... made it possible for me to attend a small private college in New York. All of these things were gifts to me that I am thankful for."

"Do you mind my asking what happened to your parents?" Claire asked hesitantly.

"I did not know for a long time, because I was very young when it happened." She began to clean up the breakfast things, her back to Claire.

"If you don't want to tell me that's okay, I'm sorry if I was intruding."

"It's alright. I can tell you." She sat down again at the small table. The morning outside the kitchen window was gray and drizzly again.

"When I was about four years old, about Patrick's age, my father left my mother and I and never came back. I found out later that he had run off with a *gaje* woman and left the Gypsies altogether. My mother was very upset. She was very fragile, like a child or a doll. She could not bear the disgrace or the pain and she took her own life by jumping off a cliff into the sea in California."

Claire winced and put her hand on the young woman's back. "I'm sorry, so sorry. And your father died, too? I remember Holz saying that your father was dead."

"Yes. Karl had gone to look for my father. They had been friends through the years and he was concerned for my mother and for me. He found my father in an awful, filthy place in Boston — not even living with the same woman he had left with but with another. They both were drinking quite a lot and got into a fight. When Karl came to he found my father dead and he called the police and turned himself in. He spent five years in prison for manslaughter. It was there he made the decision to become a priest."

Claire felt even more depressed. She stood up and looked out at the rain. "Life is just a big screwed up mess! And we're all connected somehow and we screw each other up even more than we already are! None of it makes sense. It's random and irrational connectedness." She looked down at Mara, who was as quiet as stone. "Rose says we're all involved. Yeah, we're all involved alright! Involved in what? A big screwed up mess!"

* * *

A thunderous knocking on Theo's door made him jump. He heard muffled voices outside and then he heard one voice above the rest: *"Open this goddam door, you bastard, or we'll blow it off!"*

Theo sat where he was. He tuned out the noise. He was transfixed by the image on his screen.

"There it is!" he whispered hoarsely. "The circuitry of the brain, the hard-wiring of the soul, the program of the universe!" His voice grew louder as he continued: "The entire world in a grain of sand — silica dioxide to be exact. It's the *Pathway — the Gate.* It's what Einstein was hinting at. The deeper you go inside and the smaller you get, the farther you go *outside.* In and out are the same thing! The *nervous system, the ley lines, the electron paths!* It's all connected. My testicles could be the moons of Jupiter and my stream of

consciousness the Jordan River, for Christ's sake!

What shone on the monitor appeared as an elaborate pulsating video game maze of patterns and circuits that was falling in upon itself at such a speed that the movement was almost imperceptible.

"*Now I will see if I, the Emperor, with my hand can make a move in this game!*" Theo was yelling by this time.

A small explosion and then a crash sent the old man flying off his chair and onto the floor. The door from the hallway hung on its hinges. In the thick smoke stood Treat O'Toole and James Day. Theo scrambled quickly back up to the desk and hit the keyboard with one finger before the two men could find their way to him.

"Alright, you whiny little Greek bastard! We've had enough of you!" O'Toole clutched roughly under the old man's arm and jerked him up. "*How dare you* come in here and lock us out!" He struck Kostanikas across the face full force with the back of his hand. There was a snap like brittle wood breaking. The old man cried out and put his hand to his cheek. Blood trickled onto his fingers and onto the cold dead cement floor.

"*Good God, O'Toole* … you've broken his cheekbone! What is the point of this senseless violence? He's no match for you. He's an old man. We've got what we wanted."

He walked over to the computer and looked in the screen. "What is this, Theo? Where is he? Where's Michael?" He tried to sound calm and reassuring.

"Oh, it's the *good heartless dictator/bad heartless dictator* routine, is it!" Theo sputtered in spite of his pain.

"See, Day … you're an idiot! All your coddling this nutcase for all these months and he still mouths off to you." O'Toole moved as if to strike Kostanikas again. Day held out his arm.

"Theo, you need to get some rest and somebody to fix that bump. But first tell me … where's Michael?"

"Either he's in the maze of the game somewhere or the whole thing is inside of him! It's all the same damn thing!" said Theo gruffly. He smiled slyly at O'Toole over Day's shoulder.

Chapter 42

The computer world is taking the material world and making it immaterial ...
Nothing could be more disembodied than cyberspace —it's like having your everything amputated.
                John Perry Barlowe

Material reality as the lowest formation remains in the last resort the foundation of all other reality and therefore undoubtedly the phenomenology of material nature holds a pre-eminent position.
                Edmund Husserl

  Claire flew hurriedly up the stairs, leaving Mara in the kitchen cleaning up and Steve in the parlor, still at the computer. She felt awful. Why was she always taking things out on people who were trying to help her? It all started with her mother. Her mother was always trying to help and usually made things worse. What was she doing now? Why did she have to start investigating and get herself kidnapped? Claire caught herself again. Here her mother was in trouble because she cared about her and Patrick — *so she got mad at her mother*. She felt like an ungrateful jerk. No wonder Mara's mother jumped into the Pacific. It seemed like the sensible thing to do.
  She went into the room where Patrick was still sleeping. She looked down at him. She could never jump.
  She found her overnight bag and looked into its depths to find her watch. It was very important that she find her watch. She didn't care about the time. Her fingers touched the shape of it and pulled it out. The red-haired woman still floated in the sea of time, perhaps like Mara's mother when she rose to the surface of the ocean, her dark Gypsy hair spread out by the water, her broken heart within her broken body. The second hand moved, sadly sweeping over the sun, the moon and the stars, over the form of the mysterious woman.
  Claire's hand had touched something else in her bag. After she clasped her watch onto her wrist she reached again into her bag and got it — a floppy disk. Patrick always asked why it was called a *floppy* disk, since it had none of the casual properties of say, his brown

floppy stuffed dog. She didn't know what to tell him.

Where had *this* come from? She read the label. It was one of the disks from her novel. The only thing she remembered grabbing off her computer table on her way out the door of her house in Chicago on that night was the folder she had found in Treat's office. Well, it was really *Michael's* office and always would be. *Dr. Treat O'Toole, Chairman, Irish Studies* — the lying murdering traitor! *And* sexual pervert, according to Franny. She should have listened to Franny.

So this must have fallen out of that folder into her bag when she was moving things around in one place or another. She couldn't even put a name to all the places she'd been — an abandoned motel Gypsy camp on old un-traveled highway somewhere, back roads through Indiana, a convent near the mountains, a house in Ireland. It was a good thing Karl didn't trust her with any significant information. She probably would have blabbed all to Treat O'Toole.

She ran downstairs again. "Steve, can I check something on there for a minute," she called as she came into the parlor.

"Sure, just a sec while I close this and get offline. What is it?" He turned from the screen for the first time.

"It's a disk I found in my stuff. I think Michael had it, even though it's part of my novel." She blushed slightly as she said 'my novel'. She didn't really think much of it, even though Michael and Franny both liked it. "I just want to see if it has anything on it that's of importance to us."

"Go ahead, pop it in!" Steve got up and let Claire sit at the computer. When the index for the A drive came up, she saw her headings: **ch25, ch26, ch24,** then *Wordsworth*. "What is this Wordsworth thing?" she said, clicking on it and waiting for it to come up. Mara had come in and was standing with Steve behind her.

What came up was familiar. It was *The Prelude*. "Michael must have typed this onto my disk." She was disappointed though. "Doesn't look like anything really new here, guys. Sorry, it's just a poem that Michael liked." She wondered why he had put the whole thing on there. It had been quite a task–fourteen Books or sections. Then Claire noticed something. Certain sentences or phrases were in italics. The first was in Book I, 31:

255

A prophecy: poetic numbers came
Spontaneously to clothe in priestly robe
a renovated spirit singled out.

"Well, there are some things highlighted here that I don't remember Michael pointing out to me before. It might not mean anything, but we can look through it and you can tell me what you think."

Mara and Steve both pulled up chairs and sat on either side of Claire. They looked on as Claire read. Book I was scattered with italics.

I heard among the solitary hills
Low breathings coming after me and sounds
of undistinguishable motion ....

and

But huge and mighty forms that do not live
Like living men, moved slowly through the mind
by Day, and were a trouble to my dreams.

"I do recognize this passage," Claire said and read it aloud again. "It's funny, I don't think day is capitalized here in the original."

"How about putting *James* in front of it." Steve suggested. "It seems to me that your husband's describing what happened to him."

Calling Michael her husband made her feel happy. He *was* her husband. He would always be her husband. She felt a sort of strength from the fact. Book II, 252:

Emphatically such a Being lives,
Frail creature as he is, helpless as frail,
An inmate of this active universe
For feeling has to him imparted power ...

"He might be trying to tell us something, but I can't get it. I mean, I can tell you what he thought Wordsworth was talking about, but how that would have anything to do with James Day and his own murder or anything ..."

"Just keep going and don't get frustrated. I've got some stuff to tell you that might help, after we're done." Steve as he stretched his arms and neck. "Ouch. People weren't meant to sit at computers so much. Let's go for a quick run and come back."

Mara and Claire both looked angrily at Steve. "Just kidding. Come on …" he said, putting his hands up to stop their mock punches to his head and chest. "Go ahead get back to it."

"Book III, 64:

> *O College labors, of the Lecturer's room …*
> *… some fears about my future …*
> *And, more than all a strangeness in the mind,*
> *A feeling that I was not for that hour,*
> *Nor for that place.*

"Okay, he must be talking about being at the university and getting involved with the weird cult. But what's this next line mean?"

> *… the matron temples …*

"I don't get it … keep going though," said Steve.

Claire read on. "Book V:

> *Oh! Why hath not the Mind*
> *Some element to stamp her image on*
> *In nature somewhat nearer to her own?*
> *Why, gifted with such powers to send abroad*
> *Her spirit, must it lodge in shrines so frail?*

"I always wondered if he had a clue about the plan to upload his mind. I think now that he did." Steve sounded sobered at the thought.

"Wordsworth is talking about his fear that some cataclysmic event would wipe out all *books*. It's books he's talking about as frail and perishable." Claire insisted.

"I believe that Michael was talking about himself, Claire." Mara spoke for the first time since Claire's outburst in the kitchen. Claire turned toward her, then looked back at the poem.

> *On poetry and geometric truth*
> *And their high privilege of lasting life …*

"And now comes the whole passage about the Bedouin coming with the stone, which is 'Euclid's Elements,' and the shell, which represents poetry, of course." Claire stopped. "*The chess set!* Why didn't I make the connection before? The Bishops — one's holding a stone and the other a shell …" She got up from the chair and went to the table where Patrick had left the game.

"They must be Bedouins. I always thought they were Cistercian monks … they look so foreboding." Claire picked them up from the board and felt a queer sensation in each hand. She put them back quickly.

"How about Druids?" asked Steve. "Did those spook you just then? They are very strange items, you know."

"I guess they are. Strange that is." Claire stepped away from the game and went back to the computer. "Druids — is that what *you* think?"

"That's what I know." Steve answered with assurance. "Keep going."

"He doesn't have a lot italicized here, though."

"I think it makes the effect all the more dramatic. Look." said Mara.

Mara took over reading. Her voice sounded different than usual, her accent more pronounced.

> *… at the word …*
> *… in an unknown tongue,*
> *which yet I understood …*
> *A loud prophetic blast …*
> *… which foretold*
> *Destruction to the children of the earth.*

A shudder went through them all at the thought.

There were no more italics until Book VII. Claire read again:

> *… all the marvelous craft*

> *Of modern Merlins …*
> *All out-o'-the-way, farfetched perverted things,*
> *All freaks of nature …*
> *… to compose a Parliament of Monsters …*
> *… the mighty City is herself …*
> *… reduced*
> *To one identity, by differences*
> *That have no law, no meaning and no end —*

"That's it, I guess." Claire sighed, scrolling through the rest of the masterwork and finding nothing noted "… A lot of painful imagery, but nothing really that helpful. But at least it wasn't helpful to O'Toole when he looked at it either."

"It's more helpful to us than you think." said Steve. "Let me show you what I've been doing." He got up as if to take over the position at the computer.

"Wait a minute!" Claire looked at the screen intently. "This isn't the right *end* to the poem. I know it so well. It ends by talking about the human mind being a thousand times more beautiful than the earth, 'as it is itself of quality and fabric more divine.' This is different:

> *And if my love would yet gaze into her own superlative prose*
> *She would still find the key to clearest insight.*
> *And unknown tongues that plague the island's light*
> *Would fly into her arms where I would wish to be.*

"Michael must have written this himself … to me, hoping I'd read it. It must be my *novel*. He wants me to look in my writing for something. I didn't look through my own chapters."

She went back to the disk file and clicked on **ch24** and looked at words she had not read since she wrote them last year. She was embarrassed to have Steve and Mara looking over her shoulder and she skimmed through the pages rather quickly.

"Are you sure you are not missing anything there?" Mara asked.

"Nope. Just my scribblings, or tappings I guess you'd say."

Toward the end of **ch27** they all exploded at once. "Whoa, hold on there!" Steve called out. "What's that?" Mara said. And of course Claire was most eloquent with "Holy shit!"

Here was an entire page of tiny indecipherable markings, and then another.

Steve asked if he could take over at the controls. Claire obliged him, squinting at the screen.

"If it's what I think it is, we'll be able to read it in a minute." He clicked a few times, highlighted some of the lines. "Yep. It's four point font, but even at twelve — it's not in English."

"It is "the tongue" … *Misog* … I recognize it!" Mara exclaimed.

"Yes, it does look like that note I found. But we're in the same boat with this. We don't have the lexicon." Claire said.

"Oh, yes we do!" Steve said, his voice filling with excitement as he continued to enlarge the rest of the text. "Whoa, baby!" he whooped. "What we have here … *is* the missing lexicon!"

Claire and Mara both murmured with surprise as they studied the screen in front of them.

"There's no punctuation," Steve noted, "but it's there. *English-Misog*, in alphabetical order.

They all looked together.

able grabalta above swurt across hal afraid agetul again yurt ale slan alive atap all goixil also stes Anne Grunles anus tur anvil smugal apple grula arise gre around sula ashes sloha …

"I am going to get the note I found in Michael's pocket." Claire said, jumping up and scaling the stairs two at a time. Patrick was still sleeping. *It's no wonder,* she thought as she looked at her watch again quickly. It was only seven forty and he had only been sleeping peacefully for a couple of hours. She found the note in her wallet. It was folded and rather limp. She ran back downstairs and over to where Steve and Mara sat.

"Here it is!" she said, holding it out to them. Her legs felt shaky. She hadn't run in a long time and had almost forgotten about her disease for a few hours. Ignoring the feeling, she sat down as Mara took the note from her.

"We've started to translate the first part of Michael's writing on the disk," Mara said, pointing to the monitor. It's a message to you, Claire." Mara reached over to lay her hand on Claire's. "You're shaking! Are you alright?"

"I think it's just excitement. Yes, I'm okay. What does it say ... the message —?"

Just then the front door opened and Karl walked in with Rose on his arm. The three at the computer turned to welcome them. Rose looked tired and pale; Karl seemed unchanged although they both were dripping with rain as they shook off their coats and hung them.

"You go first!" said Steve. "Then we'll tell you what's up around here." He tried to contain himself, unsuccessfully.

"Well, I'm afraid we didn't come up with what we needed." Karl said, leading Rose over to the sofa.

"We did find the gentleman's name among Ian's things, but nothing about how to locate him. Dear Ian's office is such a mess. I must get over to sort it out soon." Rose began fidgeting nervously with a thread that hung from her sleeve and went on chattering aimlessly. Claire felt a deep sympathy for the older woman who had seemed so strong and courageous the night before but now appeared washed out by the Irish rain and disturbed by the contact with her dead husband's things.

Karl stood next to Rose, rubbing her shoulder. She began to cry softly, pulling her handkerchief out from her expandable watchband. "There now," Karl spoke gently in a deep Germanic timbre. "You need a glass of warm milk and a good rest. Thank you for your help, Rose. You were a splendid accomplice."

She stood up with his help. "Oh, guess you're right. I do feel a bit done in."

The three computer whizzes had left their station and stood near Rose and Karl. There had been a silent and unanimous decision to put her first, no matter what they had discovered.

Mara took Rose's arm and moved toward the stairs. "I'll take Rose up and help her get settled."

"I'll warm the milk." said Karl

"You will not!" Claire insisted. "Even if you don't sleep at least you can sit down and rest. I'll get the milk. Do you want some, too? Or how about some hot tea?" Claire felt extremely good about doing something for Karl. She realized it might be the first time.

He looked at her gratefully. "Tea would be very nice, thank you."

"I'll stay here and make sure he sits still." said Steve.

After Rose was dry and in bed, the other four met in the parlor and sat together while Karl drank his tea. "I think she'll sleep, poor dear." Mara said, sitting lightly on a worn brocade chair.

"I've filled Karl in on what we've found … Okay, I couldn't wait! Time is of the essence, you know!" Steve said, looking defensively at the women. "But we waited for you, Claire" He nodded toward her. "Are you ready for me to read Michael's message to you … first?"

"Yes, I'm ready." They all went over to the computer. She looked at the screen.

Mo gra', Klaihed. The Midrils sridug an tan grimsher. Strofrik nid'es ng'aka beinn napin swurt.
Labi an Luba. An Luba stes fe' a a-mukin gyay mwil a thoo. A fe' nid'es ng'aka beinn a-grat'I Luba.

"Do you want me to read the translation aloud or do you want to read it yourself?" Steve asked.

"I want Karl to read it to me."

Karl took the paper from Steve.

"*My love, Claire: The Devils reign a little time (*Devils is capitalized*). Patrick can no be given up. Hide the Word. (*And Word is also capitalized*) The Word was made flesh and lived with me and you. The flesh can no be made Word!!!!* (Again Word is capitalized in every instance.)

Everyone kept silence, allowing Claire a chance to absorb the message. She did not speak.

"Michael is quoting the Bible, isn't he? Saint John?" Mara asked finally.

"Yes, it's from the first chapter of John's Gospel." Karl answered. "*In the beginning was the Word, and the Word was with God, and* the Word was God. He was in the beginning with God; all things were made through him and without him was not anything made that was made. In him was life, and the life was the light of men. The light shines in the darkness and the darkness has not overcome it." Karl stopped.

"Saint John was using the Greek word *Logos*, meaning reason as the name for Christ himself. Reason … the Word incarnate." He lifted his voice again, almost in a chant. *"And the Word became flesh and dwelt among us, full of grace and truth; we have beheld his glory."* There was silence again. Claire's eyes were locked on Karl's face which was turned slightly upward.

"But I don't think he is just quoting here," said Karl. "Do you, Stephan?"

"No, sir. I certainly do not."

"What about not giving Patrick up and my mother's note about not letting Patrick out of my sight? They know I would never give him up to anyone. Do these people want Patrick for something?"

"Before we try to answer your questions, shall we translate that other note? The one you found in Michael's pocket?" asked Steve.

"Sure," Claire agreed. "Let's get it all done."

Steve had clipped the note to the monitor already.

"Boy, this will take awhile — from *Misog* to English. How did you do the other one so fast?" Claire asked.

"I just scanned the lexicon and put it through my encryption cypher. It pulls up any code that you enter word by word." He typed in the message:

Sreikel, Bin Ain,
Tori mwi'l dumnik stroidan a bin lightie klisp a mam'rum a an sarker.
Grat Masur

He read:

Michael, Great One
Come to me, Sunday morning at daylight break, in the room of the schoolmaster (or teacher's room).
Golden Hammer

"So someone told him to come to Northwestern, it must be, at daybreak in the teacher's room … Wait. Go back to *The Prologue* a minute … one of those highlighted parts about 'a lecturer's room' or something …" Claire stood up and bent over Steve's shoulder.

"There!" she said with agitation. She read it again:

> *'O College Labors, of the Lecturer's room …*
> *… some fears about my future …*
> *A feeling that I was not for that hour,*
> *nor for that place'.*

"He must have written this all after he got the note and before he left that morning. He *did* suspect something terrible. Why did he go?" Claire asked helplessly.

"Mommy, did you find Grandma yet?"

Patrick was on the stairs rubbing his eyes, with his brown floppy dog under his arm.

Chapter 43

Franny repeated her statement, "I want to talk to Seymour," she said.
J. D. Salinger

There is an ordinary reality which suffices as a common denominator for the comparison and ordering of things. But the great reality is another.

Martin Buber

On a perfect Midwestern Indian Summer night in late October, Franny unlocked the back door of Claire's house and pushed it open quietly. She had waited for evening to come again, for darkness to fall. She was dressed all in black, which wasn't a stretch, she realized. But she knew it would help her not to be seen nonetheless.

Francine had phoned Bridget. Her father would not move from his chair in the cluttered living room. He had pulled the telephone over so it sat on the floor by his feet. Franny told her oldest sister that their mother had gone off somewhere to look for Claire and Patrick and that their dad was worried. Franny was restless and frustrated. Her father wouldn't talk to her. It was hours since she'd called Claire and still no word, nothing. She told Bridget she had some important errands to run. Bridget didn't seem too worried. Of course, she had no idea. "I'll make some dinner. Will you be back to eat? Should I set a place for Mom?" She really had no idea.

Fran had decided to look for clues. They always did that in the movies, at least the cool people did. It was the aging 'Oh-I-didn't-know-he-was-still-around' people who just sat and waited. And besides, Dad's cigar smoke was beginning to make her feel sick, so that she didn't even enjoy smoking her own cigarettes. She had to get out into some fresh air and smoke for herself. She never thought she'd feel that way, but driving over to Claire's, she realized that she did.

She and her dad smoking together had always been a thing between them. It had made her feel closer to him — probably because Grace was there to fuss and scold perfunctorily and then quickly accept or forgive (Franny could never tell whether it was pragmatism or kindness that produced the change) their 'sin.' Now Grace was missing. She had smoked half a cigarette and thrown it out the window of her car.

Franny had the idea that Grace had gone to Claire's. She had wanted to get in there ever since Patrick and Claire had left on their "trip". But Karl had left orders that it was too dangerous and she was the one who had to think up the stupid reasons why Grace couldn't set foot in the house. The extermination thing had worked for awhile, but then her ideas got lamer and lamer. Carbon monoxide leak, polyurethane drying on the wood floors, she couldn't even remember them all now. But the last one, which was the low point, was that there were 'indications' that Michael's ghost was haunting the house. "Piffle!" Grace had said. But Franny knew there was enough of the Irish in her to half believe.

Her little flashlight didn't give off much light, but that was the point, right? She didn't want anybody to notice it from outside. It was kind of creepy being in a dark house at night by yourself. Why had she said the thing about Michael's ghost? Why had she even *thought* about it? Then she *did* think about it: If Michael O'Connell was one of the best friends she'd ever had while he was alive and *did* somehow came back from the dead, he'd *still* be one of the best friends she'd ever had. She started talking to him softly as she searched through the kitchen.

"Michael, I know you're probably not here, because if you had the choice between heaven and this dark empty house, I don't know why you'd pick this house. Now *purgatory* and this house? I don't know. I don't really understand purgatory. You tried to explain it to me and I almost got it when we were talking about film editors and about how much of the movie ends up on the cutting room floor, as they say ... and how that's a painful thing for the writers and especially the actor whose whole 'big break' never makes it through editing to the theatre and how that *has* to be done to make the movie the best it can possibly be and everything ..."

She shone the light over toward Claire's work area. Nothing looked disturbed. She looked in the wastebasket for a matchbook from a roadhouse on the way out of town (what exactly was a *roadhouse* anyway? A seedy bar? A seedy motel above a seedy bar?) or a piece of paper on which she could find the imprint of the all-important phone number which would solve the whole case. But the wastebasket was empty, not even any of Claire's crumpled up 'shitty first drafts.' 'Shitty first drafts' made her think of purgatory again. She walked through the first floor rooms, searching tabletops, looking under furniture, checking wastebaskets and talking to her brother-in-law.

"I just don't get why God has to punish anybody. Okay, I know, you said *purify* was a better word. But it is suffering all the same, isn't it?"

Franny started up the stairs, turning off the flashlight because she had the railing and moonlight was shining through the window at the upper landing and she could navigate quite well. She didn't feel spooked at all anymore. "I mean if you think of it like plastic surgery, then it really bothers me. I saw this thing on TV about Debbie Reynolds and her long career and her hard life and everything, but her face was *perfect* — you know, no wrinkles and flaps or droops or anything. And you really didn't think much of it right away, because you're so used to seeing those old actresses like that, until they started interviewing her best friends from high school and stuff who still knew her …"

She looked in the guest room first, switching the flashlight back on as she checked the closet. Then she went into the bathroom. "Michael, I hope you're not in here. If you are, excuse me," she said, pulling down her pants. "I've had way too much coffee today." She saw nothing remarkable in the bathroom.

When she walked into Claire and Michael's room and shone the light around the walls, she gasped slightly. She had not remembered so many icons and religious artifacts. The flashlight illuminated them one by one. Celtic crosses with their intricate patterns and designs, The Blessed Virgin on the night-stand, the famous painting of Saint Michael the Archangel holding a shining sword and the scales of justice (or maybe it was time, she didn't know) treading on the Evil one, Lucifer, who was almost entirely engulfed in flames. Then there was Patrick. She'd always liked this statue of Patrick. It was from Ireland and was very old. Michael had bought it from someone alongside the road near the Croagh. It was not your traditional St.

Patrick, an old man in green vestments with a long white beard that fit in well with the shamrock salt and pepper shakers, but this Patrick was a younger man, muscular. She walked closer to it. It was carved out of stone. The hand at his side was holding several lengths of dead, limp snakes and the other, raised in the air, held a book with a cross. His mouth was open and he was yelling — a blessing or a curse, you couldn't tell, but there was a wild boldness in his eyes that reminded her of Michael. Looking out from behind him was carved a small deer, no doubt because of the *Deer's Cry* poem which her own nephew Patrick had shown her so many times.

"So the thing that struck me about these friends of Debbie Reynolds was that they were all old ladies and *she* wasn't, and they were all the same age …" Franny continued her talk with Michael. "The funny thing was, I liked the old ladies better. They were more interesting with all their wrinkles and puffy eyes and everything. You could kind of see what they'd been through in their lives. Whereas Debbie's face was stuck in this weird mask-like expression."

She looked in the large walk-in closet. *Geez,* she thought, *I know a whole homeless family that would love this space.* She looked on shelves and behind clothing, in pockets. You never know, there could be another *really* important message in a pocket that Claire missed!

"So I guess what I'm saying is that if Purgatory makes us all look like Debbie Reynolds, I don't get the point. I'd rather look like the other ladies with their warts and all. You take Aunt Kathleen, she'd have much more character in her face if she hadn't had those nips and tucks that make her look surprised all the time." She sat down on Claire's and Michael's bed. She flashed the light over to the top of the bureau to see the crucifix she remembered there. It was gone. It came to her that Claire had mentioned something about it missing the night they had to flee with Karl.

"Michael, I really don't know if you can hear me but if you can, help me! And get some of your *old friends* here to help me," she said, skimming the light across the pantheon of saints and martyrs. Just then a name skipped into her mind. The name of a movie that her friend Chad had made her watch one night along with some of the black and white Hitchcocks. It was supposed to be based on a true story and called *The Elephant Man*. She didn't know why she thought of it, but then it made sense. Purgatory was not like Debbie Reynolds having surgery to look younger; but it was like *The Elephant Man* having surgery to look *human*, to look like himself, the real John Merrick. "Well, Michael, thanks. I suppose our souls look a lot more like *The Elephant Man* to God than they look like Debbie Reynolds or Aunt Kathleen with crow's feet!"

Franny went into Patrick's room last. She really missed him. What a great kid he was! She looked around. It was a typical kid's room. Well, not really. He didn't go much for the trendy stuff, so no marketing genius could claim his walls. He mostly had up his own little drawings. She noticed one she hadn't seen. It must have been of her because it was this kind of scaggy looking girl with spiky black hair and a flower on her shoulder. "Oh, my tattoo!" she said affectionately.

She opened Patrick's closet. Another walk-in, but narrower. She almost didn't venture farther, but she saw that the closet was in the shape of an L, which she had never noticed before. Moving to the bottom of the L she shone the light around the corner. She was surprised to see a little altar set up. There was a board on two stacks of books. Across the board was spread a white cloth that seemed to be a pillow case. On the altar was a little cheap plastic statue of Our Lady, the St Patrick Holy Card that Grace had given her grandson on his feast day last Spring, the dry Palm crosses from the Passion Sundays he'd lived through (Michael had always done it for him — this year one of the old men at the Mission had given him one), two never-lit votives (Smart boy, Patrick), a snapshot of Claire and Michael, with a beaming Patrick on his shoulders.

Standing above it all, in the center, propped against the wall, was Michael's crucifix that had been above the bureau.

Franny swallowed hard. She knew it would break Claire's heart to know that Patrick felt that he had to have a secret place to keep these things. She picked up the crucifix and as she did something fell off the back and landed on the floor. She felt around with her hand and found a small cube of wood. She turned the cross over and saw that the piece had fallen out of a hole the same shape and size in the back of the crucifix. Fran looked carefully in the hole, but nothing was there.

Nothing in the entire house gave her any better idea about where Grace might be. She dreaded going back to her father with no clues. After fitting the cube snugly back into its space, she left things as she found them and went downstairs and out the back door.

Chapter 44

The commands you type into a computer are a kind of speech that doesn't so much communicate as make things happen.
Julian Dibble aka Dr. Bombay

They are brilliant, sordid smiles of the devil upon the face of the wilderness, cities of secrecy where each man spies on his brother ... cities through whose veins money runs like artificial blood and from whose womb will come the last and greatest instrument of destruction.
Thomas Merton

An Irish shepherd followed the trail of a stray sheep over the sparse grass and stone of the Burren. It was the second time in a week some of the sheep had wandered this way. He was in sight of the cottage. No one knew what went on there. Through the chill mist he noticed there were cars parked near the place, but the cottage itself seemed empty and nobody about. Someone said it was rich Americans using it on holiday for wild sex parties. Some said (he thought it might have been one of the bloody *Travellers* in the pub) that it was a daft scientist doing experiments and making a monster like Frankenstein. The shepherd laughed to himself. *What local people won't do to generate some excitement in the day to day routine out here.* He thought about all the excitement and violence his country had known and now with the Accord breaking down again ... who knew what would happen? *It's funny how we go about sniffin' out excitement until it blows up in our own back yard, and you might lose a hand or half your face or your only son,* he thought grimly. He, for one, would just enjoy the peace of this day and be glad of it. "Frankenstein!" he harrumphed as he turned with his stray toward the rest of the flock. One day he'd go up to the door, say 'How do ya do?' and put all the rumors to rest.

* * *

"*Your treatment of Kostanikas was inexcusable! We still need him!*" Day shouted at the younger man as they stood in Theo's room. "What if he refuses to help us anymore?" He paced the room nervously.

"You know we don't need him now." O'Toole pointed coldly to Theo's computer. "He's got the whole thing there. Except for the Word from the boy. *That's* who we need and we should have him soon enough. You've gone soft, Mr. Day. What! Have you developed an attachment to your Greek lunatic? Do you miss your wife ... *in bed?*"

"You leave her out of this, you *filthy minded son-of-a-bitch!*" Day continued shouting, his face beet red and sweat dripping off his pudgy undistinguished chin. "I think you are forgetting who's in charge around here!"

"Oh, *am* I now? Oh, yes, I believe it is Dr. Kostanikas." Treat O'Toole smirked sarcastically.

"I was planning to have Theo present when we made the final connection, since he seems to have developed a rapport with Michael." Day pulled out a handkerchief and wiped his chin and forehead.

"Will you stop calling *It* Michael? It's just a machine with human capabilities that happened to have been *borrowed* from someone named Michael!"

"Someone named Michael! Someone named Michael!" Day cried incredulously. "He was a *great man!* We thought he was *the* Great One, remember? *And* he was a colleague of yours!"

"What is this? Sentiment?" O'Toole laughed. "You're the one who sent me over there to watch him ... spy on him! You're the one who okayed the upload and the murder!"

"It was *not* a murder!" Day yelled. "It was a *sacrifice*.It *had* to happen that way or the full power wouldn't have transferred! You know that's what Rabbi Lowe believed and Pifkin, being Jewish himself, of course agreed. If there would have been any other way ... *any other way* for real and lasting peace." James Day sat down looking wistful.

"Kenneth was right. You *do* believe your own lies! If all your political cronies and your mealy-mouthed Peace-Seekers knew even half the truth about you ... The Nobel Prize winner, the Irish Statesmen ..." He began saluting and marching around the room mockingly, "... the poor grieving widower!"

Day turned toward O'Toole, his face a doughy mask with hollow eyes staring through. "That's *enough,* O' Toole. No more of your joking around. We have a sacred mission to accomplish and we can't let personality conflicts interfere."

O'Toole sat down across from him, still smirking through his neatly trimmed beard.

"Fill me in on the current status of the boy," Day asked the younger man.

"He landed in Dublin two days ago with his mother. I still can't believe the luck … that Burgmann practically brought them to us."

"So it is Burgmann who's with them. I've had some interesting talks with him. He's a very clever man, you know. He'd be a great asset … I still have hopes that if all goes as planned he may come over to us."

"Now I *know* you're delusional. But we accept each other's weaknesses to get what we want, don't we, now?"

"Yes, young man, you'll realize as you get older that compromise is a necessary and even noble thing." Day's face remained impassive despite his attempt at modeling integrity. "Go on about the boy."

"Burgmann gave our people the slip when they arrived. He is very clever at that elusive business. But it doesn't matter because we have the old lady to use for bargaining." O'Toole looked at his freshly manicured nails and then picked a bit of lint from his tweed jacket.

"And where is *she* now?"

"Flying across the ocean with one of our friendly tour guides to Shannon and her beloved homeland."

"If for some reason things don't work out with young O'Connell we could try again with …"

"Will you bloody shut up? That was all a mistake. You went soft on that one, too, now didn't you? We'll get the boy and it will all go well. Is Pifkin or McCarthy going to supervise the final connection?"

"I told you I want Theo there in case something unforeseen happens."

"Who'll be the technical supervisor? That's what I mean. Who knows the most already?"

"It would have to be Pifkin. McCarthy still has hints of scruples that could get in the way the greater good."

"Not like us, James. Not like us. Pifkin it is then." He made a note of it on the desk.

"The Circle is gathering tonight, as are the others all over Ireland."

"Not many of *them* know either, do they James, the price of peace?"

"You know most of them couldn't handle it. It's the super-humans that can see the end, the glorious end and not let anything else stand in the way. Some of those involved are intellectuals, but many are just common people, of different ages, who've seen the terrible weaknesses and inconsistencies in the Roman Catholic Church *and* the Church of Ireland. They know the long history of fighting and bloodshed between the two — some have experienced it firsthand. They're sick to death of Christianity and its 'Peace on Earth'. They're ready for a better way."

"Oh yes, James! We all know of the peace in Ancient Ireland. I am the Chairman of Irish Studies at a prestigious American University, remember! We know how the *Firbolgs* were forced into slavery by the *Tuatha De Danann,* and how the *Milesians* split the country in half, north and south and that Eremon, in the north, fought Eber, in the South. And what about the much loved Conor MacNessa who dumped his first wife, Maeve, and married another, leaving Maeve to become Queen of Connaught and set up everlasting hostility in that region?"

O'Toole, speaking fast and furiously, stood up, slipped into an exaggerated brogue, but made no break in his speech.

"And what of the great Cuchullain, the darling of the Revivalists who battled his own brother Ferdiad, and then died with him? And I could go on and on. Not to mention the practice of keeping the bloody severed head of your enemy for days on end, stinking on a pike … But that's what you've done with O'Connell now, isn't it? It's a lot cleaner nowadays. Instead of the *Assembly of the Blessed Head,* we're all standing around ooing and ahhing around a virtual brain."

He found his normal voice. "There was no more peace in Ireland before Patrick than after!"

Day seemed undismayed. "There was peace under Cormac and peace under Niall," he said, shaking his finger like an old nun. "But you must understand that even the great Druids did not have what we have. They had the ley lines, untapped solar energy, the language, some physical heads with some sort of primitive mystical properties, and a few obscure mathematical formulae." He stood up to meet O'Toole eye to eye.

"*We* will connect the intricate ley system to the infinite channels of cyberspace and infuse it with the tremendous mystical power not of a mere *severed head*, but a *pure intelligence* — the mind of a man captured, disembodied, stored in silica, chips, crystals of sand — waiting to be sent out by the Word — not the word of naming but the Word of Making — the Word that *is* the thing — the Word that is *everything*. We will Make and Un-Make. We will fit the Stone and the Shell — Form and Content — Order and Chaos. And then ... *Peace will come*. We will control it *all* — information, movement, temperaments, climate ..."

"You're as crazy as Kostanikas! You really are!"

"If you don't believe it, then why are you doing all of this?" Day asked. He sat down again, his face still almost expressionless despite his revelations.

"I'm much more honest and much more consistent than you, James. I believe in *power*."

Day picked up the receiver on the wall of Theo's room. He noticed the marks from the explosion still around the edge of the door which hung unevenly on new hinges. *Another unnecessary thing O'Toole had done! He could have gotten Theo to open the door eventually. And it had been risky too ... even a small explosion underground like that could have harmed the structure of the lab spaces or interfered with the ley readings.* He thought, only half jokingly, about the idea of sedating O'Toole instead of Theo. At least Theo was a Visionary. "Yes," he said into the mouthpiece, "Find Mr. Pifkin and send him to Doctor Kostanikas' room as soon as possible."

He did not look at O'Toole as he spoke. "Pifkin will get Theo's final program transferred to the mainframe in the Great Room. You wait for him here." He reached into his pocket for a breath mint and popped it into his mouth nervously. "I'll have to check on preparations for the Circle this evening. I shouldn't be long." Day straightened his tie and mopped his face again. "Tell Pifkin to hold off until I get back."

"Ah, yes, noble Conor!" Treat taunted, again using his mocking brogue. "We must appease the Goddess of the Night, now, mustn't we?" O'Toole sneered derisively as Day attempted to close the ruined door.

Chapter 45

To Bruce Maglish of M.I.T. the sentimental hoo-ha that "life is better than piston engines" is hubris and the "only people to believe this are intellectual Luddites, religious fanatics, humanists and readers of National Enquirer."
　　　　　　　　　Mark Slouka

Do we each, as individuals, have an aura, a unique presence, that is only manifest on site, in our immediate space-time location?
　　　　　　　　　Sven Birkerts

　　Patrick walked down the stairs with barely a limp; his normal complexion had replaced the feverish pallor of the previous night.
　　"No, little boy, we don't know about Grandma yet, but I think she'll turn up real soon."
　　Claire tried to sound reassuring as she went over to greet him at the bottom of the stairway. She gave him a big hug and whisked him off the third step and on to the floor. He was getting heavier all the time. She still couldn't believe he was five years old already. "You seem to be feeling better today!"
　　"Yeah, I do. My foot doesn't hardly hurt at all." Claire hadn't corrected a double negative since Michael died.
　　"That's great! You want some breakfast?"
　　"Mommy, you don't have to pretend with me. I know that the bad people have Grandma." He put his arms around her. Claire looked over at the other three by the computer, trying to decide what tack to take next.
　　"Patrick O'Connell, come over here!" Karl called to the boy, slapping his own leg. Patrick obeyed quickly and climbed unselfconsciously onto the big man's lap.
　　"You want to be like a man. You want to know what's going on. Is that right?"
　　"Yes, Father."
　　Claire was taken aback at Patrick using Karl's priestly title. She herself kept forgetting about it, or denying it.
　　"Alright then, son." Claire realized the exchange was more than

ecclesiastical. "If it's okay with your mother, we will take you in to our investigation. You can help us with our detective work ... *after* you have some breakfast," Patrick seemed elated, "... *if*, it's alright with your mother."

Karl looked at Claire who shrugged and nodded. She didn't really have an alternative. Patrick seemed to sense things whether she told him or not.

"Can I be Watson?" Patrick asked.

"Oh certainly, my dear Watson!" Karl said, mustering a passing British accent. "You know those stories, do you?" Patrick nodded emphatically.

"Excuse me. Excuse me. I am really hurt here." Steve put on his best cheesy acting performance, catching his breath and suppressing a sob, hand to his chest, voice quivering. "I thought I was Watson." He started blubbering. "I really did!"

Patrick started to giggle and everyone laughed except Steve who was still enjoying playing against type.

"Come Patrick! Let's find you a good hearty *man's* breakfast, as the *former* Dr. Watson seems to be losing his edge!" Mara grabbed Patrick's hand and he jumped off Karl's knee and ran with her to the kitchen.

"I do still insist on screening privileges." Claire said. "There are bound to be some things that come up that Patrick doesn't need to know."

"Of course," Karl assured her. "Of course!"

"If I still have any credibility left," Steve asked, "can I suggest we leave the messages and the lexicon for a moment and look at some of the stuff I found online? I think it might help."

"Show us what you've got, Stephan," Karl said, standing and stretching. Claire pulled her chair closer.

"Well ... I know that you know, Karl ... but Claire may not ... that the Internet is a breeding ground for every imaginable esoteric belief system that's ever existed. For instance, all I have to do is type in *pagan* on any search engine and thousands of possible sites come up. You can see here, just a partial list I gathered: *Pagans.org, Pagan Federation Online, Student Pagan Groups*, even a *Guide for Pagan Parents*, and a *Pagan Home-school Page*. Most of them are pretty interesting, some are really thoughtful, inspiring, and have very nifty state-of-the-art graphics, like the *Bardic Circle* ... I especially like the link to the old illustrations from the 1922 classic book, *The Boy's King Arthur*" ... he pulled up some beautiful full color drawings done by N.C. Wyeth, father of Andrew Wyeth, exquisite in their detail and composition. Claire was stunned by their power and beauty. "But I don't want to digress," Steve said, glancing at Karl.

"A lot of them promote good things like this *Pagan World Outreach* that sponsors Coastal Cleanups and environmental stuff. There is, as you can see, even a *Jewish Pagan Resources* site. It's ironic how these Earth religions have come to embrace this technology as a way of contacting each other and sharing information."

"Now I'm not saying that's wrong or even inconsistent. Remember, I agree with McLuhan that we as human beings have to stay on top of the technology, and even ahead of it, so we understand what's happening to us. So we can watch our demise in greater and greater bandwidths ...." he muttered out the side of his mouth. "Sorry, I'll always be a Luddite deep in my unrepeatable soul." Steve clicked the mouse and the screen changed.

"As a matter of fact, look who has an Official Web Site: *www.vatican.va*". Slowly a virtual image of St. Peter's Square and the Basilica appeared and then dissolved to a parchment background with a directory of the Holy See.

"I don't believe it! I was only kidding when I said that about you guys being on the Web! Do they have a link to you? *Cult Buster Boutique* or something?" Neither man acknowledged her.

"Yeah, Karl, JP2 even has his top forty-five movie picks on another Vatican site!"

"Franny will get a charge out of that!" Claire said dryly. "Who's JP2?"

"The Pope himself." Steve was surprised she didn't recognize the affectionate papal title.

"*Oh! Oh*, the Pope! John Paul II! I thought it was some kind of Vatican VJ, like MP3 or something." Claire was genuinely surprised. "That is strange about the movies. I still remember when they only had lists of the ones you *couldn't* see."

"Stephan, please! Let's get back to the urgent matter at hand."

Karl urged commandingly.

"Okay. So most of these Pagans seem pretty harmless. We know that they all don't put everything they're about out on the information highway for everyone to see. There is this kind of funny satirical thing, though, on one of the sites called "How To Be An Evil Cultist" where the author is lamenting the decline of fanatical henchmen, evil priests, etc. One of the tips is 'Never invoke anything bigger than your head.'" Steve laughed. "And another is: 'Plan ahead by selecting ceremonial robes that are easy to run in while still affording ample concealment.' But my favorite has to be 'The hero (or heroes) will always show up at the last possible moment to foil your plans. With this in mind, start half an hour early.'"

Karl looked at Claire, shaking his head.

"These guys crack me up!" Steve cut himself short. "I guess it would be a lot funnier if there weren't *really* evil people *really* doing evil things. Which is one thing that I wanted to show you. First, as I've been looking through sites, especially the Celtic ones, going into the chat rooms and looking on the message boards and stuff, I've found some very strange things. There are a lot of messages posted that seem to be by the same person. They are somewhat like prophecies or warnings, but almost like recruitment, too. Maybe like excerpts from a *Manifesto*. Here, I've printed some of them out.

Mara and Patrick came back in to the parlor with a tea tray full of buttered toast, jam, sausages, cheese and a pot of steaming tea and three cups.

"I had a big bowl of Irish oatmeal with brown sugar and a glass of milk! Now I'm ready to help!" Patrick turned to his mother. "I already helped get the tea and toast ready, Mom. Mara says I'm a good helper."

Claire took a piece of toast and a cup of tea gladly, as did her male partners. "Yes, you most certainly are a good helper — the *best* in the world, I'm sure of it." She took a bite.

They all focused their attention back on Steve who was holding the printout in his hands.

"So these," he told Mara and Patrick, "are the anonymous messages I found on the Web."

The 'Time of Peace' will be ushered in by the Great One. He will draw down the Power of the Air, and pull up the Power of the Sea. He will harness the Heat of the Sun, the Influence of the Moon, and the Mystical Dirt of the Earth. And all must listen to the Great One."

"It sounds like the old man behind the curtain in 'The Wizard of Oz' to me," Claire admitted.

"That was on the Pope's list, by the way." Steve said quickly.

"I liked that movie, didn't I, Mommy?"

"Yes, you did Patrick. Except for the wicked old witch — you had a few bad dreams about her."

"I still have dreams about a wicked old witch, but she's a lot fatter and not green."

"*Stephan!*" Karl called out.

"Sorry, sorry!"

"It was my fault that time, Karl. I brought up the movie, because this guy doesn't sound that dangerous or even believable," said Claire.

"Just listen further." Steve began to read again.

The True Ireland will rise up and draw all people to herself at the Great One's command. And She will be a light to the world. No longer will Hibernia be oppressed and divided, but All will be One. No longer will Ireland's sons and daughters kill each other, but Peace and Harmony will reign. The Word will be fitly spoken and the Flesh will become Word."

They all looked at one another, remembering Michael's message to Claire: *The flesh cannot be made Word.*

"It *has* to be Day! He just couldn't help himself, could he?" asked Karl. "What else does he say?"

"This was on another site."

Patrick had slipped off Mara's lap while Steve was reading and had made his way to the sofa. He pulled something out of his pocket. He placed the White Queen on the chessboard and sat quietly staring at the game.

"You, okay, little boy? Not feeling sick again, are you?" Claire asked.

"No. I can help better and think better over here."

Claire suspected that it wasn't as exciting as Patrick had imagined it would be to be 'involved' in the mystery when it meant sitting in front of a computer. She kept her eye on him. As Steve read, Patrick picked up the Black King and the Black Queen. He laid them on their backs on the table side by side. His lips were moving slightly.

Stephan moved on. "This one's a little more radical, but obviously by the same person. The same sort of stuff and then:

All who do not submit to the Great One must be destroyed. Many have been and will be sacrificed for the good of All. The Power available to Ireland will be given to all the World.
The Day is coming soon.

Is that a play on words or what? Day is coming soon, come on!"

'Be ready! Be prepared! Are you with us? Blessed be! Blessed be!' And look he gives an email address for junior evil cultists to sign up: mod@flash.net."

"MOD, what does that stand for, I wonder?" asked Mara.

"Who knows?" Steve answered. "Maniacal Old Druid, maybe? Metaphysics On Demand?"

They listened to some other messages that seemed redundant until:

It should be of no surprise that Hope will rise in the West, like the orchids and gentian that push up through the stony floor of the Burren, and the ancient wounds of Connaught will heal Her borders there.

"It would seem that he's giving away the general location where this cataclysmic event is supposed to take place," said Karl. "It seems unreasonable though for all the high tech systems that relate to all this to be possible in that area of the country. Not everyone in Clare even has a telephone."

"I remember being there with Michael. Even though it's bare, it's where most of the prehistoric dolmens are. Because of its lack of habitation, things have been left alone. There was a stark beauty to it and definitely a mystical feel." Claire had conjured up the image of Michael standing alone in the moonlit mist.

"Where's Auntie Rose?" Patrick asked, sitting up straight all of the sudden.

"She's taking a rest, honey. She's alright." Claire thought he might be worrying that she had disappeared, too.

"I think I'll go check on her." Mara said, getting up and walking over to Patrick. "Do you want to come with me?"

He looked over toward Karl as if for dismissal.

"Errr … It's alright, Dr. Watson. Check on your patient if you must!" *Karl really did relate to children well,* Claire thought. She wondered when he'd ever spent time with them–how long he'd been running around the globe.

Patrick seemed relieved. He left the Black monarch's face turned down on the table.

"Anyway," Steve continued, "MOD is causing quite a stir in the Celtic Neo-Pagan world. One of their main tenets is autonomy. They don't *want* to be joined together — they don't *want* to all believe the same thing. Some of them are reacting to Day's stuff. Listen to this:

"We are quite seriously disturbed by the growing trend within the Magical Community towards Power-over Cults of Personality. We believe these serve only the abusers of magic, and offer no true path, but rather lead the most vulnerable of Seekers into a maze of dead-ends, lost dreams, and spiritual stagnation."

"Not to mention death! I wish Michael would have read this before he got involved with these insane people!" Claire poured herself another cup of tea and went over to the sofa where Patrick had retreated earlier. "So what more do we know? Day has some kind of project going on in the West. We don't know exactly where or what? Are we any closer to finding my mother?"

"Yes, we are." said Karl. "We had people focusing in the urban areas, especially in Belfast, Day's home, and here around the new M.I.T. Media Lab in Dublin where we've seen Kostanikas. This will help us a great deal."

Mara had come downstairs and gone into the kitchen. She came out again. "Rose would like a glass of sherry, of which we have none. I will run out to get some. Any messages for Rafael?"

"No, we'll let him know if anything changes." Karl answered. "Rafael is guarding this house right now, Claire. He's in a car across the street."

"I thought you meant the angel."

"That is quite possible, too. Though I think tradition has it that Ireland is St. Michael's dominion, as far as angels go."

"Rose is delighted to have Patrick keep her company. I'll be back soon."

"Use the customary precautions."

"I do think I'm familiar with them by now, Karl."

"Yes, I'm sure you are. I'm sure you are. Forgive me."

Mara demurred and left the house.

"Now let me show you the *coup de grace*. I don't know the literal translation …" Steve admitted.

"Literally, in the French," Karl offered, "it means 'stroke of mercy.' I think you mean it as 'the final stroke, the death blow.' Not that dissimilar in some instances."

"Yeah, well, I was searching the AI sites, too. They're much spookier than the Pagan ones, hands down. McLuhan was right thirty years ago about these people. They have no idea what they're doing. They're just blind to the ramifications of their ideas. Do you remember, Karl, when I went to hear that Kurzweill talk at Borders in Boston and he was talking about Spiritual Machines? — How it was inevitable that all of us would be uploaded and rid of our carbon-based bodies by the middle of the 21st century! All the people just sat there accepting it because he told them they'd be smarter and how they could be *modified* … how with neuro-implants they'd be able to feel Mexican sand between their toes without leaving *Topsfield!* It blew my mind, I'll tell you. When I asked my question about the sacredness of identity and place, they all acted like I was from the Stone Age."

"That's what Michael's fear was and what Day's dream is — that the flesh will actually become Word — Logos — Reason — Mind.

It's the Incarnation in reverse," Karl replied quietly.

"*Exactly!* They want to suck us all up into our minds and then blow us apart all over the information highway like roadkill. I really don't believe it can ever happen, but I'm afraid they can make quite a mess in the attempt."

"No, I don't believe it can happen either, Stephan. As you pointed out earlier, each of us is *unrepeatable* and we are more than just our brains or the algorithms of our brain. Whatever they did to Michael, Claire, they didn't put him on a software program." Karl turned toward Claire as she leaned back against the cushion of the sofa. Her head was fuzzy and her own mind overloaded from the weight of these things. Stephan continued relentlessly:

"You know the Magic/AI connection is not just made from people on Day's side … Listen to this quote from Minsky's website at MIT:

> *Would it be possible to duplicate the character of a human person as another Self inside a machine? Is anything like that conceivable? And if it were, then would those simulated computer people be in any sense the same or genuine extensions of those real people? Or would they merely be new, artificial person-things that resemble the originals only through some sort of structural coincidence? … A simplistic way to think about this is to assume that inside every normal person's mind there is a certain portion, which we call Self, that uses symbols and representations very much like magical signs and symbols used by sorcerers to work their spells. For we already use such magical incantations … to control those hosts of subsystems within ourselves*"

"That guy teaches at MIT? — sounds more like Hogwarts," Claire said with her eyes closed.

"Here's the main thing though …"

Karl frowned in concentrated stress. "It seems, Stephan, that you've been getting to the main thing for quite some time now."

"Okay. Okay … This is a story from the *Boston Herald* back in August. Are you ready? The Headline reads:

MIT GRAD STUDENT GIVES A+ ON TURING TEST

Jeffrey Klein, 28, sent word to his colleagues at MIT that he had been part of a project where an intelligent agent in a computer program, i.e. Artificial Intelligence, had passed the Turing Test with flying colors. The test, named after and designed by famous technology pioneer and WWII code breaker Alan Turing, is simply a match-up between a human person and a machine, with both asked to perform the same functions. "There was a flutter of excitement about this," said colleague Keith Nalley, "but unfortunately there was no proof. We've heard the story hundreds of times, but we never get the proof." Klein could not be reached for comment due to a fatal accident that occurred during his summer internship in Ireland. "All of the AI Community is saddened by his untimely death." said one of his professors, Dr. Leon Brodsky.

Claire put her face down in the sofa pillow. She was glad that Patrick was upstairs.

"It would seem like another one of Day's sacrifices for the Good of All?" Karl intoned solemnly. *"We have to find this project's whereabouts!"* You contact who you have to on there, Stephan. I'll call Brennan and his group up in Belfast and send them down, too."

The door opened with a shove and closed with a bang. Mara stood breathless, leaning on the threshold with Rose's little brown bag in her hand.

"I'm almost certain someone followed me. I thought I'd lost them, but … I'm so sorry." Mara was obviously upset.

Karl reacted immediately.

"Stephan, call Rafael. We'll go with plan A. Mara, please go up and tell Rose that we have to move along. Claire, will you help Patrick get his things and yours? *We have to move quickly!*"

Chapter 46

"The vagrant, I think, along with perhaps the sailor, has preserved the dignity of motion."

J. M. Synge

"The mind doesn't absorb a sense of place at any speed much faster than the human body moves."

Rebecca Solnit

Some would trace the history of the Irish Travellers back to 600 B.C. when certain outcasts traveled across the country developing the specialized and excellent skill of working metal. Though willing to confine their wandering to an area roughly the size of Illinois, this group has never been able to settle down. They have absorbed, throughout the centuries, various disenfranchised individuals and people groups. There is a belief by some that they were joined, in the middle of the first millennium, by Druids displaced from their positions of esteem and prestige after the advent of Christianity in Ireland. Their secret language *Gammon*, or *Tinker's Cant*, is thought to possibly contain a remnant of the mysterious Druid tongue. *Cuinne*, the Travelers' word for priest, is an ancient term for *Druid*. Later in time, after the power of many British Acts took the land of farmers and tenants, this traveling community grew in number. Thus the Travellers have taken in others, but have never been taken in themselves.

They were called 'tinsmiths' or Tinkers. It has been said of them, by one writer, that they were able to make a living in this way despite every invasion that swept through the tiny land except for one — Plastics. Thus the modern Travellers have had to seek temporary and creative self-employment, adapting and changing in whatever way needed to escape the burden of selling themselves to someone else. 'Traveller' came to replace the terms 'Tinker' or 'Itinerant', which were equivalent to 'Negro' or 'nigger' in the States. What is said about the Travellers by the 'settled' Irish is what was once said of the Irish as a whole: "they drink, brawl, and have too many children." They are furthermore "dirty, lawless and have no work ethic."

It has also been said that this connection to the land — the passing over it but not *possessing* it in the normal way of owning property, almost like an animal staking out its primal claim, is what protected the Travellers from the tragedy of being Irish. As an itinerant Jewish poet once said, *"When you ain't got nothin', you got nothin' to lose."*

Karl and most of his current household sat in the rectory of the "Parish of Travelling People" on Cook Street, near the Liffey River in Dublin. It was a 'parish without borders', for obvious reasons, and was pastored by a friend of the German priest, who offered them generous hospitality but did not seem to understand the urgency of their circumstances.

Rose still looked tired, but Father Doran had found some welcome brandy that seemed to substitute for the misplaced sherry, and she sipped it slowly and smoked her cigarette. Steve and Mara were off setting decoys and distractions for whoever was in possible pursuit.

"They do believe," Father Doran offered as part of a rambling lecture. He focused his attention on Claire who listened politely but glanced nervously at Karl as she rubbed Patrick's back absent-mindedly. "But some are *magical* in their belief. They seem much more interested in the miracles and the sacraments than in the teachings and morality — if you know what I mean. But I love them, I do. I've been with them ten years now, or is it eleven … I can't —"

"William," Karl interrupted, "We *do* have to be going. Will our friends be here soon?"

"Oh yes, yes. Always willing to take in the stranger, they are. They obey Our Lord in that way, I suppose. 'Always take in strangers' He said, 'for ye may be entertaining angels, unaware.' They'll be here soon. Yes, they'll be here soon." The old priest's weathered face turned toward Patrick. "What's that you got there, my boy? Under your arm?"

Patrick held the square up for the priest to see.

"Ah, a game board is it? And what do you fancy playing on that?"

"It's not mine." Patrick said honestly. "But Karl and Auntie

Rose said I could take it from the house."

"He's a fine chess player, William, for one so young," said Karl, stepping in to relieve Patrick.

"Chess, huh? What was it you used to like as a boy now, Karl? I can't remember the name of it."

"*Kriegspiel,*" Karl reminded him in perfect German. "You have a fine memory, Father Doran."

"*Kriegspeil!* Yes! A lot like chess, wasn't it? You explained one evening around a campfire after Mass — somewhere down in Wicklow — at Glendalough — yes, that was it — by the Upper Lake. Beautiful Country, that! It was a summer evening and one of the men was singing and we had some whiskey to keep off the mountain chill." He laughed. "I can see it all so clear in my mind but I don't remember now what you told me of the game …"

Claire was tired of moving. She was tired of uncertainty — of her whole life, and Patrick's, and now her mother's, being up in the air. At least she hadn't been symptomatic in a while. Maybe it was all in her mind and she'd had no time to think about it … No, there had been tests. She looked at Rose who was dozing in an overstuffed chair. She was still wearing her raincoat and holding her pocketbook securely in both hands. Claire wished she could just sleep, but she kept looking anxiously at the door, watching for their rescuers.

Patrick slid off the bench by his mother and walked over closer to where the two priests were talking. He heard them talking about chess boards. Karl attempted to include him in the conversation. He pulled the board out from under Patrick's arm, asking for permission with a nod. Patrick handed it over gladly and Karl held it out before them.

"There would be three boards, one of which was shown only to the umpire." He handed the board to his old friend. "The two players sat back to back," he said turning Patrick around and himself in the opposite direction, "each with their own board and neither one knowing the other's moves. The umpire told them what moves were permissible and when a piece was taken." Father Doran held the board and had an official look about him. Karl faced the boy again and Patrick jumped in the air to land squarely back in his original position.

"No wonder I didn't remember it!" the old man exclaimed, the spell broken. "That is a strange game! Very confusing! Not seeing your opponent? Very strange!"

Karl reached down to hoist Patrick up in his big arms. "Actually, William, I think it's more realistic that way — more like the way we live. Our enemies do not always play out *their* game before our eyes."

"Ah, yes, St Paul! Yes, Karl, quite right! *We wrestle not against flesh and blood, but against spiritual hosts of wickedness in the heavenly places:*' unseen opponents! Quite right."

"Our earthly opponents can be inscrutable, as well."

Patrick took advantage of his position and looked deep into Karl's eyes. "Is God the empire?"

"The empire?" Karl smiled at the boy. "Why, I'd say he *is* the umpire! That's very wise, Patrick. How did you think of that?"

"Daddy said God could see what everybody does, but we can't. So he's like the umpire. Right, Mom?"

Claire's chin was resting on her chest and her eyes were closed. She woke suddenly, though, as did Rose, when the door of the rectory flew open.

"Is it yourself, you rovin' Jew, with the body of a German, and the heart of a Saint?" A big barrel-chested man in baggy trousers, frayed tweed jacket and a tattered cap blustered into the room with a wide smile. He was followed by a woman and several children dressed in similar but various degrees of disarray. "And him needin' the help of the likes o' me!" He laughed heartily as walked toward Karl and grabbed the priest's large hand firmly in his own.

Claire was startled by the group and thought she had awakened in the midst of a Synge play. Patrick, however, laughed along with the gregarious stranger and had a look of joy on his face.

"*Dermot Brown!* Why didn't you tell me, William, that it was Dermot who would be coming?" Karl had a genuine smile on his face, as well.

"The good Father didn't know who it would be comin'. The call just went out and I'm the plonker who answered it," Dermot explained. "And who's the fine *young one* here, ye've got?"

"This is Patrick O'Connell," Karl answered, still holding the boy in his arm.

"Aye, *Paidrig*, and that's a noble name now, isn't it?" He turned to his wife and children who all nodded approvingly and in agreement with their patriarch.

"And this," Karl said, gesturing toward the seated ladies, "is Patrick's mother, Mrs. Michael O'Connell." Claire nodded. "And Mrs. Ian McCullum."

"Oh, Mr. Brown! I believe we've met before," Rose offered with a warm smile.

"Oh yes, that we have and I knew *both* yer husbands well. Fine men they were and we're all very sorry about their passin' on." Dermot removed his hat and bowed slightly and respectfully toward the widows. "We had no idea these were the poor souls who needed our help, but we're ready all the same and we got the caravan waiting and stocked outside of town. Tommy'll be cheesed off that we stole his van, but he'll get over it when I explain."

"Well, well! I'm sure you'd all like a bite to eat before you —" Father Doran began.

"No, no, William, we have to be off. We don't want to lead our opponents in any way to *you*." Karl thanked the old priest and with Dermot Brown hustled everyone into the seventies vintage Ford van outside. Dermot jumped into the driver's seat and they sped away.

"Your opponents that are not flesh and blood — the ones you *can't see*," Father Doran spoke to himself from the doorway. He held up his hand and prayed: "*St. Michael the Archangel, defend us in battle; be our safeguard against the wickedness and snares of the devil. O Prince of the heavenly host, by the power of God, cast into hell Satan and all the evil spirits who prowl about the world seeking the ruin of souls.*"

Chapter 47

Man's evolutionary drive takes him further from animal nature. [We must] isolate our perfect machines from the irrational and hideous world of trees, birds, and animals ... They do not wish to settle for such a limited condition. They aspire to be angels, if not God.
  Bruce Maglish

Physiologically, man in the normal use of technology is perpetually modified by it. Man becomes, as it were, the sex organs of the machine world enabling it to fecundate and to evolve.
  Marshall McLuhan

"*He's not there?* What do you mean, he's not there? I thought you were watching him! Didn't you dress his wound as I asked and give him his sedative?"

Day was yelling at a nurse/technician whose customary duty was in the experimental wing with the children.

"*What is this?* Do your patients have to be caged to allow you to keep track of them?"

"I'm sorry, Mr. Day! I only left for a few minutes to use the loo. I was *sure* he was sleeping. And he was so banged up and all and seemed so old and sickly ... I didn't think he had it in him to move about."

"You don't get paid to think, Miss ..."

"Miss Baker, sir. You commended me for my work with —"

"Oh, shut up and help me look around for him and don't tell *anyone* he's missing, especially not Doctor O'Toole! Understand?" Day got himself under control and tried to act as if no angry words had passed his lips.

"Miss mm ... Baker, I'm sure we can find him. As you said, he is a weak old man. I think the two of us can handle this."

Theo sat quietly in a dark closet off the hallway. He thought he was dead. Now he was sure of it. He had no cigarettes and he couldn't see. He had always seen things — even in the dark — even with his eyes closed: *patterns,* always patterns. And it was so *silent.* There were no voices — the Voices were quiet. This is what he had longed for most of his life — was it *death* he had longed for? Why had he been afraid of death? It was cessation. He sat there in the dark in silence. But something moved inside him, deep in his bowel or the pit of his stomach — it was rising and as it did he felt as if he could not breathe. It was burning, surging, growing in volume and intensity. His whole body began to shake, like the ground before a geyser gushes or an oil strike spurts into the sky. But this was a cold, horrible, liquid that froze his lungs and his blood. As it reached his throat he began to have a faint recollection of what it might be, but never before had he felt it so overwhelmingly. Every molecule of his flesh and bone were gripped and wrapped by another force. He felt that if he did not stop shaking that he would shatter like glass.

"*The Abyss* —" Theo whispered, "— my *Master, talk to me a little while to draw me out of error. Where is the ice? It has found me, the rivulet which descends along the hollow of the rock, gnawing ... inside me. Vexilla regis produent inferni.*" It was *dread* — dread that turned human beings to stone or that made them face anything else, no matter how terrible, *anything* else. It rose up in his throat and he had to let it out — vomit or scream. *But wait!* He heard *voices*. In his head? Outside?

"Are you sure he said to meet him here?" Pifkin asked impatiently.

"Yes, I'm sure."

O'Toole stood with Herb Pifkin in the hall outside Theo's workroom directly across from the storage closet where the old man sat huddled behind some large boxes and unused equipment.

"While we're waiting we can have a little chat," the Irishman said as he led the way into the workroom and closed the door behind them.

"Tell me about yourself, Herb. We've never really gotten to *know* each other, have we? No more than a businesslike 'hello.' Mister Day says you're an absolute *genius* — couldn't have done this without you and all that ..."

Pifkin had no desire to develop a friendship with O'Toole, but he relaxed a little at the mention of his intelligence and expertise. "Well, I *have* worked harder on this particular project than anyone else. You might say I've been working on it my whole life."

"Oh, really? I'd like to hear your point of view on this. I'll bet it's fascinating." O'Toole feigned respect and took advantage of the rare opportunity of questioning Pifkin without Day's constant interference.

"Believe it or not I used to be considered somewhat of a *nerd* as I was growing up!"

Pifkin laughed and pushed his glasses up on his nose. He hadn't looked in a mirror for days and his dark hair sprouted in curly tubes from his small head.

"You're kidding!" O'Toole said facetiously. He was afraid to waste valuable time listening to Pifkin's life story. "Well, tell me how and why you got involved in this *particular* project."

"You mean AI? I guess I've always had the dream of hacking life. It's part of the *evolutionary process* for us to move farther and farther from animal nature and toward the *new nature* which is technology — to leave behind our irrational allegiance to the physical world. The idea is to take the material and make it immaterial!" Pifkin's face had lit up.

"And why does that excite you?"

"I know a lot of Jews, some in my own family, who have an attachment to *tradition,* meaning, ritual, individual morality, and so on. All of that stuff never turned me on. I get off on the 'spirituality' of the *hive* — you know, the *linkage* — subsuming the millions of isolated, dim-witted PCs into one magnificent *organism* with all minds uploaded on the Net suspended in an ecology of voltage ..." Pifkin's eyes were aglow. He pranced awkwardly about the room.

"What about our *bodies?* What do we do with *them?* And what about *sex?* You're not screwing one of *these,* are you?" O'Toole pointed to Theo's computer. On its monitor glowed a virtual image of Michael instead of the elaborate game maze construct which had been on it before. Michael's image was seated as if in a chair, but there was no chair and he seemed to be floating in a white sky. O'Toole was disconcerted by the change. Pifkin was oblivious.

"*Some* of us, not *me* exactly, refer to humans as merely 'meat on the fringe.' Carbon-based bodies will eventually be unnecessary — with implants and more and more 'smart' objects around us. For most people it will all happen so gradually, they'll hardly notice. And as for sex, it's just a matter of finding the right neuro-stimuli to create the sensation. You won't need all that male equipment." Pifkin snorted.

"I like *my* equipment just fine — but whatever turns you on, huh?" O'Toole tried to go on humoring this freak, in spite of his inability to relate to his motives: "So what does old Michael-in-the-machine mean to *you*, Herb?"

Pifkin was startled from his ecstatic state. "I was given to believe that everyone involved with this project *understood* the significance of the creation of a *truly Intelligent Machine!* Are you saying you don't understand what this *means?*" Herb was upset by O'Toole's unenlightened crassness — *shows a very primitive motivation*, he thought.

"Of course ... I understand what it means to *me*. I was just interested in *your* perspective — you being the *real* expert and you might say the *mind* behind it all?" O'Toole couldn't wait to get rid of the weasely little bastard when it was all over.

"Well, what it means to me and to all of the world-wide AI Community is that we have done the two things that we've been attempting to do for almost half a century." The speed of Pifkin's steps increased as he paced around the room. O'Toole sat listening, trying to avoid eye contact with Michael's image on the monitor.

"First let me say that the *nay-sayers* have always asserted the sentimental idea that there is something *special* about humans that makes it impossible to capture our intelligence in machines — that the transfinite induction needed to reproduce the operations of the human mind are non-computable. But *here* we have built ..." Pifkin stopped pacing and raised his voice and his hand. "We have built ... a *replication of human computational capabilities* that is the system S which defines how all minds work. S is based on the algorithm which is equivalent to the human mind. And that brings us to Step Two ..." He took a deep breath and pointed to the computer screen.

"The program is so advanced, so unparalleled that it was able to capture our friend here ..."

"He wasn't a friend of *mine*," O'Toole said defensively. "I only knew him *slightly* — I ..."

He still looked only toward Pifkin, away from the screen.

"I was using it in the *generic* sense. I never met the man myself."

Pifkin went over and sat face to face with Michael's image. "So what we were able to do, or I should say our colleagues in Chicago using *our* map of neurotransmitters, was *upload* (some still say download, but I find that so demeaning) *his* brain onto our program, which has not only amazing computational skills but *captures all the insights and judgments that a human can make*. If I were a Jew like Minsky or Sussman I'd say a wandering 'soul' from *neshamot* has inhabited our machine … But I'm not sure about that mystical stuff. I just thought we should at least tip our hats to Rabbi Loew and the whole *golem* thing …"

"Murder is a big tip of the hat."

"Lots of people have sacrificed many things for this idea," Pifkin replied with no emotion.

He reached for the computer keyboard. "I still can't believe we've actually done this!"

"*Wait a minute*, there! Day said not to touch anything 'til he got back!" O'Toole fought to keep his composure in the starkly lit room.

"Oh yes. Alright. You know why we've been successful here when no one else has before, don't you?" Pifkin asked, turning to O'Toole. "Because of James Day! He's given us the *funding we need* … with no strings attached and *no limitations* in experimentation. These advances could never have been made without human subjects. It takes a great person to understand the sacrifices that must be made."

"You don't see Day as a *mystical* person then, huh?" God, this guy was sick, but at least O'Toole was learning things.

"I don't know in what sense you mean that, but in the *strictest* sense … No. I see Mister Day as a philanthropist and a lover of science. He doesn't understand everything we're doing technically, I know, but he shares the same vision."

O'Toole smiled blankly and nodded, thinking: *You don't know what the hell you're in for, you castrated little mechanic. Day is good at keeping his right hand from knowing what his left hand is doing, that's for sure.*

Day walked into the room just then, looking very distracted.

"Well, are you ready, Herbert, to begin the transfer*?*" He too was startled by Michael's image on the screen. "Have you been *doing things* while I was gone? What happened to the graphics that Kostanikas had up? I *told* you, O'Toole, that —"

Before the Irishman could defend himself, Pifkin spoke up.

"We haven't done a thing. It must have switched over into a resting mode. *It* … or we should say *he* … will be much more active on the mainframe. I am *extremely* anxious to continue testing his capabilities without Doctor Kostanikas' erratic presence."

"Well, I think he'll stay out of the way now. Don't you, Mr. Day?" O'Toole asked.

"Uhh … yes, he'll be out for awhile … the sedative and everything. No need to worry about him."

Day was sweating again, profusely.

Chapter 48

The Annunciation was not so much a vision as an earthquake in which God moved the universe and unsettled the spheres, and the beginning of the end of all things came before her in her deepest heart … God was a child curled up who slept in her and her veins were flooded with His wisdom which is night, which is starlight, which is silence.

Thomas Merton

The church was dark except for the candlelight in the red glass by the Tabernacle and a few votives burning in front of St. Jude. St. Jude was a favorite of the wayward strays around the Mission. Franny didn't know why she had driven all the way downtown instead of going home to her father and her sister. Yes, she did. She didn't want to see her father like that — staring aimlessly, helpless. He was always the strong one. Grace depended on him for everything. But with her gone, he looked like a statue. Franny, honestly, was tired of the whole thing.

She had walked in the side door past the chapel and into the main gothic structure, which was in need of many repairs. She couldn't see those cracks and chips in the shadows. Sliding into one of the first pews she bumped into something large. She heard a groan and let out a small cry.

"Whaaahdya doin' here?" a low slurred voice mumbled. "Are you th'angel?"

Francine realized that it was just one of the street people who hadn't made it into the shelter for the night. As a matter of fact it had been her idea to leave the church open and Father Sileski had agreed to it. "I suppose God doesn't lock his doors," he'd said, "and I suppose the Blessed Sacrament can have an effect on whoever comes in even if they're fall-down drunk."

"Excuse me," Franny said, "I didn't see you there."

"Are you … th'angel?" the voice mumbled again.

"What angel?"

"Th'one I been talkin' tooo?"

Franny looked around in the darkness. "You were talking to an angel?"

The man attempted to sit up, but fell back down on the pew. "Ah-I-I don't know, I thought it wasn'angel. But I am verrry drunk. Shhhh, don't tell. Don'tttell. Shhh." He was quiet.

"I won't tell," Franny said, patting the man's arm gently and getting up to go back out of the pew to leave him in peace.

She knelt down in the dark before the statue of Our Lady. She took out her cigarette lighter, saying as she lit some candles, "Hail Mary, full of grace …" The flames flickered and caused a dancing light on Mary's quiescent face. The paint was peeling in places, especially near a crack that cut diagonally across her chest. "I don't get you — I don't know what you have to do with everything …" Franny interrupted her familiar prayer with an outburst of frustration.

"Do you really have any say with the Big Guys? Or are you just kind of a front that they put up to make our religion seem a little easier to take? I mean what kind of stuff can you really do when you're not a goddess or anything, right? You were, or are, or I don't know … supposed to be human … like us. So why does Grace spend so much time going on and on with the rosary? What's the point? Michael said you were a …" She paused to think of the right phrase, "'mystery wrapped in silence.' Well, you could say that about *anything*, right? — I mean, anything that didn't make sense." Franny stood up and said angrily, "I don't know why the hell I'm talking to you. Why am I?" She tried to look the statue in the eye but the stone eyes were looking down at her. "*Why am I?*"

Suddenly the fire in the red globe by the tabernacle began to flicker violently as if a strong wind had blown in across the altar, but Franny felt no wind. The flames in front of her died with a puff. Her eyes went from the extinguished candles back to the darkened statue. But it was not dark. It was lit as if with white fire from within — with the quality of moonlight, not sunlight, Franny would remember. She was not afraid but was completely entranced. She looked again at the eyes which were now gazing directly into hers. She could not look away. Warmth surrounded her like a breath. Without moving her eyes she removed her leather jacket and her shoes — feeling like a little girl *and* the oldest wisest woman in the world, all at once.

Vacant eyes gained pupils and the chiseled face became olive flesh. Stony lips took on the slightest pink and black hair hung on soft shoulders. Everything changed but the silver white light shining from within.

Franny's mouth moved slowly. "Mmmm …" The word *Mary* would not come out.

The Shining Woman stretched out her hands, which held a beautiful red apple. Thinking she was meant to take it, Franny started to reach but pulled back with a gasp. A writhing black worm had pushed through the surface of the perfect skin. Soon the entire apple was alive with dark worms who ate its flesh until there was almost nothing left. The Woman put the rotten thing into a thick velvet bag and when she drew it out again it was a spinning globe, like the world. This she pushed through her cloak and seemingly into her own body. Her hand came forth again, this time with a golden apple … not solid gold, Franny would say, but *living* gold. The golden fruit burst open and in it was a tiny baby, the size of a fingertip. The golden crust of the apple dropped away as the once-delicate infant grew to be a healthy radiant young boy in the Woman's arms.

Franny looked again into the Shining Woman's eyes. "Mmmother!" she whispered.

The Woman looked down once more. The Boy held in his own hands an object that gave him great delight, as a child with a cherished possession. It was the spinning globe — it was the world.

Francine was startled to hear the sound of weeping behind her and turned from the Vision to find the old drunk in his pew on his knees, tears streaming down his face. Turning toward the Woman again she saw only the statue that had borne the brunt of her earlier vexation, in darkness now except for the fluttering light of her few candles. The old vagrant's face was still bathed in light, however, and she wondered about her own as she moved and knelt down beside him.

Chapter 49

Unmediated reality is a profoundly democratic thing.
Mark Slouka

Man is the measure.
Man's feet are the measure for distance,
his hands for ownership,
his body for all that is lovable and desirable and strong.
E.M. Forster

"My name ... *Dermot* ... it means *free man*, you know. And that's what I've been me whole life." the Traveller told them as he settled them into their caravan. "You'll only be voyagin' in *this* 'til we get word from the West on the doin's around the Burren. This is a good cover, you know. Only tourists use 'em much nowadays."

The horse-drawn wagon, sometimes called a *Romany* Caravan, had been patterned after the nomadic vehicles used by the Irish Travellers since about 1840. It was made mostly of wood and canvas.

Karl, Rose, Claire and Patrick were sitting at a table in a surprisingly roomy space that was equivalent in many respects to a modern camping trailer. Dermot Brown stood toward the rear, pointing things out to his guests while his own family stood behind him outside peeking in.

"Aye, Dermot" said Mrs. Brown. "And why can't we be livin' in one a' these?"

"Cop on, Janey! We couldn't afford this now, could we?"

"Our grannies could afford 'em and we can't? That's a fine idea of gettin' up on the world, isn't it?"

"Now, Janey ... will ya listen whilst I explain to everyone, yourself included, how we came upon this caravan." Dermot clapped his hands and continued with his 'tour'.

"This friend of a friend o' mine started building these for the tourists that flock to Ireland every summer for to have a *real* Irish vacation. We all says, 'why would a rich American or some such plonker want to copy the likes o' *us?*', but he didn't listen and now he's rakin' in the money. They ain't like our grannies had, no sir.

They's all fixed up as you can see with a cooker, a sink, electric lights …" He demonstrated all the features like a salesman. " … Fold-out beds, and *still* light enough for one horse to pull. It does have the old 'common harness' used by our people for centuries and the draught horse is a beauty — out of the original breedin' pool."

"Dermot, we can compensate your … friend's friend in whatever way necessary." Karl assured him.

"No, no, he owes me a favor … honestly — not me friend's friend, but me friend, Bubby. And he woulda done it anyway, not me friend, Bubby, but his friend, because it's kind o' off the season and he understands that you're in trouble and all …"

"Aye, Dermot, couldn't we get be gettin' an off-the-season rig from Bubby's friend, too?" asked the Traveller's wife. Her children were wide-eyed at the thought.

"Janey Brown, would ya stop *yappin' on* about it? They're only usin' it a *short time*, is all!"

"Well, a short time would suit me just fine. Did ya ever think we'd like a vacation?"

"Well, *excuse me*, Mrs. Brown," Dermot said in an attempt at a sophisticated British accent, jumping down out of the wagon and grabbing his wife in a bear-hug. His children were giggling with glee. "I forgot about *us* needin' a vacation. We don't get much time off, now do we?" She didn't give in.

"Awright then, I'll be checkin' on it sometime soon, I will. I will surely." At that she hugged him back, gathered the children, said good-bye to everyone in the caravan and headed toward the truck.

"Tell Tommy I'll buy him a coupla' pints o' the Black Stuff when I get back and *I love ya, Janie Brown*."

Dermot hopped back into the caravan and landed lightly like a large-breasted bird on spindly legs.

"It's too bad your kids couldn't stay and go camping with us," Patrick said with some disappointment.

"Now yer soundin' like me dear wife herself!" Dermot winked at the boy.

"I am afraid he misses playing with friends his own age," Claire said as she pulled her son closer.

And everything else he's ever known, she thought bitterly.

"Well then, we'd best be movin' along. We'll be huggin' the Liffey out toward Naas, but we'll stay away from the main roads and on the cart roads. Ye'll be knocked about a bit more, but it'll be safer fer all concerned, even the *horse,* eh, Father?"

"That's fine, Dermot. We're in your hands," Karl answered. "And from the looks of them, I believe they're quite capable."

Dermot held up his large grimy hands and smiled broadly. "They're rough, but yer right, Father. I've grabbed more o' life than most and I've held it right *here* …" he said heartily, cupping his hands, and then pointing to his head: "and *not here.* And it hasn't got the best o' me yet." He started to leave the caravan. "If you need anything, just tap on the window there and I'll hear ye. Oh, and Mrs. McCullum …"

Rose, who had been relatively quiet since her abrupt awakening in the rectory armchair, chirped in, "Please call me Rose, Mr. Brown."

"Well, then, you can call me Dermot."

"Yes, then, Dermot?"

"Rose, I was just wonderin', are ye fer fags?"

Claire colored as she gave Karl and Rose a look of surprise. Rose laughed and slapped the table. "It's not a *political* question, Claire, dear!" She nudged Karl as he sat snugly next to her on the small bench. "He means *cigarettes* — do I need cigarettes."

"Sorry, it's the Dublin slang. I pick up languages very quickly, ya see."

"Yes, Dermot. That's very kind of you. I *am* out of them and I haven't wanted to trouble anyone."

The Traveller handed her a fresh pack. "Thank you, Dermot," Rose told him.

"Not at all, Rose. Well then. It'll be good to be with a horse again. I used to trade 'em over at the Puck Fair in Killorgan. Two thousand years old, that fair is. And a car just isn't the same," Dermot said wistfully. "But it is handy if it's time you're short of and it might come to that, eh Father?"

"I'll let you know when we get the call." Karl patted the breast pocket of his black suit jacket.

The wagon moved off rather smoothly and Karl stood up from

the cramped table-bench just as Dermot steered them onto the smaller cart road. The rolling jolt caused the priest to bump his head on the curved beam that formed the entryway into the other area of the caravan. Rose was up in no time, walking like a new sailor trying to get his sea legs.

"Oh, Father, you've banged your head and there'll be a good-size egg arising shortly. Do we have any ice?"

"Don't worry about it! It's nothing, really." Karl sounded a bit gruff with the older woman, but then changed his tone as she seemed to contemplate her uselessness. "You know a cold rag might be fine, Rose."

"What's a plonker?" Patrick asked of the adults as Rose squeezed a cloth out in the shiny small sink. "A plonker means uhh …, a foolish person," Rose answered. "Dublin slang again." She put the cloth to Karl's head, reaching to her full height to hit the spot. "Ahh, there it is, now. Starting to swell up already, isn't it?" Patrick and Claire nodded to her demand for a response.

"It was the other side I hit, Rose." Karl said, smiling and taking the cloth from her to hold on the left of his forehead. "That other bump is just part of my natural topography, I guess."

"What's a jibber?" Patrick asked. "Mr. Dermot Brown said he was glad I wasn't a jibber."

"It's someone who's afraid to try new things. So you surely aren't a jibber, Patrick! Dermot was right about that."

"None of us are jibbers then, are we?" said the boy. "We're going on lots of adventures and solving mysteries and stuff." Claire tried to look agreeable — but she felt very 'jibberish.'

Rose searched through the cupboards and found them stocked well. "There are the makings here for a splendid tea!" Claire got up to help her prepare it and Karl went back to sit down across from Patrick. They didn't speak, but just looked at each other for a few minutes while Rose and Claire chatted about ordinary things and groaned laughingly when the wagon occasionally lurched to and fro.

Patrick reached down for his bag and pulled it up on the table with a clunk. Karl, anticipating his wish, reached behind him for the chess board and laid it in front of them. They took out the game pieces from the midst of the boy's other possessions and put them in their proper starting places on the board. Patrick sat with his chin leaning on his right hand. He had chosen to put the 'black' pieces on his side and had insisted that Karl handle the 'white' pieces.

Claire glanced over at their game as she found a box of tea biscuits.

"Do you really think that this is wise?" she asked of Karl, not masking her irritation and apprehension. She also noticed that Patrick had the 'black' pieces and that unnerved her. "We all know that this is a strange game. Patrick even got sick last time he played with it. It has weird … *powers* and who knows what all?"

"I know, Mommy, I know what all. I took it out. Don't be mad at Karl."

"I'm not *mad* at Karl, really. It's just that I think you should have asked me before …"

"Don't you know that I'm doing what Daddy wants?"

Claire was stunned. She felt that she had been chastised in some way by her five-year-old son for interfering and she looked away. Rose saw the tears in her eyes and hugged her tightly while she whispered in her ear. "*And a sword shall pierce your own soul … so that the truth shall be laid bare.*"

Claire backed away from her embrace. "What are you *talking* about?" She demanded quietly but urgently. "Isn't that what my mother said in her note, about 'the truth being laid bare'? And she used to say something about 'the sword piercing her soul.' I always thought she was trying to make us feel guilty for hurting her feelings. How do *you* know about it?"

"It's referring to Our Lady, my dear. Your Mum knew the Scriptural Rosary, I take it? It is from the Bible, when the new little holy family comes into the Temple precincts in Jerusalem to follow the Jewish custom of presenting the baby to the Lord? The Presentation, it's called. It's one of the Joyful Mysteries, remember?"

"I really haven't said the Rosary since the fifth grade and all I remember is the 'Hail Mary'. I don't think I ever learned the other stuff. But let me clue you in, Rose. Having a sword stuck in your heart or your soul or *whatever*, doesn't seem to conjure up a *joyful* mystery to me."

Karl and Patrick sat silently, completely engrossed in their game.

Only two pieces had been moved.

Rose took the whistling kettle off the ring and poured the steaming water into the teapot. "It's joyful in the fact that it is another affirmation to them that they are following God's plan, and He knows how much they needed every bit of that, poor dears! So they come in and who meets them but two of the saintliest people in all of Israel, very old people, definitely pre-Vatican II." She chuckled.

Claire looked somewhat confused.

Rose apologized, "I'm sorry — dreadful time for a joke — and especially one … Well, never mind — let's get back to the story. Simeon had been waiting for years and years to see the salvation of Israel. Things seemed fairly hopeless, I'm sure, but he had been promised by the Holy Spirit that he wouldn't die until he did. So that day, in walked a young Jewish couple with a baby boy and Simeon grabs the baby from them and begins to bless God. Saying that now he could die, because he *had* seen the salvation of Israel. And who else should they happen to meet but old Anna, who'd been *living* in the temple, fasting and praying day and night, herself looking for the redemption of Jerusalem. And then she begins to exclaim over the little baby as well, telling everyone she met that this was the one."

Claire had arranged the biscuits and sliced some cheese. Rose poured out the tea, careful not to fill the cups on account of their bumpy ride. She continued, "So you see now why it was joyful to them and to us all that the Redeemer had finally come. I imagine that Mary and Joseph had looked at that little boy and wondered how he, a small ordinary-looking child, was going to save the whole world. Could it *really* be true? Well, here was some more proof!"

"But you didn't get to the part yet about the 'sword' and the 'truth laid bare'. Claire reminded her.

"Oh, well, yes." She walked over and set two cups gingerly on the table for Karl and Patrick and offered them each some food. Karl thanked her and they ate with relish, not really looking up.

"It's one of those truly God-like things — one of the reasons the Scriptures have the 'ring of truth'. I mean if, well, some fanatical Christian scribe or monk was trying to write things that were *merely* joyful …," she said looking at Claire directly, "he wouldn't have put this part in, would he? But it is the reality of the paradox — the paradox that always leads to truth — that brings the true joy."

Rose handed Claire a cup of tea and sipped from her own. They sat side by side on the cushioned seat across from the sink.

"Just when the proud parents are feeling quite secure in the glorious destiny of their son, Simeon prophesies that the Child will cause the rise *and* the fall of many in Israel — that he is a sign that will be rejected. That's when he turns to Mary and says that a sword will pierce her own soul also, so that the truth may be laid bare."

"But what does that *mean*?" Claire asked in frustration. "I don't understand what that means!"

"I've never had the good fortune to be a mother myself. Lord knows, I prayed hard enough. But it wasn't meant for me. But Ian and I've had our share of spiritual children over the years. I guess what I believe it means, and maybe what your mother meant, is that you can love your child so much that when you see them suffer it pierces you in a way that nothing else can — and I think it's meant another way, too — that you can love your child so much that you are hesitant to let them fulfill their destiny because you know the pain that will come … But sometimes the child knows his destiny better than the mother and the reminder of that can pierce the soul, as well. Like what happened with you and Patrick just now … or what happened to Our Lady when she found the young Jesus on his own with the great leaders of the Temple."

"Are you saying that this *silly game* has something to do with Patrick's *destiny*?" Claire was still talking in a low voice but with great intensity, "… that somehow he's *controlling* things with it? That's *magic*, now, isn't it, Rose? Not Christianity."

"The way Ian explained the game was not that one could control the events of life but that this was somehow a window to that place outside of time, where freedom and order meet — where choices are more fluid and yet more solid."

Claire did not reply; she had nothing to say. It didn't make sense to her. She watched Patrick take the White Queen from Karl and lay her gently on the table. Claire felt shaky and that numbness she'd had in her hands — it had been one of her first symptoms — was back and was slowly creeping up from her fingertips. She flexed her hands, opening and closing her fingers, reaching to put the teacup down on the counter. She felt faint and heard a crash …

Chapter 50

The Infinite Goodness has such wide arms that it takes whatever turns to it.
Dante Alighieri

O but we dreamed to mend
Whatever mischief seemed
To affect mankind, but now
That winds of winter blow
Learn that we were crack-pated when we dreamed
William Butler Yeats.

He awoke in the dark, shivering with cold. He had no memory of how he'd got there or where he was. A looming shape hung over him, blacker than the darkness, and his back pressed against an ungiving hardness. He lay there staring at nothing until his eyes could make a distinction. The paler darkness was the sky. Clouds were moving softly and slowly across the blanket of stars. He fancied himself among them, floating gently in peaceful silence. Each star seemed to know him — to beckon in a friendly way for him to come and take his place. In all his life he'd never had a sense of belonging — never. But the stars — had he always *been* one? He now had no sense of his body. The cold and the pain were gone. There was no time as he lay weightless, bobbing effortlessly on the waves of the clouds that brushed lightly by.

Then he made the mistake — he always made mistakes — of shifting his eyes ever so slightly to the left — it *could* have been to the right with no consequences — but he looked to the *left* and there it was — the huge black shape leaning down toward him. The dread returned. He put up his hands to hold it off, but it did not move and his arms were weak. His left arm touched something as he let it fall. It was rock. He was lying under the shelter of a large rock. Shivering, he pushed himself up so that his shoulders rested against the stone. His whole body ached, especially his face. He felt his cheek and winced. He looked out at the sky again, but it was flat and cold and dreadful in its indifference.

Theo's clouded mind could not remember all the details of his journey from the underworld. He knew that that insipid, arrogant Irish professor had struck him as DAY stood by. But *they* had not inspired in him the terror that still gnawed at him sporadically, like a hungry rat. No human being could do that.

He heard voices. He was uncertain at first if they were *his* Voices. The toe of his shoe began to flicker with a yellow-orange light. If his foot was burning, he would not try to put it out. He would rather die in the fire than feel again the icy chill seeping into him through the cosmic shunt — *no!!* — The shunt was in the Hospital … which hospital? His shoe continued to burn, but he couldn't feel the heat. The voices grew louder. Theo slid around the rock to see where they were coming from. There were moving balls of flame in the dark night. Had the stars come down to find him? Perhaps soon his whole body from his toe upward would burst into flame and he would join them in their journey back to the sky. With great disappointment he looked at his shoe which was now curled up under his leg. The fire had gone.

> *We now approach the sacred place*
> *Come stand within its hallowed space*

Theo heard a man's voice and watched as robed figures approached, dancing in spirals, forming a circle of bodies and light.

> *Earth, Water, Fire and Air*
> *We would ask your Presence Here*
> *This night between the Worlds we call*
> *All the Powers that be to fall.*

Each element was matched in separate ecstatic invocations, this time in a woman's voice, with its cardinal direction — East with Air, South with Fire, West with Water, and North with Earth — Theo realized he must be observing the casting of a Magic Circle.

> *By the power that blesses thee,*
> *The Circle's cast, and Blessed Be.*

In all his years as a mathematician, Theo had ridden the cusp of mysticism, studied the *Tao* of physics, lapsed in and out of numerology and the mystery of the Aleph, but he had never touched the occult. He never had met anyone who had. Oh, yes, in the hospitals there were always some. Once he had almost believed the man who called himself Lucifer to be the true article. His descriptions of the perspicacious schemes he had planned for mankind throughout the centuries were fascinatingly evil. But then he killed himself and Theo had seen the blood on his sheets before the attendants could close the door, and he had stopped believing. He knew that Lucifer would never die, and he would never bleed.

Let the Mystery of Samhain begin:

At this point an ordinary Irish voice interjected: "The true White Lady could not come to us tonight because she is not feeling well. Her part will be enacted by another worthy lady." It reminded him of an offstage voice at an amateur theatrical production, making a change in the printed program.

Theo almost smiled, but his head was pounding. His mouth was dry and his lips tasted of dried blood. He continued to watch though, as a hooded figure called out into the night, in a vaguely familiar voice:

> *I am the Old King strong and right*
> *And I invoke the Lady White*
> *The Lady's key will turn the year*
> *Winter's door will open here.*
>
> *The Crone will help me on my way*
> *To find a resting place this day*
> *For there is nothing that I lack*
> *The Lady's song will bring me back.*

He couldn't pick up everything, but the hooded 'old king' walked around the circle in one direction, stopping at different points to pick something up or put something down. Two women, one pretty and young, hoodless and dressed in white — the other, most likely the older Crone, but her head and face were covered, moved about the circle in the other direction. Chants were chanted and songs were sung. Theo desperately wanted a cigarette. When the 'old king' and the two women met, they grabbed his hands and he fell to the ground as if dead. The old woman sat upon him and there seemed to be some confusion and whispering in the circle. A new male voice called out:

> *Summer's gone, the Lady reigns*
> *Now Winter can return again.*

Everyone in the Circle turned to watch as the young woman dipped her hands in a cauldron and sprinkled something on the 'old king'.

The Circle began to murmur again. "Well, come on then. What's happened?" and "This is when he comes back to life, isn't it?" Even the young woman called out, "Isn't this where my Cauldron brings him back?"

The new male voice called out once more:

> *Do not break the Circle's Power*
> *For you've been called here for this hour*
> *A new thing's happening now among you*
> *That's the song the Old King's sung you.*

The group had quieted and was listening intently.

> *He is showing with his mime*
> *That he shall break the bonds of time*
> *So leave us now until he's through*
> *Eternal Summer waits for you.*

Whispers and sighs echoed around the Circle.

> *Blessed be!*

"*Blessed be!*" they all answered.

Slowly and silently the group dispersed. As Theo watched them walk down the hill, he realized where he was. The homely cottage sat atop its hellish cellar and the members of the Circle went down to it and climbed into their automobiles and drove away on rough country roads to their own destinations.

The only ones left were the 'old king' and the three people who stood above him. One was the pretty young woman who held a torch. The other two were hooded. Theo could not hear what they were saying until the young woman said loudly, "Well, if I'm standing in for the White Lady, I certainly should be able to help the Old King break the bonds of time!" Soon she was turned away and walked reluctantly in a huff down the hill to scatter like the rest.

She left the others with no light, but they seemed comfortable in the darkness, Theo thought. He could see their shapes against the starry sky. They conferred quietly and then walked hurriedly toward the cottage, leaving the 'old king' miming his Winter sleep alone in a rumpled heap.

Cautiously, Theo arose and hobbled over toward him. As he moved closer, the air grew heavy and oppressive. When he reached where the Circle had been, Theo's body quivered and tingled and buzzed as if he were stepping into a stream of electric current. He stopped suddenly and looked around, making sure he wasn't being watched. He thought about going back to the shelter of the rock. But he would die there if the morning came, the stars would stop their searching and someone else would find him.

He knelt by the motionless body. He felt a wrist. It was cold, like ice, and there was no pulse. He patted the dead man's chest and hips, searching for his own life — the one reliable, calculable proof of his existence — but he found no cigarettes, only a small package of breath mints. He pulled the hood from the 'old king's' head, but could not see properly in the starlight. He took out his lighter and held it in the air above the face of James Day.

He snapped his lighter shut and for some reason looked upon the near horizon. At first he thought he saw the silhouette of a cross, but as he stared, he saw that it was the dolmen that Day was always going on about when he talked of ley lines and energy. The stones slanted and stuck in an eternally precarious balance, the inner shape of which seemed a golden rectangle. He realized with a casual blink that under those stones was where he himself had lain and seen his place among the stars … The air changed again and was cold. The old king was dead forever and winter would come and never end. A wailing horrible cry rose up out of the ley line, out of the cracks of the Burren, from the underworld beneath the ordinary cottage that pierced the night and tore at Theo's soul. He jumped up and ran away feebly into the darkness.

Chapter 51

Cramped or terrified, we must in any conceivable world be one or the other. I prefer terror.
C.S. Lewis

The Theory of Games invented by Von Neumann in the 1920s attempted to construct a systematic theory of rational human behavior by focusing on games as simple settings for the exercise of human rationality.
Sylvia Nasar

Rose was dabbing Claire with a cool cloth — her forehead, her wrists. Patrick was sitting beside her head as she lay on the cushioned seat within the perimeter of light from the kerosene lamp which hung from the ceiling of the wagon.

"What happened? … Did I —?"

"A little fainting spell — and no sherry in the wagon. Or should I say 'on the wagon'," Rose mused, a bit self-consciously. "Here now, drink this tea and have some cheese and a biscuit. Lack of nourishment, that's all."

Claire looked at Karl who stood over her; she caught him with a helpless expression that reminded her of her father's look when her mother had taken things in hand. Understanding passed between them and she realized that she was glad that he knew of her illness. She remembered the first time she'd seen him on the beach in South Carolina, her mistaken first impressions, his kindness, his strength. She did begin to feel better as she ate and drank.

"See, the apple's back in her cheeks, and the sparkle in her eyes once more," Rose observed.

"Pretty as a picture," Dermot sighed. "Should we start up again, Father? It'll be slower goin' in the dark, but the headlights work some even if they're a bit dim and a mite shaky. The road's been quite smooth, for dirt and stone, that is."

"I think we should gain more ground, Dermot, if you feel good about it."

"Gainin' ground's the story of my life. I just never *keep* it is all, Father." Dermot laughed and popped out of the door into the darkness.

"I'm sorry, Claire. Did you want some air before we start again?" Karl asked.

"No, I'll be fine …" She sat up as the wagon lurched into a roll. "I'm sorry I've held us up this long. How long have we been stopped?"

"Not that long, my dear, not that long," said Rose. But Claire sensed that it had been night for awhile. Yes it had been dark for a very, very long time. She was so weary of it all.

"Are you *really* better, Mommy?" Patrick to the rescue again.

"Yes, little boy, I'm *really* okay!" Claire tried to reassure him.

"Then can we play our game again?"

Claire smiled, shaking her finger at him. "Aha, so it's the *game* you're concerned with and not me after all!"

"Mommy!" Patrick's voice trailed down. "You're *in* the game!"

"I am? And which one would I be?"

"You'll see. You'll see, Mom."

Claire shook her head and browsed in the dim light through a day-old Irish newspaper that she had found in a trash bin under the sink. The news was depressing, as usual, especially regarding the 'Peace Accord' that was stalled once again. Rose paged through an outdated fashion magazine from a cupboard drawer and eventually smoked a cigarette, blowing the smoke through a slightly opened window. "No one is too chilly now, are they? Because I *can* close the window and not smoke at all …" No one was bothered but she asked several times anyway.

They rode for a couple of hours and then the cart took a tremendous lunge to the right and stopped. The chess pieces tumbled off the board and some fell onto the floor. Patrick and Karl both exclaimed like children at the forced end to their game. Only one of them had an excuse, Claire thought. She was glad to see it over.

"Do you remember where everything was?" Patrick asked. "I *think* I do."

"Oh puhleease, don't play any more now. Just put them away, okay? Okay?" She got up to help them find the pieces on the floor.

"Do what your mother says, Patrick. We'll come back to it

again."

Dermot hopped into the caravan with a wind-burned face and condolences. "I *am* sorry for the jolt. It's the dark and all ... and we hit a crooked rut. The horse Jim — he's ready for a breather as well, I'm thinkin'."

"That's what it will be then, Dermot. You're in charge." Karl answered.

"No ringy-dingin' on your little black phone, then?"

"Not yet. Is this a good place to camp for the night?"

"As good as any! I'll just pull us off the road. It might just help if ye all could get out and walk about a bit — make it easier on Jim and me to get this rig movin'. Ye'll maybe be wantin' yer coats. There's no rain, but the wind is keen and since ye're none of ye cultchies, or Travellers, it could bite ye."

Claire put on the coat she'd put on over her nightgown last summer when they'd fled Chicago in the middle of the night. She bundled Patrick in a parka that Mara had brought him. Rose donned her blue raincoat which had dried from her wet mission with Karl the night before. Karl merely wore his black suit jacket — *his all-season basic black*, Claire thought. Well, he was a priest, so it wasn't just a fashion statement. It was so well-cut, though. She wondered if Armani did priestly garb.

The outer coach lights, two lantern-like ones on the sides and the headlights in the front, gave them all enough light to walk around a little in the woods, and along the roadside. They could see their breath in the air. Some of the leaves were still colored, but faded now and most of them were on the ground. Karl helped by pushing the wagon as Dermot pulled it forward.

They all were for a campfire, which Dermot started up nicely in spite of the earlier rain. "If ye find a pile of rubble, there's bound to be some dry logs underneath. And I told Bubby we'd need peat, so he told his friend and there ye have it — a lovely fire, if I do say so meself."

Claire remembered the smell of peat fires from her summer with Michael, as the earthy aroma filtered into the air. She explained to Patrick about how peat was dug and how important it was in the West where there weren't so many trees. The small company was glad to let Dermot do most of the talking. He told stories of his travels in Ireland, adding with relish that the one time he went to England he vomited. "Could have been the Channel crossin' or some bad food. But I ain't never been sea-sick in my life and never bit into anything that bit me back … So you can think what ye will."

Back in the caravan, the women read again and Patrick begged to set up the chess game before he went to bed. Claire was amazed that Patrick was not sleepy and would have sent him to his cot anyway but Dermot was very intrigued with the pieces and Rose's tale of their history. She did not interfere. He got so involved in the game then, "them pieces bein' part of his heritage and all …" that Karl had to ask him politely not to comment on every move.

"Check *mate!*" Patrick said finally, with relief. He had switched sides with Karl, this time. Patrick told him he just couldn't be the 'black guys' any more, and Karl had readily let him off the hook.

"Yes, I believe you're right, young man. I believe you're …" He stopped, looking intently at the board again.

"Excuse me, good fellas, but you're wrong. Look at the black Bishop!"

Karl rubbed his chin. "I could have sworn you had it. You didn't bump the Bishop by mistake, did you, Patrick when you made your move?"

"No, sir, I don't think I did."

"Nobody bumped anything. It never was a shot." Dermot declared.

"I think we'd better leave it for the time being, son, and let everyone get some sleep."

"But …"

"It will be alright, Patrick."

Claire sighed.

The two fold-out double beds — Claire swore they were one and a half at most but only to herself — forced Claire and Rose together and Karl with Patrick. Although Karl tried unsuccessfully to give Dermot the bunk and sleep in the small pup tent, the intrepid Traveller had set himself up outside.

"I'd be doin' ye the favor to let ye *have* the tent, ye know. It's much healthier in the open air, but yer not used to it and all."

Everyone slept in their clothes, except Patrick who insisted on his own pajamas, his floppy brown dog under one arm, and his backpack on the floor by the bed.

Claire wished that *she* was five years old again — falling asleep in the old brick house, hearing her family talking, wearing the seersucker pajamas with the pink top and unmatched lavender bottoms that had once had other mates but had been passed down from sister to sister and separated along the way. And later in the night, knowing that her mother and father were in the next room protecting the whole house with their presence — and while they slept, Our Lady — whose likeness was in the very corner of her own room, surrounded by plastic flowers, candle remnants (she was *never* allowed to *light* them), a Barbie doll she had wrapped head-to-toe in black fabric to look like a nun, and other little gaudy trinkets and treasures — *She* would never sleep but would always be watching over everyone who believed in her. God and Jesus, on the other hand, watched over everyone in the whole world, even the ones who didn't believe in them. Claire, of course, did believe then, and even if she hadn't, she was safe — *everyone* was safe.

The wagon was quiet with each passenger's private half-waking thoughts.

"What's a cultchie?"

Dermot was sure to have heard the laughter out in his tent, for it was Karl's deep German voice this time asking the question and not Patrick's.

"It's a country person, Karl, and not one of us is that," Rose answered. "Not yet at least."

Faint chirping sounds broke the silence of sleep in the caravan before Karl answered his phone. It was still dark outside, with no sign of the dawn.

"Yes? It's alright. Of course, we understand ... *You can't mean it, Stephan!* Where? Unbelievable! You'll have to hold on for a moment while I rouse our friend, Mr. Brown. He'll have to tell you where we'll be and how to find us ... we'll look for her then, when they come ... Just a moment."

"Is it about my mother? Have they found her?"

"No, not yet," Karl said on his way out the back door, "but

we've a much better chance of it now. It's Stephan. Some of Dermot's people, some Travellers have found *Kostanikas* … in a ruined twelfth century monastery on the Burren."

Chapter 52

There was something magnificently wild in this stupendous scenery, formed to impress the mind with a certain species of terror — savage and dreadful.
Arthur Young

Satan [to Milton] is a creature living on the void and breathing it in with relentless gluttony as a drug addict might consume opium.
Robert Lowell

The old Econoline van reached its destination in County Clare just after dawn had broken on the eastern horizon. Dermot and his honorary Travellers had waited for an hour or so with the horse and wagon for the faster vehicle to locate them. He did not accompany Mara and the driver who had come and whisked the others off for points West. *Someone* had to get the rig and Jim back to Bubby's friend, and after all it *was* rented for a few more days. Janey would get her wish after all — the Brown family would be accidental tourists. *Who'd know the difference*, Dermot had asked himself as he rode off toward Dublin again, smiling. He'd ask if Father Doran could drive his family down to meet him in Wicklow and they could have a sunrise Mass in the fresh open air. It would be a fine thing.

Most of the little company had dozed during the several hours it took them to cross the country on main roads and side roads and finally the unpaved path that led to the Traveller camp west of Kilfenora. The autumn sun ascended slowly above the Burren, accentuating in blackened silhouette the stark forms that protruded from the dry barren land before spilling out and then flooding everything with a crimson stain that was lifted and absorbed when the full spectrum of light appeared in the sky.

Memories of Michael engulfed Claire. It was here in this strange place, during that one unregrettable summer, she felt that she had known him best. It was their pre-Christian time — before Michael had — She stopped herself. As her tired sluggish mind awakened from fitful sleep, it was as if the sun were breaking upon her for the first time. She saw things and knew things she had not seen and known before. Or maybe they were things she had forgotten and now remembered.

She and Michael, no matter how much they tried, were never 'pre-Christian'. Christianity had been a part of their lives forever — surrounding them, inside them, behind them. They could never go back and start over without it. They could not pretend that it wasn't. The same thing was true of Ireland. The Neo-pagans could never *really* be pagans. The evidence and influence of 1600 years of culture and belief could not be wiped away with revisions, or solstices, or even web sites. The druids had been real pagans. They were looking for the truth in any way they could. When Patrick came, most of them embraced the message that he brought. It was not, they believed, a rejection of their way of life, but a fulfillment. It fit. That was why Ireland was converted entirely within a few hundred years. Claire thought she remembered Michael trying to say something like this once, but she had tuned him out and he had stopped trying.

Many of the Neo-Pagans were anti-Christian, reacting, sometimes violently (she shuddered) and defensively to their own heritage. She stopped again. She wasn't *really* thinking about Ireland. She was thinking about herself. She didn't know what the hell Neo-pagans thought. But she *did* know that she had been reacting defensively since adolescence. Michael had grown up and she never had. It didn't matter that he'd gone back to the Church and she hadn't. That wasn't the point. Michael had grown up enough to accept what he believed to be true. She had lived for years in a reactionary world of non-belief — proud, fearful, lost — grasping tightly to the nothingness in her fist. That is what the rising of the Irish sun had shown her as it spread its blood-red stain on the white Econoline van and her pale body and then washed them in flashing, shimmering, almost unbearable, sheets of bright gold.

Karl got out of the van quickly and talked to a man who was expecting them. Claire could not hear their exchange. Rose and Patrick were barely awake. None of them had made much progress when Karl returned.

"Stephan is still out at the Abbey with Kostanikas," he said to Mara, looking into the front seat. "Our friend here is going to take me to them. You stay here with Claire and Patrick and Rose and help them get settled. We'll bring Kostanikas back soon, I hope. Evidently he was badly beaten and utterly exhausted."

"I'm coming with you," Claire said resolutely as she stepped onto the running board and out of the van. "This man knows something about my husband's death."

"I don't think that would be wise at this …"

"I'm going with you." She looked at Karl directly, then turned to Mara more gently. "Will you see to Patrick?"

Mara turned toward Karl. He nodded slightly.

"Yes, certainly," Mara said, sliding out of the van and embracing Claire. "*Akan mukav tut le Devlesa*," she whispered in her ear.

"And I leave you *and* my son to Him, as well."

Claire felt tears well up and almost changed her mind about going. But Karl held out his hand with great kindness in his eyes. She reached for it without resentment. He helped her into the blue Ford pickup.

"Where is it we are going?" Claire asked as they were underway.

"Would you like to tell Mrs. O'Connell where we're headed, Richard? You know the land better than I do," Karl said to the young man driving.

"Oh no, Father. It bein' an abbey an' all. I'm thinkin' you'll be tellin' it right."

"Corcomroe is the ruin of a Cistercian abbey," (Claire thought fleetingly of the hooded figures in her recurring nightmare) "actually called the abbey of *St. Mary of the Fertile Rock*, founded by King Donall O'Brien in the late 12th century. I've visited it several times in my life. It's a beautiful spot — an unlikely place for Kostanikas to show up!"

"Aren't ye goin' to tell her, Father, about King Conor's bones?" Without waiting for Karl to speak, Richard went on looking sideways at Claire every few seconds. "Right in the wall he's buried, King Conor O'Brien, and it's almost like he's stickin' out some. He was killed in his youth in a bloody battle on the Burren and folks say he tried to get out o' the wall to fight some more but didn't quite make it."

Karl was hoping the young man's graphic folklore wasn't making Claire uncomfortable.

"It's an effigy, Richard, you know … in the wall."

"Yes, Father, I know that. It's a terrible effigy when a young man is struck down like that in th' prime of his life."

Claire turned to Karl and smiled softly and discreetly to let him know she was alright.

"My mother is an O'Brien," Claire said, almost as she remembered it herself. She thought painfully of her mother's plight and closed her eyes briefly, thinking Mara's prayer in her mind and intending it for her mother.

"The O'Briens have always been the most powerful Claremen." Richard said, looking somewhat impressed. "But they'll have none of us. We're not land people. I'm from the Waters. Good name for us. We flow around as we please." He moved his hands around in a wavy motion and laughed. "Yer comin' from King Brian Boru then!" he said to Claire. "And ye must know about *Aoibheall*, then?"

"Are we getting close, Richard?" Karl said abruptly.

"We're almost there, Father. Some heard her last night shriekin' til yer blood ran cold."

"Who is she?" Claire asked.

"*Aoibheall* is the O'Brien banshee, the Death Messenger. She …"

"This is it!" Karl interrupted sharply as the Abbey ruins came visible in the lonely vale ahead.

Claire was still thinking about the O'Brien death banshee and shivering as she stepped out of the blue pickup and viewed the skeletal remains of a once-magnificent structure. She followed Karl and Richard into the west end of the nave, passing under the belfry. The cloud-studded sky was the only ceiling as the sun poured in to illuminate the interior of the cruciform building. Her eyes flew up to the beautiful arches above the choir and the two side chapels. On the ground in the open area in front of a large heap of rubble were huddled a small group of men which now included Karl and Richard. She walked toward them slowly. It wasn't until she was almost upon them that she made the unsettling discovery that the heap was made up of what appeared to be ancient human bones, chaotically scattered among toppled stone monuments and fragments of rock. Propped against this assemblage lay a battered old grey-haired man with sunken cheeks, wearing a soiled plaid sport coat, smoking a cigarette and mumbling to himself. The rage that Claire hoped to vent at one of her husband's killers dissipated faintly as she saw the pathetic figure.

"Before I tear myself from the Abyss, my Master, talk a little with me." Theo now leaned forward and pulled on Karl's pant leg. "To draw me out of error. Where is the ice?" His eyes looked intermittently wild and then vacant. "And how, in such a short while has the sun made transit from evening to morning?" Kostanikas gasped and then cried out, "The Worm that pierces the world!"

"The poor old man's daft." Richard said quietly to his two Traveller friends who had discovered Theo in the Abbey. "I'm afraid he's more bats than the belfry!" one of them responded nodding toward the steeple.

Karl put his hand up to silence them. He looked at Stephan and then at Claire. "He's quoting Dante, the last Canto of *Hell*. Shhh" The old man continued.

"*A place there is below, which is not known by sight, but by the sound of the rivulet which descends here along the hollow of a rock that it has gnawed with its winding and gently sloping course.*" He sat back against his resting place once again.

"He knows the Burren alright with its hollow underground rocks and streams. He's makin' sense of it now." Richard said, trying to be more supportive.

"Yes, yes, that could be his intention," Karl answered thoughtfully, "but he's still quoting. Dante was talking about the streamlet of sin from the Mount of Purgatory ..."

Claire looked again at the grisly pile of rubble.

"Which finds its way back to Satan," Karl concluded.

Chapter 53

And for all this, nature is never spent
There lies the dearest freshness deep down thing
And though the last light off the black West went
Oh, morning at the brown brink eastward springs —
Because the Holy Ghost over the bent World broods
With warm breast and with Ah! bright wings.
Gerard Manley Hopkins

Patrick watched his mother drive away in the truck with Karl. He felt lonely and frightened. In his small but strong heart he knew something. It wasn't clear. It was almost like a dream he couldn't quite remember or a picture before him that would dissolve into wisps of colored dots just as he was beginning to see it. It was confusing sometimes to know so much and yet not have lived life long enough to have the experiences or even the words to attach things to. Huge ideas hung suspended in his mind like glistening balls spinning around and around, brushing him lightly or drawing him into their core and then flinging him out again, breathless.

There were children playing. He stood silently. Mara knelt down beside him.

"Patrick, do you feel okay?" she asked.

"Yes, I'm okay."

"Do you want to join the other children?"

"No, thank you."

"Are you tired? Do you want to take a rest?" She stroked his head affectionately as she would her own nephew.

"No." Tears welled up in Patrick's eyes.

"Patrick, dear! What is it? Do you miss your mama? She'll be back soon." Mara hugged the little boy to her.

"I'm afraid." Patrick began to cry now, wiping and licking his tears away and turning so the other children couldn't see him.

"That's alright."

"Daddy said not to be afraid." He choked back a tiny sob.

"But he didn't mean that you *couldn't* be afraid! Or that you should feel bad when you are. I think he meant that … Look at me

Patrick, and please believe me!" She waited until the boy looked her in the eye. "He meant that Goodness is much, much greater than the Badness that we are afraid of. And that even if all we see is the Badness, it's just because we're too small to see the whole thing. But your daddy knew you were small and that you would be afraid sometimes. Do you understand me?"

"Yes."

"All of the messengers that God sent from heaven to talk to us, the angels — they all said 'Don't be afraid!' — all of them — the first words out of their mouths — 'Don't be afraid.' And Jesus told us not to be afraid. But you know what? I get afraid, too … Even with all of those important people telling me not to."

"You do? You never look afraid."

"Grown-ups can go more places by themselves. You just don't see me."

A gnarly brown freckled hand gripped Mara's shoulder and she looked up, startled by the touch. Standing by them was a very old man. He had white hair, still tinted in some places with the rusty color it used to be. He looked thin and frail despite the layers of sweaters and jackets that he wore and the strength of his grasp. His face was weathered, brown and freckled like his hand. He had no teeth but his green eyes shone like emeralds.

"Don't be afraid now, young lady." Mara and Patrick looked at each other. Mara stood up.

Mara held out her delicate hand to the old man. "Hello, sir. I am Mara and this is …"

"I know who ye are." The old man's voice was hoarse now. He took her hand and shook it firmly. "Ye're a beautiful Gypsy girl, that's who ye are."

"Do you know who *I* am?" Patrick asked, looking up at the emerald eyes.

The man hesitated and then spoke in a tired whisper. "*Yes, I do. And I've been waiting a long time for you to come.*"

"We made pretty good time, actually. We weren't far from Dublin. Did they tell you we were on the way?" Mara asked.

The Traveller camp sat on the barren western landscape like a wagon train huddled in a desert of the American West. But a chill autumn wind blew harshly and no California dream beckoned these folk further westward. Only sheer cliffs and a plunge to the cold Atlantic would they find.

There were no old Romany caravans here — only cars, a few battered trailers and a tent or two. Some fires were lit for cooking and for warmth when the sun was hidden behind the thick clouds that rode the wind.

The old man looked at Patrick. "They told me you were coming. I am so glad that you're here."

Patrick reached up for the man's hand. Mara was glad to see a smile break across the boy's face again.

"I am Patrick Michael O'Connell and I'm not afraid."

"I'll bet ye're hungry though, and I just made meself some good Irish oats. Would ye like some?" He pointed with his left hand to a fire near a small tent.

Patrick walked slowly with the old man, limping again, and dragging his pack.

"It's yer *heel*, isn't it now … Does it pain you much?" Patrick shrugged and turned to Mara.

"It's okay," said Patrick. "He's not a stranger." The two went hand in hand toward the fire.

Mara glanced back toward the van to see Rose standing in bewilderment, holding her handkerchief and her purse.

"Alright then, Patrick. I'll see to Rose. Eat up!"

Chapter 54

It has been truly said that the use that Dante made of ... his huge heathen fragments only give a hint of some enormous natural religion behind all history and from the first foreshadowing the Faith.
G.K. Chesterton

Claire bumped along in the back of a pickup, bundled in a large ill-fitting jacket and a striped wool blanket. Of course she had insisted on riding in the back. Steve had to drive while Karl tried to get the dazed Kostanikas to remember any landmarks on this lonely expanse of the Burren that might help them find the lab. After all, she had insisted on coming — it was only logical ... but cold.

"I know you're tired and sick, man, and we'll let you rest after we find Day and the others," Karl said coaxingly.

Theo sat hunched in the middle of the seat, not even looking out the window, but down at his feet, throwing his arms up periodically to ward off unseen attackers. He guzzled some warm tea from the lid of a thermos. "Are you Jewish?" Theo said, turning slightly toward Karl.

"Yes, I am."

"Then I can tell you. It's *not* the Golem! It's *not* a soul! They don't understand!"

Theo became more and more agitated. Through the rear window of the truck Claire could faintly hear his ranting. She saw Karl put his strong arms around the older man's stiffened shoulders. Theo struggled at first, but then seemed to relax as Karl's lips moved slowly and deliberately. He released him then.

"*We understand*, Doctor, that it is a *very urgent and serious* situation," Karl said gently. "And we want to help you stop it. We don't want anyone else to get hurt. We need you to simply look out the window and tell us if you see anything familiar."

Theo looked up cautiously. "The black birds are gone, then? The ones that were after my head?"

"Yes, they're gone for now." Karl answered.

Steve held a wrinkled piece of paper that had been stuffed into his hand by a very old man at the Traveller camp. It was a map, of sorts, but the lines on it did not seem to have any correspondence to the minimal road system on the Burren. He drove slowly in the general direction, he thought, of where the lines seemed to intersect, but nothing stood out as extraordinary on the moon-like terrain. Scattered shrub-like trees, random stones, some intentional monuments, a diminished herd of scrawny goats.

"There!" Theo called out. "That's where I left him!" He pointed to the crest of a small hill in the distance to a dolmen that was larger than other monoliths they had seen. "Park over there behind that old fence and cover the truck with bracken from the bushes. I know they're looking for me. They need me. I am the Greek!"

Claire left the blanket behind as Karl helped her out of the truck and explained what they were doing.

"He's not a villain, Claire. I'm sure that Day has used his mental weakness for his own purposes. He's defected and he wants to help us."

Claire did not find it difficult now to pity this abused and exploited man who could barely stand without Steve's support. Theo stared at the map in Steve's hand.

"Are you working with them? How did you get a guide to the *ley system*? That's it!" he said, pointing to the dolmen and then to the intersection on the map.

"No, someone gave this to me at the Traveller camp. I had no idea what it was," Steve answered. "Looks like First Down for us!" Claire and Karl both groaned. "Well, football was my first love, okay? Give me a break!"

The sun that had shown briefly was gone again and a massive grey shield of endless cloud cover had moved into place. Claire shivered and held the borrowed jacket close around her.

"Where is the lab?" Karl asked Kostanikas.

"Follow me," the old man said, "and stay low." He moved slowly and laboriously up the hill. As they neared the stone structure Theo said, "This is where the stars called me to dance. They knew my name."

Claire gazed up at the steel-colored barrier that covered the earth like a dome and wondered if the sun had ever shown here or the stars had ever danced. They all knelt behind the cold slabs of stone and looked down the hill on the other side. There sat a well-kept whitewashed Irish cottage with a bright blue door. The blooms were gone from the fuchsia hedge and the remaining leaves dangled and swayed in the intermittent gusts of wind. The dirt road up to the house was empty and the few outbuildings looked deserted and unusable for anything but the rudest shelter. There seemed to be no one about.

"*That* is the lab?" Steve asked incredulously, staring out on the homely setting.

"The Circles are deep in the earth … *Wherefore I think and deem it for thy best that thou follow me, and I will be thy guide, and will lead thee hence through the eternal place where thou shalt hear the despairing shrieks, shalt hear the ancient spirits woeful who each proclaim the second death.*"

Karl answered him: "*Art thou then that Virgil and that fount which pours forth so broad a stream of speech?*"

Tears fell over Theo's bloody cheek. "Am I not Pythagoras, then? He was wrong! The game was all wrong! But Virgil was Roman! I am Greek!"

"Roman, Greek, Jew … those walls have been broken down, Theo. We can walk together now." Karl continued from Dante: "*Poet, who guidest me, consider my power, if it be sufficient, before thou trust me to the deep pass.*"

Claire and Steve listened in amazement and silence as the two men spoke.

"*Now let us descend here below into the blind world. I will be first and thou shalt be second.*" Theo spoke.

"*How shall I come, if thou fearest?*" Karl asked, looking into Theo's eyes.

Theo reached out to touch the blonde man's strong shoulder. "*Because I am wroth, be not thou dismayed, for I shall win the contest, whoever circle round within for the defence. This, their insolence is not new, for of old they use it at a less secret gate, which is still found without a bolt.*"

"Wow, how did you both memorize all that? That's impressive," Steve whispered to Karl, nudging Claire for a response. She nodded, still in awe of the timelessness of the words quoted here, kneeling by a stone in Ireland over seven hundred years after they were written.

"Celibacy has its advantages," Karl whispered back to Steve.

"You two stay here. I will follow my guide to see what lies below. We'll let you know what we find."

Karl lifted Theo to his feet and peered boldly at the old man. "Let's go to Hell!"

Theo smiled as they made their way gingerly and cautiously down the hill.

"*But huge and mighty forms that do not live*
Like living men, moved slowly through the mind,'" Claire said softly.

"Dante?" asked Steve.

"No, Wordsworth. Remember? Michael's passages on the disc?"

"You all are show-offs, you know, with your eerie poetic forebodings … but I have the scariest quote yet," he said as they looked down at the humble Irish dwelling. "'*The computer, literally, could run the world from a cottage.*' Marshall McLuhan, 1970."

Chapter 55

Gimme shelter, before I fade away.
Mick Jagger

…only in the song a recurrent code showed the child already initiated.
Charles Williams

Patrick and the old man ate their oatmeal in silence. The boy felt warm and comfortable sitting by the fire with a full stomach.

"What's your name?" Patrick asked finally.

"I'm called Eamonn."

Patrick sighed with relief. "I'm glad you found me, Eamonn."

"It seems like *ye* found *me*, now doesn't it, Patrick? Well, it doesn't matter now that ye're here. Is that yer sack there?"

"Yes, and it's been very hard to carry all over *everywhere*. But my daddy said I could only give it to you — no one else."

"You're a brave one, *Oisin*. But of course, you must be. It is a heavy load for one so small to bear."

Mara had seated Rose on a stool in front of another fire and now as the old woman smoked a cigarette, she was doted on by some other Travellers who had discovered that she was Ian McCullum's widow. "Yer husband was a fine man, Rose," one middle-aged woman said fondly. "He wasn't only into his books, ye know," she added, poking a nearby friend, "but he worked all over this island for Travellers' rights. He was a true champion, he was."

Mara bent down next to Rose as she basked in the good memories of her husband. "Patrick's made a quick friend," she said, gesturing across toward Eamonn's tent. "He seems himself again. It's been a bit rocky for him, I think."

"Well, of course! Poor lamb!" Rose spoke softly out of the side of her mouth, so as not to distract the flow of compliments that were coming her way. Along with the words came a stream of smoke that Mara brushed away discreetly. "That old man with Patrick looks *so familiar* to me. I can't place when or where I've seen him, though. Must have been *another* friend of Ian's."

Mara stood and took a little walk around the camp. She was

restless and sorry to have been left 'behind the lines.'

Patrick and Eamonn had moved into the small tent; the ancient chess pieces were set up.

"I'm sorry I didn't bring the board from the camper," Patrick apologized. "I forgot, 'cause I was tired."

But Eamonn had his own board. "This is the board where they were meant to move."

Patrick watched in amazement as the pieces began to shine and then vibrate slightly.

"*Misog, sang?*" asked Patrick.

"*Stes*, I understand The Tongue."

Chapter 56

What is the price of a thousand horses against one son where there is only one son?

J. M. Synge

The shell in my hand is deserted.
Anne Morrow Lindbergh

"You left his body right here?" Karl was shocked at the news.

"*I* didn't leave him here!" Kostanikas whispered impatiently. "I told you there was a *Magic Circle* around this area." He gestured feebly. "He was the *Old King* and *they killed him.*"

"It's a ritual enactment. Do you understand that?" Karl asked.

"Don't be condescending with me! I felt his pulse! *Zero!* Nothing! He was dead!"

"And you're sure it was Day?"

"No, it was the middle of the *night!*" Theo laughed to himself. "Of course I'm sure! I lit my lighter in front of his face. That was after my foot was on fire and the stars came down to find me."

Karl was having a hard time sorting through Theo's mind. "Can you crawl a bit, Doctor? I don't want us to be seen. But lead the way … you are still my guide."

As they crawled behind the hedge Theo said, "You don't look Jewish! I knew them all; you know — the great ones — Lefschetz the first Jew at Princeton, Von Neumann, Einstein! No … You look more like *Birhoff,* the President of Harvard who refused to *hire* Jews! Are you German or Jewish, then?"

"I'm both."

There was a pause.

"God, I thought *I* was schizophrenic! Which part does your power come from?"

"I am also a Catholic priest. Any power that I have comes from God."

"Jesus Christ!" Theo exclaimed.

"Yes, more specifically, yes. I told you the barriers have been broken down."

Just then the two men heard a noise in the distance — a faint roar. "I think someone is coming," Karl whispered and lay flatter against the ground. They lay motionless along the back hedge as two cars drove up the dirt road to the cottage. They heard voices but could see nothing from their vantage point.

"As soon as they go down, assuming they do, I think that we should go back to the camp and get some more help. Then we'll come back after nightfall," Karl said quietly into Theo's ear.

"Whatever you say, but God's power must not be so great if he needs reinforcements!"

"We're not supposed to tempt God by forcing his hand. He means us to use our reason, as well."

Theo laughed almost too loudly. "If you're a reasonable man, then why are you lying on the ground in the middle of this forsaken place following a certified lunatic?"

"Because you know Dante."

"Maybe *you* are crazy, too!"

"A lot of people think so."

Their bodies were cramped and cold by the time the voices finally faded. They made their way back up the hill slowly and told Steve of the new plan. Karl waited to tell him about Theo's version of Day's death until they were alone. He still didn't know what to think of it. The sun was already making its westward descent when they returned to the Traveller camp.

When they pulled in, Mara ran up to the truck. Others joined in a knot behind her. She had a frantic and helpless look on her face. Claire saw her first. Karl had taken the outdoor ride on their return trip. Claire jumped out of the truck, her heart beating wildly.

"What is it, Mara?" she grabbed the young woman's hands. She named her worst fear: "Is it Patrick? Has something happened to Patrick?"

Mara wiped tears away from her face and nodded.

"What's happened? *What's going on?*" Claire yelled before Mara could say anything more.

Karl stepped next to Claire and put his arm around her. "Let's hear what Mara has to say." His face was tense and his jaw twitched.

"He's gone! We've searched everywhere! He was with the old

man — and *he's* missing, too. I don't understand it. There's no way Day's people could have gotten in here undetected. But they must have! It's all my fault — I was not paying attention." She began to cry again. "I'm so sorry, Claire." Claire let go of Mara's hands.

"Are there any new vehicle tracks nearby?" Karl asked of anyone who could hear. Richard Waters was the one to answer.

"No, Father. We've spread out and looked on foot. Maybe a few animal tracks. Nothing more."

Rose had pushed her way into the front of the crowd and stood on the other side of Claire, and put her arm around her.

"Who was this old man who's missing with Patrick?" Karl asked of the crowd again. "Did anyone know him well?"

"Name's Eamonn. That's all I know," said a woman with a baby on her hip.

Richard spoke up again. "He showed up here just the day before ye arrived, Father. None o' us knew him well, ye could say. But he seemed like a kind ol' fella."

"*Now* I know!" exclaimed Rose. "I remember where I've seen that old man before! It was the man that Ian got the *chess set* from. Remember, Karl? We found his name among Ian's things. Eamonn, it was Eamonn!" Rose crossed herself. "And Eamonn means 'Blessed Protection'. It's paradoxical … or is it ironic? — anyway, it doesn't seem to help much in this case."

"What the *hell* are we standing around for? What is this place? I thought we were going back to stop those fools from *ruining the universe!*" Theo was obviously regaining some strength after dozing in the truck. He looked at Karl. "If I have to go myself, I will. Now that Day is dead, that *other* Irish bastard's in charge …" He touched his cheek where O'Toole had struck him. "… He's worse than all of them put together. He's *cold*, that one — like ice."

Claire, Mara, Steve and Rose all reacted with their own kind of gasp and surprise at the mention of Day's death.

"What? Day is dead? What's he talking about, Karl?" Steve demanded.

Confusion spread as people murmured through the crowd. Claire was overwrought and Theo still looked exhausted in spite of his agitation. Karl took charge.

"Mara and Rose! Would you see if you can get some help to bandage up the good doctor's face? And get him some food and drink! You'll let them do that won't you, Dr. Kostanikas?"

"You can call me Theo! You must have studied Theo-logy! You know all about me then, Father Volkstein. That's a good German-Jewish name now, isn't it? Yes, I'll be good while the ladies attend to me. *Quickly*, though, quickly, Yes?"

As Theo hobbled off with Mara and Rose, Mara turned and glanced sadly back at Claire.

"Now, Richard, you and Stephan round up the best team of specialists you can to get us into the lab …" Karl turned to Claire, who was expecting to be left behind and no longer had the energy to care, "while Claire O'Brien O'Connell and I decide what our plan should be."

Claire roused out of her stupor at this vote of confidence and respect. Karl led her over to a fire that was burning nearby. "Let's have something to eat while we talk," he said as he dished them something from a pot close to the fire. "It will give us strength."

Claire ate the spicy stew and felt the warmth spread through her. "Why do they want Patrick? And who are *'they'* if Day is dead?"

"I don't know if Day *is* really dead. It might be Theo's misunderstanding of a Druidic ritual. And he *is* delusional, you know, even though he's extremely perceptive. So let's say that Day is dead. The only person I know who might have taken over is O'Toole … the aforementioned Irish bastard. I wouldn't put it past him. He did a lot of dirty work. My only question is how O' Toole could have supplanted him, earned the respect that Day had with all his followers …"

"So why does Treat O'Toole want my son?"

"I think they all believe that Patrick is the Great One." Karl looked gravely into her eyes.

"What? Why that's crazy! A *five-year-old* is going to run their cult? A *little boy* is going to bring peace and harmony to the world? Why would they possibly believe this?"

"I believe it, Claire." Karl still looked steadily at her.

"You *what?*" She recoiled.

"I believe that Patrick …" A chirping sound came from Karl's pocket. He pulled out his cell phone.

"Hello, Karl? It's me Francine? I hope you're doing well and everything, but … can I talk to my sister? No offense, but I want to tell her something directly and …"

"It's alright, Francine. It's fine! She's right here."

Karl gave the phone to Claire.

"Hi, Big Sister! How's it going?" Franny was trying to sound chipper.

"It's going," Claire said. She dreaded answering questions right now about Patrick or her mother.

"First — this is going to sound kind of spooky and weird and not like me at all — I had this *vision* type-thing at the Mission Church. I'm not going to tell you all about it now — it would be kind of degrading, like phone sex or something … well not like that … anyway, the main thing is that I know now that no matter what happens — everything is okay. You probably don't believe me and I wouldn't believe me either if I hadn't been there. I'll tell you more when you get home. I miss you guys so much. Claire, are you still there?"

"Yes, Little Sister. I'm still here. I love you, Franny."

"There's something else that might be nothing or it might be something. You just never know in these kind of situations," Fran added, as if she had been facing 'these kinds of situations' her whole life.

"What is it?"

"I went to your house to try to find out some clues about Mom. I thought she might have gone there before … whatever … and I was in Patrick's closet. You know the part that curves off, where you can't go without bumping your head? Well, Patrick had this little *altar* in there with little religious articles … you know kid-stuff like you used to have in our room? But I found Michael's crucifix, the one that used to be over the bureau in your room …."

Even though it made her even sadder to think that Patrick felt he had to hide the things, she was relieved that the 'cult' people hadn't stolen it as she had feared and weren't using it for a 'black Mass' or whatever it was they did. "Is that it? Is that what you wanted to tell me?"

"Well, that and the fact that there was a removable piece in the back of the cross, like a place for hiding something."

"Was there anything in there?" Claire asked expectantly.

"No, it was empty."

"Oh."

"I just thought you'd want to ask Patrick about it. It might be significant, you never know."

"You never know."

"No news about Mom?"

"No." Claire felt sick. "How's Dad holding up?"

"He still sits there in his chair. Falls asleep sometimes. But he prays the rosary all day long. It looks so funny. I've never seen Dad with a rosary. But Mom asked him in the letter to pray, so he does. He has to look in Mom's little book since he doesn't remember what comes next. I don't either, but I'm getting better. I love you, too, Claire. We all do. You *and* Patrick. I better go. Let me know if there's any news."

Chapter 57

Adhuc nox est. It is still night.
St. Augustine

I will not leave you as orphans; I will come to you.
St. John, quoting Jesus

Patrick didn't feel so sure anymore.

Since he'd been separated from Eamonn he was afraid again. The place where he was felt like a cage — like the ones in his picture book of the traveling circus that held the lion, the monkey and the bear. But those cages were brightly colored and the animals looked happy on the circus train. Here it was so dark he could barely see — he thought he could make out other cages like his own around the room in the faint light of a dim blue bulb somewhere along the wall. His cage had a pillow and a blanket. Maybe there were animals in the other cages, though. He'd always wanted a dog ... In the stillness he heard an occasional whirring noise, like Sean's remote control car. He missed Sean and Molly and ... everybody. He listened quietly. He heard a growl and snort.

"Hey, any animals in here?" he said, but not too loud. He didn't want the doctors and nurses to come back. At least they had *looked* like doctors and nurses, but they weren't nice. Except for one lady in a blue nurse coat. She seemed sad. "Hey, animals! I like you."

"AAHHIIII wan gedddd out! You bbbbaddd maaaannn!"

Patrick was startled and afraid again. The voice sounded human and strange. Then there came a banging noise.

"Hush, David! You'll make them come," a girl's voice said softly. "Hush, it's only another boy."

Patrick's eyes were slowly growing accustomed to the lack of light. The other cages were filled with *children*. Most of them were asleep, but some were stirring.

"What's wrong with *you?*" It was the same girl's voice. Patrick turned toward it. A dark-haired girl in a pink nightgown sat leaning back against the bars of her cage, her knees bent; they were too long to stretch out. He thought she was pretty. She was a lot older than

Patrick. She looked about Devin's age, he thought; and his cousin was in fifth grade.

"Nothing's wrong with me, I mean, I'm bad sometimes, but … what do you mean?"

"All of us have something wrong with us. That's why we're here. Are you an orphan, then?"

"What's an orphan?"

"It means that your mother and father are dead or that they didn't want you."

"I'm part orphan, then. My daddy died. But my mom's okay and everybody wants me."

The girl didn't respond.

"What's wrong with you? Are you an orphan?" asked Patrick.

The girl was quiet for a moment. Then Patrick heard the whirring sound again as the pink sleeves of her nightgown rose and the weak blue light reflected off the metal that shown where hands should have been.

"I was born without arms, they say, but I think it was a tragic accident, like in a car or something. I don't believe them."

Patrick stared at the mechanical limbs as they whirred slowly down again.

"I hate these. They do experimentations on us. No orphanage was ever this bad. Some of us have died. They don't say that, but I know."

"I-I-I almost died." A nasal, high-pitched voice spoke in short clipped phrases. "They test my bbbrain … I don't remember … I have con … con …."

"He has seizures. See his head? It's half metal. They hook us up to computers and do experimentations. And we're *all* orphans. Some can't speak English. They got blown up in wars and maybe their parents, too. But mostly nobody wants us. Here, he calls us *damned formori*, the worst Irish one — the meanest one. I'm glad he doesn't come here too much."

"*Formorii* are the sea gods who were all violent and misshaped. That's in an old Irish Story I heard from my daddy." Patrick said. "That *was* a mean thing to say. The *Tuath da Dannann* — the Golden people — got rid of them all."

"*Sshh* … I hear somebody in the hallway," the girl whispered.

Loud voices passed by, but no one entered the room.

"I'm Patrick. What's your guys' names?"

"I've changed my name a lot," said the dark-haired girl. "Nobody cares, so I can be whoever I want. Right now, I'm Christina. After the singer. I saw her dance once on TV in New York. I'm American. They brought me to the place in Ireland a while ago. That's when all the bad stuff started. I hate Ireland. Anyway … that's Elliot." She pointed to the small boy with the metal in his head. "David's asleep again, I guess. They give him lots of shots to make him quiet. He has Down Syndrome. I heard them talk about him. They said it was very mild … his syndrome … and they were trying to cure him. But he keeps getting worse and worse. They give him shots all the time now. Some of us they give pills to make us tired. We don't take them a lot," she said, looking over to another girl with a conspiratorial half-smile … "Do we, Mary?"

A little girl with bright red hair, somewhere in age between Patrick and Christina, smiled back. Her face was almost featureless and terribly scarred. She had no arms below the elbows and Patrick saw only one leg.

"They haven't gotten to Mary yet. I keep praying that they won't. Even though I know there isn't a God because he wouldn't allow all this experimentation. She got blown up right here in Ireland. Right, Mary?" The little girl nodded.

"T'was *Omagh*. Maybe ye heard of it. It was quite the thing awhile back. The bluddy *Unionists!*" She spat out the name and continued in her small but angry voice: "Me whole family dead but me!"

"Yu fookin' Cath'lics started the whole fookin' thing. So shut yer hole." This outburst came from a boy the size of Patrick. He was legless, but had one steel arm that whirred like Christina's.

"That's Kenny! They're both from the North. They hate each other," Christina explained to Patrick.

Mary said in her wispy voice from her disfigured face: "At least I wasn't *born* wrong. God punished yu from the start, then. It was the bluddy Unionists who did me in."

"God used the Unionists to punish yer Cath'lic arse!"

Mary started to cry.

"Shut up, now the both of you," the older girl said. "You see why I don't think much of God? If he is there, he doesn't care about us like everybody else. Or he's just mean like the doctors and nurses and just wants us for experimentations."

"My friend, Matthew, doesn't have any arms and he can climb the slide faster than me!" Patrick said, trying to cheer her.

"Is he an orphan?" Christina asked.

"Oh no. He has Mother Mechtilde and lots of Sisters!"

"And no experimentations?" She made one arm go up and down again. It whirred and looked like one of the robot toys the kids had at pre-school that he had never liked.

Patrick sat sadly in his cage. He wished Eamonn were there. He'd been braver and stronger with the old man — like when his father was alive. That felt like a dream now. Had he dreamt about Eamonn? He pulled the wrinkled piece of paper out of his pants pocket.

Chapter 58

The Big Lie is individual identity.
Kevin Kelly

The profound similarity between the individual and the nation lies in the mystical nature of their givenness.
Aleksandr Solzhenitsyn

"Do you mind telling me what she had to say? Or isn't it relevant to the situation?" Karl asked when Claire had sat silently for several seconds after handing him his phone.

Claire shook her head to clear it.

"It's your decision, then, let's —"

"No … I mean yes … I was just getting some of the Irish fog out of my brain."

A chilled foggy mist had settled in with the setting of the sun.

"She wanted to tell me that she'd had a vision that she couldn't explain right now …" Claire left out Fran's analogy for Karl's sake. "… but she said that the upshot of it was … that no matter what happened that everything would be okay."

"Juliana's vision."

"No, *Francine* is my sister, You know Franny?" Claire was afraid that Karl was as disoriented as she.

"Of course I remember your sister's name. St. Juliana was an English mystic in the fourteenth century. The whole mystery of Redemption and human life were made clear to her. Even the evil did not trouble her. She was told in her vision, '*Thou shalt see thyself that all manner of thing shall be well.*'"

"I thought that was Eliot," Claire answered, "*And all shall be well and, all manner of thing shall be well* — from the end of the *Four Quartets?*"

"Eliot read St. Juliana."

Claire sighed. "Karl, I appreciate your quotes and *everything* you've done. I don't have the faith that you do, *or* Franny, *or* anyone else. All I know is that my son is missing, my mother's missing and my husband is dead. You and I were going to think out a plan."

"Yes, you're right."

"One more thing — Fran didn't know if it made any difference, but she found Michael's crucifix in Patrick's closet. You remember the one I told you was missing from the bureau the night you rescued us? I thought the people who were after us had taken it … Well, anyway, there was a removable piece in the back — like a place to hide something, Fran said. Only there was nothing in it. It's funny now, I remember Patrick spotting crucifixes everywhere we've been. He would say things like 'Jesus is here, it's alright, Mommy.'" She started to cry again. "Karl, I feel so ashamed that he had to build his little altar in the closet to hide it from me. It was like with Michael. Patrick had to hide the things he loved most away somewhere — away from me." She cried, her face on Karl's black jacket that was already damp with foggy dew.

He held her. "Patrick loves *you*. He loves you more than anyone or anything on earth. Don't worry about having faith right now. The rest of us have enough for you." He gave her a strong, firm shake and then his handkerchief. She blew her nose loudly.

"As I said, these people believe that Patrick is the Great One they've all been waiting for. Day believed that the Great One would know the Ancient Language — The Tongue, *Misog*, innately, without ever being taught. First, they were convinced Michael was their savior. When he disappointed them, they moved on to Patrick. According to the legend, the power can be weaker in one generation than another or skip a generation entirely. But it comes down through family lines and the O'Connells are a strong line."

He continued, though Claire had a questioning look on her face.

"According to the things we've been able to piece together from Michael's secret messages to you and from Ian's discoveries and the egotistical diatribes by M.O.D. at the various Internet sites etc., they are looking for a Word — a special Word — from The Tongue that is the key to implementing all their research, all of their experiments and magic circles and rituals. It's something that they think will connect the mystical power of the Druids to the technological power of some sort of Artificial Intelligence. There has always been speculation that Pythagoras and his cult had some kind of connection and interchange with the Druids. I think Day thought Theo was the

Pythagorian figure he needed to add the mathematical element to his myths and magic. I actually think, if we can be patient and discerning enough, that Theo can help us to know more before we go in."

"I remember that whole idea from a book I picked up here in Ireland that summer with Michael. It all seemed very fascinating … But now … Do you *really* believe, *you* — Father Karl Burgmann — whose connection to the Vatican and to the Roman Church is still not clear to me, although I do believe it's there — *You* believe that my five year old son, Patrick, is the Great One?"

"Haven't you noticed, Claire? Haven't you seen the look in his eyes? The wisdom beyond his years? The way he 'knows' things? He does try to hide it, not just from you …" he hesitated, then added, "Michael believed it."

"He talked to you about it?" Claire asked.

"He told me that he had discussed it with Patrick to try and help him if anything ever happened."

"So Patrick believes this, too?" Claire was alarmed.

"He knows he's special — that he has certain gifts."

"Well, did anyone tell him not to let these people think he had what they wanted? My God! He could be with them right now and not understand the enormity of the situation and might go along with the thing thinking it was a game of some sort. Like the stupid chess set!"

Claire stood up from the fire and realized that darkness had come in earnest and there was a drizzling rain.

"I don't *need* to rest." A voice came out of the night.

"Resting is an *illusion*. Everything is always in motion. Every molecule in our bodies …" Theo broke into their conversation with Rose and Mara trailing behind. "Thank you, ladies for the first aid. Now I will go back to war! The Emperor needs me, as you can see." He pointed toward Karl.

"I'm not the Emperor, Theo!" Karl said in an attempt to calm the old man down.

"Well, you've some connection with a Pontiff and that's the closest thing to the Byzantines we'll find on the moon. Are we on the goddam moon?" He took a deep breath. "Lots of oxygen. We've been misinformed all along. I knew those pictures back in the sixties were fakes. Special suits and all that garbage — and those capsules in space! What a charade! All of us at the hospital knew they were simulations! And it's even raining," he said with his face turned upward. "Raining on the moon!" He did a jerky little dance.

"Theo, come and sit down with Mrs. O'Connell and me by the fire." The fire sputtered lightly with the misting rain. "Rose! Mara! Come sit with us!"

Kostanikas lit a cigarette and Rose followed suit.

"Where's Stephan, Mara?" Karl asked.

"Brendan and Gerry came in from Belfast. He's briefing them. Do you want me to get them?"

"That would be good. Two more smart ones!" Karl tried to keep as steady a tone as possible to keep Kostanikas on an even keel. "So, Claire! It seems wise to you then to go back again under the cover of darkness." He acted as if he and Claire were picking up a conversation where they had left off. Claire went along with it.

"Yes ... but we'll need to know more about the lab, though — its layout, its entrances. And what exactly might be going on? I wish we knew more!" She refrained from looking at Theo, hoping he'd take the bait.

"What do you need to know? I know *everything!* I know more than Day, than O'Toole, than that weasley little Fifkin or Ruxpin or whatever his name is!"

"What can you tell us then, Theo?" Karl asked.

"There are three entrances. I'm one of the few who knows about the third one. It's how I get in and out without them. The main room is down a long corridor. It's directly under the Dolmen. Day had it all planned with the intersection of the Ley lines. He didn't know I knew but I heard things ..."

"Theo, do you know why they wanted the boy? Patrick? Michael's son?"

Mara, Steve, Brendan, and Gerry appeared and took places in the circle, their faces illuminated in the firelight. "Where are all these damn people coming from? I thought this was a secret mission!" He looked around at all the unfamiliar faces. "ACCESS DENIED!" He stopped talking and continued to smoke, coughing vigorously.

Karl tried to go on with the meeting. "For all of you who don't know, we're only about three miles from the underground lab where we believe the Project is taking place. We also believe that Claire's mother, Grace, and Claire's son, Patrick are being held there for some purpose. It might be that they lured Patrick there with his grandmother, threatening her or something to that effect."

"*They need the boy to break the code!* They want the *Word!*" Theo joined in forcefully. "But they don't know about the NAND gates!" He was getting visibly upset.

"That's good," chimed in Rose, who was trying to help calm her patient. "Then those're the gates we'll use then. Don't you worry now!" She waved toward him with her cigaretted hand, as if trying to smooth away over sixty years of his mental anguish with one loving gesture.

Steve broke in. "The NAND gates have to do with computer architecture. They're circuits of programmable logic that …"

"8-Input, CMOS-triple 3 input — MILITARY! — *NONMILITARY* > *ACTIVE: YES! YES!*"

"Theo." Karl said calmly. I'm depending on you. You are my guide. Remember? You must think clearly. And don't be afraid. All of us are here to help." The old man quieted somewhat. "Tell us about the NAND gates. *What* don't they know about them?"

"They are the entrance to the 'Pure Intelligence,' the Angels and the Electrons … We don't have time for the whole story." Kostanikas closed his eyes. He began clutching his chest.

"Dear Lord! He's having a heart attack!" Rose exclaimed and rushed over to him. He pushed her away.

"I was only looking for my cigarettes …" He looked up at her blankly. "Do you have any, woman?"

Rose smoothed her hair and skirt, brushing off light droplets of water. "If you could ask *nicely*, Doctor, I would be happy to loan you a whole package." Karl almost intervened.

"For extending my life by twenty, my dear lady, I am eternally grateful." He coughed again as he took his 'life' in his hands.

Richard, meanwhile, had been unobtrusively constructing an impromptu shelter from the rain over the group while they talked — a makeshift tarp-tent with a hole in the middle for the smoke from the fire, which burned more steadily now.

"Thank you, Richard. That's much better. Now, Theo. We do have time for the whole story if it can help us to rescue our friends and stop the Project. The more we know before we go in, the safer everyone will be. Please tell us."

The rest of the band of Travellers were getting out of the weather in one way or another. The temperature was dropping. They commented on the coldness so early in the season.

Theo spoke: "I don't know where to begin — there really is no beginning or no ending … That's why I get confused." He scratched his dirty head.

"Just jump in wherever you think might be relevant to us here … now." Karl coaxed, but with respect.

"Very well, then, Father. I will jump in with Aquinas, a friend of yours, no doubt — with the necromancy of books." Karl nodded in the firelight.

"Aquinas states that the human intellect obtains perfection in knowledge of truth by a kind of *movement* … discursive operations, if you will. He also states that angels have knowledge from a *known* principle and they immediately perceive as *known* all its consequent conclusions … with *no* discursive process at all — no movement." Theo dragged again and blew smoke up in the air to join the smoke from the fire.

"Do you know what the Greek word *daemon* means, Father?"

"Yes, it means *knowledge*. Augustine says the demons are 'knowledge without love'."

"Well, these entities of knowledge," Theo waved his hand, "whether loveless or not, go from one place to another, according to Thomas, without traversing the intervening space and without the lapse of time." He raised his arms in excitement. "Do you see that he understood this long before Einstein? Electrons, says quantum mechanics, jump from the outer to inner orbit of the atom *without taking time or passing through the orbit!* Can you see, then? They are *connected somehow!* Day and his people think they have somehow given human logic to a machine — Michael's mind, his soul. But it's much worse than that."

Suddenly a distant shriek split the heavy air like a scythe. There was a collective jolt through the whole camp as everyone stopped what they were doing and listened.

Richard was upon it in a flash. "It's *Aoibheall*, the O'Brien death banshee again, it is. And so soon. That's not a good sign." There was muttering from around the camp. Claire was pale as the moon. The assembled circle was quiet, except for Theo.

"*Thou shalt hear the despairing shrieks, shalt hear the ancient spirits woeful each who proclaim the second death.*" The old man shivered uncontrollably and coughed a wheezing cough.

Karl was angry at the disruption, no matter what its source. He felt certain that Kostanikas had more to tell. He enjoined with Dante.

"*Master, thy discourses are so certain to me and so lay hold on my faith ...* Finish the story, Theo, about the demons and the machines."

"Matter is an exception in the universe," the old professor continued. "It is prime real estate. Almost everything is a vacuum. But it is not empty — it is a plenum. Quanta are being created and annihilated continually. A quantum that goes in and out of reality is *virtual* and can only become *real* with a certain type of energy ..." He looked around at his listeners. "Do any of you understand what I'm saying?" The unlikely company nodded in various degrees of truth.

"What I'm saying, and this is ironic, is that the demons — who have always known the scarcity of matter — are looking for new ways to *possess* it or at least influence it ... maybe even through electrons or hadrons ... and Day and Fifkin and their band of Jewish techno-spiritists are trying to upload everything and make it virtual. And the Portal for it all, what will open the NAND gates for both sides is the Word of a boy."

Rose had taken up a position next to Claire at Theo's brusque dismissal and was trying to comfort her by holding her hand. Claire's face had not regained its color since the unearthly wail. But she spoke to Dr. Kostanikas.

"Then what exactly happened to my husband?"

"I'm afraid I don't know you or your husband." Claire had not registered in Theo's world.

"You sent a letter to my husband at our home in Chicago. Michael O'Connell." Claire looked at the old man intently and coldly.

"You? You are Michael's wife? I had no idea ... I don't know what to ..." he fumbled with his pockets. "I never met him, really ...

until they loaded his data into my program … I …"

"How did he die?" Claire finally was able to ask.

"You have to understand that I was not there. Day said it was an accident. But he was drugged and O'Toole pushed him into the street. I heard him bragging to some whore about it when he was my bodyguard. *Prison* guard's more like it. I gave him the slip." Theo broke into a sly smile.

Claire's face was expressionless as she went on. "What did you mean when you said in the letter that Michael wanted 'out of the box'? Do you really believe that he is in the computer, that his mind is somehow replicated there?"

"I don't know where he is. I guess you'll have to talk to your priest here about that. I don't know about the computer — I thought he was —" Fear gripped him again. "No, it's *not* Michael."

"How do all of your theories, however fascinating, relate to Druids, Celtic mythology, Neo-Pagan networks, and magic chess games?"

"You have to understand, Mrs. O'Connell," Theo said, lighting another cigarette. "I was intended to be only one of the pieces in the game. I never knew their whole plan. *He denied me access!*" Theo yelled. "Access to *my own program!* But the game is bigger than them or me. We could all be destroyed!" The old man jumped up unsteadily and started to pace around in the rain.

"It's alright, Theo. We're going to stop them." Karl got up and followed him. "We'll be leaving shortly."

Chapter 59

I see a great man on the plain:
He gives battle to the armies; ...
He has set out towards the battle.
Unless heed is taken there will be doom.
Tain Bo Cuailnge
Central epic of the Ulster Cycle

The body, that scoundrel.
Samuel Beckett

The convoy of trucks and cars groped along the ill-defined Burren roads in the darkness and steady rain. It had been decided that a back-up contingent would come behind the main group who would try to make the first entry. Karl had intended that Rose stay at the camp and rest, but she insisted that she felt 'compelled' to go, even if she just sat in the car and prayed. She sat in the back seat now of an old mud-colored Ford with Mara and Claire. Steve drove, leading the foolish but hopeful regiment, with Theo and Karl.

Theo was the first to see the glowing eyes ahead of them through the sweep of the wiper blades in the faint beam of the headlights. He let out a yell. Steve slammed on the brakes as a deer and a group of fawns darted across the road. The other vehicles came to a screeching halt behind them.

"I don't see how these animals survive in this place," Steve said as he resumed the slow pace.

"There must be a lovely little green and succulent pasture somewhere that makes it worthwhile," Rose chimed in.

With headlights doused, the vehicles lined up along the old fence. Richard, Brendan, and Gerry were to wait at the top of the hill with Steve's cell phone. They would be called when needed and alert the other Traveller volunteers, who waited in their cars ready to assist. Rose was to stay in the car and out of the rain.

"I feel compelled to go down with you!" Rose called through the mist as the group began to climb. She came running after them in her raincoat.

"It's not possible!" Karl commanded. "It wouldn't be safe."

"We're not safe anywhere except in God's hand … Claire is going. She's not a trained 'operative' or whatever the rest of you are."

"But Claire is —"

"They killed my Ian, too." Then Claire reached for the older woman and embraced her firmly, thinking how useless they *both* would be if any real conflict developed.

Karl paused for a moment, then relented. "Alright Rose … alright. But you won't need *that!*"

Rose held her purse tightly. "I certainly may."

They began the ascent of the hill.

"See, Father," Theo said, breathing laboriously. "You are *not* a reasonable man."

At the Dolmen, the group split up.

"If you don't hear from us at all by midnight, call the police," Karl ordered. The three men settled under a tarp as the invading party went down the hill. It was a treacherous descent as little streams formed before they were absorbed in the porous limestone and the few patches of earth were slick with mud. Rose tried to help Theo, who would have none of it, and almost slipped herself, whereas everyone reached for Rose. They could use no flashlights until they were sure there was no one about above ground. Everything was dark and empty. The white of the cottage was ghostly, blurred by the rain.

"I count six cars and a van in the outbuildings," Steve reported as he and Mara returned from a quick reconnoiter of the area. "But everyone must be below."

Mara was silent until she moved next to Claire and said softly. "I *do* feel it was my fault. I was brooding and not attentive enough. Forgive me, please."

Claire realized with that appeal that she had no forgiveness in her heart. It was her anger that she was depending on for strength. Without Patrick, she was bitter and resentful without relief. If she said yes to Mara now, she would have to forgive everyone for everything — her mother, Michael, God, herself, and maybe even Treat O'Toole. And she would crumble there. She could not say yes.

"I was the one who insisted on leaving him," she answered, with no warmth. "Let's just hope he's alright." Mara left her side then. The rain turned to sleet and they all pulled up their collars to the icy wind.

"Can you show us the way, Theo?" Karl asked the old man.

"Over here!" Theo started moving along the front hedge of the cottage. Karl grabbed his arm and shone a slim point of light from his pocket torch in a line ahead of them. The sleet slashed the point again and again, conspiring with the darkness to cut off their progress. Mara and Steve flanked them, alert to any noise or movement. They each held something in their hands. Claire couldn't tell if it was guns or unlit flashlights. She and Rose brought up the rear.

"*Hail Mary, full of grace …*" Rose said as they walked arm in arm. "*Blessed art thou among women, and blessed is the fruit of thy womb, Jesus. Holy Mary, Mother of God, pray for us sinners now and at the hour of our death. Amen.*" She went on with the Our Father and Hail, Holy Queen. The familiarity of the prayers, their rhythm and poetry were of some comfort to Claire as they prepared to go down into the earth. She paid no real attention to the words until the last prayer, '*… To you do we cry, poor banished children of Eve, mourning and weeping in this valley of tears …*'

Claire felt like a banished child, destined to wander forever, losing everyone and everything that was important to her along the way. Rose tried to light a cigarette but the match kept going out.

Theo stood for a minute then moved off to the left by himself a few paces. "Here we are — by this bush. There's a cover over a hole right *agh* —" The old man gave a cry of pain as he fell. Karl leaned down to find him straddling the hole and rubbing his leg. "The damn cover is gone!"

Karl tried to calm him down and assess the injury to his leg.

"Doctor Kostanikas! Are you all right?" Rose came up next to him.

"Keep that woman away from me until I need a cigarette."

"Will you all keep your voices down to a whisper, *please*," Karl said with frustration. He shone his light into the hole. "It's a fortunate thing it's not deep. It's slanted inside, like a ramp."

"They probably used it to roll in their bigger equipment. Then sealed it off." Steve suggested.

"And I have the little key" Theo said in a high pitched theatrical voice as he swung it in front of Karl's light. Then in mock penitence: "Forgive me, Father, for I have sinned. I stole it from a lab technician who was torturing little children."

"You're forgiven, Theo. What happens next?"

"Are you serious about torturing children? What do you mean?" Claire had thought of Patrick. "I thought this was a computer lab." She hoped this was one of Theo's hallucinations.

"It's another thing they didn't know I knew. They do experiments on Day's crippled orphans!"

The group recoiled. "It sounds like the Nazis!" Rose exclaimed.

"You see why Science, Politics and Mysticism don't mix," Karl said.

"Maybe they're trying to *help* the children." Steve offered. "There are some technical advances that are unbeliev …"

"They tortured them. I heard them moaning and crying with my own ears!" Theo insisted.

Karl said patiently again. "Theo, what happens next? We must move on. Where will we enter the layout?"

"We'll go down the ramp and come to a door that leads into a storage room that's hardly used. That opens out into a corridor that leads eventually to the main room."

Claire was still in shock. "Where are the children kept?"

"They're in a corridor off that one. But we can't get to them. That door to that room is always locked and I *don't* have that key."

They crept down the ramp. Theo had his key ready, but the heavy door was ajar. "It's not even *closed*, let alone locked!" said Theo, almost with disappointment, as they went into the darkened storage room. "Very strange!" he exclaimed under his breath.

Karl peeked out into the hallway and turned back to the old man, whispering now. "Is there any way to kill the lights in these corridors?" Karl hoped that Theo's lucidity, which had been amazing for a long period now, would continue.

"If I knew I would have killed them already. They burrow holes in my brain and sizzle and crack."

Steve went out stealthily and found a power box. The overhead lights in the corridor went off and in their place tiny foot lights spaced at distances along the floor came on. The group moved along, finding another closet and ducking in to listen for any sounds. Nothing.

When they passed a corridor that went off to the right, Claire asked quietly, "Are the children down there?"

Kostanikas looked at Karl. "We can't get in, I told you!" He was getting agitated.

"I just want to go to the door. If Patrick's in there, even if *I* can't get in, he'll know I'm here."

"There could be an attendant in there with them." Karl said.

"Then she'll open the door and we'll overpower her — six to one," Claire responded. Rose held her pocketbook up as if preparing to use it as a weapon.

"Claire, it's risky for us to all wait here." Karl felt he was losing control of the whole situation.

"*My* room is there, too. We could go in there and wait and I could check on my things. I don't think they can lock the door since O'Toole blew it off." he cackled softly.

They followed Theo only a few steps to a door on the left. Steve and Mara tried the door and went in first. It wasn't locked and did hang askew, with blasting putty marks still on it. Theo had been right about that. Everyone but Claire tiptoed quickly into the room. She walked down to the door where the children were held. Karl went out after her. She felt no fear.

In his room, Theo tried the light on the wall switch and nothing happened.

"I want to use your flashlight to look around my room," Theo said, tapping Steve on the shoulder.

"Okay." said Steve. The old man searched the room with the single beam.

"*They've taken everything!* My computer! My table! Maybe …" He shined the light on the only thing left in the room — a bed. "*Holy* —"

"Mary, Mother of God …" Rose finished.

Karl heard the muffled commotion from down the hall but he stayed beside Claire.

She knocked on the door softly. "*Patrick! Little boy!*" she whispered as close to the door as possible. "Are you in there? It's Mommy!" There was no answer. No sound at all. She tried the door, hoping Theo was wrong. It was locked. She tapped again. *"Please, Patrick! If you're in there, make a noise — anything!"* Still nothing. She moved away in discouragement, Karl by her side.

"It's a *corpse!*" Rose exclaimed. "God rest his soul!"

"How do you know it's a man? It's covered with a sheet!" Theo retorted fearfully. Claire came with Karl into the room where the beam of light exhibited the covered body. She fainted into his arms.

"Dear Lord!" Rose said reaching into her handbag. "I do have the brandy I got from Richard!" She pulled out a silver flask. "This might help." She took a big swig herself, then went over to where Karl had gently laid Claire on the floor. Mara was trying to get Claire's feet higher than her head. Karl propped up her head briefly to see if the sip of Rose's brandy helped. Claire started to come around.

"Oh no! Oh no! Oh no!"

Mara shined her light onto Theo, who had collapsed against a wall and was rocking back and forth, moaning.

"*It's me!* I thought the cigarettes were foolproof. But it must be me! I'm dead. I am dead. I never escaped. It was a trick."

Karl was ready to leave everyone there but Mara and Steve. "It's *not* you, Theo." He left Claire to Rose and walked over to the bed and pulled back the sheet.

"No, No. I don't want to see myself dead!" the old man whimpered.

"It's not you, Theo. It's James Day." He was struck by the pallor of the skin and felt his neck. "And he's not dead, either."

Chapter 60

Myth is the mountain whence all the different streams arise which become truths down here in the valley; in huc valle abstractionis. *(in this valley of separations)*
C.S. Lewis

Up on the Burren the wind died down and snow began to fall until the ground was white. Two pig keepers ran into each other on the wintry plain.

"And what are ye doin' out in the night, Rucht? Ye're ol' woman pitch ye out again?"

The two men, middle-aged, stout and hardy, were bundled up in almost identical clothing–wool caps, scarves, and jackets with baggy pants stuck into worn leather boots. They looked like brothers, but they had a hard time even being friends.

"I wouldn't talk, Fruich! What brings ye out this far and in a snow storm?"

"It's a strange thing, isn't it? Snow on the Burren and as early as All Souls Night?"

"Ye didn't answer me question!"

"Well, ye didn't answer mine!"

"I'm looking fer me bloody pigs. They ran off. I thought maybe ye took them."

The two men were covered with snow as they stood, for it was falling heavily. They both shook all over like great dogs. The snow flew off in all directions.

"I wouldn't steal yer bloody pigs! I was goin' to see if ye stole mine, as they ran off from me!"

The two men stood and quarreled until they were each completely covered in a mound of snow. Other things were covered that night — the Abbey ruins, the ancient stone monuments, the village homes, the rural cottages, the statues, the graves of heroes and villains, of kings and peasants — the wires of electric current, the crosses, the gun shops, the post offices, the book shops — the houses of terrorists, of priests, of poets, of thieves — the stones and shells that washed up from the sea. Almost the whole island was white, they say, and it reflected into the sea and some saw it rise from the sea like a mirror and hover like a watery land between the worlds.

Suddenly the snow fell away from the two pig-keepers and there on the Burren Plain stood two bulls of different colors. The Brown Bull was huge, dark, proud and ferocious. The other had White Horns, white head and feet, and his body was blood-red. They both stamped the snow-packed earth with their great hooves. At least that's what the old shepherd said, who himself was out that night looking for his own lost sheep.

Chapter 61

They followed the light and shadows
And the light led them forward to the light
and the shadows led them to darkness.
T.S. Eliot

"James Day was dead! I told you — he *had no pulse!*" Theo was adamant. "Where's the damn woman with the damn brandy?" He looked around the room.

"You can't have a bit, if you don't ask nicely," Rose said, holding the flask before him.

"What! Does everything have to be 'pretty-please-with-sugar-on-it' for you?" Theo asked with irritation.

"No, you just need to learn to be a gentleman," Rose said resolutely. "I don't care if you are schizophrenic! Both of you need to learn some manners!"

"Rose," Karl intervened, "please give the man a drink. It's a delicate —"

"Obviously everyone has *given in* to him for years. He deserves to be respected enough to be called to account!" Still, she held the flask out toward Theo.

Kostanikas tried to stand a little straighter. He attempted to smooth his greasy hair back from his face. "My dear, Rose! May I have a bit of your brandy …? Please?"

"Why, certainly." She took his arm and they moved away from Day's bedside.

Claire still watched everything from the cold cement floor where she leaned against the wall. She saw Karl pull the sheet further off the body while Mara and Steve looked on. Day was wearing a long black robe. Karl spoke deliberately as he examined Day.

"His pulse is very slow and faint. He must have been given a drug that slows down the body's processes to an absolute minimum. No wonder Theo thought he was dead."

"*Like Juliet,*" Claire whispered. She remembered when the policeman had come to her door. In her heart of hearts she did not believe that Michael was truly dead. Even at the morgue — most of his injuries had been internal — it was so hard to think him dead. He was still the most handsome man she had ever known. It was different at the funeral parlor. The mortician had done his ghastly work and turned her beloved husband and friend into a stiff cold wax figure with sterile fluid in his veins instead of his own red blood. Even then, though, she secretly and fleetingly hoped that it was a wax figure and that the real Michael was alive somewhere …. Poor Romeo!

Had it not been for Patrick, what would she have done? Could she have gone on? She had no real independent life. She was always latching on to other people's dreams or else criticizing them. She didn't have any of her own. Except for the ship, the beautiful majestic ship in her recurring dream. Michael and Patrick were on the ship, but it was *her* dream. If she could find it and get on everything would be alright.

"Yes, like Juliet," Karl answered Claire. "I fear not for such a noble reason as Juliet's is James Day lying in this room."

"Can we wake him? Should we try?" Steve asked.

"I think it's best if we leave him here. It's one less person to worry about," Karl said. Everyone agreed.

"I can't believe this place is so *empty*. There is *no* one around," Steve commented again.

Theo came back to the conversation. "They're all involved in the ceremony. It must be tonight."

"What ceremony, Theo? You didn't mention that before," Karl asked the old man.

"They want to install my program in the main frame computer! Without me there! They can't do it without this!" He reached in the inner pocket of his plaid sport coat and pulled out something wrapped in a piece of newspaper. He unwrapped a CD-ROM. "Then I suppose they'll do their casting of circles and spells and adjustments for ley lines and …" he turned to Claire. "They must have your boy. They'll try to make him say the Word." He looked at the figure of Day on the bed. "He'll be sorry he slept through *this* one!"

Suddenly Theo's demeanor changed. Karl noticed it in the light of the torch as he spoke again: *"We can't go there!"* His face was contorted and full of terror.

"Where can't we go?" Karl asked quietly.

"To the gates of Hell! The Portal of the second death! We'll be unmade! You don't understand!"

"The person I work for was given the keys to a power that can overcome even the gates of Hell. He's given me the okay to use them." The group had to admire Karl's attempt at soothing logic.

"Oh, yes … the Emperor," Theo reminded himself. He became calmer again. "But why do you need those stinking gypsies up above the ground again?"

"Theo! Remember your manners!" Rose scolded. "Mara is a gypsy and God uses her all the time. He uses all of us who let him. And even some that don't."

"*Go on, Master, lead the way, for I am stron*g *and resolute.*" Karl hoped to engage Theo in another pertinent Dantean dialogue, but just then the body on the bed groaned softly, almost imperceptibly.

"Let's go!" Karl said, leading the way out into corridor.

They reached the big double doors that led into the main room. It was decided that all but Karl and Steve would go into the dreary empty break room and wait while the two men listened at the doors for any sound. They were surprised to hear nothing. They pushed the door slightly. The large room was empty, too. Steve went back for the others and they all stepped in cautiously.

"This is really weird!" Steve said as he looked around the darkened room at the different monitor screens lit with virtual images. "It's like a ghost ship. Maybe they've all uploaded themselves."

"What time is it?" Karl asked.

Claire looked at the floating red-haired lady on her wrist and was the first to answer. "I have 11:00."

"I'd better give Richard a call and —"

A loud creaking, scraping sound of hinges and metal on metal interrupted everything. They stood entranced as a large panel of the wall in front of them rose up.

"*Come in!*" a powerful voice beckoned from within. "*We've all been waiting for you!*"

Chapter 62

Would it be possible to duplicate the character of a human person as another Self inside a machine?
Vernor Vinge

The leader of the deed is a woman.
Virgil

No one in the group was more surprised than Theo. "I've been in this room dozens of times … they never told me there was *another* one!" They stood close together, not sure what to do next. Karl, Mara and Steve were conferring about weapons when the double doors pushed open behind them and four brown robed hooded figures burst in, one with a strange looking spear.

"*Gae Bulga*," Karl said to his small band. "A druid weapon with alleged mystical power."

Claire recognized it as the same kind of spear she had seen briefly on the sidewalk in South Carolina.

"It's the spear of *CuChulain*." Rose added with awe.

The four hooded figures surrounded them. Karl had no idea what awaited inside. He didn't think a skirmish in the anteroom would be best. Quickly and roughly one figure grabbed Claire from the huddle and held the barbed point of the weapon close to her throat. The other three slap-searched Mara, Steve, and Karl, took their stun guns and threw them across the room. Rose clung to Theo, whimpering softly.

"*Would you get off me, please!*" Theo whispered loudly. "I have *myself* to think about."

"I'm just doing it so they think I'm a weak old woman," she whispered back. "That way I might be able to surprise them later." Theo thought that a good idea and he began to cower and cling to Rose.

"It worked!" Theo said in Rose's ear after they were barely searched. "They didn't get my program!" He patted his pocket and smiled.

They were prodded into the secret room. Claire was released and

364

pushed in with the rest. They were not prepared for what they saw.

It resembled the throne room of an ancient castle and was of enormous proportions. There were no electric lights. Candles and lanterns were everywhere, set on various stands and tables, hung from hooks in the wall. A fire burned in a hewn stone fireplace at the left end of the room. The expansive floor was made of large black and white squares that appeared to be marble. Revolving crystal panels hung from the edges of the tall vaulted metal ceiling that reflected the light of flickering flames. On the walls were swaths of silks and brocades and gold and silver shields and torques with intricate Celtic metalwork that gave the stone-walled room a sense of luxuriant opulence.

The six invaders stood with mouths agape at the sheer accomplishment of creating such a place underneath the ground. All was quiet except for the low thrumming and whirring from a dark corner.

There were many people in the room. It was hard to distinguish distant faces in the dimness of the firelight. The heads of the twenty or so brown and grey hooded figures lined up and facing them across the floor were completely hidden. In the middle of that line and as tall as the figures was a black velvet cube. Behind them was a wide dais that supported several elaborate throne-like chairs.

"*Come closer and meet the family, Claire!*" a male voice called out with an Irish accent and a mocking tone. Claire and Karl knew him immediately. "Put down the spears!" O'Toole ordered.

The guards backed away.

The little band moved ahead together, though Claire had been the only one summoned.

"*Everyone else stay back!*" the voice shouted from the shadows, "This is family business!"

Claire stepped forward indignantly. "Who are you? The Great Oz? Come on out of the shadows Mister, excuse me, *Doctor* O'Toole and stop trying to intimidate everyone." Her anger was giving her courage. "It sure isn't hard to tell who was writing those meglo-maniacal things on the Pagan Internet sites. So you *are* M.O.D!"

Karl stepped forward and attempted to talk to Claire. She shook his hand off her arm. "What's it stand for?" she insisted. "Master Of

Deceit, or of Disgust, or how about" she shook her fist in his direction, "*Death!* You … you …"

A strong, low resonant female voice spoke with a heavy Irish accent from the same direction. "No, ye are mistaken. *I* am M.O.D.!"

As the woman spoke she stood up and moved a lamp so she could be seen clearly. The first thing that struck Claire was her size. She was tall and heavy and imposing. She was an older woman, though her hair was wild and raven black and she still emanated a fierce and haughty beauty. Her chair was like a box in which she stood. The front flashed with bronze metal-work and on each side was a wheel. Out of each wheel stuck a sharp and flashing blade. Claire realized it was like a chariot and knew then why the image was familiar. She was the Black Queen from the mysterious chess set. Well, at least she was dressed up to *look* like her — long blue robe with a heavy brocaded silk overdress, the chariot throne — all the trappings were there. Her face too, Claire thought, her face is remarkably like the carved game piece.

"*I am the Queen of Connaught!*" the woman's eyes blazed and her voice roared.

Claire felt a tingling sensation in her fingers. *No symptoms!* Not *now*, she thought, swallowing hard and pressing on.

"I thought you were *M.O.D.*? And what does *that* stand for?" Claire yelled back at the woman though her legs were trembling.

"Maeve O'Brien Day!" a voice said weakly from behind them.

The 'Black Queen' shrieked.

Claire and her company turned around. Leaning against the doorway stood a feeble James Day.

"He's alive!" Maeve Day shrieked. "How can it *be*? *I killed him myself!*" A murmur ran among the hooded figures. The imposing woman turned to O'Toole, who stepped into the lamplight with her. He, too, wore a hooded robe like the others but his was black, like Day's. His hood was down on his neck. Claire saw his insolent face. *Franny was right*, she thought, *he did look like Norman Bates*. He whispered something to his partner while rubbing her arm affectionately.

"Maeve! Maeve! How could you conspire against your own husband? *I* am the King!" Day called out to his wife. He stumbled forward. "All these years ... *our plans!*" He collapsed on the black and white floor.

"Take our esteemed Druid back to his bed!" O'Toole ordered the guards. "He seems ill and in need of some rest."

"I'm not going anywhere, you filthy traitor!" Day pushed himself up on his knees. "I'll tell everyone here the treachery that has been done and the deceit that ..." He paused and panted for breath.

The Black Queen had sat down, her arms folded across her chest. O'Toole took charge. "Bring Mister Day to a seat along the wall." Those who already had lifted him under each arm followed O'Toole's instructions.

"Now ... all Bards, Ovates, and Druids must leave until the ceremony begins. We have some very important matters to discuss with Mister Day and with our guests. Wait in the outer room until we require your assistance."

The hooded figures tried to exit ceremoniously, walking slowly, single file out the double doors, but Claire heard them muttering to each other under their breath as they passed. "This is very irregular!" and "I'm not at all pleased!" and "Did she say she *killed* him?"

Karl, Claire, Steve, Mara and Rose were still shocked by the presence of Maeve Day. Her death and funeral had been an international event. Theo remained quiet, just happy that no one had come after the software he carried in his pocket. He suppressed a cough.

"*I killed ye because ye were weak!*" Maeve screeched at Day after the last druid had left. "Ye *are* the Old King! Ye have no power and no spine. Fergus is the New King. He carries the virility and the strength that ye never had!"

"*Fergus!*" Day said, attempting outrage but barely able to sit upright. "He's your *lover*, then? It's not possible!" Maeve pulled O'Toole to her and kissed him grotesquely on the mouth. Day held his head in his hands.

"It's from the Legend of Connaught," Rose told her companions softly. "Queen Mebh or *Maeve*, as we say now, took a lover, Fergus, and they killed her husband Ailill, the King. They're acting it out, or somethin'."

"I don't care *who* you all are pretending to be!" Claire said hotly.

"You said something about my family. Where are my mother and my son?"

"You're forgetting about *me!*" said Queen Maeve in sarcastic disappointment.

"What do you mean?" asked Claire.

"Why, I'm your mother's cousin, dear." she cooed. "Our fathers were brothers. Both O'Briens. This is our land here."

Claire was stunned. "That can't be … she never said …"

"There're a *lot* of things ye don't know, ye cheeky little bitch." Maeve said.

Karl stepped next to Claire. "Haven't you done *enough?*" he interposed. "This is all useless. You murder and lie and still you'll not get what you're looking for. It's not going to happen."

"*Shut up, Burgmann!* You couldn't save Michael *or* McCullum!" O'Toole taunted him. I know we're going to get what we want. *You're* the impotent one! You have nothing but a useless thing between your legs!"

Rose became indignant. "You, sir, are a *filthy, disrespectful reprobate!* How dare you speak to this fine priest and gentleman that way!"

O'Toole was inspired. "You going to let the old lady fight for you, *Father,* like you did her old man? Never like to get those nails dirty, do you? Or that finely tailored suit? Does the Pope take you shopping? '*One of every color, sonny*'" he switched to quivering, aged voice as he bent over and shook a palsied hand. "OOOps. It's only black, isn't it? That's my color, too."

Karl's jaw was clenched and his whole body shook as he contained the rage he felt for another human being. "Is this your gift, O'Toole? Your bardic gift of withering satire? None of us have succumbed!"

Rose grabbed hands with Theo and Mara. "Sticks and stones may break our bones but words will never —" Theo pulled loose and hid behind Steve.

Claire spoke again. "Where are my mother and my son?"

"Well, cousin, once or twice removed as the case may be, "said Queen Maeve, "why don't we take one thing at a time …"

She walked over to another throne that was still in the shadows and slowly lifted the lamp to enlighten it … "I'd like you to meet

Brigit, the White Queen, or *Arianrhod*, as some would call her — the Silver Wheel."

This seat was silver with a huge frame behind it, like a fan, made of thin hazel rods and filled in with ferns and rushes. On the chair sat a fragile woman with flowing red hair that bore a silver crown. She was dressed in a snowy white robe and silver brocaded silk overdress. In one hand she held a golden apple and in the other was a velvet bag. Her face beautiful, but drawn and pale as the moon and older than it seemed at first. Claire realized with a sudden bolt of shock that the White Queen was her mother.

Chapter 63

At the door of life, by the gate of breath
There are worse things waiting for men than death.
Charles Swinburne

Whatever else we have grown accustomed to, we have grown accustomed to the unaccountable. Every stone or flower is a hieroglyphic of which we have lost the key. With every step of our lives we enter into the middle of some story which we are certain to misunderstand.
G.K. Chesterton

"*Grandma is a silver wheel* …" The words flew into Claire's mind from Patrick's poem. And something about 'her new dress' … Patrick had *known* somehow about this. About *what*? What was going on?

"Mother? Is that you?"

The 'White Queen' was silent and still as stone. A drum continued to beat from the left corner of the dais. A beat and a whir, a beat and a whir — the rhythm never changing. It bothered Claire terribly. It seemed like the same cadence she fought against when she had one of her spells — when everything felt mechanical and artificial, when her own movements became jerky and self-conscious. It was oppressive and slavish. Was it affecting her heartbeat? Is this how they would take over the world? With the beat of a drum? Or was she going mad? Hallucinating this whole hellish fantasy? She looked quickly at Theo behind Steve. He seemed surprisingly undisturbed.

"That's your mother, Claire?" Rose said, breaking the spell for a moment, in her now-perfected stage whisper, "My, she's lovely! You take after her — you do."

She *was* lovely, Claire thought. She hadn't seen her mother's hair down since she used to beg to brush it as a little girl, in the early morning before it was wound up tightly in the twist or knot at the back of her neck. The red hair now fell over her shoulders and softly framed her small canescent face.

"Mother! Are you alright? Are you ill?" Claire stepped closer to the right side of the dais where her mother sat.

"Of course, she's ill." Maeve said shrilly. "Brigit has the malady that cannot be healed. She is the Mother-Goddess of Ireland who takes upon herself the wounds and pains of the land. See? She holds the world in her velvet bag." The Black Queen gestured toward her cousin.

"Brigid was not a goddess but a saint!" Rose called out urgently. "And she *did* have a malady, Holy Brigid, and she was on her way to a physician when she fell and struck her head against a stone and blood poured from her eyes that healed two lame women who went to her aid. Before that …" Rose pressed on, "she founded the nunnery at Kildare and she is the great protector of women in childbirth, along with Our Lady!"

"That's what the *Catholics* did to her." Maeve said with scorn. "They even took the Pagan festival of Imbolc, the worship of the goddess and her son, and turned it into Candlemas. They took *everything* from us!" she wailed.

"What are you saying *'they' and 'us'?*" Rose protested, holding her handbag tightly. "You're *baptized Catholics* — the lot of ya." She pointed also to James Day, who slumped in his chair.

"*We reversed that long ago!*" Maeve yelled.

"But you can't … unless …" Rose put her hand over her mouth and gasped softly.

"And who are you, Mrs. McCullum? Who's never had an original thought in her mind! Who held on to the coattails of a *man* her whole life. A *cowardly* man, at that. Right, Fergus?" She turned to O'Toole who was seated now on his own throne, usurped or not. He nodded.

"These cruel and senseless insults *have got to stop!*" Karl broke in, his German accent very noticeable because he was upset.

"*Yes, Commandant!*" O'Toole retorted, mockingly imitating his voice. "Ve'll bring some *Jews* in for you to intimidate and torture shortly. *Heil, Hitler!*" He laughed at his own joke. Claire looked at Karl's face, touched with a sudden sympathy for him.

O'Toole switched again to his own Irish brogue: "Or will you have the *women* play and speak for you then, as well? Oh, I forgot again, Father, you're not really a man anyway. You need the Ladies

371

Aid Society, the Altar Guild and all that!"

"I'm not afraid to let women speak, especially when they're as able and wise as the women I have with me here. Why do you keep asking me that? I thought you Druids had no problem with female leadership. *You* seem to have no trouble taking orders from a woman." O'Toole looked around nervously.

"And why won't you let Claire's mother speak for *her*self?" Karl asked. "She is a Queen, right? Or do you have her drugged, too?"

"What time is it?" O'Toole asked, looking around. "We have to pull everything off by midnight. According to Day that's when the Ley Energy will be optimum." Claire looked at her watch. Eleven fifteen. She did not volunteer the information.

Day groaned as if on cue and sat up again before Maeve could answer. "You can't do this without me! *I am the Archdruid!*"

Maeve shrieked again. "I am the *Archdruidess!* You never had any power in you! It is through *my* family — the O'Briens — that the power has come down! You were just … useful!" She turned to O'Toole. "Why isn't he dead? I gave him the poison!"

"I thought, my dear," O'Toole said sycophantly, "that it would be best to get him out of the way, but not do him in. We may need him for new experiments — new brain patterns — or more likely," he continued, "we may need to prop him up for Public Relations." He laughed. "I switched the potion you gave him."

"*What?*" cried Maeve.

Claire interrupted. "You never answered Father Burgmann's question! Why can't my mother speak?" She started to walk toward her again. She wanted to hug her, to cry on her shoulder and have her say all the wrong things. She wanted her to make tea and prattle on about why 'her father' was worried. Claire wanted to go back to her old red brick house for Easter with all the family. She wanted to tell her mother about her illness — about how much she loved her.

"*Stay back, Blodeuwedd!*" the Black Queen cried out. "You'll have your chance with Brigit. You are part of her, after all!"

"I'm not playing your silly game! I'm Claire O'Connell and that is my mother Grace Daly. You people are *nuts!* You're *delusional!*"

"It's not *just* a game, Blodeuwedd … *You* know that." The whir and the low pounding in the corner kept rhythm with the turning crystal panels and the flicker of the flame. The smell of peat from the fireplace was overwhelming. Or was it just peat? Claire looked around at her friends. They all looked like she felt. Tired, depleted, with a terrible need to sleep …

Rose put something to Claire's lips. It was the silver flask from her purse. She took a sip. Rose took it around to each companion. They all perked up and came alive again.

"Alcohol is really a depressant and not a stimulant," said Steve, who'd barely moved since they'd entered the secret room, but now stretched his arms and legs freely.

"Well, nobody ever told the brandy that, thankfully, and the lot of you have improved greatly!" Rose said cheerfully.

"Are you kiddies done with your snack break now?" Maeve mocked.

"Go ahead! Drink up!" O'Toole added. "You're done. You've lost. It's inevitable. Let's get on with the ceremony, shall we, dear?"

Maeve walked over to O'Toole's chair and rubbed his shoulders and chest. "Too bad it's not *our* kind of ceremony." She leaned her large body down and kissed his neck. "Are you sure we need all this electronic stuff if we have the Boy? With his power and mine and the Ley system …"

Claire's heart leapt at the mention of Patrick, but she listened on without comment.

"No," O'Toole said, pushing her off. "Your husband was right on that. He might have been a genius in fact. We have the union of the Pythagorean deities and the Celtic pantheon and even the added bonus of the cabalistic aspect of the *Golem* thrown in for good measure. Where is our little Jew again?" He reached up for her hand again but she had walked back to her chariot throne.

"He's in the room, over there." She pointed past Grace to a side door. "Waiting."

O'Toole got up and went over to the door and opened it. He pulled out Herb Pifkin, whose hands were tied and mouth taped shut. He threw him into the room. Pifkin stumbled and fell to his knees.

"Is there anything you vant to do to him, before I untie him, Commandant?" O'Toole used his German voice again, looking at

Karl.

"I *am* a Jew, O'Toole. My mother was Jewish." Karl answered. "Even if I wasn't, I would have no desire to inflict any more pain on this poor man. I'm afraid that is *your* fantasy, not mine."

"Oh, this *poor* man? He's the one who implemented all your crazy professor's brilliant but purely theoretical ideas so that we could *load Michael O'Connell into a computer!* And this *poor man* is the one who experiments on *crippled orphans* and makes them scream. Are you proud of your fellow Jew, Father or should I say, Rabbi?" O'Toole said, adapting his taunts quickly, as only evil can, with no loyalty to any cause. He lifted Pifkin up by the armpits, took him off the dais and sat him in a chair in front of the black cube.

"What are *you* proud of, O'Toole?" Karl asked. "Do you think that you're better than this man? How many people has *he* murdered?"

O'Toole did not reply. He untied Pifkin's hands and ripped the tape off his mouth. The young man screamed with pain. "*I refuse* to work for someone who treats me like this! Where is Mister Day? I only work for Mister Day."

"He's over there taking a nap." O'Toole said, pointing. "He told me to go ahead."

O'Toole then pulled the black velvet cover off the cube, revealing a computer monitor that was taller than he was. He turned Pifkin's chair toward the keyboard. "Get everything set up while I send for the Boy!"

"I told you I will *not work for you*. I will only work for Mr. Day." Pifkin insisted.

"Will you *die* for Mr. Day?" O' Toole asked, pulling a gun out from under his robe and holding it to Pifkin's head.

"Fergus, you know we agreed to use only ritualistic weapons! *Authentic druid weapons!*" Maeve yelled.

"You must have made that agreement with the *Old* King! I like to choose my weapons freely."

The Black Queen stood and raised her hand with cold fury in her eyes.

O'Toole let out a yelp and the gun fell to the marble floor. "*My hand!* It's frozen!"

"Don't forget who has the power, my love!" she cooed hoarsely. "*Use a knife.*"

"Parlor tricks!" Rose whispered to her friends. "Mere parlor tricks. She calls that power?"

"*I* was impressed." Steve whispered back.

Maeve reached above her chair and pulled a cord that sounded a clanging bell. Two hooded guards with spears appeared through the double doors.

"Bring the Boy here *now!*" she said in a strong commanding voice, invigorated by her display of power over O'Toole.

"Alright, Pifkin, get it running!" O'Toole said as he held the knife to the man's throat.

"Okay, okay, I'll do it!" he said quivering. "But take the knife down. I have to concentrate! Why didn't I stay at MIT?" he groaned as he booted up the system.

"Because nothing *really* exciting ever happens there!" O'Toole answered. "Just endless talk and theory. With *real* excitement, there's always risk." He was still rubbing his frozen hand against his cloak.

The huge monitor lit up and characters scrolled down. Buzzes and beeps echoed as Pifkin punched the keys. "It's the Face Recognition security system. It won't let me in. We need Mr. Day to —" Theo began to fidget and move around.

"Come over here, my Queen," O'Toole said to the older woman. "Let it see your beautiful face!"

Maeve came down heavily off the dais and stood by O'Toole. She was a good foot taller than her young King and twice as wide. She pulled Pifkin off the chair and sat facing the monitor. "If you insist, Fergus …" she cooed with an incongruent girlishness. "You know how I have no *head* for machines!"

The unintended pun did not escape Theo or Rose who chuckled together. She gave him another sip of brandy after she had one herself. Theo went back to pacing.

A series of icons and patterns appeared on the screen and the Greek let out a yell. "Those are *my* patterns, *my* icons!" He broke toward the computer but Steve and Karl stopped him.

"Icons are *windows to heaven,* Theo. Don't you know your Greek?" O'Toole spoke snidely. "You can't *own* windows to heaven.

They should be available to *everybody*."

"It's not possible!" Theo struggled to free himself. "How did you get it? I have the only authentic copy here in my pocket!" He patted his sport coat.

O'Toole let out a great laugh of satisfaction. "This one *is* a very convincing fake, Pifkin! *That* part was fun, now, wasn't it, Herbie?" He laughed again. "You played right into our hands, Doctor Kostanikas. Thank you ever so much!"

Queen Maeve clanged the bell again and two more hooded armed guards came in. Steve and Karl still held Theo protectively.

"In case you're getting any bright ideas, Burgmann, I've got a whole lot more where those two came from," O'Toole warned. "You'd better just hold on to your crazy professor while we get what we need. Otherwise, we'll get it anyway and someone will get hurt. And that would be *tooo* bad!"

"*No! No!*" Theo shouted, writhing uselessly between his two younger and stronger allies.

"You don't understand! It's not Michael! It's one of the Ancient Ones! The Angels! The Pure Intelligence! We can't let *them* have this! It would be better to be *killed* than … than …"

Karl and Steve held on to Theo as one of the figures reached into his pocket and took the CD. The old man managed in his flailing to pull the hood down off the head of one his enemies. It was not a man, but a large woman with coarse features and hair pulled tightly back from her face. Claire shivered. She recognized her assailant from the encounter in South Carolina. The woman quickly covered her head again and walked toward O'Toole with the disc.

Theo moaned, "*Thou shalt hear the ancient spirits woeful … Strange tongues, horrible utterances … voices high and faint and sounds of hands with them, making a tumult which whirls always in that air forever dark, like the sand when the whirlwind breathes!*"

Karl spoke firmly but calmly in his ear. "*If I have rightly understood thy speech, thy soul is hurt by cowardice, which often times encumbers a man so that it turns him back from honorable enterprise, as false seeing does a beast when he shies.* Remember, Master! What were you saying to comfort me?"

Theo stopped struggling. "I have considered thy power, my son! *Here it behooves to leave every fear; it behooves that all cowardice should here be dead."* Theo shook his head. "I forgot that I was Virgil! It …" He looked around in wonder. "It slipped my mind." His lips continued to move as he quietly talked to himself. Karl and Steve released him.

Pifkin slipped the software into the computer. Similar patterns and icons popped onto the screen. The demoted member of the *digerati* lost track of his status as he entered into the euphoria of control and warmed to his personal contribution to the phenomena of mediated reality.

"Wait a minute, Pifkin!" O'Toole stopped him. "How do I turn on the other special effects?"

The scientist pointed to a button on the table. "I think *that's* it. I didn't install those. It was McCarthy. Where is McCarthy?"

"He took a vacation with your other Jewish buddy, I think. Shut up and keep working!"

O'Toole pushed the button. Monitors lit up on the ends of the dais — each portraying different virtual druid rituals. The light from the left monitor lit dimly the corner where the drumming sound was coming from. The drummer could barely be seen; the whirring and the unnerving beats continued.

Suddenly, two guards burst through the double doors. "*The boy is gone!*" one of them shouted in a strong Irish accent.

"*Gone!*" shrieked the Black Queen and O'Toole together.

"What about the attendants?" O'Toole asked, rushing toward them. "*What happened?* What was *their* explanation?"

"There are no attendants, sir!" another higher-pitched rural accent added excitedly. "The whole place is empty — except for us Druids in the other room."

"You're not all druids *yet!*" Maeve pronounced arrogantly.

"Would you shut up, woman!" O'Toole yelled.

The Black Queen raised her hand at him again.

"Of course, I didn't mean that, my dear!" he demurred, rubbing his hand, which had barely and painfully thawed. "It's just the stress of the moment!" She relented.

"All the children are gone, sir!" the first voice said. "The room is empty."

"*That can't be!*" O'Toole shouted. "They were sedated and some of them couldn't even *walk! Pifkin,* do you know anything about this?

Did *you* do something?"

Herb Pifkin was oblivious to anything but the images, numbers and text coming up on his screen.

"*PIFKIN!*" O'Toole shouted louder, shaking the little man. "*Where are the children?*"

"What children?"

"Your *guinea pigs!* And the boy, Patrick!"

"If you'll remember, I was tied up cruelly in the closet until a few minutes ago. How could *I* know?"

Maeve went back to her throne and sat down angrily. O'Toole spoke to his men. "Organize a search party, then. They can't have gone far! A bunch of crippled children!"

"We looked outside, sir! And there are no tracks at all in the snow," said one of the guards.

"Snow!" exclaimed O'Toole. "There's *snow* outside?"

"Ah, yes!" said Maeve with satisfaction.

"Oh, yes, sir" said the other. "It's deep! And it blew in the door that was left open at the end of the corridor. That's what took us so long. We had to dig out!"

"I will speak now!" said a lighter voice from the right side of the dais. The White Queen was standing regally with a white hazel rod in her hand.

Chapter 64

From the fixed place of heaven she saw
Time like a pulse shake fierce through all the world.
Her gaze still strove within that gulf to pierce its path;
And now she spoke as when the stars sang in their sphere.
                    Dante Gabriel Rossetti

We need a poor mother, for we ourselves are poor …
Through her weakness we are healed.
                    Karl Adam

"*Silence!*" screamed the Black Queen. "Sit down, Brigit!"

"You have no power over me, Maeve, now that Patrick has escaped. You have never had any *real* power over me! It was only your threats to dear Patrick that kept me quiet all this time. Now … you cannot silence me while I hold the hazel rod."

"Oh rubbish!" spat O'Toole. "Go find the Boy, you idiots! And hurry!" The guards ran out again. "Maeve, we don't —"

"Of course, she is right, Fergus! You *must* know of the spirit of utterance that rests upon the white hazel!" said Maeve with dismay. "You know much less than I thought of the Old Ways."

"But the *time* —"

"Quiet!" commanded Queen Mebh. "How did you get the rod, cousin?"

"I found it secreted in the folds of my gown when you had me dress. I don't know how it got there."

"Mother?" asked Claire. "Mom? What's happening?" Claire felt like a child.

"Come here, darling Claire!" the White Queen said gently.

Claire walked past O'Toole and Pifkin and the giant machine, stepped carefully up on the dais and collapsed at her mother's knees.

"Mom …" Claire broke down and began to weep in heaving sobs with her head her mother's lap. "*Why are you here?* Why are you dressed like this?" she pleaded. "What have they done to you? They're lying about all of this, right Mother?" Grace smoothed her daughter's hair and patted softly the head that lay in her lap. "Do you know where Patrick is?" Claire asked, looking up into the colorless face.

"I don't know where he is, but I feel that he is safe." the White Queen assured her. "These people lie about many things, Claire, but not entirely about who I am."

"But Mother," Claire said in shock. "You're *Grace Daly!* You're married to *John* Daly! ... You live in Chicago, Illinois and you have five daughters and ten grandchildren!" Claire spoke desperately. "You're a *Catholic,* not a goddess? This is crazy!"

"Let me try to explain quickly. I only have a short while left ..." Her breathing seemed labored. She put her hand on her chest and inhaled deeply.

"Are you really ill? Are they lying about *that?"* Claire demanded.

"*Of course, she's ill!"* Maeve screeched from across the dais. "Her heart was pierced by her son, Dylan, who drowned in the lonely sea."

"My mother never had a son!" Claire said loudly back to the Black Queen

"I did have a baby boy, Claire dear." Grace looked bitterly at Maeve for a moment. "Between you and Francine ... John Patrick Daly." Grace spoke with effort and emotion. "He died within me before my pregnancy was evident or the news was shared. He was the tiniest thing. They let me see him. It saddened me so that I never talked of it, except with your father, of course. It broke his heart, too — his only son and all."

"Why didn't you tell *me?* At least after I was older? I could have ..."

"You had your own burdens to bear." She looked deeply into her daughter's eyes.

"So that all made you sick or something?"

"It was my heart —"

"But you have your medicine and you went on ... and you had Franny and everything's been fine!"

"There are things we have kept from each other."

Claire looked up at her mother, wondering if ...

"Just get to the story, Brigit!" Maeve urged. "So she knows this whole thing's *legitimate*. She's got a part to play, too! Get on with it!"

Grace began. "I've known since I was a little thing on my

granny's knee that I was special. Not that everyone isn't special in Our Lord's eyes — but I knew I had special gifts and powers. I saw pictures in my mind of things — and sometimes those things I saw came to pass. I *knew* things. It was almost like dreaming. My granny could sense it and she told my father. My father was very angry with me and told me that I was wicked and that I had the O'Brien curse upon me, left over from the ancient days before the Church."

"*My* father was *very* sympathetic of *my* gifts!" Maeve boasted.

"Your father was a weak-willed man who spoiled you with all your family's ill-gotten British blood money!" Grace spoke and then seemed drained by the outburst. She turned back to Claire.

"My father told me to pray all the time or I'd go to hell with all of the other pagans." Grace said. "So that was one good thing he told me, at least — to pray. Whenever one of my 'seeings' or any other signs of the 'curse' would come up, I would push them down and pray. They eventually went away and I almost forgot all about it …" She caught her breath and went on.

"Then one night I stayed late, after a Lenten Mission at St. Rita's, to pray for you girls. I lit a candle before the Blessed Mother and while I was gazing at her likeness I had a vision unlike anything I'd ever had before. Our Lady turned from stone to skin and she shone with a light from within and she was brilliantly white. She handed me a velvet bag and a golden apple and told me not to be afraid, but to hide these things 'until the truth shall be laid bare.' She was gone then, leaving only her lovely stone likeness, and these gifts …" She gestured toward the velvet bag and the golden apple that were near her chair on the dais.

"Then one day when I was at your house — it was before Patrick was born — you were at school and Michael was there alone — I saw a picture in a book on his desk of a Shining Woman and she was holding a velvet bag and a golden apple. I let out a little cry as she reminded me so of Our Lady in my vision. I asked Michael who it was. He told me the ancient legend of Brigit, and Arianrhod, and Blodeuwedd. I asked him how he could reconcile the study of these pagan things with his own Catholic faith. He said that all of these myths and legends were *true* in the sense that *they pointed to their own true fulfillment.* He said that what was good in these had come to our human imagination through divine power and that God had a way of using that good for his own glory. Nothing good was to be lost. He asked me if I knew about Guadalupe. I had to admit that I hadn't paid much attention because I wasn't Mexican." She laughed softly. "I was so foolish then."

Maeve held her tongue and waited with the others, though reluctantly, for her cousin to continue.

"God uses the truth for his own glory. I wouldn't be here if I didn't believe that. I know that this is the time for me to use the gifts that I have kept hidden."

"After Patrick was born, I saw the signs in him even stronger than my own — in his eyes, his hands, his face. So I spoke to Michael about it. I told him my secrets, for Patrick's sake. It was then that he knew for certain about Patrick. This was only weeks before he died. He never told me his whole story — only that I shouldn't tell anyone of Patrick's true lineage, as it might put him in danger. But they guessed it."

"*Look out there!*" Karl yelled. O'Toole had come alongside the White Queen's throne. He tore the hazel rod from her hand, then held it in his fists and cracked it over his knee into two pieces. Maeve shrieked. He ran across the room and threw the pieces in the fireplace.

"*Seize him!*" the Black Queen shouted at the two guards in the room. They were conflicted about what to do but decided to follow the noise and the power. "We will put the *real* King back on the throne!"

She ran over to where Day was moaning in his chair. She lifted him up and dragged him, barely walking, to the throne nearest hers where O'Toole had been. She dropped him down in the seat.

"*Maeve!* What are you doing?" O'Toole called from between the guards who gripped him.

"You were only using me. I know it now. You don't even really know or believe in the Old Ways, do you? You just want power!" she wailed.

"And what do *you* want, my dear? Tea and scones in a whitewashed cottage?"

"Of course *I* want more power. It is my *due!* It's in my *blood*. You are *nothing*. Tie him up over there!" She pointed to the chair where Day had slumped before.

"Maeve! You can't do this? What about our love … our …?" He was tied fast.

"You!" she said low in her throat. "You broke the hazel rod — the rod of utterance!" Her voice was rising in pitch, "I should cut out *your* tongue! Be quiet or I will!"

She threw some water from a pitcher into her husband's face and slapped him quite brusquely. "James! *Ailill!* James! *Wake up!* I'm sorry I killed you, dear! It was all a mistake! Wake up!" She fluttered around him in clumsy movement.

James Day sat up as straight as he could and looked groggily around the large room. "What time is it?" he asked.

"It's quarter of twelve!" Maeve answered him, looking at her watch.

"Do we have the Boy?" he asked.

"We did, but due to Mr. O'Toole's ineptness we've lost track of him again!" she answered.

O'Toole was seething silently.

"Well, get everything ready and if we have to we'll do Plan B! Why is *she* on the dais?" Day pointed at Claire.

"Things got out of hand without you!" Maeve Day cooed, then turned. "Get back with your group, Blodeuwedd," she ordered, speaking to Claire like an Activities Director. "We'll let you know when we need you."

Claire clung to her mother, but the White Queen freed Claire's hands from the folds of her gown and nodded to her daughter to step down from the dais. Claire reluctantly left her mother on the crystal throne.

Chapter 65

All moveables of wonder, from all parts,
Are here — Albinos, painted Indians, Dwarfs,
The Horse of Knowledge and the learned Pig …
The Waxworks, Clockwork, all the marvelous craft
Of modern Merlins …
All out o' the way, farfetched, perverted things
All freaks of nature …
All jumbled up together to compose
A Parliament of Monsters.
                William Wordsworth

"The *Fianna Fitchell!!* Where are they? Why are they not in their places?" Day's voice had grown stronger since he sat on his throne.

"O'Toole sent them out because they were clamoring for *your* leadership again!" the Black Queen said coyly.

"Call them in! It's time to assemble!" Maeve clanged the bell.

"What is he talking about?" Rose asked of Karl. "I know the *Fianna Eiraan*, the Warriors of Ireland, and the *Fianna Fail*, Warriors Together … but they have nothing to do with any of those *political* groups, do they?"

"Those groups got their names from the game pieces of the ancient Celtic chess game, *Fichell*. Each piece had a cosmic significance and they were called called *Fianna Fichell*." Karl answered, trying to string it together himself.

"We all know *that* game!" Rose replied. Karl wasn't so sure.

"All right!" called Day, even stronger. "*All of the rest of you off the board* until we place you!"

"The board?" Theo questioned. He noticed those around him looking down at the black and white squares on the floor.

"Move!" Day yelled again. "Over to your left! Against the wall!"

They were herded over to the side of the room — nearer to the incessant drumming and its shadowed drummer. *Beat-whir … beat-whir.* The group insisted that Rose and Claire take the only two chairs along that wall.

The line of hooded figures came back into the great room

silently and stood waiting for instructions. A ripple of 'ahhs' and 'ohhhs' went through them, however, when they saw James Day on his throne. They could also see O'Toole in humiliation tied to the chair on the right.

"Yes, my *filid!* Bards! Ovates! Druids!" Day said. "It is finally time to take your places!"

The hooded figures in brown and gray broke into two even groups and stood as pawns on a chess board, facing each other, with a space between them running down the middle of the room from the giant computer screen to the double doors. The back row on each side was empty except the places for the 'rooks' or 'castles', which were filled by hooded members.

Pifkin, looking up from the computer, as if coming out of a trance, spotted Day sitting in his chair. "*Mr. Day!* We'll have to talk! I was terribly mistreated while you were ... incapacitated." He stared around the room at all the robed and hooded figures. "What's going on here? Mr. Day? I thought this was a more *private* project ... I thought it was just you and me and Stein and McCarthy ... *What happened to McCarthy?* I could use him in case there's a bug in the system or something ..."

"He's *dead*, you imbecile!" yelled Theo from the side. "And you will be, too! Refuse to help them! You don't understand! It's not artificial intelligence! It's *Pure* Intelligence — looking for a gateway! Looking for a *Host!*"

"Theo!" Day said. "Mr. Pifkin would never abandon a project of this magnitude right before its crowning success!"

Pifkin answered in a different tone. "No ... I must see it through for all of my colleagues."

"Of course you must." Day encouraged him. "I'm so glad everything is happening so peacefully, just as it should." He turned toward the rebel band along the wall. "You all realize, I can see, that there is no use in resisting. We can use force if we have to, but please don't make it necessary."

Whir-beat ... whir-beat ... Claire looked closely at the drummer. He was small — at least it looked like a he was — a boy, a child. She could not make out his features, but by his size she thought him to be only a few years older than Patrick. He moved his arm up and down in the shadows like a mechanical monkey — like the old toy ones. Karl studied him, too. He stepped behind Claire and put his hands on her shoulders. He leaned down and spoke to her softly.

"Claire! I know that your mother's appearance and her story are a great shock to you. But you do know that she is here for good and not for ill. She is here for the love of you and Patrick and … for the world."

"I know." Claire answered him with emotion. "I know!"

He looked again into the shadows. "There may still be other revelations that will be hard for you to bear. I'm not sure of it. But if so, *be strong* — in the love of your mother … if that's all you can believe in right now. And listen to me then. Listen to me."

"But what …?" Claire reached up for his hand on her shoulder. He squeezed it firmly.

"*We must move quickly!*" Day called out. "Everything must be precisely coordinated."

He stood up.

"Burgmann — yes, so nice to see you — *You* shall take the place of a White Bishop" Karl walked slowly to his spot on the floor. "… and Mrs. McCullum — yes, hello, to you as well — *You* shall take the place of the other White Bishop." Day sounded as if he were organizing a game of croquet.

"*First* of all," shouted Rose, who had become slightly tipsy from her medicinal ablutions, "how *dare* you greet me as if we were having tea, when you killed my dear husband … And secondly, I *cannot* take the place of the White Bishop for I am a woman and *cannot* be ordained."

"*It's alright, Rose!*" Karl whispered loudly. "Take your place. It's a game. And you really are the best one for the part. It's for Ian!" She shrugged her shoulders and walked to her square, still clutching her handbag.

"Now, quickly! You two young people" he said pointing to Steve and Mara, "You are the White Knights!" They looked to Karl and then took their places … slowly, stalling for time.

"I hope you don't think I am going to join this idiotic childish charade!" Theo yelled.

"Oh yes, Dr. Kostanikas!" Day spoke grandly, "You have the

great honor of being a Black Bishop ... along with Dr. O'Toole."

"Black Bishop!" Theo shouted. "I'm staying on this side!" Two figures grabbed him again and dragged him to the opposite side of the room. "I am not Pythagoras, I tell you! *I am Virgil.*" he screamed as he went. "Tell them, Alighieri! Tell them!"

Karl called after him. "*This one, who guides my eyes on high, is that. Virgil ... Teacher, now canst thou comprehend the sum of the love that warms me to thee, when I forget our emptiness, treating the shades as if a solid thing.*"

Claire, sitting alone now, looked again at the drummer.

"What are they doing? What are they saying?" Queen Maeve screamed. "That's not part of the myth! Make them stop!"

"It will be fine, my dear. Everyone has gone to their places nicely."

Theo still struggled with his handlers; O'Toole was taken to his square still bound in a chair.

"*Are you ready, Mr. Pifkin* ... when I give the go?" Day asked formally.

"I think so, Mr. Day. Everything is loaded onto the mainframe and the connection is made on the Net. We're ready to virtualize the entity and begin communication." Pifkin stood up in front of his terminal in anticipation. He was only two thirds the size of the huge monitor.

"*Now* we will open the *first* gateway!" Day intoned as he pulled a lever on the floor beside his chair.

A great creaking and scraping of metal and the loud clicking of gears in motion startled everyone in the room. All eyes went up to the slanted ceiling which shuddered and moved. Clumps and dustings of snow fell down in the chamber as the roof began to open. Two massive doors in the side of the hill were being swung out. There were gasps and cries.

"*What the hell is going on?*" Pifkin yelled as some of the cold white stuff fell on his machine. This is totally *unnecessary!* All the connections can be made from underground! *You'll ruin all of my things!*"

"*Your* things!" Theo shouted. "*Your things?!*"

"Oh, James! ... I mean, Ailill! ... This is masterful! It's magnificent!" Maeve crowed.

"I wanted to surprise you! The snow has fallen as we knew it would on this night of nights, but now it has stopped!" Day said to his queen. The two talked like sweethearts, with no betrayal or treachery to remember.

Out of the lower part of the roof, just past the thrones, the cottage could be seen in the near distance, covered in white snow and drenched in moonlight. The sky above was dark and clear and bright with brilliant stars.

"Look!" Day said excitedly, turning around and pointing up the hill. "Look! *The Dolmen! The monument, Pifkin!* Keep your eyes *there* – as your push your buttons!"

"*I refuse to stand on this square!*" Theo shouted again, lifting his feet so he hung suspended from the arms of his two captors. "I certainly am not on the same level as this degenerate sadistic murdering bastard to my left!" he looked toward O'Toole. "Black Bishop, my ass!"

O'Toole spat toward the old man.

"Since the boy has not been found," Day called out again, "and so many of the *right* players are here, we will go with our *other* plan! We don't have much time! Maeve!"

"Yes ... alright." She said hesitantly but with a certain heightened tone to her voice. She turned to the shadowed corner on her right. "Come forth, Bran!"

The drumming ceased. A young child, a boy, walked out into the light of the lamps and the moon. His body was profoundly deformed. He moved in a jerking motion with a whirring of electronic prosthetic devices that protruded from his body. Half his face was a silver mask, but the other half was quite handsome — clear skin, one dark beautiful eye and black hair. He moved slowly and, it seemed to Claire, painfully. Her heart went out to him immediately. *A poor orphan ...* she thought. *They're experimenting on him with those hideous appendages.*

He was dressed nobly in blue glossy silk breeches, bordered in gold. His shirt was scarlet, covered with a leather apron and over that an iron apron that was touched with red enamel and glowing crystal. He came and stood beside the Black Queen. She put her hand on his shoulder.

Grace was leaning on the arm of her chair and weeping. Her tears were wetting the velvet bag.

"Claire!" Maeve called. "Take your mother's place on the board. She doesn't seem to be well. And you *are* Blodeuwedd, after all. It's time to take up your destiny!"

Karl and Rose both motioned to Claire. She got up and stood by Karl. She desperately wanted to go back to her mother. Maeve addressed her again, looking directly into her eyes.

"This is *my* son!" She took his false hand and lifted it up as if preparing to bow.

O'Toole finally broke his silence. "It's not going to work, you crazy fools! He's *deficient!* We've already tried things with him. He doesn't know '*Misog*' at all. He can't even remember what he's been *taught*. He can barely speak *English!*"

"*Shut up!*" Maeve screeched. "It may be just a matter of maturity and timing."

"And *this* is the right time, if there ever was one!" Day said, looking up again at the Dolmen which stood against the starry night.

"He has all the right *blood!*" Maeve said, looking at Claire again. "The O'Brien's *and* the O'Connell's!"

Karl grasped Claire's hand tightly.

"This is my son," Maeve repeated malevolently, *"and Michael's!"*

Claire gasped. The White Queen let out a cry of pain.

Chapter 66

Hear the voice of the Bard!
Who Present, Past, and Future see
Whose ears have heard The Holy Word
That walked among the ancient trees.
William Blake

The miracle that gave them such a death
Transfigured to pure substance what had once
Been bone and sinew; when such bodies join
There is no touching there
Nor straining joy, but whole is joined to whole
For the intercourse of the angels of light
Where for its moment both seem lost, consumed.
William Butler Yeats

Somewhere within herself Claire had sensed the impossible truth that this *'shade were a solid thing'* and he was part of Michael — even before she saw his half face and the mysterious familiar likeness that inhabited it. What she couldn't bear was the thought of the inevitable circumstances which must have brought it to fruition.

Karl was holding Claire, reminding her steadily, "This is what I feared would be revealed. Listen to *me*, Claire!" His breath was warm in her ear and seemed to dispel to some degree the cold which was settling upon the room from the open sky-doors to the snow-covered Irish night.

"It's all *Michael's* fault, you know … the boy's deficiencies!" … Maeve continued taunting Claire. He just didn't have what it *takes!*" She laughed haughtily. "At least for *me!*"

Claire felt sick to her stomach. Her chest heaved. Karl spoke again with power in his low whisper. "This is what Michael hoped you'd *never* know. It was *against his will*. It —"

"The boy is deficient because *you're a dried-up old woman who shouldn't have been conceiving children!*" O'Toole shouted from his chair. "*And* because of the drugs —"

"They *weren't* drugs! They were natural potions!" Maeve shrieked.

"*Silence him, James!* Before I —"

"Tape his mouth, *filid!*" Day ordered. "I think he may serve his purpose now without speaking."

"He didn't even know the boy existed until just before he died, Claire!" Karl went on. "He had dim horrific memories of the rituals surrounding his conception, sexual rites that haunted him …"

"My son was his *first* born, you know. He had a great preference for him!" Maeve attempted to wither Claire with her words.

"*Stop!*" the White Queen cried out. "Your wickedness is beyond belief, cousin!" She stood to her feet with difficulty. "… But the truth shall be laid bare — you … *Destroyer of Souls!* You *Mother of Lies!*" A righteous fury seemed to lift and strengthen her fragile frame.

Karl supported Claire, as he had that day on the sunny beach in South Carolina — to Claire it seemed centuries ago. "Day told Michael," he said, "about the child and then tried to pressure him to join them again. He was never certain that it was not a hoax. He asked to meet the child. They refused. He tried to find some records of the birth in Ireland. There were none. He suffered much over this uncertainty."

"Take your rightful place then, Bran — on the board!" Maeve pushed the hapless child a little to get him moving. He faltered and stepped down with uncertain mechanical motions.

"He never met him," the priest continued in Claire's ear, "but I can see, as you can, that it is true. This may be how they lured him to his death."

Claire surveyed the tragedy displayed before her and the evil that had spawned it. She also saw in her mind's eye how seemingly harmless choices had been swallowed up by greater and greater evil. How a desire for peace and freedom, for progress, for family and even national pride had changed into control and lust, ambitious greed, arrogance and selfishness. The whole vicious circle hung now over this poor creature who made his way down from the dais. A product, not of love, but of distortion.

He walked over to stand on the square next to Claire. She realized with a fleeting thought that she had lost somewhere her phobia about 'imperfect' human beings. The child stood staring straight ahead to the middle of the board. Claire could see the 'good' side of his face now in profile and her heart softened. Karl still held her as she reached out to lay a gentle hand on the boy's shoulder. He flinched slightly and she felt him shaking uncontrollably under his clothing.

"Don't be afraid!" she said soothingly. "It will be alright!" She heard the words out of her own mouth and wondered if she possibly believed them.

"We must go down ourselves now, Queen Mebh!" Day called out.

"Yes," Maeve answered. "The White King, The Youth of a Thousand Summers … is in his place!" She heralded this accomplishment, gesturing dramatically toward her ill-begotten son.

A new and unexpected gust of warm wind blew through the open doors.

"*I* am the White King!" a voice declared from somewhere. Everyone looked around and their eyes landed on the lower edge of the opening in the roof.

Patrick stood on the snowy threshold at ceiling level, dressed in a glowing white tunic with a golden breastplate. On his head was a crown of gold and he held a golden shield that caught the light of the moon and spread it across the room in dazzling rays. His right hand held a straight white hazel rod. A golden sword hung in a belt at his side. The snow that had stood in drifts at the bottom of the gateway was melted away by his presence.

Claire would never forget the way Patrick looked that night against the Irish sky. He looked like himself, but *not* like a mere boy. It almost seemed he had grown a little taller. His face had taken on the solemn expression of maturity that had only passed over it fleetingly before. His voice had a ring of authority that resonated throughout the room. Everyone was stunned.

"*Mwilsha's gater,*

swurht asturth Nyedas a Daalyon!" The White King declared.

The words seemed to have shape and weight.

"What's he *saying* and what about Bran, now?" Maeve whined.

"He's been installed and —"

Day was flushed with excitement, ignoring Maeve completely.

He mumbled and stuttered, paging frantically through a booklet he'd picked up. "Aaahhh, where is Great? Oh, yes and One? ..." He cleared his throat. "*Bin Ain!* ... Yes, yes, let's see," He looked at the booklet and said. "*Gralta! Gralta!*"

"*Swudal Duilsha' Linska,*" the Shining Youth continued.
Duilsha's Sreedug toari,
Duilsha's Lag gray died,
shedi Ladu arark asturth Nyedas a Daalyon"

"I've got it!" Steve whispered to his fellow *Fianna*. "I've got my printout from the lexicon."

He held a wrinkled wad of paper in his hands. "I guess I'm faster than Day! ... It's the Our Father! '*Upon earth ... same as ... in Lodging of God*' It's the beginning of the 'Our Father'.

"He *does* know The Tongue!" Day announced happily to the assembly. "It's something about 'names', and 'kingdoms' ... He's probably talking about us, Maeve ... and ... let's see ... 'heaven' or 'lodgings' of some sort" He threw the booklet down. "Let's just speak English for now shall we? Until the crucial time, that is. And that time is drawing near! Is that why you are here?"

Claire stood on her toes and strained to see her son more closely.

"I am here because I was sent!" Patrick answered.

"And who sent you, Cuchulain?" Day added the mythical name hopefully.

"*Eamonn* told me to come and gave me all that I needed."

"Eamonn? ... Well ..." Day paused. "... whoever it was, *we've* been waiting for you! Do you understand what is required?"

"I know that you want me to say the Word."

Day almost swooned.

"He could be making this all up!" Maeve shouted. "Learned it from his father!"

"*Quiet!*" Day ordered his wife impatiently. Then to Patrick in a honeyed tone, "Yes, the *Word!* One simple Word that will bring happiness to so many and it will bring your ..."

"He must fight his brother first!" Maeve yelled desperately. "It's in the myth! Cuchulain and Ferdiad! They must fight to the death!"

Patrick looked sadly at the boy who stood on the board in his place.

"You are *crazy!*" Claire shouted and broke through the living game pieces to stand in the middle of the board. "You would have your own son risk his life for this … this …" She motioned to the monitor.

Day was sweating in spite of the cold. "Both of you stop! No one is going to fight or die. It will be a *White battle*, Maeve, remember? No blood!"

Patrick stepped into the room, his golden armaments glowing as with fiery heat that radiated to even the farthest corners. Claire thought of him standing in her bedroom doorway in his pajamas with his plastic sword and shield held high.

"It's time, Mr. Day!" Pifkin called out urgently.

"Yes, pull him up on the screen, Pifkin!" Day said. "It's your *father*, Patrick! You can make him real again when you say the Word."

Claire was edging forward toward the dais, wild with anger at the attempt to manipulate Patrick with promises of his dead father's 'resurrection', when a life-sized image of a man appeared on the monitor. It was Michael. He smiled and seemed to look into her eyes. Claire froze in her tracks.

"Your mother wants you to say it, Patrick! Look! She wants to be see your father again, to be with him."

Then the image spoke in a voice that sounded like Michael's. "Claire, tell Patrick it's alright! … I love you both."

Claire dropped to her knees and stared at Michael, who was reaching out to her. It *was* as if he were alive again. She ached with love for him. She could only weep. She lifted her hands toward him.

"*No! Stop!*" It was Kostanikas. "It's a *trick!* The NAND gates are opening to the Pure Intelligence — the *'majestic intellect!'* It's the Fibonacci sequence! I knew it all along — the numbers are entities. *Phi* will unlock the Platonic solids!"

"*Shut up*, old man!" Herbert Pifkin cried out with a look of urgent ecstasy on his face. "It is a *Spiritual Machine!* Rabbi Loew *was* right!"

"It's *not* Michael!" Theo warned. "Patrick! It is *not* your father!"

Then everything happened all at once and no one remembers it completely. O'Toole had hidden the knife in his sleeve, had cut himself loose, then crept unnoticed to the back of the dais. He grabbed Grace Daly and held his knife to her heart.

Claire ran toward Michael and Patrick, but was stopped abruptly and held by two hooded figures.

My dream, she thought, *it's my dream!* She desperately tried to wake up.

"Say the Word, you little bastard, or I'll *kill your granny!*" O'Toole shouted.

"*Don't do it, Patrick!* This is all of the evil one!" Grace begged him. "The power in you is meant for *good!* Use it for good, my dearest boy!"

"Say it, Patrick!" called Day. "He means it! He'll kill her. *Say it!*"

O'Toole lifted the knife.

"Always obey the Almighty One, Patrick! *No matter what happens!*" Grace cried out.

Karl, Steve and Mara broke toward the dais. Rose began praying the Hail Mary loudly holding the hand of Michael's unfortunate son.

A force seized Patrick. He lifted up his hazel rod. His red hair stuck out like nails from his head and there was a spark of fire at the end of each hair. One eye was nearly shut and the other open wide. He bared his jaw almost to his ears and his mouth opened so wide you could see down his throat.

"It's the *Riastrad!* The hero's battle frenzy! I told you he was the real article, Maeve, I —"

Then an unearthly sound came from Patrick's distended mouth.

"***TOIRIADI!***"

"*No!*" cried Kostanikas hunched on the floor, his arms over his head. "Have mercy, God! Have mercy!"

Great black birds flew into the room, swooping and diving and screeching loudly. The hooded *Fianna Fitchell* ducked and scattered. Claire, now freed, walked toward Michael and as she did the image stepped out of the screen and onto the black and white floor. Her heart pounded madly as she reached out to him. As their fingers almost touched, she recoiled in horror.

There stood not Michael, but a hideous and repulsive creature the size of a man, but with the body of a serpent and great horny wings that flapped with such a force that no one could stand upright in the wake of their beating. The air in the room became colder again and swirled around and around. The whirlwind was now filled with opaque glimpses of unnatural misshapen things that howled and shrieked.

Patrick in his powerful state whisked his Grandma from O'Toole's weakened grasp and set her on her throne carefully.

The foul, cold, ghoulish wind circled again and again, seeming to suck all life and breath from the room.

"In the beginning was the Word" Karl yelled, his hands raised. He knelt down and raised his open hand. *"Enemy of the human race! Source of death! Robber of life! Twister of justice! Traitor of nations! Inciter of jealousy! Cause of discord! Despicable Serpent! You cannot STAND against the ancient strength!"*

He continued, *"And the Word was with God, and the Word was God."*

James and Maeve Day clung desperately to their thrones, but they were held high in the air, flopping like two heavy banners. They shook like rag dolls, gasping for air as the whirlwind blew and raged. Treat O'Toole tried to make his escape into the night, clawing his way along the floor, but he was taken up and slammed down again and again.

"Through him all things were made; without him nothing was made that has been made. In him was life, and that life was the light of men. The light shines in the darkness, but the darkness has not overcome it!" Karl finished and remained kneeling on the floor.

Patrick, with his golden sword now unsheathed, leaped and ran toward the repulsive shape of the winged serpent. He issued a mighty thrust into its dark reptilian body as he roared another word out of his wide mouth:

"D'ONADU!"

The giant beast then seemed to be drawn back and swallowed by the computer, dissolving almost instantly, leaving for a brief moment a faint outline of itself on the huge monitor. The wind slowed. The black birds flew out into the night. The disembodied apparitions moaned and cried out with shrill pleas and finally settled on the herd of curious and truant pigs that lined the edge of the gateway in the hill. Some say the pigs ran all the way to the Cliffs of Moher and into the frothing sea. They were never seen again.

"Mommy!"

Patrick stood empty-handed in his borrowed winter jacket, asking, "Mommy! Are you, okay?" He sounded like a child once more. Claire rushed to him, hugging his five-year-old body tightly and repeating, "I love you, little boy! I love you!"

All of the hooded filid and druids, bards, and ovates had run from the massive room as soon as they were able to stand. James and Maeve Day were found on the Burren the next morning with no breath. Even though the snow was gone and the unseasonable chill was replaced with an equally unseasonable warmth, their bodies were frozen stiff, each corpse covered with a powdery crystalline frost.

Treat O'Toole's hollow chest had been stabbed by his own knife as he fell and died by the threshold of the door in the hill.

Herbert Pifkin disappeared completely. Theo said that he saw him walk into the monitor after the virtual beast. No one else could corroborate that.

After her joyful reunion with her son, Claire turned to her mother's throne. It was empty.

The White Queen lay motionless on her back in front of her chair. Karl felt her neck. He quickly reached in his pocket and pulled out a small black leather case with tiny vials. He touched Grace's eyes, ears, lips with oil, saying final words. Her eyes opened briefly and Claire took her hand to her own breast. Grace whispered something inaudible, looking at her daughter. Claire put her ear to her mother's mouth as Karl continued his prayers. The white hand that Claire held gave off a surge of heat that Claire felt through her whole body as her mother spoke.

"But Mom, I can't be ..." Claire gasped

Then Grace Daly was still.

Claire moaned with grief. She saw a jagged rip in the bodice of the White Queen's dress. *"O Toole!"* screamed Claire, "He ..."

"No, Claire" Mara said gently, opening the dress to show Grace's soft white skin. "There is no wound."

"Grandma's heart is broken on the inside." Patrick said. Then he silently cried his boyish cry into his mother's shoulder.

Steve watched silently from the foot of the dais.

After a few minutes, when she and Patrick had both quieted Claire said, "Patrick?"

"Yeah?" the boy answered, wiping his face and looking up into her eyes.

Claire didn't know where to begin with questions or even if she should. She wasn't sure how much Patrick himself understood of what had just happened.

Before she could ask anything, Patrick spoke.

"I didn't say the Word."

"You didn't?" she said with surprise. "Did you know it?"

"Daddy asked me that, when he found out about my … you know … the way I … I —" He was unsure.

"It's okay, little boy, I know what you mean."

"I told him I didn't know what word he meant … 'cause lots of words came to me. He said that this was a special word that was different … and I would know. He said if that Word ever came to me, that I should never say it, and something was hidden in Jesus that would help me to never to even think of it again."

"Hidden in Jesus?" Claire looked to Karl.

"In the crucifix?" Karl asked.

Claire remembered then Franny's discovery. "Did you have to find what was hidden? In the cross?"

"Yeah."

"What was there, honey?"

"I can't tell you, Mommy."

"What did you do with it, then?"

"I ate it."

"You ate it?" Claire asked.

"Yeah."

"And you never thought of it again?"

"No, Mommy." He hugged her tightly.

"So what did you …?"

Patrick was crying softly again now. Claire stopped her questioning.

Steve spoke up. "He said two words from the Ancient Tongue. They were in the lexicon."

Everyone turned to him, waiting.

"He said, *Come* and then he said *Go*." Steve still held the folded printout in his hand.

Patrick nodded.

"And the deer and fawns we saw crossing the road?" Karl asked.

Patrick nodded again. "That was us. I prayed the prayer Daddy gave me, like Eamonn said to … All the kids are at the Travellers' camp. Eamonn came and helped us get there. It was all like a dream … but I knew I had to come back …" Silent tears rolled down his face which he tried to lick and wipe away.

Claire rose to her feet, bringing Patrick with her, and reached out to Mara. The young woman came willingly and kissed Patrick and Claire on both cheeks. They stood arm in arm, keeping a silent vigil as Karl prayed again for Grace.

When Claire looked down on her mother, she saw the White Queen — her red hair thrown wildly about her head — her white gown flowing luxuriantly out from her body, as if she were floating. Then in amazement she noticed the painted designs on the floor of the dais. Above her mother's head was the sun and beneath her feet, the moon. Stars surrounded her body like jewels. Her arms were still and pointing like hands on a clock.

Chapter 67

The myth sovereign in the old age was that everything means everything.
The myth sovereign in the new is that nothing means anything.
           Thomas Howard

What is this place where dreams and myths are made, and poets go? Where numbers live in terrible beauty? Is it true what some have said, that there is a place between the worlds — a place of 'making,' of 'huge shapes' that leads to either Heaven or Hell? Or perhaps back again to this world, destined to be forever misunderstood — jolted with electric shocks in sterile brick buildings, screaming 'I *am* a human being!' or shot to the inevitable bondage of fame and illusion, screaming: 'I am *only* a human being!'

Did the Ancients cross the borders more easily with less distraction from theories to explain away the obvious connections? Or did they in their ignorance bring that unnatural place into this and then pay the price in fear and appeasement?

The Celts, the Greeks, the Navajo, the Jews, the Romans, the Germans — every nationality has its stories, its shared memories and apocryphal nostalgia. The Nations, it is said, will bear witness to the ultimate sovereignty of Lord and King, of individuals and of themselves, as they are among the joyous throngs gathered when time is no more. But now they fight and cling possessively to their earthly boundaries, ignorant of their birthright and resentful of their innate dependence — like unhappy children in an orphanage.

Does everything mean something? Are we delusional to think so? Our songs and stories, our paintings and sculptures are constantly claiming ground from the Abyss, and we still treat them tenderly, wrapping them in paper, passing them on to our children, hiding them from harm against unbelievable odds.

But where do we live? Our own stories, our everyday lives, give us shelter from the unrelenting chaos that grins at the fringes of our world. And so we pass our days making of them what we will, finding comfort in routine, in ritual, and simple courtesy.

Yet each moment is an edge, from which we can drop this way or that. So many forces compete for the chance to choose the place of our landing. We have to trust someone.

Chapter 68

*The winter's rains and ruins are over
And all the seasons of snow and sins; ...
And time remembered is grief forgotten
And frosts are slain and flowers begotten
Blossom by blossom the spring begins.*
　　　　William Wordsworth

Many who knew [her] thought it a pity that so substantive and rare a creature should have been absorbed into the life of another, and be only known in a certain sense as a wife and mother ... But the effect of her being on those around her was incalculably diffusive: for the growing good of the world is partly dependent on unhistoric acts; and the things that are not so ill with you and me as they might have been, is half owing to the number who live faithfully a hidden life, and rest in unvisited tombs.
　　　　George Eliot

It was a brisk spring day in Eastern Tennessee. The mountains rose smoky gray in the distance, reaching into clear blue sky. All the children at play still wore their sweaters or light jackets, but it wouldn't be long before that first day would come when those could be gloriously shed as welcome warmth overtook the last chill of winter.

Three figures sat bundled on outdoor picnic benches. Claire's bulky white sweater was pulled down over her knees, which were tucked up tightly to her chin. She watched the children, scattered among the black and white habits, squealing with delight on the playground.

"This *is* a beautiful place!" Franny exclaimed, sipping her coffee and cupping her fingers around the warmth of the mug. "*And* ... I love your shoes!"

Mara laughed in response. "I got them from a leather vendor in Rome — for six dollars! I almost felt bad, but then I guess the Gypsy in me took care of that."

"I'm *so* glad I met you!" Franny effused. "I think you've influenced me, *fashion*-wise, more than any other single person."

Claire shook her head, smiling, and looked down at her own worn jeans and sneakers fondly.

"You've made me see," Fran continued quite seriously, "how fad-conscious I was and how totally peer-oriented. I mean, spiky hair and black leather — how immature was *that?*" She grabbed a handful of granola and tossed some into her mouth. "I'm definitely into the more Classic-Euro thing now — like you! And if I might be *working* with you sometimes …"

"What?" said Claire. "Working with who?"

"Well, I just mentioned to Karl that I'm very good at detective, mystery, edgy-thriller-type situations … and he said he'd definitely think about it."

"Who'd think about what?" Karl asked as he joined the three women at the picnic table.

"Just girl talk!" Franny said, hurrying to the next topic. "So is it all set? All the paperwork finally done and everything?"

"Yes," Karl said, looking at Claire as he sat next to her on the bench. "He's free and clear."

Patrick ran up to the table beaming. "Remember I told you, Mom? I'm happy when my most favorite people are together?"

Claire nodded.

"Well, *here you are!*" He ran around to hug each one.

"I'm glad we're here for Easter, too! Sister Catherine …" He giggled to imitate her. "… is gonna hide all the eggs we color today and we get to hunt for them *tomorrow!* Now I gotta go find my brother!" He ran off again, looking very pleased at the thought.

"I know we've had this talk before," Karl said to Claire after Patrick left, "but are you *sure* you're okay with this? No one expected it. It's still not too late."

"Of course it is," Claire replied with a smile.

"He'll require much special attention and care. The surgeries he needs will be ordeals in themselves. Mother Mechtilde is perfectly willing to keep him longer with the others until he's more stable …"

"We're ready, Karl. We're *all* ready. Michael's mother and his sister Mary have been down to visit more than once. Both of our families want to do everything we can to make this child happy. We love him and he loves us."

"Yeah," Franny said. "But how can such a sweet kid come out of that nightmare! I'd adopt him myself, if I could. But … I might be *traveling* a lot." She licked a few sweetened grains off her finger.

"Karl, did you really tell Fran …"

Patrick was back, pushing a small wheelchair, with a friend on either side. Claire said hello to Matthew, who seemed to have grown another inch or so since her first visit. On the other side was a dark-haired girl, perhaps ten years old, with glasses and no arms. She had on a long yellow flowered chiffon dress and a bright green sweater with the arms tied over her chest. The little girl who had greeted Patrick in her miserable circumstances under the Burren was barely recognizable.

"You remember Christina, right, Mom?" Doesn't she look pretty?"

"I may change my name again," Christina told the adults. "Mother Mechtilde says that a name is a very powerful thing. And if I become a nun and all … She says it will be a while before I know that."

Claire remembered her own burning and romantic desire for a vocation when she'd been this age. Maybe a 'Brian McCarthy' would never ask *this* girl to dance and change her plans. But there was definitely a plan for this brave young lady and it might just involve dancing.

"Mother Mechtilde gave me this," Christina said, twirling around, watching the flounce of the dress skim the tops of her hiking boots. "It's the first dress in my history. The glasses are kind of dorky, but I can see a lot better now … and at least they took off those horrible noisy arms."

She rolled her eyes knowingly at Matthew.

"Don't worry about the glasses!" Franny reassured her. "*Fake* glasses are actually cool among older kids now — childish, faddish I know, but what can you do?" Mara and Claire glanced at each other and smiled.

"Do you like it here, Christina?" Karl asked kindly.

"Like it! I don't think there is a word to describe how much we *love* it here, really. I said it was like we were saved from Hell, and Mother says that's *exactly* what it was. And I said if that was Hell then this is *Heaven* ... and she said that we ain't seen nothin' yet. But all of us are sure glad that there aren't any experimentations. We *all* made it here, you know — David ... Elliott. And Mary and Kenny don't fight anymore, well, *most* of the time. I say it's because there's no experimentations, but Mother says it's the love and peace of God. And I do believe in God now because everything is alright!"

Claire looked at this garrulous stately armless girl, and around at the disfigured and deformed children who filled the playground. "Somehow it is, Christina, somehow it is ..." The two armless friends ran off toward the play yard.

The quiet boy in the wheelchair looked nothing like the child he had been. His robotic parts had been carefully and expertly removed. His bandaged stumps were covered by jeans, a plaid flannel shirt and a navy blue sweat jacket. Half of his small face was also in bandages, but the part that was uncovered beamed at them all.

"We're going home tomorrow, Brandon!" Claire said happily, going over to the boy and kneeling beside him. "Your Grandma O'Connell and all your cousins and aunts and uncles are so glad you're coming!"

"And I'm glad, Mom, don't forget. *I'm* glad." Patrick added.

"Aahheemmm ggglaahhd ttoo," Brandon said slowly and deliberately.

Claire gently embraced the seven-year-old with great tears in her eyes. Everyone silently praised the accomplishment themselves, for the boy had not said a word since that awful night. They weren't certain if he ever had.

"It's a surprise!" Patrick yelled with delight. Mother Mechtilde got the speech ther ... sera ..."

"Therapist?" Karl helped him.

"Yeah," said Patrick, "She's been helping him and he can say lots of words now and Mother Mechtilde says it will be even better after the plastic surgery ... and I told Brandon not to worry 'cause she says it won't be plastic but *real*. Mom?"

"Yes, little boy?" Claire was dabbing her eyes on her sweater

"Can Brandon and I get a dog?" Molly and Sean have one and so do Devin, and Meghan and ..."

"We'll see!" Claire laughed.

Patrick turned to Brandon. "We'll see *usually* means no! Remember that, Mom? But it doesn't have to any more, right? We'll take care of the dog *all* by ourselves, won't we, Bran?" He looked at his brother for support.

"Yyessh! Wwee wwwill … PPPaaahttrricckk!" The boy spoke confidently with half a smile that looked just like his father's.

Patrick wheeled Brandon away again, bumping over the newly thawing earth at breakneck speed, both boys yelling with glee.

Steve walked up to the group carrying an envelope. "Well, we've got to be off soon, you two!" Franny put her hands up to her chest with astonishment and mouthed, "*Me?*"

Steve shook his head, smiling at her. "You and Claire are taking the boys home tomorrow evening, right?"

"Oh, yeah," Franny said, almost with disappointment, but then brightened, "but that's a very important mission, isn't it, Mr. Bond?"

Karl laughed and nodded. "Just don't ever call me Hercule Poirot. Or Lord Peter, either!"

All three women *and* Steve were incensed. "Lord Peter Wimsey rules!" Steve said. "And Bunter! My hero!"

"Lord Peter's the *ideal* man!" said Mara.

"He and Harriet have the perfect relationship!" insisted Claire.

"His fashion sense is exquisite!" said Franny. "If you weren't a priest, I'll bet you'd definitely be as natty as Lord Peter! Definitely!"

"Alright, please!" Karl said and changed the subject. "Stephan! What have you got there?"

"Well …" He handed the envelope to Karl. "It looks like a letter from Rose."

They all were anxious to hear any news from their friend. It was several pages of beautiful old-fashioned penmanship. "Why don't you read it to us, Stephan?" Karl asked as he handed the envelope back. Steve read aloud:

My dearest ones,

I know you tried to get me to come to the States but I couldn't leave my home. Now that the danger is past, I have been able to resume my life and have fellowship with my friends and spiritual children here.

As you've no doubt read in the papers, the Peace Accord is all but buried and the funeral said. But I have hope yet that one day it will come. I pray for it every day, along with the Unity of the Church. I truly feel that that awful being in that machine was meant to possess our whole country. Can that be, Father? A nation possessed? And then who knows what could have happened to the whole world with those NAND gates and all. I pray for dear Grace's soul every day and remember her sacrifice, and of course, for my Ian and Michael, too. I believe they went straight to God, because they were all martyrs in a way. But still I pray.

The dear Sisters of Mercy here have taken all the poor children from Day's orphanages — which were closed down by the way, even though the truth of him and his wicked wife never got out. I suppose that's for the best — it might have given ideas to some other lost souls. It is good, Father, that you had everything removed from that underground "inferno" and the place sealed up. They tell me that stories in Clare abound. I'm going over West with Dermot and the Browns one day soon to loll around the pubs and hear some of them.

I'm working, as I may have told you before, with 'Travellers' Rights'. Sort of taking up where dear Ian left off. It's a shame the way they're treated in their own land — a land that almost belongs more to them than to us, although they don't want possession of it.

Theo's doing quite well! It was a stroke of genius, Father, to put him in the Dominican Hospital here in Dublin. Everyone there treats him so kindly. Of course, I don't let them spoil him! I make them give me an account every day when I visit and I set him straight if I have to. He still can be stubborn and resistant to my helpful comments. The doctor told me to let you know, Father, that Theo's made so much progress since you were here last that he may be able to live in one of the assisted living residences and perhaps teach part-time at the university. He's eating well and looks quite handsome and distinguished in the suit you picked out for him, Father.

"See, Karl!" Franny interrupted, "It's the fashion sense. You can't help yourself!"

"Is there more, Stephan?" the German priest asked with a hint of a smile.

"Just this!" he held a newspaper clipping in his hand and read on,

I found this item rather buried in the Daily last week and thought you all would be interested.

"Then" Steve said, "it's love to each one of us and promises of prayers for everything, including Bran's adjustment to his new home and family."

"What does the article say?" Karl asked.

Steve read it also:

LONDON

The British Museum has reported the mysterious return of a valued but obscure treasure to its collection. An ancient chess set was found set up in the same area from which it was stolen some seventy years ago and presumed lost forever. The set has a mysterious history and it should be no surprise that mystery still surrounds it.

In 1831 a high tide on the coast near Uig in the Isle of Lewis washed away a sand bank and exposed a cave in which there was a small beehive-shaped building rather like the little domestic grinding querns to be found in the Highlands. A labourer working nearby found it, and thinking it might contain some treasure, broke into it. He found a cache of eighty-four carved chessmen ranged together. They had an uncanny look, and he flung down his spade and ran, convinced that he had come on a sleeping company of fairies. His wife, the tale goes, was of sterner stuff and made him go back and fetch them. The greater part of them were given to the British Museum.

'Replicas have been made of them, but the originals, all mustered together, are much more impressive,' said the overjoyed curator at his happy discovery.

Before they disappeared a tradition had arisen about them. It was said that the guards who took the guard dogs around at night could not get them to pass the Celtic chessmen. They bristled and pulled back on their haunches.

Perhaps the Highlander's superstition can be excused, especially after this unlikely reappearance.

The curator says there will be a slight fee to view the returned pieces.

"So did Eamonn …?" Claire scratched her head and looked quizzically at Karl, Steve and Mara.

"We just don't know." Karl replied. "What does Patrick say of that time in Ireland, Claire? I've tried not to interfere with it."

"You have never interfered with anything!" Claire said. "You've *only* helped!"

She paused for a moment.

"I think he knows what happened. But he still says it is like a dream and maybe one day that's all it will be to him … a terrible and wonderful dream. He talks about Mom being in heaven with Michael and how happy they must be. I actually see him being more of a kid than he ever was. I think he's relieved, in a way, that the great things that were demanded of him are done … They are done, aren't they?" Claire asked Karl.

"We just don't know!" Karl said again, "We don't know when great things will be demanded of any of us."

"I still can't believe Dad actually sold the old house!" Fran said.

"How is your father doing now?" Mara asked both of the women.

"He was devastated at first," Fran answered, "but he wasn't like the rest of us. He'd known how bad it was. He had so wanted to be with her…" She blinked and took another sip of coffee.

"The funeral was such a celebration of her life, as all of you know — of course, because you were there!" Claire went on. "So even though he went around then saying 'Life without Grace is not worth living!' — and still does occasionally — I know that all the stories of what she had meant to everyone and the knowledge of how rich and full her life had been have helped him to go on one day at a time. I know it's helped me … although I've had my regrets to deal with. I don't think he has as many."

"All wise people have regrets. Regrets, if they are fully realized, are the things that give us hope," Karl said.

Claire knew that Karl wasn't preaching but speaking to himself as well. She responded. "And gratitude for life — a chance in this life, to try again."

"Dad said he couldn't stay in the house without Mom," Franny said, "but I didn't think he'd go through with it. I'm gonna miss that place — maybe I'll buy it back some day and have an orphanage there or a mission or something!"

"He's taken me up on my invitation to live at our house," Claire told Karl, "... even though the other three girls and their families asked him to come. He insists that he wants to help with the boys and that there should be a 'man in the house'!" Claire lowered her voice in an attempt to sound like her father, and banged the picnic table with her small fist which in no way resembled his massive one. She laughed. "Honestly, I don't know if I'd have really taken Bran on if Dad hadn't been so insistent about being there."

No one had mentioned Claire's illness since they left Ireland. She hadn't gone to Doctor Quinlan once since she'd come home. She almost had, but changed her mind at the last minute. She'd had no symptoms. She would wait to see.

"I've promised Mother I'd stay and celebrate the Easter Vigil Mass," Karl said to Steve. "Is there any reason we can't wait and leave after that?"

"The meeting with Father Wang is scheduled for one o'clock tomorrow in Connecticut. As long as we can get a flight — it's up to you."

"*Ahh!* Chinese intrigue!" Franny interjected. "I'm *very* up on all the martial arts. I do Tae Bo and I love Jackie Chan and Jet Li movies!" She looked at Karl hopefully. He ignored her.

Back in her room, Claire knelt by her bed and reached into her small suitcase. She took out two items and laid them on the bed before her. She looked at the crucifix on the wall, covered still with the small purple Lenten shroud. She stood, reached up and pulled it off, folding it reverently. She still was no theologian. And she wasn't devout. A lot of things made her mad or uneasy about the Church, but as she looked at the cross and the figure upon it, she did know now that it was not suffering that Catholics were enamored of, as she had once believed. What held it all together, what kept the world turning — was sacrificial love. This man's, on the cross — Michael's, Karl's mother's, Karl's, her own mother's, so many others ... Claire looked back down to the bed. She had already given Patrick her mother's well-worn O'Brien rosary with the smooth green glass beads. After all, it had been blessed at the summit of Croagh Patrick and she was sure it was meant for him. But the mysterious things on which she now looked with awe had been given to her. She picked up the golden apple and the velvet bag that held the world within it. She would show them to Franny one day because of her Vision, but for now she would hide them and ponder them along with the other secret things in her heart.

*   *   *

Claire came upon a circle. In the center was a flaming fire in a golden bowl. The priest was dressed in a brilliant white robe bordered with golden brocaded silk. His arms were outstretched over the fiery bowl. They were in the midst of the ritual.

Father Karl Burgmann prayed aloud as the Sisters and children and their guests surrounded him outside the darkened chapel:

> *Father,*
> *we share in the light of your glory*
> *through your Son, the light of the world.*
> *Make this new fire holy*

His hand moved, tracing the shape of the cross.

> *And inflame us with new hope.*
> *Purify our minds by this Easter celebration*
> *and bring us one day to the feast of Eternal Light.*

The huge nail-studded candle was lit from the sacred flame and all the faithful followed its light into the darkness.

Beachhead Books

Forthcoming Titles:
Broken China